THE 9/11 MACHINE

GREG ENSLEN

GYPSY
PUBLICATIONS

Published in 2013, by Gypsy Publications
Troy, OH 45373, U.S.A.
www.GypsyPublications.com

Second Edition

Enslen, Greg
The 9/11 Machine / by Greg Enslen
ISBN 978-1-938768-18-7 (paperback)

Library of Congress Control Number
2013937151

Edited by Diana Ceres
Cover by Pamela Schwartz

For more information, please visit the author's
website at www.GregEnslen.com

PRINTED IN THE UNITED STATES OF AMERICA

DEDICATION

This book is dedicated to those who lost their lives on 9/11/2001 and to anyone who lost a loved one, family member, friend, or acquaintance that day. Even ten years later, the losses suffered on that day are still being felt.

This book is also for my children: Xander, Annabelle, and Katie. Kids, this book is about 9/11, an event that took place before any of you were born. It feels strange to write that, but it's true—for you, the attacks in Washington, D.C., and New York City are as much a part of ancient history as Pearl Harbor or the Great Depression.

Many lives were lost that day, and the rest of us dealt with it in our own ways, struggling to move past the loss and the shock and grief of those events without allowing them to define us. None of you were alive ten years ago, but now it's impossible for me to imagine a life without you. You children are a testament to the fact that, above all, life goes on.

I love you.

Books by Greg Enslen

Black Bird

The Ghost of Blackwood Lane

Tipp Talk 2010

The 9/11 Machine

Tipp Talk 2011

A Field of Red

Tipp Talk 2012

Tipp Talk 2013

FOREWORD

This book is intended to be a work of speculative fiction about the events of September 11, 2001. I have always thought that 9/11, the worst terrorist attack in the history of the United States, could have been a lot worse.

World Trade Center. The hijackers struck the twin towers of the World Trade Center, destroying both buildings and shaking the nation's financial center to its core. But they struck very early on a Tuesday morning during a mayoral primary, and a sizable number of people who should have been in the towers had not yet arrived at work. Normally, upwards of 50,000 people worked in the buildings on a daily basis, with another 100,000 passing through the seven-building complex and the large shopping mall built underground beneath the towers. Yet on the day of the attacks, only 2,606 people were lost, along with 147 passengers on the two airplanes. For purposes of comparison, I will not include the hijackers in any of these calculations.

Conversely, in 1993, while only 6 people were killed when a car bomb was set off in the basement, it took well over two hours to evacuate the 50,000 people that were in both towers at the time of the attack. Improved evacuation systems implemented after the 1993 bombing, along with the primary and the fact that the hijackers struck very early in the morning before some employees had arrived, certainly contributed to a lower death toll on 9/11.

Pentagon. The hijackers managed to crash a passenger jet into the Pentagon, the heart of the American military. But they somehow managed to hit the only part of the building that had been recently upgraded to much stronger construction materials, blast-resistant glass, and other improvements. The Pentagon was, at the time, undergoing an extensive retrofit. The location of the plane strike was the only "wedge" that had been upgraded. In addition, personnel had not yet moved fully back into this section, and be-tween those two reasons, the loss of life was much lower than it could have been.

Also, in 2001 the offices of the Secretary of Defense and other high-ranking military leaders were reportedly located on the up-permost floors of the E ring on the eastern side of the building, which faces the Potomac River, a large marina, and downtown Washington D.C. Yet the hijackers struck the western side of the building, far away from these important offices. If they had struck the Pentagon from the east, coming in over the Potomac, they would have been much more likely to strike near the offices of Secretary of Defense and other high-ranking military leaders.

Flight 93. The fourth hijacked plane, United Flight 93, was heroically brought down by the passengers as they attempted to regain control of the hijacked airliner. One of the reasons the passengers were in the position to attempt to retake the plane was because the flight departure had been delayed 41 minutes, taking off from Newark Liberty International Airport in New Jersey. After the plane was in the air and the hijackers took control, the 41-minute delay allowed the passengers and crew to learn about the other planes that had been hijacked and that those planes had been used as missiles to strike important targets. If the passengers had not acted or if the flight had not been delayed in leaving Newark Airport, the plane likely would have, according to congressional reports, targeted either the Capitol building or the White House. The loss of either of those buildings would have been a crippling blow to the American psyche.

I began to wonder what a person with foreknowledge of the event could, or would, do about it. Would they intervene and try to stop the attacks from happening altogether? And what if the authorities did not believe them?

Fortunately (or unfortunately) as a writer, when I get an idea like that in my head, my brain will not stop churning until I write it all down. My thoughts, speculations, and extrapolations about politicians and ordinary people's reactions to that foreknowledge transformed themselves, over several years, into this book.

I offer one clarification. This book is not meant to belittle the suffering of anyone who was affected by the events of that tragic day. I think every American, and many people throughout the world, has been affected in some way by 9/11.

This story is also not meant to second-guess any of the decisions made by those in charge, either before or after 9/11. As they say, hindsight is

20/20, so it's easy for me to write about what might have been.

One thing people rarely discuss when talking about 9/11 are the hijackers themselves. It's still very difficult for some to believe that 19 men, armed with nothing more than box cutters, could have carried out such a devastating attack. It's difficult to believe how four very inexperienced pilots with minimal training could have managed to pilot the massive airliners so accurately. Many professional pilots have stated that it would have been difficult to strike the targets as they did, especially in the case of the Pentagon attack, which required the plane be flown very close to the ground at over 500 miles per hour.

The hijackers and terrorists used surprise against us. They took advantage of our open society to take flight training and acquire the basic knowledge they would need to use our own airplanes against us. The hijackers were clever, and their planners and supporters bold, in bringing the fight to our shores and using our own technology—and, in some cases, our own bureaucracy—against us. But their plans did not cause as much damage as they had hoped, and one has to wonder whether it was incompetence, poor planning, or just dumb luck that saved so many people that day.

For those interested in 9/11 conspiracy theories, you'll find them in this book aplenty. I think there are so many conspiracy theories surrounding 9/11 because no one wants to believe that 19 men with little more than box cutters and a martyr's zeal could have such an effect on history. People want to believe that larger forces were at work. I incorporate several theories in the book and discuss my skepticism about the major conspiracy theories in the afterword. But I don't begrudge those who believe we haven't heard the whole story. I understand that there's a comfort in imagining that we were all victims of some grand scheme. The truth is probably closer to this—that we were all taken by surprise.

For those interested in making a donation to support the families of those who fought and died on 9/11, I would suggest researching charities or donating to one of the few described below:

9/11 Memorial: This amazing memorial at Ground Zero, located in the footprints of the towers, is dedicated to those who died on 9/11. I toured the perimeter on a trip in 2010 with my wife, when it was still under construction, and it was a humbling experience to see the construction firsthand. To make a donation, visit www.national911memorial.org. There is an interactive guide to the memorial, including detailed maps and animations and a detailed 9/11 timeline.

Flight 93 National Memorial: This memorial is dedicated to the passengers and flight crew of United Airlines Flight 93, who fought back against the four hijackers aboard their plane, causing the flight to crash into a field in Shanksville, Pennsylvania, instead of striking the intended target in Washington, D.C. Visit www.honorflight93.org.

Friends of the Firefighters: I mention this great organization in the first chapter of the book. This organization was created in the wake of the 9/11 events to offer support to firefighters and their families. Their website can be found at www.friendsoffirefighters.org.

I apologize if something in this book offends you. I tried to take what I know about our historical figures and extrapolate what they might have done in alternate universes. I'm not saying that 9/11 wasn't horrible—it was. But I am saying that, looking back on it now, ten years later, I think we dodged a proverbial bullet. It changed our country, reminded us about the importance of foreign policy, and brought about many long-needed upgrades to our military and intelligence infrastructure.

The events of 9/11 changed this nation and affected many people in many different ways. It rocked our nation to the core and is still, to this day, affecting people on a daily basis through increased security and the costs of waging two ongoing wars. But in this work of fiction, I propose a disturbing concept.

It could have been worse.

"THEY ALWAYS SAY TIME CHANGES THINGS, BUT YOU ACTUALLY HAVE TO CHANGE THEM YOURSELF."

ANDY WARHOL

PART ONE

1.1
QUIET READING

Don sat on the edge of his daughter's small bed, reading carefully through one of her favorite books. In this one, she had drawn curls of red crayon in the margins and over the pictures.

He marveled at the thin, looping lines as they twirled around the blocky words that made up the page of text.

The room was silent, as always.

Don had tried to leave everything exactly as he'd found it; her toys and stuffed animals were just where she had dropped them. The nose of a green plastic frog peeked out from under the bed. The small jade plant she had won at school looked bigger now, of course, and the tree outside her window was taller. But inside, her room was preserved, as untouched as he could manage.

There had been days when Don would just sit in her room, sometimes for hours. He would make plans, or ponder some particularly difficult engineering problem, or allow himself to daydream. Sometimes he would sit in here when he was trying to extrapolate future events from past occurrences, following the loops of time and predicting what might happen based on a particular set of circumstances.

He did some of his best thinking here, sitting on the corner of her twin bed.

It was nice, remembering what his life had been like. Sometimes, he even smiled.

On occasion, he dusted her room and tidied up a little bit, but it was difficult to decide what to clean and what to leave alone. Two years ago, he'd finally washed the "Dora the Explorer" bedspread—it had grown too dusty, sending up little clouds every time he sat down on her bed. But he'd hated himself for washing it. He didn't want any part of her to be gone.

Last summer, Don had finally given in and reorganized her bookshelf. Princesses and Sesame Street and Elmo and dozens of other titles.

He'd read many of them to her, but he'd been too busy to read them all. He hadn't known at the time that there was a limited window of opportunity. Of course, no one would have blamed him—he had had his work and papers to grade and his plans and gizmos to tinker with in the basement office. Sarah had picked up the slack, reading to Tina every night before bed.

But Don didn't want to think about Sarah.

Don liked to flip through the books, concentrating on the fact that he was probably the first one to do so since Tina had held them in her small hands. The books had been a mess after five long years of him taking them down and reading quietly through them, so in 2008, he'd spent a long weekend dusting and organizing the books.

But Don tried not to move many of her things. This was his sanctuary, where everything was still the same. It was a museum to his past. It was a time machine—when he was in here, he could pretend that Tina would come walking through that door at any moment.

In this room, he could pretend Tina and Sarah were still alive.

Don stood slowly, putting the book back. He looked around the room, smiling, and walked slowly out of her room, closing the door gently behind him.

He wanted to linger, but he couldn't. He needed to get on with the myriad activities and errands that his life had become. He had things to do before he could leave for work. Don was also on edge because of the date. He thought every single person in the nation was probably nervous today.

Ten years ago. It seemed like only yesterday.

Don walked down the hallway, passing the walls decorated with faded pictures of his family. Sarah had put those up. He shook his head and pulled the front door open, stepping outside.

Today was sunny, nice. And it was a nice neighborhood—Jericho, New York. A nice little town on Long Island, about a half-hour from the University of New York and an hour from the city. A funny name, he'd told Sarah the first time they'd walked through the home. A little too biblical for his tastes, he remembered telling her. She had giggled—he suddenly remembered, as clearly as if it had happened yesterday. They had been following the agent, who was busy pointing out the home's features, and Sarah had giggled and thrown him one of those looks she used to give him.

Don's stomach turned over.

Sarah had loved the home, the lawn, everything, from the start. She'd made up her mind, even before they had gotten to the expansive kitchen, the room that ended up being her favorite in the house.

Don leaned over and picked up the paper, flicking off the rubber band and pulling it open. He glanced at the paper and was reminded again of the momentous date—huge headlines screamed about the anniversary and memorial services to be held at Ground Zero and in D.C.

Don glanced around at the grass between him and the street. Not long after she had died, Don had gotten a lawn service to take care of the yard. He told himself that he was simply too busy to be out here, mowing and pruning, but he knew that, on some level, he needed to preserve the yard as she'd liked it. She had always been out here, planting and pruning in the yard around their home, a habit that had given her so much pleasure. He didn't have the heart to let the flowers and bushes die.

He tried to not look at the flowers around him. Now, he paid the service, and they kept her gardens up. He would occasionally glance out a window and imagine her out in the yard, hunched over some flowers or digging in the dirt in her ridiculous gardening outfit—faded jeans and a silly shirt with a fig leaf pattern that she had said reminded her of the story of the Garden of Eden.

And then, of course, after a moment, the ghost would be gone. It wasn't even a ghost—it was more like a shadow, moving over the grass.

Don turned and went inside, heading into the kitchen. He flipped on CNN on the big TV in the family room and started his breakfast. He hated quiet rooms, as a rule, but quiet kitchens were the worst.

"Anxiety levels remained high amid more warnings from the federal government concerning additional terrorist attacks," the news anchor on the TV said as the commercials ended. "Homeland Security Director Tom Ridge assured citizens that everything that could be done was being done."

On the screen, the video changed to show Ridge, looking tired.

"As we mark the tenth anniversary of the 9/11 terrorist attacks in Washington, D.C., and New York, I want to assure the American people that we are more prepared, more ready than ever for any eventuality than we were on that day that, for many, seems like yesterday. The government, including the reconstituted Congress, is working hard to protect you and your children."

Don finished chopping up the ingredients for his omelet and heated the pan.

The TV changed back to the announcer.

"President Cheney is scheduled to make a prime-time speech tonight on the tenth anniversary of the terrorist attacks of 9/11," the male anchor said soberly. He turned to another camera and continued. "In news from the war front, today marked the 35th straight day of bombing, as coalition forces from the United States and Britain pounded entrenched forces near the Iraqi city of Mosul. The U.S. Army Forward Command acknowledged their use of infamous ground-penetrating 'bunker busters' to flush out top-level Iraqi and al Qaeda personnel, hiding in deep concrete bunkers beneath Mosul, Baghdad, and other major Iraqi cities, despite international outrage."

The scene changed to show a military helicopter landing on the lawn of the White House. "In Washington, D.C., General Franks has returned from the front lines in Iraq today to meet with President Cheney to discuss the progress of the war. Last week, during a press conference with the pool of embedded reporters in Kuwait, Franks mentioned that the use of tactical nuclear weapons was on the table for the first time. The weapons are now being considered to end the stalemate in Baghdad and other entrenched locations in Iraq. Known as Battlefield Nukes, these smaller, portable nuclear weapons have a variable yield of between 40 and 80 kilotons. Dr. Hawkins, an expert in such weaponry, joins us now to explain why the U.S. military is turning to these types of weapons to halt the Iraqi stalemate, now entering its fifth year. Tactical nukes were used to win the war in Afghanistan in 2004, paving the way for the beginning of the war on Iraq, which started the same year as victory was declared in Afghanistan."

Don muted the interview and finished cooking his breakfast. He carried it over to the table and read the paper and ate, looking for anything out of the ordinary. The headlines were the same as always—war. War in the Middle East, war in the Balkans, war marching across the globe like a cloaked figure with a scythe.

The war in Afghanistan had gone well, quick and successful, except for the guerilla holdouts in the north. President Cheney had taught them a very valuable lesson, "glassing" the area in and around the city of Mazar-i-Sharif, the fourth largest city in Afghanistan. Something like 40,000 people had died instantly, with a hundred thousand more sickened by the nuclear cloud that had drifted north into Uzbekistan. A hundred square miles now made up the "Cheney Zone," as the uninhabitable stretch of desert was known.

But that brutal, horrendous attack ended the war. The Taliban had fallen, and every insurgent captured was executed by Hamid Karzai's forces. But oddly, the tactical nuclear obliteration of Mazar-i-Sharif had emboldened the rest of the world for more fighting, including the United States. A dozen smaller wars, brewing since the months following 9/11, grew in breadth.

Cheney had then laid out his case against Iraq. Chemical weapons, weapons of mass destruction, al Qaeda training camps, active terrorist funding. Only months after victory in Afghanistan, as the troops were coming home to a grateful nation, the president embarked on another war. Weary, but understanding the need to fight terror anywhere in the world, the American public had backed the invasion, cheering as forces gathered in Kuwait and stormed across the border, hell-bent on racing each other to Baghdad.

But in Iraq, the invading United States and British forces had found an embedded and embittered enemy who would seemingly stop at nothing to repel the invasion and, more importantly, maintain Saddam Hussein's stranglehold on power. The front page in Don's hand said it all:

SADDAM'S CHEMICAL WEAPONS
UNLEASHED AGAIN

Riyadh, Saudi Arabia (AP) – Saddam Hussein announced on Monday the use of chemical weapons again, this time on a battalion of U.S. forces, saying that "the infidels must be pushed back into the sea." There have been several reports of casualties from the attack, thought to be mustard gas or some other highly-toxic nerve agent. The U.N. further condemned Iraq's use of banned chemical weapons and munitions. After the fall of Afghanistan in August 2004 and Basra in May of this year, U.S. military planners had expected to take the country by summer, but resistance forces from neighboring Iran and Syria have poured into the country, stemming the invasion and...

The story continued onto another page, but Don shook his head. He didn't need to read the rest—it was always the same. He flipped through the rest of the paper and finished his breakfast, then stood to do his dishes.

On the TV, he saw images of car bombs and turned up the sound to hear the report.

"Three more car bombs ripped through the newly-occupied Palestine Territory," the anchor said over footage of wreckage from car bombs and mass casualties. "The exiled leader of Israel, Yasser Arafat, again called for Israel to withdraw from Palestine. In the months after the terrorist attacks in New York and Washington, Israel invaded and occupied the Palestine territories, citing security reasons. Since the 2002 invasion, more than twelve hundred suicide bombings have taken place, as the Israeli government takes more divisive and controversial preemptive action to counter terrorist threats. Forcible removal of Palestinians resulted in Yasser Arafat's resignation as president of Israel in protest. Most of the leaders of Hezbollah were assassinated in the months after 9/11. Israel also has accelerated construction of a controversial security fence around the occupied..."

Don flipped the TV off, disgusted. The situation around the world had been unstable enough after 9/11, with the United States temporarily occupied with a constitutional crisis.

Of course, the Israelis had gone off the reservation and used the 9/11 attacks as an excuse to take back the Palestinian lands. Now, it was an all-out war, with air strikes on one side and waves of suicide bombers and Iranian-made missiles on the other.

And Israel had nukes.

Don wondered how long the Israelis would be able to control themselves before resorting to wholesale slaughter of the Palestinian squatters. Or how long the Iranians would sit on the sidelines—of course, their focus now was sending as many "martyrs" into Iraq as possible to fight the Americans. But they were reportedly close to developing their own nuclear weapons and recently had successfully tested a short-range ballistic missile. He was sure the Iranians had already picked out their list of targets in Israel.

Don didn't know a lot about politics, or geo-political movements, or international relations—he was a physicist. He didn't want to know anything about this stuff, but it had been important for him to steep himself in it, to learn enough about international relations to understand it and, more importantly, accurately predict future events. He'd called on a few of his former colleagues at the university, political science and international relations professors, to give him a crash course in the thinking that drove national leaders and dictators.

Don preferred theoretical physics, and meson particles, and string theory. Those concepts were cut-and-dried, true-or-false constructs, not abstractions based on mood, or revenge, or petty political gain. Next to trying to ascertain and predict shifting political allegiances and back-room deals, quantum entanglement was easy to understand. Don was far more comfortable in the world of the real. But he was learning enough to wander his way through areas that, just a couple of years before, would have been unnavigable.

And now, his research was complete.

Don gathered his keys and briefcase from the side table near the front door—he double-checked to make sure he had his USID. The checkpoints were bad enough without trying to explain that you had left your card at home.

Sarah had always been good at remembering where he'd left his keys. One time, she'd found a printout of a wayward PowerPoint presentation that he'd spent a solid and panicked half hour searching for; he'd inexplicably left it on the top of the refrigerator. She'd always needled him relentlessly about the time, when they'd first started dating, that she had found his car keys in the freezer. To this day, he still didn't understand how they could've gotten in there.

On the small table next to his keys and cell phone sat a dusty, framed certificate:

THE 1999 SAKURAI PRIZE FOR THEORETICAL PHYSICS

AWARDED TO DR. DONALD ELLIS

FOR DISCOVERIES RELATED TO THE PROPERTIES OF SPONTANEOUS AND REPEATING SYMMETRY IN FOUR-DIMENSIONAL THEORY AND OF THE CONSISTENT GENERATION OF GLUON AND MESON MASSES.

Don glanced at the framed certificate—he remembered that dinner. He'd been presented the award at a very fancy black-tie dinner in the city. He'd been so nervous, but Sarah had calmed him. The university had sent a limousine for them, the first and last time he'd ever ridden in one. He remembered sitting in the back of that limo, sweating bullets and agonizing over his speech.

She'd climbed into the car next to him, looking amazing in a slinky black number that he hadn't seen before. Sarah had taken away the note cards he'd been nervously fingering. She'd held his hands and told him stories of her youth in the Texas panhandle as the long black car glided into the city. Those were the stories that he remembered, goofy tales that she'd told him over the years. They had always helped him get through the tough days or long nights of research. Without effort, Don could recall several. He missed hearing those stories.

Don glanced around the house, seeing the pictures on the walls and reminders of her everywhere. Tina and Sarah. Sarah's old leather coat still hung on the hook by the front door. He never had people over—who would want to visit the house anyway, a mausoleum that he maintained in their memory? It was just creepy: the preserved rooms, the coat hanging by the door, as if Sarah would return at any moment, annoyed that she'd forgotten it.

Don could just imagine the looks he would get from visitors, sideways glances that made it clear how strange they thought the whole situation was.

And then there was the living room.

Don spent most of his time in there, anyway. Three walls were hidden behind bookshelves, next to the large fireplace she had loved. He slept many nights on the couch in the living room, when he wasn't sleeping at the warehouse.

He hated sleeping in their bed.

But the fourth wall of the living room was the one he imagined people would notice first. It was covered from floor to ceiling with newspaper clippings and photos and articles printed from the Internet. The collage now covered the whole wall, with strings tacked into articles and running down the wall to other articles. Pages torn from newspapers, with sections circled and handwritten notes in the margins. Printouts and mathematical formulas and a large "timeline" of events leading up to 9/11 covered the wall. Even to him, the wall looked like the lair of a crazy person, someone pathologically obsessed with the events of 9/11.

But the articles and pictures and research were important—there was no way for a visitor to understand what he was doing, or why it was important that he study these things, to commit them to memory, to capture scans and PDFs of all of the facets and details of the months and years leading up to 9/11.

Don didn't think any visitors would understand, and he didn't really care. He knew that afterward, the cops would search his home and find all of his notes—well, not *all* of his notes. Not anything really important and certainly nothing to give away what had really happened. But Don was pretty sure they'd look at the wall of his living room and shake their heads and assign him the official label of "nut job."

Don knew it was bad to surround himself with their things, but he had been unable to remove them, even though they had both been dead for ten years. Leaving all of this behind would be the hardest part—Tina's room and her books. Sarah's closet, filled with clothes that somehow smelled like her, even after all this time. Don still kept his things on his half of their closet. He still slept on his half of their bed.

Sometimes, in the morning, he still absentmindedly started her coffee for her. Once, his mind so distracted with a new set of calculations on the machine, he'd even made her an omelet, setting it out for her on the dining room table. It had been there, untouched, when he'd returned that evening from the warehouse.

Don sighed and opened the front door, stepping outside. It was a beautiful, blue sky day. He'd washed his car once on a day like this, a crisp September day ten years ago. While he'd washed his car, the most important people in his life...

Don shook his head. He turned, looking for a long moment down the dark hallway of a home that had become a museum.

Quietly, he closed the door behind him.

When Tina had been a baby, Sarah had always asked him to close the front door quietly, so as to not wake her. He'd gotten into the habit at the time.

It was a habit that he could not break, no matter how illogical it seemed.

1.2
LIBERTY, TEXAS

The smartly-dressed Asian man in dark sunglasses was watching a cloudless Texas sky when his earpiece cracked. He reached up and tapped at it.

"Yes?"

"Lin, it's Tuan," the speaker said in Korean. "We have the tower. There was only one American, and he's dead."

"Good," Lin answered. "What about the plane?"

"It should only be a few more minutes—they're on approach now. I'll be contacting them soon."

"OK," Lin answered, using the American idiom that had become universal, even in his home country. "Once they're down, direct them to the hangar."

Lin stood near the open doors of the airport hangar, watching the skies to the north. After a moment, he turned and glanced at the boxy white van inside the hangar—two Asian men stood next to it with machine guns. Lin could see Hyun at the back of the van; both doors stood open. The man was still tinkering with the large device inside—it was covered with wires and was the result of hundreds of hours of work for Lin and the others. Now, it rested quietly in the back of a van in a dusty airport hangar. It had traveled quite a road. And Lin saw no reason why Hyun should still be fiddling with it.

Lin tapped at the small earpiece/microphone in his ear.

"Hyun—can we lift it?"

Hyun turned and walked over. "It weighs almost six hundred pounds," he began, his English excellent. He'd schooled in California. "It will take all of us to get it into the plane. If that doesn't work, I found a small forklift at the back of the hangar, but that will delay takeoff."

Lin nodded, smiling. "Excellent."

"Are they approaching yet?"

"Tuan's directing them in now. His English is almost as good as yours, my friend."

Hyun nodded, taking Lin's arm.

"Are you sure about this? The remote operator will work—I've perfected it. There is no need for you to fly..."

"No, I want to," Lin answered quietly, tapping the back of his friend's hand. "It's the only way to be sure." They had been on this assignment together for a long time, and it was now coming to the end.

In the distance, they heard the sound of a small plane.

Lin nodded. "Here we go."

He turned and walked out of the hangar.

Turning to look to the north, Lin watched as a small plane approached the small airfield. The Cessna 182 turned, gliding in over the low trees and scrub that surrounded the landing strip. Lin noticed that there were oil wells pumping on the rise above the airport.

The plane slowed, the engine purring. The unseen pilot feathered the plane expertly to bleed off speed as he approached the runway, the wheels touching down lightly. The plane moved slowly south and then turned, taxiing to the only hangar at the tiny airport. It was one reason Lin had chosen this strip, a few miles outside of the small Texas town of Liberty.

The Cessna buzzed loudly as it taxied up to the hangar and came to a stop. Two large men climbed down from the plane, one of them wearing a cowboy hat, just like in the movies.

Lin walked up to them slowly, greeting them. "Welcome to Texas," he said, producing a handgun from his coveralls.

The pilot and passenger stopped—the look on their faces was comical. The other Koreans emerged from the hangar and escorted the men inside as Lin climbed into the plane and fired up the engine, taxiing it into the hangar. It only took a few moments. When the plane was in place, as close to the back of the van as he dared, Lin cut the engine. He secured the plane and climbed down, getting started on the pilot seat.

Across from him, the passenger door opened and Hyun poked his head in, smiling. He nodded and began using a large wrench to remove the passenger seat. The Cessna was a small plane, a four-seater, but to get the bulky device in, all of the seats would have to come out. Lin worked on the driver's side at the same time. Within minutes, all four seats had been removed and thrown on the floor of the hangar.

Lin walked over to the two men who were now tied up on the floor.

"You know," Lin said, looking down at them. "I've always wanted a cowboy hat." Lin leaned over and took the man's large hat, trying it on. He looked at the other Koreans. "What do you think?" he asked, giving them a thumbs-up.

One of them smiled. "You are cowboy!" he said, his accent thick.

Lin nodded and gave his friend a big smile, then drew two imaginary six shooters from his belt and started shooting with his fingers. "Bang, bang!" The others laughed as Lin walked over to the van, joining Hyun.

"Ready?" Lin asked. Hyun nodded.

Together, the men worked to pull the large device out of the back of the van. They and the three other Koreans lifted the device gingerly and slowly walked the device over to the open doors of the Cessna. It wasn't as heavy as Lin had feared, especially with five men carrying it. They slid it easily into the plane. Hyun went to work, connecting the final wires. Lin took a small folding chair out of the back of the van and walked over, standing it up inside the airplane.

"Not much of a seat," Hyun mumbled as he finished securing the device inside the plane. It was important that the device not move around in flight—managing the center of gravity in a small plane like this was difficult enough without a quarter-ton amalgamation of metal and wires moving around.

Lin smiled. "This seat will be fine." He climbed up into the folding chair that had replaced the pilot's seat, nodding as the other Koreans gathered around the door. Hyun finished and slammed the passenger door closed, coming around the plane to join the others.

"Good luck," they said together, and Lin smiled again and nodded.

"What should we do about the Americans?" Hyun asked quietly.

"Wait until you're ready to leave, and then kill them," Lin said. "And burn the hangar and the van as well. It might have some residual radiation. Take Tuan's van and go north."

Hyun glanced outside. "The prevailing winds are to the southwest. We'll be fine. Are you sure you don't want to use the remote? I spent a lot of time making it work, and I'm sure—"

"No, no. We've wasted too much time as it is," Lin said, patting his friend on the arm.

Lin started up the plane and expertly taxied it out of the hangar. He spoke to Tuan in the tower, who had already informed the Houston Air Route Traffic Control Center of the incoming flight, working to clear the airspace. Remarkably, there didn't appear to be any additional precautions from Houston. Lin and his group had assumed that, with today being the tenth anniversary of 9/11, there might have been a few additional hoops to jump through. They had prepared a back story and sufficient paperwork, just in case they were questioned by Houston. But Tuan had said nothing was out of the ordinary; he'd gotten Lin a clear corridor all the way in.

Finally, Lin throttled up the engines and the plane raced down the runway, picking up speed. It took a moment or two longer than Lin had expected, but the overweight plane finally nosed up into the sky. The rickety pilot seat leaned back as he pointed the plane into the sky. The seat wasn't at all comfortable, and it wiggled around a lot from the vibration of the engine, but Lin didn't really mind.

He knew the discomfort wouldn't last long.

1.3
A WAREHOUSE IN RED HOOK

Dr. Donald Ellis drove into the city on the Long Island Expressway. The tall buildings of the Manhattan skyline, forever altered, took up the entire front window of his car.

For years before 9/11, he'd driven into the city and never thought about the World Trade Center buildings. They were just there, two more tall slabs of metal and concrete in an uneven skyline. Now they were gone, but he still glanced in their direction. Sometimes he saw a shadow of them in the corner of his eye, a reverse image memory of where they had been, like when you stare at a dark object in front of a light background. For him, there would always be a dark smudge of an afterimage in his vision where the two hulking towers had stood.

He passed through two U.S. military checkpoints between his home in Jericho and Queens, with a third one at the interchange from the LIE onto I-278. It was overkill, to say the least. The backups were just a fact of life now, but there was always a longer backup at this checkpoint than most—it was the last one before the Brooklyn Bridge. The military never moved the checkpoints—in fact, the "temporary" buildings the Army had put up to house security personnel were starting to look like permanent additions to the urban landscape. Atop one of the military buildings, Don saw a menacing machine gun pointed down at the highway full of Volvos and Hondas and Mercedes, each inching their way to the checkpoint.

After *posse comitatus* was suspended as part of the First Patriot Act, the U.S. military had been called in to assist police forces around the country with various security operations, including checkpoints, airport and seaport security, and border patrols.

While he waited in line, Don got out his USID, the American eagle hologram reflecting in his eyes. There had been so many "show us your papers" jokes at the beginning, all uttered in horribly fake German accents, when Homeland Security had begun instituting the U.S.

Identification System, but Don didn't think the jokes were funny. It was just one more personal freedom gone, one more thing about American life that had been surrendered to the terrorists. What had Ben Franklin said? "Those who would give up liberty to purchase safety deserve neither," or something like that.

And it wasn't even real safety—it was an illusion. Folks sitting in their cars at checkpoints, or lined up at the airport for screening, felt better, right? "Well, look at how much effort the government is putting into protecting me. Wow. That really does make me feel safer!"

It was crap. In Don's mind, it was the terrorists' way of destroying the United States from the inside. They couldn't beat us with guns, or bombs, or invade the country, so they had to get at us another way—turn us on each other.

It sickened Don, but there was nothing he could do. All of the people around him were just a product of their times and their circumstances. For things to be different, history would have to be different. Army checkpoints and USID and war—it was just the logical outcome of the events of 9/11. Don could see that now.

Don shook his head and glanced over at the other cars around him. Most of the other drivers were on their cell phones—he saw several Apple iPhones and smiled. Don couldn't control the Army or national politics, but he could certainly try to watch the trends and make money. Money was one of the few things he really needed—money and time and privacy.

Apple had hit it big, and that stock had done very well for him over the last six years, especially since they'd launched the iPad. It was taking the tech world by storm, which surprised him, considering it had been a rumored product launch for a year and a half. Didn't everyone know it was coming? Hadn't everyone seen the brewing excitement? Making money on Apple stock seemed like a no-brainer. Apple's iPhone was cleaning up at the market as well as people snapped up the handsets. Apple was on its fourth version of the phone, and new versions of the iPhone and iPad were scheduled to come out in 2012.

Don glanced over at Queens and Brooklyn beyond, stretching off to the south of the freeway. There were blocks and blocks of apartment buildings, intermixed with warehouses, restaurants, and a few parks.

His car edged up to the checkpoint and, after a short conversation with a soldier, he was waved through. Big dogs were led around his car, sniffing at it from all angles at a secondary bomb check, and then he drove on. Don shook his head and continued on 278 South, heading toward Brooklyn. Off to his right, downtown Manhattan disappeared as his car weaved through low tunnels and overpasses.

He took 278 through Brooklyn Heights and got off at Columbia Street, heading south. All of the property to his right, along the waterfront, was owned by the Port Authority. Don made his way through the neighborhoods and cut over to Van Brunt, passing the beautiful red Friends of Firefighters building—they were a nonprofit organization set up after 9/11 to help care for the families of lost firefighters. Over the past nine years, they had grown into an organization dedicated to helping firefighters and their families through community support and fundraising. A lot of people didn't realize that many retired FDNY members volunteered to return to service after 9/11 and the devastating losses inflicted on the number of active firefighters in New York City. It made Don happy to know that there were so many good people out there in the world.

But the 9/11 attacks had changed everything for so many people. So many lives were changed—loved ones lost, lives disrupted forever. Entire families killed.

After abruptly leaving the university after 9/11, he'd set up shop in a quiet warehouse in Red Hook, a run-down neighborhood on the west side of Brooklyn. The ugly-looking building was located among a dozen others, but it afforded him three things that would be essential in his work.

The first was unfettered access to the high-power electrical lines that his equipment would require: power lines and transmission lines.

The second thing he needed was privacy; the warehouse district was notorious for being full of crime-ridden lairs for squatters and troublemakers. He had been careful to choose a location that could be easily secured, with no large windows. The entire facility was surrounded by razor-topped fencing.

The third reason he'd located in Red Hook was that the row of warehouses afforded an exceptional view of the Manhattan skyline. Governors Island stood in the water just offshore, and no bridges or towers obstructed the view of where the World Trade Center had stood.

A last, important detail he'd considered might not have made any sense to an outside observer, but to him, it was very important. When he'd been negotiating with the local commercial real estate agent to secure a location in the blocks of warehouses, he had asked to see the lists of previous tenants in the buildings. She'd looked at him strangely—clearly, she wondered why he would care. He'd explained that he was concerned about contaminants from previous tenants interfering with his chemical experiments, and she'd bought the story. But he was actually researching previous tenants, or lack thereof, and factoring them into the purchasing decision.

Don continued down Van Brunt Street and turned on Wolcott, following it until he reached the waterfront and a nondescript warehouse that sat next to the water. He used the remote on his keychain to open the security gate. A security guard appeared as soon as the gate began to open—one area where Don had spared no expense was on facility security. It was no secret that he was working on some type of physics experiment inside the warehouse, and he'd hired the best security agency in the area to keep the curious away—and anyone looking to strip out two hundred feet of copper tubing to sell for recycling.

Of course, no value could be placed on the machine inside the building, if things went as planned.

Don nodded at the guard and directed his Volvo around to the large parking lot. At one point, this building had been a cannery, so the parking lot could hold eighty or ninety vehicles. On this sunny morning, as was usual, it was only his Volvo, Terry's red truck, and a dozen more cars for the other technicians and security personnel, surrounded by a weedy expanse of empty spaces. Beyond the East River stood the Manhattan skyline.

Don climbed from his car and headed inside. The front reception area held a guard desk, where two guards checked IDs and waved people through a small metal detector. They waved at Don as he passed them and unlocked a set of doors marked with signs that said

POWER BLOSSOM PHYSICS RESEARCH FACILITY
NO GUESTS OR VISITORS ALLOWED.

Beyond the locked doors lay the expansive main floor of the warehouse and several small rooms that he had had built on the main floor, including an office for himself, a large computer lab, a galley and break room, and a small machine shop for fabricating parts. Above these was a small, second-story apartment where he occasionally slept when he was too tired to make the drive home. Even the top of the second floor was dwarfed by the high warehouse ceiling, and the constructed rooms on the eastern side of the main floor took up only a small portion of the space.

The rest of the main floor was taken up by a massive machine. As Don passed through the working spaces and out onto the main floor, he stopped to look at it, a massive assemblage of tubes and structural components and hundreds of miles of thick cabling, running off to various parts of the warehouse.

Don was really only using about a tenth of the space, but he had been unable to estimate the exact size of the project when he'd been shopping for locations. He walked across the wide, concrete floor, stacked with massive wooden crates that had held many of the specially built parts he had procured from all over the world. Now, the packing crates and boxes served to fill the empty rooms and visually block the machine from prying eyes.

He passed the last of the boxes and saw their working area—he'd essentially built another small building on the main floor of the warehouse and housed his equipment, offices, and support systems inside it. Another guard stood outside as he waved and entered, then went down a small hallway and into a room marked OFFICE. He sat his briefcase and keys down on a desk covered with electronics. He glanced at the SEPTEMBER 2011: WE'LL NEVER FORGET! calendar on the wall and left, heading out into the larger open room.

Don had managed to convince the university and some of its donors to fund the initial phase. He had been convincing in his presentations, promising a whole new field of energy production resulting from his experimentation. The university had been sad to see him leave the teaching position but had supported him in his new work, going so far as to allow him to poach most of his staff and research assistants from the school.

Now, years into the project, many of his recent successful experiments had added greatly to the bottom line of Power Blossom, LLC, the corporation that he had set up to hold all of the assets and financial interests of this new venture. The LLC was doing well now, fully funding the operation. He still owed the university a sizeable amount of money from the initial investment, but he didn't think they would see their money. It was for the greater good, what he was doing here, and he hoped, on some level, they would understand.

Don smiled, remembering how he stifled a crazy grin when sitting across the desk from his lawyer as they set up the LLC and its component parts. Don had explained the structure, including the fact that he was donating his personal accounts to the venture. Don had then added another mortgage to the house and had taken out several other personal loans in the last two years, over the protestations of his lawyers and accountants.

Of course, the men were not working with the full knowledge set. They didn't have the whole picture and, as a result, didn't understand the full implications of Don Ellis donating his personal fortune, as it was, to an LLC. Don had given the accountant enough of an explanation to make the transfer of funds palatable, not going into the details. And Don had hidden a smile when he'd explained that he wanted to call his post-university research venture Power Blossom. He hinted at the idea that the research might result in a radical new power source. It was the same explanation he'd given to the university and the donors.

He hadn't explained to his lawyer that Power Blossom actually came from the Powerpuff Girls and Tina's favorite member of the cartoon superhero team, Blossom. He'd assumed that working in the names of the other two characters, Bubbles and Buttercup, might raise too many eyebrows, so he'd left it at that, content in the knowledge that, in the end, the entire multi-million dollar project was dedicated to his young girl.

The machine stood in the center of the huge warehouse. It was an impressive sight, even if it was impossible to guess what the machine did just by looking at it. The central particle accelerator stood in the middle, surrounded by support structures and scaffolding, and Don could see two of the research assistants climbing on the outside of the accelerator. Large pipes and tubes and wires ran across the floor to a large computer terminal.

The machine itself, coincidentally, resembled pictures he had seen of the Large Hadron Collider, now under construction in Switzerland. Of course, Don's machine was much smaller and almost eight times as powerful. The LHC, funded by an international coalition of governments and research facilities, was being built to test theories about physics and quantum mechanics on a subatomic scale. The Ellis machine was being built for a much more specific purpose. But only Don was privy to that information.

He found Terry sleeping on the couch in Don's office.

"Terry?" Don asked, waking the man. "Seriously, you shouldn't be sleeping here. The others won't respect you, and it's my office. I prefer to keep it locked up, you know."

The large man sat up, rubbing his eyes. Don saw a plate of pizza crusts on the side table, next to the remote for the large-screen TV that hung on the wall of the break room.

"I know, boss. Sorry. The testing team stayed late, running that last set of figures," Terry said, nodding at a sheaf of large computer printouts on a table in the center of the room.

Don nodded, taking the papers and flipping through them.

"Plus," Terry continued, "I'm in trouble at home. Too many late nights."

"Katie giving you a hard time?" Don asked, not looking up from the figures.

Terry nodded. "Yeah, she thinks I work too much. We had a date last night—it was a Saturday, but I forgot. And I can't really tell her a lot about what we're doing here, so it's hard for her to understand. You know what I mean…" he began, but stopped abruptly, looking at Don.

"No," Don said quietly. "I don't." His voice sounded tired, even to himself.

Don knew the technical support staff avoided the subject of his family—everyone knew what had happened to them. But people often brought up the subject of their own families and then hurriedly stopped talking. Whether out of guilt or embarrassment, Don couldn't say. Either way, he didn't really care.

Terry looked at him strangely, but Don knew he wasn't going to say anything.

"Just be glad you have someone to worry about you, Terry. It could be worse," Don said, looking at Terry.

Terry nodded slowly, his eyes wide.

"Now," Don asked. "Are the calibrations done?"

Terry nodded vigorously.

"They're complete," he answered. "The last three tests we ran last night were in the green. The margin is now down to 0.52 percent, which is within acceptable parameters, based on the planning documents."

Don walked out of the room, not saying anything, and Terry followed him to the computer lab, where Don sat at a large monitor and began tapping at the keyboard. Presently, a set of schematics for the machine appeared, spinning slowly. Don tapped at the keyboard, stopping the schematic and zooming in on the round red object in the middle of the machine. "And the accelerator—how did she do?"

"Great, boss," Terry answered, excited. "I think we got those wave formation problems solved, and it's taking in all the power it can. 'We're giving her all we've got, captain!'" Terry said weakly, but Don didn't smile at the Star Trek reference. One thing he would not miss about Terry would be his cheesy movie references.

Don pinched the bridge of his nose, something he did when he was tired. He wondered if anyone else ever noticed. "Good, good." Don said, nodding at the screen. "This margin of variance is much lower than on our last five experiments, and those were all positive, so I'd say we're on the right track."

Don was referring to the five earlier times that they had operated the machine with positive outcomes. They had actually powered up and fired the machine on twenty-seven occasions over the past nine weeks, but only five of those "events" could be construed as positive.

In each of those cases, an item was retrieved from the future.

Actually, in each case, a test item was sent into the future and then retrieved successfully. All five events had been recorded and documented, and now the items were stored away in a safe in Don's office.

"Did you update your research notes?" Don asked, looking up at Terry. "It's very important that everything be written down, or we'll never be able to prove our work for the patent office. We need to catalog every step of our work, especially the failures." The five successful events had been interspersed with failures—in fact, they had experimented with so many different wave forms and tweaks to the machine that, until last night, they had gone two weeks since the last success.

"Did you send anything through?" Don asked.

Terry shook his head. "No, I'd never do that without you here. We were just verifying the wave form and the field variance, trying to get it down to zero."

Don nodded. "I don't think it'll ever get down to zero, but we're close. Close enough, I think."

Terry nodded. "That's why I was up late—the notes are all up to date, including last night's testing numbers and the solution to the wave formation issues."

Don nodded. They were ready, or as ready as they would ever be. "Good. Let's set up for another test. Can you get it ready?"

Terry smiled and left the computer lab as Don went back to the computer, verifying that the latest lab notes and every other scrap of information that he had gathered over the last five years was saved on the mainframe and in three other locations, including a cloud-based encrypted backup system. He'd have to remember to delete all of the data sets and backups before he left—

"Excuse me, Dr. Ellis?"

Don looked up to see Peter Burg, the head of security, peeking his head inside the computer lab. Burg was the perfect person to be in charge of security: huge, bald, burly, and without a shred of curiosity about what Ellis and his team were building.

"Yes?" Don asked.

Burg waved his walkie-talkie—all the guards carried them.

"You better turn on the news, sir." he said. "Thomas outside said he heard something on the radio that you need to know about."

Don thanked him and walked into his office, switching on the news. Images of fire appeared on the screen, with the CNN logo in the bottom right corner, and a news anchor spoke over the video from a helicopter flying over the city.

"That appears to be a bus or truck of some sort, but I can't see any buildings yet. There is too much dust and debris. Just to repeat our top story, it appears that a massive bomb, possibly nuclear or radioactive in nature, has been detonated in the airspace above Houston, Texas."

Oh, God, Don thought. Not again. Not another attack.

"Initial reports indicate that a small plane had been flying above the city, and air traffic controllers at George Bush Intercontinental Airport had been unable to raise the pilot. What you are seeing now are the first pictures we're getting—apparently, the device aboard the plane was detonated over the Garden Oaks area of greater Houston, the northwestern portion of the city."

Terry and another technician ran into the room to see the news report, joined by several others.

"Homeland security officials are just reacting to the event, and a press conference is scheduled in the next few minutes. It may be some time before we start to receive initial casualty estimates, especially because of the need to factor in wind patterns. If the weapon does turn out to be chemical or nuclear, the device may have been intentionally detonated upwind from downtown Houston to increase the number of casualties. We're joined now by..."

Don switched it off.

Terry and the other technicians looked at him, incredulous.

"What are you doing? Don't you want to find out—"

"It doesn't matter," Don said tersely, looking at Terry and the others, who were confused. "We need to keep working on the machine."

Don turned and walked out of the office, heading back to the computer lab. Behind him, he heard the TV switch back on. The other technicians stayed in his office to watch the news, but Terry followed him.

"It doesn't matter?" Terry asked, his voice low as they entered the lab. "How can it not matter? There might be 100,000 people dead by the end of the week. How can *that* not matter?"

Don ignored him, sitting back down at the computer.

After a few long moments, Terry shook his head and walked away.

Don didn't blame him. Terry had no idea what they were working on here, really. None of them did—they were all under the impression that they were working on a particle accelerator that was capable of transmitting objects and items over distances. If Terry knew what they were really working on, he might've understood what Don meant.

He didn't see Terry for the rest of the day—Don poured over the results from last night's tests, trying to pinpoint the reason for the 0.52 percent variation. It was within acceptable parameters, but any variation meant a problem in the machine, something that Don needed to solve.

Of course, if things started to go south in a hurry, Don was comfortable enough to use the machine, even with the variance.

1.4
LATE HOURS

Don looked up some time later and realized that the warehouse was silent. Above his head, the windows were dark—it was nighttime. He'd worked nine hours straight without noticing it or noticing that everyone else had left.

No one had said goodbye, either—probably a reaction to his odd behavior. He needed to watch himself. He needed to keep it all under control. It was only for a short time, anyway.

Don walked to the front security doors and found a guard seated at the main desk, watching a small TV. On the screen, Don saw a news report.

"Everyone gone home?"

The guard looked up from his desk, nodding. "Yes, Dr. Ellis. Most—well, most of them went home to watch the news. And to be with their families, sir," the man added quietly.

Don nodded. "Thanks for staying. When is your relief?"

"6:00 a.m., sir."

Don nodded again and turned, heading back inside.

Hours of work, alone, and he hadn't noticed. On his walk back to the lab, he decided to try another test and then knock off early tonight. He would head home before his usual quitting time of 8:00 or 9:00 p.m.

In the computer lab, he ran another computer simulation then walked out to the machine. Don leaned over the main terminal, tapping in his credentials and powering up the machine—it took almost twenty minutes for the capacitors to prepare to fire—and left, heading back to his office, closing and locking the door behind him.

Opening the large safe, he took out the small pad of yellow Post-its and the five notes with writing on them. He ignored the large duffel bag and a strange, drum-like device.

He'd run the other tests at night, after everyone had gone home, and these five small notes were the proof of his successful tests.

The first night, back in July, he'd tried the first experiment. He had taken one of the Post-its and placed it on the machine's primary target area, below the particle accelerator. On the paper, he had written "7/9/11: Top NYSE percentage gainer for the day." Below those words, he'd drawn a box and signed his name inside.

He'd stepped back to the computer terminal that operated the machine and typed, "Send +86440 seconds," or 24 hours. After a second of hovering his mouse over the red EXECUTE button on the screen, he had clicked it.

At first, he thought something had gone wrong—the machine emitted a sound that sounded like breaking ice on a frozen pond. He thought something was breaking loose from the machine.

The machine worked primarily by using a wave formation, combined with advanced quantum entanglement, to collapse space and time in a very small area into a series of synchronized and entangled energy waves. The particle accelerator then, using massive amounts of power, pushed the object or objects inside the target area into the wave space. Conversely, the accelerator could "interrogate" the coordinated wave space anywhere along a finite time period for the object and return it to this reality.

The theory was that, due to the proclivities of quantum entanglement, the wave in this universe and the identical wave in a universe moving parallel to our own would be connected momentarily, allowing the object to pass through. The variance issue made it difficult—only when they had been able to get the wave formation variance below 0.5 percent were they able to generate a stable enough field for the waves to "sync up" and allow an exchange of physical objects. And the mass of the object passing through determined the amount of energy required—so far, they had only sent through and retrieved tiny objects. When Don started to experiment with increased time differences between the synchronized wave spaces, his power consumption rates would probably increase exponentially.

As he watched, the small square of yellow in the target area faded out of existence.

He got up and walked over, running his hand over the flat metal area right under the particle accelerator aperture—the machine created a wave form and directed it through the accelerator and down onto this small metal platform. Anything sitting on the platform would be affected by the wave formation, but the metal platform, as it was part of the machine, was not affected.

Now, the note was gone.

He walked back over to the terminal and began typing:

"Retrieve +172880 seconds."

After another second, he clicked EXECUTE.

Immediately, the cracking sounds filled the air, and Don looked around as the lights flickered in the warehouse. The machine was drawing massive amounts of power from the capacitors, which drank up power slowly from the local utility and discharged it all at once to power the hungry machine. He was using enough power to light up the entire neighborhood for a day, and all in just a few milliseconds.

The note faded back into existence.

He walked around and looked at the blank Post-it for a long moment before reaching out with a Geiger counter, waving the wand over the small object. The readings were low but showed some residual radiation, something that his theories had predicted.

He set the counter aside and picked up the piece of paper, flipping it over.

"Gap shares, up 18 percent, 7/9/2011, 6:00 p.m."

It was in his own handwriting. And it was dated tomorrow night.

The other notes were similar—in each case, he'd sent Post-it notes into the future, getting stock tips. It was a ridiculous use for the first operational time machine. But it proved that the machine worked.

The investments made on the knowledge had paid off very well. He'd disguised the stock purchases by buying blocks of several stocks at a time—none did as well as the "target" stock of the day, of course. In some cases, he'd bought groups of random stocks that had gone down, but the stock always paid off handsomely. Power Blossom's accounts were growing quickly.

Don had tried sending the notes farther into the future, and they had always come back with no problems.

Tonight, he asked the future version of himself for the top ten stocks for September 13, 2011, forty-eight hours in the future.

The sixth experiment went uneventfully—the Post-it disappeared, but this time he had attached it to a one-foot square metal cage, containing a sedated mouse. He then sent it forward, waited a few seconds, and retrieved it with no problems. The additional mass had required more power, which he made note of—he would need to calculate the power needed to project himself in time and ensure that the machine's capacitors could handle the energy output.

As usual, the note came back filled in with the pertinent information, in his own handwriting, attached to the cage. The mouse returned alive and awake, running around the cage. There was a half-eaten carrot in the bottom of the cage. Evidently, someone had seen fit to feed the little guy.

He returned to his office and, after locking away the Post-it notes, he logged into his brokerage account and bought stocks. He used the list of top ten gainers from today and the list from the future, buying substantial amounts of twenty different stocks. By buying them ahead of the large gains to come in two days, he hoped it wouldn't look too suspicious. He had also bought today's gainers, which were statistically likely to go down over the next two days. A loss was fine, especially if it turned curious eyes away. Either way, he should be able to turn his last major profit. Or prophet, depending on how you wanted to spell it.

According to his latest theory of branching timelines, every time Don sent a Post-it into the future, the future version of him that found the note remembered only having sent it to himself in the future—he never received a note of his own. When the note came back, it reentered the original timeline and returned to the previous location on the time machine.

But as soon as someone, such as himself, found the note and acted upon it, a new timeline was created. That meant that every time Don read a note and acted upon it, he was creating a new timeline. The item from the future was just an object out of time. It didn't create a break in space-time or form a branching timeline—only his actions, or someone else taking an active interest in the Post-it, could create a new timeline.

It was hard to imagine that he had the power to create whole new universes, but it seemed to be the case.

So far, he had not received or filled in any Post-its from days past. That meant that each time, they were going "uptime" to his future, but when they came back "downtime" and he saw the note, a new timeline was created.

So much power, contained within a stupid yellow square.

But if an alternate timeline were created every time he successfully communicated with the future, then he was now in a seventh timeline. Every other timeline involved him sending a note into the future, finding it the next day, filling it out, and watching it disappear as the machine retrieved it from the future. In those other six timelines, the other Dr. Ellis' would never know if the machine worked or not, because once a person had proof that the machine worked, it would create a new timeline.

And if his branching timelines theory was correct, then he was concerned. If he was able to travel through time, projecting himself backwards, then whenever he acted in a way contrary to original events, he would be creating alternate timelines. If that were true, then he would never be able to actually improve things in this world, his only reality. In this version, he had lost his wife and child.

Because as soon as he went back in time, a new branching universe would be created. Nothing could ever affect the original timeline. Nothing he did could ever save his wife and child. But it was just a theory, at this point. He would need to be sure.

Don shook his head, all of the timelines and Post-it notes and alternating theories filling his head. He needed a good night's sleep, but he didn't feel like sleeping at the warehouse again. Instead, he gathered up his things from the office and headed out.

He locked up the double doors to the lab and waved at the guard as he walked to his car. He glanced up at the skyline, as he always did. It was just a reflex now, an impulse, but the Trade Center was always gone. No matter how many times he looked, it was always missing.

The news on the radio from Houston had gotten even worse, if that could be imagined. Apparently, the air burst over the sprawling city had contaminated a larger portion of the city than previously expected. CNN had the initial casualty count at 21,000, but their numbers were changing by the hour as new reports came in.

Don slowed at the checkpoint to get onto the LIE—three Humvees full of Marines were checking cars before they were allowed to get onto the highway, east or westbound. He saw other Humvees racing into the city, full of troops—they were probably increasing security on the bridges and tunnels, just in case. The additional security meant a slower checkpoint.

He knew better than to be impatient. Today's events in Houston, along with the significance of the day, had put everyone on edge, he assumed, and the military would be extra diligent. An efficient organization would have two lines of cars, with one for people like Don who were heading to Long Island and the other for cars headed downtown. But, as he'd been reminded a thousand times over the past nine years, the U.S. military was designed for efficacy, not efficiency.

Don rolled his window down as he finally made it to the front of the line of cars, waving his USID.

"Evening, sir," the soldier said, his hand resting casually on the butt of his rifle as he leaned over. "Heading into the city tonight?" the young man asked, his eyes roaming Don's face, the plastic card, and the interior of the car with one long, practiced glance.

Don shook his head. "No, just headed home. Jericho, on Long Island."

The soldier looked at him for a moment and then smiled, standing. "You have a good night, sir," the young man said, waving him through. Don directed his car onto the expressway, heading for home.

It had been this way since 9/11. The U.S. military had been obliged to take on an expanded role in homeland security during the chaos that followed the attacks on New York and Washington. People understood, with Congress essentially wiped out and the Pentagon half destroyed, that the country was on the edge of anarchy. President Bush had made the difficult decision to suspend the time-honored rule of *posse comitatus*, which prevented the use of U.S. military troops for law enforcement on U.S. soil.

The fall of 2001 was a traumatic period—anxiety about more attacks, the Anthrax scare, war breaking out around the world. Most people had welcomed the U.S. military with open arms, wanting to feel safe and protected and reassured, warm in the bosom of American might. As had happened during the 1992 Los Angeles riots and many natural disasters, the National Guard and military troops had been called in to calm a tense situation.

It had worked, making the nation feel safer, more protected. But the years had marched on, and the military stayed, establishing more permanent "temporary" checkpoints and forming completely militarized cordons along the northern and southern borders of the continental U.S. And many wondered why there were still checkpoints outside many of the major U.S. cities, ten years after 9/11. The Houston attack would go a long way toward silencing any of the brave civil libertarians that had spoken up about the increasing "militarization" of the U.S. mainland.

But Don still didn't like it. He didn't like the idea of the military checking people as they tried to drive into New York or military security at every major airport. The First and Second Patriot Acts had changed this country, and he wondered if it would ever be the same.

Now, the Third Patriot Act had introduced USID cards, universal identification cards that you were supposed to carry with you, everywhere you went. Don was against the new USID cards, too. The U.S. was involved in two wars, and there was talk that the government might have to institute World War II–style rationing. President Cheney was a warmonger, surrounding himself with similar-minded people after ousting Bush in the spring of 2003, having him declared mentally unfit for the presidency. He was subsequently elected on his own in 2004 and 2008. There were many that would have agreed with him about President Bush's mental state after the chaos of 9/11, but now it seemed they had traded a president unsure of how to proceed, stunned by the loss of Congress and his wife, for a new president that looked to pick fights around the world.

There was even discussion, in some circles, of repealing the 22nd Amendment, allowing President Cheney to seek a third term in 2012.

When he got home, Don tried to watch the news, but it was just too depressing. Instead, he started the coffee maker. He knew he wouldn't sleep if he tried to go to bed—he was unable to fall asleep before 2:00 or 3:00 a.m. usually, so he spread out the blueprints on the dining room table and started up his laptop. He might as well get some work done.

But the silence in the house was oppressive. He put the news back on and turned the volume low, just so the house wouldn't be silent.

1.5
NORTH KOREA

It took less than three days for the U.S. government to conclude that North Korea had been behind the deadly Houston attack—evidently, the one-engine plane used to deliver the device had been stolen from an airport in eastern Texas. The device had been loaded into the plane and then flown by a suicide bomber to its intended target. The name on the rental receipt on a white van, found at the airport, was traced back to a community in northern California. After the FBI and U.S. military had moved in and begun interrogating everyone in the community, it was discovered that the plot was instigated by agents from North Korea, who had been planning the attack for months.

President Cheney held a primetime news conference, something he seemed to love to do. He announced the findings and warned the United Nations and the North Koreans that actions were being considered. CNN reported that the FBI had a very strong case against the North Koreans, and it was just a matter of time before the United States retaliated. The initial casualty numbers were over 30,000.

Houston was devastated, to be sure, but it looked like much of the radiation cloud would be drifting out over the Gulf of Mexico and away from any populated areas, dissipating before it could reach either Mexico or Florida. In a twisted sense, it seemed like a lucky break that the terrorists had chosen a target like Houston.

But it was another attack, another blow to the American psyche that was so fragile. Even now, ten years later, the attack on 9/11 still rattled people's hearts and minds.

21,502 had been the final tally for the 9/11 attacks. There had been 17,429 people killed in the attacks on the World Trade Center complex in New York City. The city had been brought to its knees—losing their leaders, including the mayor, along with the towers. The financial district would be crippled for months. And the attack on the Pentagon had left it half destroyed, with another 2,641 dead. The attackers had crashed their fuel-laden jumbo jet into the aging symbol of American military power and crippled it. Fire had raced through the 1940s-era construction, and hundreds had perished, partly due to outdated emergency systems and a substandard sprinkler system.

But the part of the attack that had the most prolonged affect on the nation was the destruction of the Capitol building, along with the 1,432 souls lost on Capitol Hill—senators and representatives, along with policemen and visiting tourists. To see the U.S. Capitol building brought down was a devastating blow to the American psyche, not to mention the fact that over half of the working members of Congress had been killed.

The nation had been brought to its knees.

It would take Bush and the remnants of Congress months to fill the empty seats, find meeting locations and alternate working areas, and reconstitute Congress. But it would take much longer to restore American's faith in the promise that we would rally and succeed.

It was no wonder Bush had crumbled under the pressure just months later. And it was no wonder the American people had embraced the militarization of the U.S. homeland to such an unprecedented scale.

This new attack in Houston had reminded people just how vulnerable we were. In some ways, it was amazing that President Cheney hadn't already nuked North Korea off the map.

Don was not watching the news any more—the numbers coming out of Houston were just too depressing, and he didn't need to hear about the American ships steaming off toward the coast of North Korea. It was clear that they would be invading soon, so instead of going into the warehouse to work, he'd decided to stay home and exercise his other passion. Unrelated to his current experiments with stock investments, he was working on another financial aspect of his project.

After getting the mail, he walked down the hallway, passing a table near the doorway to the kitchen. On it stood a dusty plaque from the city of New York. It was adorned with a picture of Mayor Peter Powers, expressing the city's regret at the loss of Sarah and Tina Ellis, lost in the terrorist attacks of September 11, 2001.

He stepped into the living room and walked up to the wall covered with tattered, faded clippings and newspaper articles. There were magazine covers, newspapers screaming the horrible news: the collapse and destruction of the World Trade Center, along with the destroyed U.S. Capitol dome in D.C. Photographs of hijacked planes frozen in the sky, just before they hit their targets, littered the wall.

The front page of *The Washington Post* showed a large picture of the smoking Capitol dome, collapsed in on itself, a picture that would come to symbolize that horrible day. The headlines below the pictures noted the hundreds of Congressmen and staff that had been killed. Other papers detailed the attack on the Pentagon—one picture showed a burning Pentagon in the foreground and a collapsed, smoking Capitol dome in the background.

Another large color photograph showed the banking second plane just as it hit the South Tower, spraying a fireball of jet fuel out the other side. Next to that photograph was one of the North Tower falling, destroying most of the other buildings in the World Trade Center complex. That included WTC Building 7, which had housed New York City's Emergency Management Center—everyone inside had died, including Mayor Giuliani, the Chief of Police, and a dozen other high-ranking city officials. Their deaths in the crushed building had ended the chances of any coordinated local response to the attacks.

Other newspaper headlines mentioned the essential decapitation of the U.S. Congress, with the loss of so many senators and representatives. Several months later, there were still so many vacancies that the country had been seriously crippled, and the First Patriot Act was passed with a rubber stamp from the gutted Congress.

A hundred other articles hung on the wall, with information about the terrorists, their funding, their motivations. Don's scratchy handwriting in red Sharpie could be found in the margins, circling items of particular importance: structural reports on the World Trade Center, including post-attack examinations of why the towers fell. Reports on the Pentagon's 1940's-era construction, including archival photos of the building under construction—on these, he had written and underlined "improved construction techniques, bullet-proof glass, sprinklers." Continuity of government documents, detailing several new procedures were put into place after 9/11 to designate backups for every Congressperson and create alternate meeting locations during an attack. There were even listings of the most popular conspiracy theories out there, including the one that espoused that the U.S. government itself had been behind the attacks. Don didn't put any stock in any of the theories, but he wanted to see the story from all angles.

Don shook his head and walked back into the dining room. The blueprints for the machine and his other papers had been moved off the dining room table and replaced with books and printouts bearing titles such as *Making Money in the Stock Market* and *Trading Derivatives in a Turbulent Market*.

Don was working at his laptop, a small silver Toshiba he'd recently bought for his upcoming trip. The tiny machine was the top-of-the-line laptop available, yet the styling was similar to Toshibas from ten years ago, an important consideration for him. Don tapped away at it, downloading reams of historical and financial data and using off-the-shelf and customized financial software to scan for investment opportunities.

The company he'd hired to write the customized scanning software had been confused by his initial email requests. He'd had to explain to them that he was interested in finding investment opportunities at various points over the last fifty years.

"I'm trying to figure out the optimal investment windows for these securities," he'd told the young female programmer who had called him after several fruitless days of emails back and forth.

"You're scanning for opportunities to invest, but using historical data?" the woman asked. He could tell she was confused.

"That's right," he'd said. "I'm researching the optimal entry points for a course I'll be presenting at the university this year," he'd lied. "I'll be instructing students on how to recognize windows of opportunity in historical data, so they can find correlations in the current data."

That had done the trick—two weeks later, he'd received a CD in the mail with his customized program, which was chugging away right now on his machine, crunching historical stock quotes and other data that he was downloading from Yahoo Finance through an anonymous web query server, to avoid having his search tracked back to him.

Of course, after he left on his "trip," certain people would be intensely interested in talking to him—mostly the FBI and the U.S. military as well as a host of creditors.

Don had already maxed out several dozen credit cards, purchasing materials and sourcing parts from a dozen different countries under several different names. He had taken out second and third mortgages on the house, money he never planned to pay back. Nor did he plan to return the $2.1 million in seed money that the university had provided him to fund the initial phase of his research project. He'd told them that that the investment would be returned within two years and that they would receive payments on all future sales of his research. His former employers and the endowment lawyers had seen dollar signs and written him checks.

All the money had gone into the LLC. It was really too bad that the creditors would never be able to collect. But where he was going, he wouldn't be able to send them a check.

His computer was crunching numbers, but Don wasn't paying attention. He stood at the back door, which looked out from the dining room into a modest backyard. Tina's Powerpuff Girls playhouse was still out there, leaning heavily to one side after nine years of disuse. Two of the neighbors had offered to come over and remove it, assuming that he been too emotionally broken to take it down himself, but he'd explained to them that he'd preferred to keep it up. That was about the time most of his neighbors stopped talking to him—before, he'd been a normal member of the community, a working dad with a wife and a child. Now, he was the strange, sad interloper who had never taken down his dead daughter's playhouse. His was the house that folks avoided.

He didn't care.

Like he'd told Terry a few days before, it didn't really matter anyway. Nothing here, in this world, really mattered.

Things were almost ready.

1.6
0.11 VARIANCE

Two weeks later, Don was ready. He'd done what he could to prepare and, at this point, he was just stalling for time, waiting for improved results in the machine's calibration. He pulled into the parking lot, thinking about the items in his trunk and those stored at the warehouse.

He parked his car next to Terry's red truck and climbed out, but on this morning, he spent an extra few minutes looking at the Manhattan skyline before going inside. Even ten years later, it looked like there was something missing from the jagged rows of buildings. Don opened the trunk of the Volvo and pulled out a box of items, heading inside.

Terry was smiling and greeted Don as soon as he entered the primary work area. He was clearly excited about something.

"What is it?" Don asked, setting down the box of items from his truck. "You look like you're about to burst."

Terry nodded, beaming. "We ran another two more simulations last night, after you left. The variance is 0.11 now."

Don nodded, looking at the graph Terry was pointing at on the monitor.

"Wow, that is good," Don said. "Very good. Can I see the printouts?"

Terry handed the thick stack of paper over—it was bound by one of those super binder clips. Don started flipping through it as Terry excused himself and left the room.

Don looked through the charts. He'd given Terry permission to work on the variance problem, even though Terry didn't really know why—but the man had taken to the problem and solved it.

Terry came back into the room and Don looked up at him. "Vibration?"

"Yup, that was the problem," Terry said, smiling. "The accelerator was moving too much, and it was creating the variance. We stabilized the supports and added another series of welds."

"This is great, Terry. Really great," Don said, smiling and setting down the report. "The numbers look right. Good work."

Terry was beaming.

"What's up?" Don asked.

"Oh, some of the guys are watching the TV in the computer lab. The news," Terry said, grinning. "It looks like we're finally bombing North Korea. We're taking the fight to them."

Don nodded but didn't say anything—he needed to remember to control his reactions.

"I wondered when Cheney would get around to that," Don said, making up his mind. It was time. The geopolitical situation was getting less and less stable, and he was ready.

Don looked up at Terry. "I'll tell you what—why don't you send the others home?"

Terry looked at him. "Are you sure?"

Don nodded. "Yeah. And if you and I can work for a little while longer, to update the schematics, I'll let you off as well."

Two hours later, Don was standing by the machine, in the central area beneath the massive red particle accelerator—it looked somewhat like a CAT scanner, a large open area in the middle with a horizontal, hollow tube surrounded by wires and fans. Beneath it was a large metal table. Don worked on a monitor attached to a control panel, tapping away at a keyboard, and behind him, the machine began to rumble, powering up.

"Good," Don said to himself. "This is very, very good."

He turned to the machine's primary control panel, a ten-foot expanse of buttons and gauges that control various aspects of the accelerator and its sister components. Don opened a small door on the control panel— inside were a recessed key and a big green button labeled ACTUATE.

He turned the key. The green button lit up, ready.

Don stepped away to the open area adjacent to the machine and opened a metal cabinet. He took out a small cage containing a hamster, crossing back to the machine. He held up the cage, regarding the hamster inside it for a moment, and then placed the cage on the flat stainless steel platform directly under the aperture of the particle accelerator.

Don returned to the controls and, consulting his printout and a clipboard of jots and calculations, adjusted a few controls. He double-checked his figures one more time and then opened small door, his hand hovering over the ACTUATE button.

He sighed deeply and pressed the button.

The lights in the room flickered and dimmed. Massive amounts of energy poured from storage batteries into the bulky machine. As he watched, a hazy blue glow began to surround the flat table and the hamster cage upon it. The room started to vibrate slightly, and he grabbed his clipboard and printouts as they began to slide to the floor.

Suddenly, huge booming cracks, like ice shattering, echoed through the room. It sounded like the floor was tearing itself apart beneath the machine. The overhead lights flickered and, as Don watched by the glow of the machine, the hamster cage began to fade out of reality. It didn't disappear all at once—instead, it appeared to evaporate. The top of the cage paled, and then the rest of the cage faded and was gone. The computer, following the preprogrammed cycle, began slowing down the machine's power consumption, and the overhead lights flickered again.

Terry raced into the room.

"You tested it? We've got so much more refining—"

Don pointed at the screens.

"0.11 variance. It worked." He picked up a handheld radiation detector and waved it around the metal table where, only moments before, the hamster cage had sat. "Nothing. No residual K-band energy."

Terry looked over the monitors, and Don knew what he was doing: looking for problems to overcome, mysteries to solve. Terry was a valuable research assistant. It was too bad.

"Jeez, boss," Terry said. "I can't believe you went ahead and tested it. Our development plan says we don't try for a live animal test for at least another two months. Where did you send the cage?"

"Two minutes, uptime."

Terry glanced back at the metal table. "Wow."

Don nodded. "Can you check the power consumption?"

Terry nodded and went into the computer lab, returning in a moment.

"You're not going to like it—we used seven megawatts. That's like three months of power usage in twenty seconds."

"Con Ed?"

Terry shook his head. "Nothing yet, but I'm sure they'll be calling. Our batteries are still nearly full, but it will take six hours to build them back up to full without causing a blackout," Terry said, nodding at the massive power transformers on the far end of the main floor.

Don looked at his watch and then pointed at the table. "Here it comes."

They watched the empty table as the room began to vibrate again. This time, it wasn't the machine or the massive amounts of power coursing through it—no, this was something different. It felt like nature itself was vibrating around them.

"There it comes," Don said.

He and Terry watched as the cage began to form. At first, it looked like a trick of the light. To Don, it looked like a shadow that grew darker and darker until it took on details and sharp edges and finally resolved into an ordinary cage. Don walked up to the table, seeing the hamster scooting around in the cage. Terry picked up the cage and took out the hamster, checking him for any problems.

"He looks good," Terry said, smiling. "Well, it's no Delorean, but it'll do."

Don smiled. "Yeah. I guess that makes me Doc Brown."

"Then I'm Marty," Terry said. "And if you're Doc Brown, you need much wilder hair."

Don sighed, looking at his watch, and decided. The project was as complete as they could make it, considering how much time and effort had gone into it. Now, it was just a matter of executing the plan.

Don turned to Terry. "Are the schematics updated?"

"Yeah, I just finished entering the last changes related to the stronger accelerator supports. We just used the last settings, and they worked, so I think they're finished, finally."

"Good, good," Don said, glancing around at the machine. His mind was racing now, a hundred things to think about. "Can you burn those to a CD? Actually, make me five copies of the whole set of plans and all the testing data. And double-check the CDs to make sure the files aren't corrupted. I want to do a full off-site backup tonight."

Terry nodded and headed off, then stopped. "CDs or DVDs? DVDs will hold a lot more."

"Yeah, but make it CDs, okay?" Don replied. "Five full sets of all the data."

Terry nodded and walked out.

After he left, Don tapped at the keyboard, making a few more notes on the clipboard, then went into the office. Don spent a few minutes scanning the office for any paperwork, schematics, or drawings that he had inadvertently left, but he found none. He took a moment to sit at his computer, where he checked his email a final time, then stood and disconnected the laptop from the monitor.

Turning, he kneeled down and spun the dials, opening the grey safe that stood on the floor behind his desk. He took out a large black duffel bag, stuffing his laptop and the final notes from the clipboard inside. Then, he turned and carefully removed a black, drum-shaped device from the safe and walked out to the machine, setting the drum on the floor next to the particle accelerator—he'd had the device made years ago and had forgotten how heavy it was.

Don returned to the office and made a call to the front desk, asking the only guard on duty to walk the building's exterior perimeter. Don said he'd thought he heard noises coming from the river side of the parking lot. After the guard said he would investigate, Don hung up and got his bag, turned off the lights in his office, and took the bag out to the machine, setting it on the table.

To an outsider, the items contained in the bag would seem a strange collection, even if he knew Don was leaving on a trip. First was the Toshiba laptop, three large binders of printed materials and schematics related to the machine, and an empty CD storage case, which he took out and set on the table. There was a small case of toiletries and, rubber banded together, ten sealed boxes of contact lenses. There were also several thick, padded envelopes containing four iPads and various other electronics, along with several thick paperback books.

At the bottom of the leather duffel bag was a silver attaché case. Don took out the silver case, set it on top of the bag, and carefully opened it. $500,000 in small bills, along with a small black velvet bag of uncut diamonds and three small containers of ten-ounce platinum bars. The case contained one more item that Don removed and slipped into his pocket.

Don closed the attaché case and put it back inside the bag as Terry walked in, shaking his head as he handed the small stack of CDs to Don.

"It all fit on three CDs, so you've got fifteen there, five full sets," Terry said.

Don nodded and began sliding the CDs into the storage case.

"I was checking the Internet while I was burning those disks," Terry said. "Looks like the U.S. military is massing ships offshore. Supposedly, the Marines are preparing to land forces, or at least that's what Fox News is saying. There's a big uproar from the U.N., but Cheney isn't listening."

Don nodded and went back over to the table.

"I swear," Terry continued, "I think this world is just going crazy. What's the bag for?"

Don sighed. This was the worst part of the whole plan, but it couldn't be avoided. The machine was ready, he was ready, and this world was going down the crapper, and fast. How long until there was another attack? What if the Houston bomb had been detonated over Manhattan instead? If that had happened, then it would already be too late. Don couldn't delay any longer. There was no turning back.

He had to.

Don turned, a small gun in his hand.

"Sorry," Don said quietly to his friend Terry, and shot him.

Terry's eyes went wide, his hands going to his chest. The red stain spread fast across his white shirt, and he fell awkwardly to the floor.

"Sorry, Terry, but I've gotta go." Don said to the man on the floor, and fired again, the sound of the gun louder this time.

Don turned away and slowly put the gun and the CD case into his duffel bag, and zipped the bag up, placing it on the machine's target platform.

He walked around Terry's prone figure, over to the control panel, and activated the program. Don tried to ignore the smell of gunpowder hanging in the still air. He tapped at the machine a final time, setting the coordinates and maximizing the power usage. It would probably cause a temporary localized blackout, but it couldn't be avoided. He needed the power more than these people could possibly understand.

He tried to ignore the moans coming from the floor nearby.

Don walked over to the drum-shaped device and opened the top of the unit. He could hear the contents sloshing around inside—there were two large containers of methyl alcohol, a central explosive, and a timer, which he dialed to ten minutes and pressed START. The bomb began counting down. He placed it between the control panel and the primary electrical systems of the particle accelerator, near the target platform.

Don walked back to the computer lab one more time, tapping instructions into the small networked server station to begin a full system wipe. There was no way to be sure that the fire would destroy the computers, so he detached the network storage units and brought them back into the main room, setting them on the floor next to the bomb.

Don suddenly remembered to check his wallet.

Quickly, he pulled it out of his rear pocket as the timer counted to eight minutes remaining on the bomb. He fished frantically through his wallet and finally found something, a small folded scrap of paper. Don relaxed and smiled and looked at the scrap of paper for a long moment, his eyes shining, and then put it away.

He glanced over again at Terry, but the man wasn't moving.

There was nothing more to do.

He looked around one more time and then walked to the control station. He started the sequence, then pushed the large green ACTUATE button.

Immediately, the machine began to cycle up again, faster and louder this time. He was using a lot more power than during his experiments with the Post-its or the hamster cage. His calculations needed to include the heavy duffel bag along with his weight.

Don walked over and lay down on the table, clutching the bag to his chest.

The lights in the room dimmed as energy poured into the machine from the batteries and the live power conduits. Above and around him, a hazy blue glow began to surround his table. He saw the room around him begin to vibrate, but strangely, he and the duffel bag and the table they were on were perfectly still. The table was connected to the machine—only items *on* the table should be affected by the temporal fold. Suddenly, there were the huge booming cracks, but much louder this time, coming from inside the machine. It sounded like ice shattering, or his eardrums—he couldn't be sure. He wanted to reach up and cover his ears, but he didn't want to loosen his grip on the bag—without the contents, he would be a newborn, naked in a new world.

The room around him began to fade, and one of the fluorescent lights above the machine exploded in a shower of sparks. He turned on the table to look at them, dropping, so many of them, dancing off the floor and the batteries and the exterior of the particle accelerator and—

PART TWO

2.1
A Positive Outcome

—fell two feet onto cold pavement.

For a moment, he just lay there. The room swam around him, the floor tilting like a carnival ride. Don held onto the bag, gripping it tightly, until the room slowed and finally stopped spinning altogether.

Slowly, he sat up.

The massive warehouse was empty.

The machine, the computers, the batteries that had stored up massive amounts of electrical power—they were all gone, evaporated into the timeline.

No Terry, bleeding to death on the concrete floor. No security guards, no technicians, no lab assistants.

"Damn."

Dr. Donald Ellis stood gingerly, his legs wobbly, and walked slowly across the expansive floor of the warehouse. He had to know, right away. Don approached the large rusty doors nervously and put one hand on the door and paused, sighing.

"Come on. Be there."

He pushed the doors open, stepping out into a parking lot that he already knew would be there. He shaded his eyes from the bright sky and looked.

He saw the expanse of the East River flowing beyond the shoreline. And across the river, rising against a beautiful blue cloudless sky, the twin towers of the World Trade Center dominated the Manhattan skyline.

2.2

MIKEL'S THEORY OF NON-INTERACTION

Ellis stood outside his old home in Jericho, New York. He'd been holed up in the warehouse for the last seven months, but now it was time. His key worked, as it should. He slid it in the door and let himself inside.

The house looked much like Don remembered it, only messier. The floor was littered with toys, and there was a pile of unmatched shoes in the foyer next to the door. He'd forgotten what it was like to have a child around the house—nothing was ever in the proper place.

Dr. Ellis wandered around a house that was his and yet, at the same time, completely alien. Everything he recognized, yet everything seemed different. All the detritus of normal family life—an empty glass on the coffee table, piles of papers and books and mail on every flat surface, toys strewn about the living room. He stepped on one of Tina's toys and jumped.

There was a stack of Sarah's magazines on the coffee table, magazines that he had forgotten she liked to read. Tina had left drawing materials spread over the entire dining room table, the same table that he'd used only days ago for stock research.

Actually, the stock research hadn't happened two days ago—it had happened ten years in the future. It had already happened, and yet it was a decade before it would happen. Or maybe in this timeline, he would never use the table for that purpose at all.

He'd heard once on *Star Trek* that time travel can play hell with verb tenses.

Ellis had checked his schedule from early 2001 and chosen this stretch of days around April 5. It was a time when his younger version would be off work for three days because of some construction and painting in his building at the university. He remembered those three days well—he had enjoyed playing tennis and doing projects around the house that Sarah was always after him to finish.

Unfortunately, this time around, his younger self would be too busy to tackle the honey-do list.

Actually, there were three theories about this aspect of time travel, and he wasn't sure which one would be proven in the next few minutes. He had high hopes for the first theory and was dreading the second. The third, he'd already disproven.

The first theory was that everything that ever happened and ever would happen was confined to a single time stream. Any potential "travelers" through time would enter the same time stream and be incorporated into it. This was the classic "go back in time and kill your grandfather" time conundrum that people loved to quote.

The second theory posited branching timelines. In this scenario, time streams would overlap, unless a major event caused a break; if that happened, the time stream would branch into two distinct futures.

A third theory stated that a time traveler wouldn't be able to interact with the past, because "time" itself would prevent him from changing things. To the time traveler, everything around him would appear much like a three-dimensional hologram that he could observe but never interact with. One version of this theory supposed that ghosts were time travelers, destined to endlessly observe the world without being able to change it.

Ellis had already disproved theory three, Mikel's Theory of Non-Interaction: over the last seven months, he'd secured a lease on the warehouse, created multiple investment accounts, and begun staffing and construction efforts. Most of the money from the duffel bag was already at work, growing in value on investments that seemed to be making enormous amounts of profits and funneling those gains into another LLC he had set up, this one named "Blossom Investments."

But had he already created a new universe, or was he just changing the one he was already in? He tended to think of the original world where he was from as Timeline #1 and this as Timeline #2. That would mean he was Ellis #1, and the man driving home from the tennis club right now would be Ellis #2.

Nothing Don had done yet since he'd gone back in time had affected his previous life, as far as he could tell. It had taken months to get everything rolling—a new identity, the money, the warehouse. But it came down to this—when he finally talked to his younger self, there would be three possible outcomes.

One, he would cease to exist.

Two, he would suffer a brain aneurysm and die.

Three, nothing would happen, other than extreme confusion on the part of his younger self.

Dr. Ellis cleared Tina's mess off of the dining room table and set a couple of things down that he'd been carrying. He heard the sound of a car and turned, watching it pull into the driveway, and walked around the counter and bar stools that separated the dining room from the kitchen. He continued into the family room—the wall-mounted TV wasn't there yet; instead, a painting hung.

Sarah had bought the painting at an auction, but he hadn't been able to bear having it up after she died. He remembered how excited she'd been—

The front door opened, and Dr. Donald Ellis walked in, carrying a tennis bag with a racquet handle sticking out. He set it down, closed the door behind him, and walked through the living room without looking up, flipping through a stack of mail. Then he glanced up and saw the items on the dining room table.

One was a pile of CDs, along with a box of contact lenses. On top lay an Apple iPad 2. The other pile was made up entirely of banded stacks of money; the pile about six inches high.

"What the hell?" he asked, glancing around. He set the mail down and picked up the iPad, turning it around, flipping it over to look at the back.

"Hi, Donald."

The younger Dr. Ellis glanced up and saw himself, an older version of himself, walking around the refrigerator, his hands raised.

"What? Who the hell are you—oh Jeez!" the younger Ellis began, stumbling backwards. He backed up against the sink and his hands, moving on their own, knocked a plate from the counter onto the ground. It shattered, loudly.

The older Ellis kept his hands up.

"Don't lose it, Tiger," he said.

The younger Ellis looked like he was moments from throwing up.

"Mom used to call us Tiger, remember?" the older Ellis said slowly. "It's me—you, just a little older."

"What?" the younger Ellis said, looking down at the plate and bending to pick up the pieces. "This can't be happening—it's a dream, or a goddamned nightmare," the younger man said, putting the broken shards in the trash.

"Ask me something only we would know," the older Ellis said, smiling and putting his hands down.

The younger man nodded. "Cognitive deduction. OK, but it won't prove anything if you're a simple hallucination. Do you remember the Sadie Hawkins dance in sophomore year?"

"I thought you might ask that," the elder Ellis said, smiling. "She made quite an impression on me as well—her name was Linda. She dumped us after a couple of weeks, if I recall. I always considered her my first love. You?"

"What do you mean, 'you?'" the younger Ellis said, shaking his head. "There is no 'you' and 'me,' there are just two 'me's."

The older Ellis shook his head. "No, I've already disproven Mikel's Theory on Non-Interaction. I've been in this timeline for months, setting up a new identity."

The younger Ellis nodded and turned, walking around the chairs and sitting down in the living room. He sighed and pinched the bridge of his nose between his thumb and forefinger. The older Ellis joined him, sitting in the chair by the fireplace.

"I always loved this chair," he said, sitting down and rubbing the arms slowly. It was a wonderfully comfortable chair, dark brown leather. What had happened to it? "I don't remember for the life of me why I got rid of it."

The younger Ellis looked up. "So, you built the machine," he said slowly, looking at him. "And it actually works."

The older Ellis nodded. "Obviously."

"And you've entered your old timeline or created a new one. Which is it?"

The older Ellis shrugged. "Not sure yet. Though I know this didn't happen to me on my vacation, so—

He felt a sudden, sharp pain in his head that doubled him over. The headache was so intense—

"You're getting an echo," the younger Ellis said calmly. "Your brain is hearing what you're saying and what I'm saying and wondering why it doesn't remember. Theoretically, of course.

The older Ellis rubbed his temples. "It doesn't feel theoretical!"

"That's because you and I are different. As soon as you entered the timeline, you must have caused a branch off the original. We're in a different reality than the one you're from. But your brain is trying to put it together, trying to make sense of it."

The older Ellis nodded. The pain backed off a little. "Heisenberg's theory. It's like I'm saying something, and then for a moment I remember not hearing it before, or hearing it but not remembering it. I had hoped to be in my original timeline—it would have made things easier." He paused. "It's getting better."

The younger Ellis glanced down and realized he was still holding the iPad. "Artifacts from the future, money, and medical supplies," he said, glancing at the table.

The older Ellis nodded, and they sat quietly for a few moments. The younger Ellis had figured out how to turn on the iPad and was touching the screen, playing his fingers across the black surface.

"Pretty neat."

The older Ellis looked at him. "Yes, it's all touch-based. A real breakthrough. When I was leaving, they were getting ready to bring out a fifth-generation phone and a third-generation iPad. It was sweeping through the PC industry, causing a lot of disruptions."

The younger man nodded. "I like the responsiveness. It does feel like magic, doesn't it? Asimov was right."

The trick was obvious.

"Clarke, you mean."

His counterpart looked up from the iPad. "What?"

"Arthur C. Clarke. He said that any sufficiently advanced technology would look like magic to the unskilled user. You said 'Asimov.'"

The young man nodded, smiling. "Just testing you. If you are from the future, who knows how far ahead you're coming from, or what kind of technology they have. You might be an evil future me, back here to replace me."

Don nodded slowly. "Well, I have to say I had given the notion some thought."

The younger Ellis smiled. "Or you could be some kind of cyborg, right? But you are me, I think. An older version. Fifteen years?"

"Ten. I'm from 2011."

"Oh," the younger Ellis replied. "You look older than that."

"The years have been…difficult. And now these headaches."

"Headaches. Remember that paper we wrote? We called it 'reintegration'—the period of time when your mind is adjusting to an alternate timeline, catching up to the fact that events are skewing away from your memory."

"I remember coming home on this day from tennis," Don said. "I remember looking at the mail and then starting some project, something I don't even remember."

"Garage," the younger Ellis said. "Sarah wants it cleaned up before spring."

The older Ellis smiled, remembering.

The younger Ellis stood, walking back over to the dining room table. "Money, lots of it. You've been planning this for a while. Are those the plans?" he asked, pointing at the CDs.

"Yes," the older man said. He picked up the CDs and handed them to a younger version of himself when, suddenly, his nose started bleeding. He stepped hurriedly around the younger man and went into the kitchen for a paper towel.

"Damn, that's a lot of blood. Let's get you horizontal. Come on."

The younger Dr. Ellis led his older self down into the basement to a large office. Every flat surface in the room was covered with electronic equipment—it looked like a smaller version of the warehouse. Don dropped down onto the couch and held the wad of paper towels to his nose.

The two men sat quietly for a moment.

"Something terrible is going to happen," the older man said, his voice strange. "You have to stop it. "

The younger man looked briefly at Ellis and then walked back upstairs. He returned with the CD case. He opened the case and pulled the first one out, labeled "Machine," and popped it into the computer.

"Bad enough to motivate you to finish the machine," the younger Ellis said quietly, looking at monitor. "And faster than it should've taken. You're using the machine for personal gain? If you are..."

"Shut up," Don said gruffly. "You haven't seen what I've seen."

The younger man was quiet for a moment, thinking. "But you—we can't use the machine to benefit ourselves. It's only for research. Plus, it doesn't matter. You can't change your original timeline anyway—only make new ones."

"I know, I know. Just look at the CDs. I'm tired. Look at the CDs and then tell me what you think of my... er, our 'research.'" The older man reached over, pulling open a cabinet drawer and taking out a bottle of Advil—he knew where the bottle was without asking. He downed several dry and nodded at the screen.

"The password is 'Buttercup.'"

Don sat back on the couch and watched as the younger man pored over the schematics on the computer screen of a machine that was, even now, being built again at a quiet and familiar warehouse in Red Hook. There were blueprints, photographs, testing information, even a section on the explosive device Don had used to destroy it.

Then the younger man put in the second CD, labeled "Incident." Don watched as he pulled up a series of images and headlines from September 11, 2001—the destruction of the World Trade Center, the U.S. Capitol building collapsed in on itself, the Pentagon in flames. Headlines flashed up—*21,502 dead in attacks on Washington and New York City. Congress wiped out. Bush declares unilateral powers to fight terrorism. New York and Washington brought to knees.*

Tens of thousands dead—and the elder Ellis didn't need to see the images again. He'd seen them all, too many times. And the Houston incident dwarfed these tragedies—the final casualty estimates were upwards of 100,000 people—men and women and children. The numbers were too staggering to even comprehend. And North Korea was being bombed back into the Stone Age as President Cheney exacted his pound of flesh.

The younger Ellis looked through the files on the CD slowly, eventually getting to the final one—a picture of the plaque that hung in Ellis' living room. Not the living room above their heads, but another version of the same room in the future.

The plaque read "The City of New York wishes to express our sincerest condolences at the death of Sarah Ellis and Tina Ellis, lost in the terrorist attacks of September 11, 2001."

"Oh, Christ." the younger Ellis said quietly. "No."

2.3
COFFEE BREAK

The Starbucks at the corner of K and 16th streets bustled with activity—life on Capitol Hill seemed to be fueled in equal parts by caffeine and power and attitude. Baristas shouted orders for pick-up, and customers jostled for position in the long line that reached to the doors. Every table was taken, and no one wanted to be outside; a June heat wave was baking the Washington, D.C., area.

Dr. John Marburger walked into the Starbucks and saw the long line, but he didn't turn around and leave. He could only shake his head and get in line. One of the things he'd learned in academia was just how bad office coffee could be. He'd developed a taste for more expensive stuff after too many late nights doing research.

But he hated standing in lines.

"Dr. Marburger?" a voice called from behind him. He turned to see a tall man, dressed nicely, sitting at a table for two. He was indicating the open chair across from him.

"Please join me—I've already ordered for you."

Marburger frowned.

"I'm sorry, I think you have me confused with someone else," John said, turning back to the line.

"Has the president made up his mind yet about the nomination?" the tall man asked loudly.

Marburger quickly stepped from the line and walked over to the man.

"I don't know what you're talking about," John said, trying to keep his voice down. "I just want to get a coffee and be on my way."

The seated man nodded, smiling.

"Triple venti extra-vanilla latte, right?" he said, nodding at the barista behind the counter. "I've already ordered for you. Do you find it pretentious, sometimes, that they insist on your ordering their drinks in such a specific manner? It reminds me of that Seinfeld episode about the Soup Nazi. Do you remember that one?"

Marburger stared.

"Sorry about the intrigue, Dr. Marburger. I've been waiting to meet with you, and I thought you might enjoy a drink while we chatted. Nothing mysterious in that, right?"

Marburger wasn't sure, but he nodded and slowly sat down, setting his briefcase between his feet.

The tall man sat and sipped from his cup. There was a manila folder on the table. "I'm Dr. Donald Ellis—I'm a researcher at the University of New York. Particle physics and applied fourth-dimensional field space, mostly. I won the Sakurai Prize in 1999 for my work on fourth-dimensional field theory."

Marburger leaned back, waiting for the pitch.

"Well, you have your meeting, Dr. Ellis. How can I help you?"

John got twenty of these a month now, ever since the president had called. None of the others had been so out of the blue like this, or in a coffee shop with his drink preordered, but they were all similar in intent. Researchers, applied science guys, nut jobs—everyone wanted ten minutes of his time to pitch some new idea or new experiment that they insisted should be funded by the U.S. government. A friend from his days at Brookhaven had called him up only days ago to pitch an alternate use for the National Ignition Facility, a high-energy laser being built at Lawrence Livermore National Laboratories (LLNL).

Another guy last week had launched into a long and detailed proposal for capturing icebergs as they calved off of glacial sheets in Antarctica. He wanted to attach motors to them, pilot them into warm-water harbors, and sell the melting fresh water. John had been intrigued, until he'd done ten minutes of Internet research and found out that the idea had been lifted from an '80's movie called *Brewster's Millions*.

But some of the ideas he'd been getting were interesting. At least this guy was buying him a coffee.

Dr. Ellis smiled.

"Why are you smiling?" Marburger asked, curious.

"Oh, just the look on your face," Ellis answered, smiling. "I know you've been getting a lot of bad ideas thrown at you since the president asked you to be National Science Advisor. I assure you, Dr. Marburger, this is not one of those meetings."

John wasn't sure what to say. The presidential appointment wasn't a secret, but it wasn't public knowledge yet, either. "How do you know about that?"

Dr. Ellis smiled again and slowly opened the manila folder, handing two sheets of paper to Marburger. John took them slowly and glanced at them, then started reading.

"Triple venti extra vanilla latte!" the woman at the counter announced. Ellis stood. "I'll get it—you read. It's good stuff."

The first sheet of paper was incredible—it was the entire text of the president's announcement that would come next Monday, June 25. Marburger hadn't read what the president was planning to say, but it sounded like him—his cadence, tone, and delivery.

Ellis sat back down, offering Marburger coffee. "I know that you'll be nominated—Bush will be announcing it this week. Rumors are already out there, which is why people are starting to pitch you ideas."

John stopped reading and looked up.

"I don't know how you know this, but anyone could get this information off the Internet if they looked hard enough. And a good writer could fabricate a speech by the president—"

Ellis nodded.

"That's right—it's not hard to create a speech. But the nomination isn't fabricated—you will be nominated to be the president's science advisor. He'll make the announcement on Friday—there's a copy of the announcement that he'll read, along with the second page, which are photos of the nominating ceremony. See, there you are with the president."

John looked at the second sheet—there were indeed photos of him, standing behind the president in the Rose Garden along with a few other people, some of whom he did not recognize."

"How do you have these photos?"

Ellis nodded. "Well, any good journalist could have those created, along with the president's speech."

John nodded, sipping at his coffee. It was excellent.

"But why?" he asked. "Why go to all that trouble?"

Ellis nodded. "Quite right. One only needs to buy you a cup of coffee to get your attention—this is something more." The man leaned forward, speaking again in a low voice. "Something will happen this fall that will change this country forever," Dr. Ellis said quietly. "Something that will shake this country to its very foundation."

Marburger looked at the man slowly, sizing him up. He appeared completely serious.

"So, this is how you know about the appointment—you know the future?" John said quietly, smiling. It was funny, hearing himself say the words. "Really?"

Ellis nodded slowly. He rested his hands on the manila folder.

"And you know something 'bad' is going to happen?" John asked, incredulous. "How do I know you're not the one planning something bad?"

The man across from him nodded.

"Dr. Marburger. As hard as it is for you to believe, I have foreknowledge of what is to come. Just as I have this information," he said, taking another item out of the manila folder and handing it to him. "The top is a copy of your statement to Congress, which I'm sure you've already started formulating. Under that is the congressional report."

John took the bound report, disappointed. This had started to get interesting, and then it had suddenly devolved into a bad episode of *Star Trek*. The man had intrigued him, but now he'd gone completely off the rails. For a moment, John was glad he was in a public place. He glanced at the paper—it was his speech.

"The good news is, you'll be confirmed," Ellis said, smiling. He took a sip from his coffee cup and sat back, waiting.

The president's chief of staff had explained the entire process to Marburger two weeks ago—first, there would be the president's official nomination, and then three months later there would be a congressional hearing. Marburger would appear on Capitol Hill, and a group of legislators would ask him to present his credentials and answer questions. Chief of Staff Andrew Card had said that the questions might be challenging—the congressmen liked to look like they knew what they were talking about for the cameras.

John had taken the words to heart and started formulating his speech, but this sheet had the entire finished speech, something that he would have needed another week or two to complete. The speech included a nice part at the end about science promoting democracy and freedom— he'd been thinking about going into that topic, but here it was, finished.

The speech sounded great. Stranger still, it sounded like him.

There were also several mentions of "the events of September 11," a date that held no particular meaning to him.

Behind the speech was the bound congressional hearing report, which read, "Nomination of Philip Bond to be Under Secretary for Technology at the Department of Commerce and John Marburger to be Director of the Office of Science and Technology Policy, Tuesday, October 9, 2001."

"October?" John looked up at the man, frowning. "You got this part wrong. This is supposed to happen sooner than that. Early September, I heard."

Ellis nodded. "Yes, that's when it should have happened. But then 9/11 happens."

John looked at the speech again.

"Is this '9/11' the 'bad' thing you're talking about? With your foreknowledge?" he asks, his voice laced with sarcasm.

Ellis' face darkened, and John wondered if he'd made a mistake, indulging this man.

"Yes, Dr. Marburger, it is," Ellis said as he leaned forward, his voice low, insistent. "9/11 will bring this nation to its knees. 21,502 people will die, half of Congress will be wiped out, and both buildings of the World Trade Center in New York will fall. The Pentagon will burn. It will be the worst day in our nation's history. It will be remembered along with Pearl Harbor and the assassination of Lincoln."

John sat back slowly—this man was serious. And, incredibly, he seemed to really believe what he was saying.

"And I will lose my family," Ellis said, looking down at the table. "My wife and daughter will die in the South Tower. Many people will lose their families, Mr. Marburger. Of course, now that I know what's coming, I've taken steps to protect my family."

The two men sat at the table, silent, as the customers and staff bustled around them, ignored. John heard several drink orders called out as he read through the speech again.

At one point in the congressional record, there was a nice statement from Representative Grucci of New York—John had worked with him for years at the Brookhaven National Laboratory. Grucci mentioned a difficult and expensive environmental restoration of the facility that Marburger had overseen. The tone of voice in the transcribed document was distinctly Grucci's, something that John thought would be very difficult to replicate, unless you knew the man personally. His voice had a Brooklyn accent that was very distinct.

The preponderance of the items in the report added up to the genuine article. But how could that be?

The man across from him finally spoke up, sighing. "You will be confirmed, but it will be too late."

John Marburger nodded, glancing at the report and reading quietly. "Near the end of my testimony, I say that 'The most pressing of these needs is an adequate and coordinated response to the vicious and destructive terrorist attacks of September 11.' I don't know what to say."

Ellis nodded, sitting up. "You'll only get into power after it happens—you'll be on cleanup duty. We need to go to your office and get started. Now."

"I don't have an office—" he started to say.

"They've set you up in the Old Executive Office Building," Ellis interrupted, "while they're waiting for the nomination to be announced."

John looked at him.

Ellis continued. "I have the information that you and the Bush administration need to prevent this thing from ever happening."

"What knowledge?"

The tall man reached into his jacket and took out a single CD, placing it on the table between them. On it was written "9/11."

2.4

FOREKNOWLEDGE

Ellis followed Dr. Marburger as they exited the coffee shop and walked toward the ornate Old Executive Office Building. Built next to the White House in 1888 for a growing war department, the building was now used to house White House support staff.

Marburger entered and signed him in. "You were a professor of physics and electrical engineering for three decades?" Ellis said to Marburger as they stepped onto an old elevator.

Marburger pushed the button. "Yes."

"So what do you think of the idea of a machine that can project items or people through the time barrier?"

Marburger looked at him—they were alone in the elevator, or Ellis wouldn't have asked.

"I'd say you were crazy."

Ellis smiled. When the elevator dinged, they got off and walked down a long, ornately appointed corridor, passing two security guards, who nodded at Dr. Marburger. The carpet was plush, muffling their steps. They reached a door with a temporary sign on it that said "OST/SA Appointee" in hand-drawn letters.

"Can't they get you a better sign than that?" Ellis asked, smiling.

Marburger shot him a look and they entered the office. Marburger sat at the computer, and Don handed him the CD case. Marburger put the CD in the tray, and the computer began reading it.

"The password is 'Buttercup,'" he said. "One word."

A prompt appeared, and Marburger entered the code. Detailed schematics appeared on the screen. Ellis watched, narrating what he saw.

"These are the machine schematics. I spoke with the man who built and used it—he said that the machine took him almost ten years to construct, but that they were improving and refining it as they went. He estimated it would take about three years to build it again."

Marburger tabbed through screen after screen of complicated

schematics. Ellis knew he was looking for details and subsystems to give him a better handle on the veracity of the plans.

Ellis continued. "It uses a small particle accelerator to fold the quantum field at the specific location where the item or person is located. Only objects inside the fold are displaced in time. The amount of power placed into the quantum field determines the actual amount of displacement."

Marburger nodded.

"Is it multidimensional?"

"No, but the other Dr. Ellis said in his notes that he thought it could be perfected to do that. Time machine and teleporter, all in one. But his machine could only move objects through time, not spatial dimensions."

Ellis walked around and sat down in a folding chair. The office appointments left a lot to be desired, but it made sense—this wouldn't be his office after the nomination, but it would do for now.

"And it works. Clearly." It was a statement, more than a question from Marburger, but Ellis nodded anyway.

"It works. Or worked, at least the one time," Ellis said. "I watched the man die right in front of me. We only had a few minutes to talk before the other Ellis died, or whatever it was that happened. Temporal physics is my specialty, but it was still very disturbing. I've theorized that two versions of one person cannot coexist on the same timeline, and this person was an older version of me. Still, watching another version of yourself fade out of existence is…disturbing."

Marburger looked at the screen, then at him.

"Have you started it yet? Building a machine?"

Ellis shook his head, obviously waiting for the question. "No. I'm not building it, not without the government's help. I can't afford it—the only reason my counterpart could finish it was because he was so driven."

"By the loss of your family," Marburger asked.

Ellis nodded, looking out the window, quiet for a long moment before speaking again. "I can't even imagine it. Now, I hug them both every night, can't get enough of them. Can't tell them why, of course. They must think I'm nuts."

Marburger smiled. "They're not the only one."

"Pull up the second file, John. Same password."

Marburger tapped at the keyboard. Ellis couldn't see the screen, but the look on Marburger's face said it all.

"Shit," the man said quietly.

Ellis gave him a few minutes to look at the information—he'd been through it all a dozen times, incredulous at first but absorbing more and more information with each pass. It was a horrible day in this country's future. Anything done to mitigate it would be a blessing.

After some silence, with Marburger tabbing through the headlines, short video clips, full-color photos of so much loss, Ellis spoke up.

"That's why he came back—not because of his, ah, our family. The government was, or will be, crippled, with the loss of half of Congress and so much damage to the Pentagon. The economy will take years to recover. It will take months to replace the congressmen lost on that day with appointees and new, emergency elections that, in some places, violate the constitution. The Bush administration will founder in the darkness, shocked by the enormity of their challenge and without the steady guidance of Congress, who is reeling from its own tragedies. Cheney will take power in 2003 but not before—well, there are roads this country should not go down. This is one of them."

Marburger nodded.

"And the damage to the country will be long lasting," Ellis said. "The economy will be broken by the loss of the World Trade Center, and New York City's economy will go into the toilet. Mayor Giuliani and the rest of his emergency team will be killed inside Building 7, the location of their emergency bunker on the 23rd floor, when it collapses after being hit by debris from the falling North Tower. But the psychological effects of the sneak attack are the worst. The U.S. military, riled by a massive and deadly attack on their headquarters, follows a hawkish president on the road to war. Afghanistan, Iraq, the Philippines—anywhere where al Qaeda is seen as a threat. The U.N. protests, governments fall, Cheney seizes control.... The list goes on and on."

Marburger stared at him.

"It's too much to even fathom."

Ellis nods. "I know. I know just how you feel. Take the information, digest it, and then make a suggestion to the president—he needs to meet with me, with us, and discuss the next steps. This attack must be prevented."

Marburger nodded, agreeing, but then looked up at him. "I don't know the president that well. I don't know how he would react. I can't get in to see him unless it's scheduled a month ahead of time. They aren't going to let—"

"No, that isn't going to work," Ellis shook his head. "You'll convince them. Or thousands will die."

Marburger nodded, looking at the screen again.

"And after the attack is averted—do you think you can build it?"

Ellis smiled. "You think like I do. Yes, I think I can. I had a little time to talk to him before he died, and all of the improvements are there, in the schematics. Take them, discuss them with your counterparts, and then please contact me—I'm staying at the Willard."

2.5
DR. RAINES

He had been having an early breakfast in the Windows on the World restaurant, but now the entire world was on fire. Smoke poured from every vent, and three of the windows had been broken out. The staff was gathered around the open windows, gulping at the fresh air. Others had crawled into corners of the room, waiting for rescue.

But, somehow, he knew rescue would never come.

As Ellis walked to the windows, a woman standing too close to the edge lost her grip and fell away from the open window. He heard her screams as they faded into the deafening wind that buffeted those of them gathered around.

"We should climb down the outside," one person said, panic in her voice.

"No, it's too slippery," another person said.

"What about the stairs?" another one asked.

A tall black man shook his head. "They're blocked. Jammed—too many people."

"When will the firefighters get here?" the woman asked.

Ellis shook his head, speaking up for the first time. "They're not coming. They won't make it—this entire building is going to collapse."

The others looked at him, their eyes wild.

"No, no!" she shouted at him.

"It's true," he said. Ellis felt the tears streaming from his eyes—the smoke was too much, and the wind was roaring in from outside. "It will all fall down. Nothing can be done. The firefighters will be killed, too."

He stepped around her, to the open window, his legs not under his control.

"I don't want to die that way," he said, and stepped to the open window, which used to stretch from the floor to the ceiling. The wind pulled at his clothes.

He looked out—the entire city of New York was spread out before him like an endless, living blanket of streets and buildings. It was like looking down at the most detailed model one could possibly imagine—the moving cars, the little people, the boats creating wakes on the distant Hudson. Ellis looked straight down between his shoes—it was impossibly far down to the fire trucks and police cars. He saw 5 World Trade Center below him—people were streaming from it like ants. He knew that when the building he was in collapsed, massive pieces of it would fall on the other building, crushing it, killing everyone inside.

Out of the corner of his eye, he saw another person at another open window. She was clinging to the metallic skin of the skyscraper, panicked, but when she saw him, she seemed to calm. She looked at him steadily, nodded and then let go, falling backwards into the air. He watched her fall, and her eyes held his for a long moment until she disappeared into the smoke.

Don turned to say something to the people inside, to warn them about jumping and how he had seen the others fall on the videos he had seen, videos of the tragedy that had run over and over again on the news. A sudden gust of wind lashed him, and he lost his grip.

Falling.

The wind was deafening. He could finally breathe. Between his feet, already far above him, he saw the twisted scar near the top of the building, smoke pouring out. It looked like a blackened wound, the size and shape of the plane that had struck the side of the building only minutes before. Ellis twisted in the air like a cat and saw below him the buildings and the cars and people and—

"Are you Dr. Raines?"

The elder Dr. Don Ellis was standing in the warehouse parking lot. He tore his eyes away from the World Trade Center. It was not on fire—it stood proudly against a blue sky. No one was on fire or falling to their deaths. Or leaping from shattered windows. There were no sirens or exhausted firefighters gasping at oxygen masks as the towers fell around them.

There were no casualties.

He turned. There was a short delivery driver standing next to him, holding out a clipboard.

"Ah, I have a delivery you need to sign for, Mr. Raines," the short man said. He jerked a thumb over his shoulder. "They said you were out here."

The elder Dr. Ellis nodded slowly and took the clipboard, remembering to sign his new name. In this timeline, he was not himself, and the younger Ellis was telling everyone that the time-traveling "original" had died. It seemed everyone had bought the story, although he couldn't be sure. He still got some odd looks from staff when he and the younger Ellis were chatting.

"Beautiful city, isn't it?" the delivery guy asked.

Ellis smiled and handed the clipboard back. "More than you know."

The delivery man turned and headed back inside the warehouse. Ellis watched him go and looked at the warehouse—it looked much as it had in the first timeline, but Dr. Ellis had noticed a few differences. It was slightly newer, looking only a little less abandoned. The parking lot that surrounded it looked newer.

In the first timeline, he had found and rented the warehouse in 2004. It had taken just over five years to build the machine and get it functional. This time, he hoped to build it faster and to make it smaller and with greatly reduced power requirements.

In this timeline, it was still 2001. He'd noticed upon leasing the warehouse again that there was a large pier, jutting out into the river from Governors Island, the squat military installation that sat in the river between Brooklyn and Manhattan. At some point, over the next three years, the pier would be removed, assuming everything progressed unchanged.

But some things were the same. Dr. Ellis walked back inside the warehouse and a young man nodded at him from up inside a large metal scaffold—it was Terry, or a younger version of Terry. Dr. Ellis had felt horrible about shooting the other version of him, so he'd found Terry slogging away at a dead-end research fellowship in Newark and asked him to come work for him at Blossom Investments, the new umbrella company.

"Hey, Terry, how's it goin'?" Don asked, nodding at the familiar-looking machine above him. Several other men and women bustled around the red and yellow support beams of the particle accelerator. There were differences between the first machine and this one. The particle accelerator was not as wide as before and would require less power. With a completed set of plans and no trial and error or testing required, he could build a machine much more quickly and efficiently.

Terry looked up and smiled. "We're looking good, Dr. Raines. The anti-vibration supports are installed under the accelerator. But are you sure they're really necessary?"

Ellis smiled. "Yup. Once those are done, get the techs working on the power conduits."

Ellis walked off, looking for Stevens, the facilities manager. Ellis had decided that, this time around, he could afford to hire someone else to handle site construction, security, and staffing, as well as help the facility fly under the radar. Ellis had put out feelers at the university campus, asking around for references, and Bruce Stevens had popped up on the radar as a solid man, one who could be trusted. Ellis had liked him immediately and hired him on the spot.

Stevens was helping keep prying eyes away from the facility. Upon entering the timeline, Ellis had decided there was no need to get the government involved with this machine. He'd tasked his younger version with interfacing with the government, with passing along the important information about 9/11 and the time machine, but they'd agreed to keep Don's existence, and the existence of their machine, a secret. Don prayed the younger Ellis would be able to convince the Bush government to step in and prevent the horrible events to come. If not, well, that was why they were feverously working to complete this machine—a multimillion-dollar insurance policy, hidden in a nondescript warehouse on the Brooklyn waterfront.

Dr. Ellis found Stevens at the front desk, talking to the guards. Stevens had a background in project management, having helmed several large construction projects up and down the eastern seaboard. Ellis found Stevens' mix of talents very useful. This was a smaller project than most, Ellis knew, but it was surely the most complicated project Stevens had ever been involved with. And more secretive.

There was a large sign behind the reception desk, where two security guards sat, that said BLOSSOM INVESTMENTS, LLC.

"Stevens," Ellis said, and the man turned.

"Ah, Dr. Raines. Good."

They walked together back into the primary testing area.

"This looks great," Ellis said, indicating the machine under construction.

"Yes," Stevens agreed. "The primary construction should be done soon, and you and Terry and the team can get started testing. Terry looks to be finishing the reactor containment system within the week."

Ellis nodded, impressed. "Good—that's well ahead of schedule. With enough money, you can do anything, right? How about the power?"

"All set up, Mr. Raines," Stevens answered, pointing at the massive power storage batteries that took up a good portion of the floor of the warehouse. In this timeline, the battery technology wasn't as advanced as when he'd sourced the batteries and capacitors in 2006 for his first machine. Here, in 2001, he was forced to buy what was available and jury-rig it. Of course, he had also used his knowledge of future technology, including battery production, to set up a shell manufacturing company in New Jersey to exploit his future tech. The company would have a "breakthrough" in battery capacitance and size later on this year and bring the "2006" batteries to market in 2002. And Ellis would be his own first customer.

Stevens continued as they walked the perimeter of the warehouse floor, circling the growing machine. "I told ConEd we were testing some large centrifuges for separating DNA. They didn't have a clue what questions to ask after that, so they just approved it, especially when they saw your $10,000 deposit and the indemnification paperwork."

They walked in silence for a moment, passing the machine and walking back into the suite of offices that Ellis had had constructed again within the warehouse.

"And our new 'friends?'" Don asked.

Stevens smiled.

"Reaching out to the locals was a great idea. They control this part of the waterfront anyway, but bringing them on cemented the relationship. The Italians are going to be great for external security—they're tied in to the local police, and they're not scared of anything. Your generous donation impressed them, as did that tidbit about the police sting that was planned for last week. I'm not sure how you knew about that, but they really appreciated it. As you asked, their organization has been put on a weekly 'retainer' and will be providing security for the exterior of the building, including the lot."

Ellis nodded. "Perfect."

Stevens nodded. "I did a little digging before approaching them—apparently, they have some family connections to the Luciano and passed along an interesting story. Did you know the U.S. Navy got help from the mob in World War II to protect shipyards here in New York?"

Don shook his head. "They have a lot of history here—guess I shouldn't be surprised."

"Apparently they helped out with the invasion of Sicily as well, supposedly in exchange for a lighter sentence for Lucky Luciano," Steven said, smiling. "The things you learn. Anyway, our new friends are on board. They also offered to have a group of men regularly walk a four-block perimeter out from the facility, just in case. They're also rotating personnel in and out so no one gets too curious about what's going on here. So they're watching the outside, and the private security group will handle internal security as well as emergency procedures."

Ellis nodded. "Good. How did Brinks take it?" he asked, referring to the security agency.

Stevens smiled. "They're not sure what to think. I can tell they're not used to working with a 'questionable' element. But splitting up the workload will help out. And they're all on the same frequency, so we'll know if anything is happening."

"Excellent. Things will really start to ramp up once we can start testing, so I'm glad to see that this is all in place now. Thanks, Stevens."

The man nodded and took the opportunity to make his exit.

"Thank you, sir. I'll go check on things. See you tomorrow."

Ellis nodded and watched for a few long minutes as the interns and construction workers climbed over the exterior of the machine—it was quite a bit smaller this time around, with the improvements in the schematics and less of the trial-and-error approach that had defined the look of the first machine. As Ellis watched, Terry welded another support under the particle accelerator. This time, they were adding even more anti-vibration support to reduce that 0.11 field variance that the first machine had experienced. More calculations after the test showed that more structural supports for the accelerator could further reduce the vibrations he had felt during the last time incursion.

Soon, they could begin testing.

The younger Ellis was anxious about the machine and wanted to visit when they started testing. Don thought it was probably because his younger self had never seen a machine in action—maybe on some level, the younger man didn't think it would work. When they'd chatted at his house three weeks ago, the younger Ellis had wanted to oversee the machine's construction, but Don had kept that job—he was the only person in the world to have ever built a time machine, as far as he knew. But Don was worried that the younger Ellis wouldn't be able to convince the government to avert the disaster.

But he hadn't been there. The younger Ellis hadn't seen the bodies falling from the towers on that day, people jumping to certain death to avoid asphyxiation at the top of the burning towers. He knew the story, but he hadn't sat in a darkened room, listening to the television reporters speaking in hushed tones as they watched the smoke rising over the smoldering remains of the collapsed U.S. Capitol.

Ellis hoped that the younger version of himself could convince the people in this world—lately, he'd begun to think of this timeline as another world, and he as just a visitor—to intervene, before it was too late.

2.6
WILLARD HOTEL

The Willard Hotel was the crown jewel of the ornate, 18th century hotels that still existed along Pennsylvania Avenue. Built in 1850, the renaissance hotel had hosted a gaggle of presidents, Hollywood starlets, politicians, and Washington luminaries over its storied years. It stood next to the Treasury Department building, a stone's throw from the White House. In recent years, it had become a hangout for the Washington elite and members of the Press Club.

Dr. Don Ellis' hotel room was amazing—large and lavishly appointed, with antique furniture and a breathtaking view.

But Don wasn't enjoying the accommodations. He was sitting in one of the soft green chairs next to the window that looked out over the White House, only a block away, and wondering when the Bush administration would begin to take him seriously. It had been four days since his meeting at Starbucks with Marburger, and Ellis had talked to him on the phone and in the hotel's opulent lobby on several occasions since. So far, no one at the administration seemed to want any more information other than the machine schematics and the CD of photos and video clips from 9/11.

It was still hard to believe what was supposed to happen in just a few months—the Capitol destroyed, the World Trade Center gone. Last week, Ellis had visited the Red Hook warehouse to see the construction of the new machine, and he had tried to look at the skyline and imagine those two massive, towering buildings gone. It was difficult to do, even after the other Dr. Ellis had shown him the pictures and videos over and over again.

It was the videos of the towers collapsing that bothered him the most.

Of course, the destruction of the Capitol dome and the loss of half of the sitting Congress had been the real blow to the nation—he knew this intellectually. It would lead to months of governmental floundering and an administration with no checks against its aggressive response to the

9/11 attacks. And, of course, it led to geopolitical instability around the world.

But it was the towers falling that affected Don the most. He knew that his wife and daughter were trapped inside. Not his wife and daughter—some alternate version of them, doppelgangers, exact duplicates, but not his wife and daughter. It was crazy, thinking about different versions of his loved ones existing.

Don remembered last week, when the older Dr. Ellis had taken his wallet out and slowly, carefully removed a small, wrinkled piece of paper. He'd laminated it somewhere along the line. It was at least eight years old, but Don had recognized his wife's handwriting immediately:

> *Gone into the city to visit Elaine at the Trade Center. Be back for lunch. Tina was excited, so I took her too.*
>
> > *Love you,*
> > *Sarah*

The older Ellis had treated the scrap of paper as a treasured relic. He'd put it back in his wallet, turning away, but not before Don saw the tears.

In this timeline, Don's wife and daughter would be safe. Don had seen to it. They would have no reason to visit the towers on September 11. Without any warning, Elaine, the woman they had been visiting, had received a surprising (and very lucrative) job offer at the University of New York, working for a colleague of Don's.

So there would be no need for his family to visit the Trade Center on that fateful day, even if he was unable to convince the Bush administration to change anything.

Even if they packed him away to a mental institution, Sarah and Tina would still be safe.

He sipped at his coffee and tapped on his iPad—the elder Ellis had loaned it to him for his meetings with the government. Don hoped they wouldn't confiscate it—he'd grown used to accessing the Internet on the amazing device. The Willard didn't have wi-fi available for guests, so Ellis had set up his own hotspot in the room using the latest 802.11b technology.

When he'd told the other Ellis, the older man had laughed at the "ancient" wi-fi setting. The elder Ellis had altered the device's operating system and wireless connection enough to spoof any curious Internet servers about the device and its operating system. Every computer that accessed the Internet identified itself through a series of codes, but the codes for the iPad, or the Apple iPhone that the older Ellis had also described, did not exist yet. The wireless speed also operated at the non-existent "N" setting, but the older Ellis had changed that to the much slower "B" setting. There were no routers or modems in existence that could yet accommodate the "G" speed, which was just being discussed by regulators to become the new standard in 2003. The "N" speed, the iPad's default wireless speed, wouldn't be widely available until 2009.

There was a quiet knock at the door. Ellis glanced at his watch—6 p.m., just as Marburger had promised. Well, we'll see about that.

Ellis stood and straightened his tie, crossing to the door and opening it.

"Dr. Ellis?" the man asked. Don thought he looked like he might be chiseled from solid granite—all of these Secret Service types looked the same.

He nodded.

The Secret Service agent nodded at Don's coat hanging on a hook by the door. "You might want to grab that."

Don looked at the coat and slipped it on. He put the iPad and two books into a small bag and followed the agent, closing the door behind him.

The agent spoke into his wrist radio as they walked to the elevators.

"Okay, we're coming up."

Ellis was surprised. "Up?"

The agent smiled as they stepped into the elevator. He pressed the button labeled "Terrace Restaurant."

After a moment, the doors opened onto the rooftop of the Willard, revealing a large open area with tables and chairs. The restaurant was in full swing, with scores of people enjoying the unique experience.

The view was stunning—in every direction, Ellis could see monuments and famous sites, glowing in the setting sun. To the west was the White House, the crenellated roofline of the Old Executive Office Building, and beyond, the Kennedy Center. To the south, he could see the Washington Monument and, closer to the low river, the Lincoln and Jefferson memorials.

The agent directed him to a pair of tables near the rooftop railing. John Marburger sat at a table with two other gentlemen who rose to shake Don's hand as he approached.

"Hi, Dr. Ellis. I'm Andrew Card, the president's chief of staff," the man said, smiling. He was tall, taller than Don, with an open demeanor and gray hair that edged down over his ears.

"Hi, Mr. Card," Don answered, shaking his hand.

Card's grip was firm, and for a moment, the man looked at Ellis, sizing him up, before continuing.

Card pointed at the seated man. "That's Ari Fleisher—he's rude. He's also the Press Secretary."

Fleisher dabbed at his face with a napkin and offered his hand, shaking it as Don sat down in an open seat next to Marburger, who nodded at Don.

Don shook Marburger's hand. "Congratulations on the nomination today."

Marburger smiled. "No surprise there."

"Sorry about this," Card said, indicating the food. "We were having a working dinner and discussing the topic with John, and we decided to cut to the chase and chat with you. We ordered you a steak—oh, here it is."

A waiter's arm appeared over Don's shoulder, lowering a massive plate in front of him. It looked like the world's largest porterhouse. He wasn't sure what to do about it.

John looked at him and laughed.

"Don't worry, go ahead," John said. "This is an informal meeting."

Fleischer leaned forward. "That's right. We're trying to figure out if you're crazy," he said, not smiling.

Card shook his head. "Just ignore him," he said and held up the red CD that Don had given Marburger four days earlier. "So, this is all true?" Card asked, and the others quieted.

Don looked at them. "I think I should discuss this with the president."

Fleischer shook his head. "He's not available, Dr. Ellis. You'll have to talk to us."

Don nodded.

"That's fine—I'm sure he's busy getting ready to go to the ranch," Don said, smiling. "Tomorrow is a big day for him. He's got that speech in Birmingham to finish writing. Plus, he'll release the Comprehensive Trade Package for Poland, announce those three ambassadors, and finish that Tax Relief speech for the presidential dinner next week. I'm sure he's far too busy to meet with me about such a trivial matter."

Card and Fleischer looked at each other for a moment, and then Fleischer leaned forward, curious.

"What ambassadors?"

Don smiled, taking a bite of his steak before answering. This was fun. "It will be Gnehm for Jordan, Napper for Kazakhstan, and Huddle for Tajikistan, I think. Of course, maybe I got that off the Internet. I'm sure it's widely available info—"

"No," Fleischer said. "It's not. The names of the potential ambassadors are public knowledge, but there are ten names in the running for each, and you just picked the winners. That's a 1 in 1,000 chance you could get them all correct, without even mentioning the Birmingham and Tax Relief speeches."

"And he knew I'd be nominated today," Marburger added.

Don nodded. "It doesn't matter. What I'm telling you is true. The question is, are you going to do something about it?"

Andrew Card leaned forward. "We don't know yet. Ari and I want to hear you out. We've been through all the evidence you gave John, but we're curious about you, Dr. Ellis."

Don shook his head.

"You don't need to hear me out—you've got the proof in the information I gave Dr. Marburger. I can't give you any more than that. This event *will* occur—it's up to you to figure out what, if anything, to do about it.

Marburger leaned forward. "Couldn't we just release it to the press?" he asked Andrew Card.

Card shook his head. "Release what? Sources inside the White House are saying they have knowledge of the future? They've got a feeling that something bad will happen in three months and are trying to determine what to do about it?"

"It's the truth," Ellis said quietly.

"It doesn't matter," Fleischer added. "It's preposterous. No one will take us seriously again. Dr. Ellis, there are worse things that can come from this information."

"Like what?" Don asked.

Fleischer sat taller, not used to being challenged. "Like we act on it and nothing happens. Have you thought about that? Maybe this is all fiction."

Card shook his head. "I don't know what to think. If your information is genuine—"

"It can't be. It's impossible," Fleischer interrupted. "The Clintonites wouldn't have missed something this big. How can al Qaeda possibly pull off something like what you've claimed?"

"Can I get something out of my bag?" Don asked.

The Secret Service agent, who had been standing nearby but supposedly not listening to their conversation, immediately stepped over to Don, glowering.

Card waved him off. "It's OK, Fletcher. I trust the man."

Don reached in and took out the iPad and a book, one with a red, white, and blue cover. It read *9/11 Commission Report*. He handed the thick book to Card.

Andrew Card took the sizeable volume and began flipping through it, reading passages and flipping back and forth between sections, reading the congressional summary of what happened on that morning and the years leading up to it.

"I'm sure you've been through all the information I gave to Dr. Marburger," Don began, nodding to John. "That is a copy of the official congressional report that will be published in 2007, after years of investigations and committee hearings. I only have the one copy, so please take care of it. It outlines everything leading up to the attack on the Capitol and the Trade Center, including extensive information about the al Qaeda network in Iraq and Afghanistan."

Don turned to Fleischer, handing him the iPad. "You might find this interesting," he said. "Apple will develop a phone in 2007 that uses a touch-screen control interface. Two years afterward, they will release this tablet computer, called an iPad. It puts today's laptops to shame, doesn't it?"

Fleischer took the iPad and, after wiping his hands, began tapping at the screen.

"What's a 'Facebook'?" Fleischer asked.

Don shook his head. "I have no idea."

"This says that the attacks were planned as early at 1999," Andrew Card asked, looking from Fleischer to Don and back. "Is that true?"

"Yes, they've been receiving flight training," Don said quietly. "The hijackers are in Germany now, but will return to the U.S. in early August to begin the operation."

"Jesus." Marburger was sitting next to him.

Fleischer grumbled under his breath and looked up at Card.

"And this is all true?" Card asked, handing the book back. "This is all really going to happen?"

Don felt his face growing hotter. "Yes, it's going to happen," he said, his voice rising. "The question isn't if this is going to happen—the question is, what are you going to do about it? You and the president need to be taking this seriously—" he started to say when Card put up his hand to stop him.

"Don't worry," he said calmly. "We believe you. We've been through all the information that you gave to Marburger, and it all checks out, up to this point, obviously. There is no way to corroborate future events."

Marburger nodded and turned to Don. "They are just trying to get the measure of you. We're meeting with the president tomorrow."

Fleischer looked up from the iPad, not paying attention.

"Can I keep this?" he asked.

2.7
PRESIDENTIAL BRIEFING

Later that evening, Card and Fleischer met the president in the briefing room, recounting their dinner meeting with Dr. Ellis. Printouts of some of the newspapers and magazine covers from the CD were arrayed on a large table in front of them.

"And we think this is legit?" the president asked—even though it was after 9 p.m., he was still in his suit and tie.

"I'm not sure, sir, but there are a lot of details he cannot know. He had a handwritten copy of Dr. Marburger's acceptance speech, and the handwriting matches. Dr. Marburger had just started drafting his version the day before, and comparisons of the two documents, including the punctuation and writing, were uncanny."

Bush nodded, looking at *The 9/11 Commission Report*. Card handed it to the president, who began thumbing through it.

"I've done some preliminary work on this," Card said, "which Dr. Ellis just turned over. There are stunning amounts of detail in the book, including classified intelligence from the Clinton administration. So far, everything is 100 percent accurate. This book says that the hijackers trained here in the United States for their piloting duties. Most of them are currently in Germany, completing their plans before coming to America in early August. It's really very frightening, if this plot were to come to fruition."

Bush nodded. "What about this *other* Dr. Ellis—what happened to him? The one who supposedly came back in time and delivered all this stuff," he said, indicating the table in front of them.

"Dead. Died upon entering our timeline, according to…our version of Dr. Ellis," Fleischer said.

"'Our version?'" the president smirked. "Really? Different versions of the same person running around?"

Card shook his head. "No. According to Dr. Ellis, two people can't occupy the same space together. He described it as saying you couldn't have two trees growing in the same space—either there is one tree or no trees, but not two trees or a hundred. Once the second version enters the timeline, according to Ellis, the first one remains and the second one fades. He said the other Dr. Ellis started bleeding from his nose and mouth and then died on his couch," Card said, pointing at the CD. "The body faded out of existence moments later."

The president looked incredulous. "'Faded out of existence.' Sounds like an episode of *The Twilight Zone* to me, boys."

"I know," Card said. "But to answer your earlier question, his background checks out. The FBI did a quick check on the guy—it shows exactly what we thought. He's a famous, brilliant theoretical physicist whose specialty is quantum mechanics. He's been happily teaching and doing theoretical research for ten years. But if someone were ever going to be successful in building a time machine, this would be the guy. Or an older version of this guy, with ten more years of research and a really good reason to succeed."

Bush nodded. "And no ties to terrorism? How are his finances?"

"No, finances are normal, nothing out of the ordinary," Card replied. "Pays his taxes, owes money on his mortgage, etc. He's the real deal. And he's never had any contact, as far as we can tell, with any questionable entities or persons."

Ari Fleischer leaned forward. "What about Marburger? He seems to believe the guy. Wants to go ahead and start building the machine."

Bush shook his head. "We don't need any damned time machine. Sounds like a load of bunk, anyway. What worries me is this stuff about what happens after the attack. I don't like that sound of that President Bush. Sounds like an asshole."

The others said nothing.

The president smiled, looking at them both. "No disagreement? Interesting. I love the way Cheney gets him declared unfit and moves into the driver's seat. What about his other information? How close is it?"

They were quiet for a moment, and then Card flipped open another folder. "So far, it's been dead on. This guy knows what's going to happen and when. We can use this."

"Notice how he only hits the high points," Fleischer said, tapping the reports. "Too bad there aren't any stock tips in there."

"Or baseball scores," Bush agreed. "I'd love to know how the Rangers do. But seriously, if we move forward with him, then we have to assume this information is credible. What do we know about these supposed terrorists?"

Card looked at him. "There's the problem."

"What do you mean?" Fleischer asked.

Card looked at them both. "Well, we really only have one chance to verify the information in the report and make it work to our advantage. We don't get a second chance."

Fleischer looked confused. "Why?"

"Because this information is of use to us only as long as we don't change anything," President Bush said, understanding what Card was driving at. "As soon as we change something, we're flying in the dark."

"Right," Andrew Card said, nodding. "This information comes to us from a time when no one did anything to change it, because no one knew to change it. Once we change something, new stuff may start to happen, events and other things that we can't predict."

"The more changes we make, Fleischer said, "the less valuable this information is."

Bush nodded. "So, what you're saying is, we pick the right time to intervene?"

Card nodded. "Right."

"So, we only get one shot," Bush said.

"And we have to wait a while," Card added.

"Wait? Why?" Fleischer said.

Card leaned forward. "Well, if we just go in and stop this, no one will give us credit for stopping something *huge* from happening. It'll just be a random arrest of a bunch of Middle Eastern thugs."

Bush read part of the next section of the summary report in front of him. "Who is this Mohammed Atta? Do we have any info on him? He's the leader, right?"

"Yes," Fleischer began, looking at his report. "He's supposedly the leader. He'll fly one of the planes—the first plane—into the World Trade Center's North Tower. And Dr. Ellis' information matches what the FBI knows: In July 2000, he enrolled at Huffman Aviation International in Venice, Florida. In December, he was back in the Miami area, practicing on a Boeing 727 simulator. He returned to Germany and left again in May 2001, first travelling to Spain. He's in Florida right now."

The room fell silent. A navy steward entered, quietly setting down some coffee and a small tray of pastries before exiting.

"Kinda scary, thinking about it, huh?" Card asked, looking up from the report. "What if these guys were successful?"

Bush nodded. "They're using our own free society to get the training they need."

"Bastards," Fleischer said low, under his breath. "Over 21,000 dead, including half of Congress. Did you see those pictures of the Pentagon? It's half gone."

"No one will believe any of this," the president said, shaking his head.

They were quiet for a few long moments as each read parts of the report. Bush sipped at some of the coffee the steward had brought in.

"Couldn't we... oh, I don't know," Fleischer began. "Could we release what they were planning—maybe even some estimated casualty numbers?"

Card shook his head. "It wouldn't have the same impact. No one knows how this would affect the economy."

"Did you guys read the magazine headlines from a year after the incident?" Fleischer asked. "*Time* said that the president was a lock for reelection."

Bush looked at him sharply. "You're not suggesting we let this happen..."

"No, no, no, of course not," Fleischer said, waving his hands. "I could never live with myself, if we could've done something to prevent it and didn't. I'm just saying that no one, outside of the people who've seen this information, will truly appreciate how big a bullet we dodged. Or will dodge."

Bush smiled. "This time travel stuff really plays hell with the verb tenses."

"So what do we do?" Fleischer asked.

"I suggest that we do what we do best in D.C.—form a super secret committee to study this," Card said, pointing at the files. "Then we decide when to act. I'm guessing we intervene the day or a few days before, when all the terrorists are in place and the operation is a go. We storm the planes, seize the terrorists—they'll all be carrying small box cutters. We parade them out and then announce exactly what they were planning to do."

"Good," the president said. "No one will believe us."

No one answered. After a moment, Fleischer asked the question that was on all their minds.

"What about Marburger? And Dr. Ellis?"

Card nodded. "I say we hold them close to the vest. Put them some-place quiet—let them run the intervention committee. Get them and some guys in a think tank and figure out the perfect time to step in. After that, I suggest we have them start building. It took the other Dr. Ellis years to build his, so we might as well get started."

2.8
A Messy Desk

Cassandra sat at her desk, reading through FBI reports and taking notes on a small yellow pad. Her desk was surrounded by dozens of others, but hers was a complete mess. Books were piled precariously on the edges, and papers sprouted from every drawer and in plastic and paper bags on the floor.

Seeing something in a report she was reading, she turned and scooted some papers out of the way, revealing a keyboard. She tapped at the computer on her desk and reached up to adjust the monitor, and, in the process, knocked a stack of papers off the desk. They cascaded to the floor like a waterfall. A fellow reporter snorted as she walked by. Cassie ignored it, tapping away at the computer, when her phone rang.

"*Washington Post*. Cassie O'Neil."

She listened for a long moment, still typing, then stopped. She turned slowly and rooted for a pad and pen, or anything to write with.

"Hang on. OK. Today?" she asked. "No orders on the books?"

She jotted more information down, then continued listening. After a minute of nodding and a few more quick, bird-like questions, she hung up the phone and stood, knocking over another stack of papers. She ignored them and walked across the large room, where a score of other reporters were working, hunched over their own computers, and stuck her head in an office. The nameplate on the door read: MIKE FOREMAN, EDITOR, CITY DESK.

"Mike," Cassie said quietly.

The man looked up at her and grunted.

"I need to talk to Jenkins over at the Pentagon. Might be on to something. Anybody have any contacts at the FBI?"

Mike nodded, reaching for his Rolodex. "Yeah, I do. Why?"

Cassie shook her head. "Not sure, yet. Something's getting investigated, pretty high level. A source just called me. I need to know if it's on the books, or if it's coming from the Bureau."

Mike looked at her for a moment, and then nodded. "OK. Let's meet in ten minutes."

2.9
TEA

In Fort Lauderdale, Florida, on the evening of July 6, three men were seated around a small table in a dining room. Middle Eastern music played quietly in the background. They were eating flatbread and sipping hot tea and discussing a series of plane trips they had recently taken—each had been able to successfully conceal a small, metal box cutter on them and had made it onto their flights with no difficulty.

The three men had been taking intensive flight training over the past six months. They were quietly discussing the relative difficulties of flying large passenger jets when a phone on the wall in the kitchen rang.

One man stood, answering the phone.

"This is Atta," he said in Arabic.

After a long pause, he replied back into the phone.

"God is Great. This is excellent. Thank you. Praise be to Allah."

Atta walked back over to the table and sat down, regarding the others. They remained silent for a long moment, before one of them, Marwan al Shehhi, spoke up.

"Is that the news we've been waiting for?"

Atta nodded.

"Yes, my brothers."

The third man, Ziad Jarrah, nodded and smiled.

"The other teams have passed through Canadian customs without incident. God is Great. We are now in the final stages."

Groups of other Saudi Arabians were entering the country—each pilot had a team of people under him. "Are we to help get them settled?" Shehhi asked.

Atta nodded. "I'll be traveling in a few days to Madrid, so you'll need to get them settled. Get them new IDs, and the younger men seem to enjoy going to the gym."

Shehhi nodded. "Madrid?"

"Yes, to meet Binalshibh. I'm sure he'll pass along the final instructions."

Jarrah spoke up. "I agree with you—I think the Capitol would be a better target. Why does bin Laden want to strike the White House?"

Atta shook his head and ate. "I'm not sure. He prefers it, so it shall be."

"Will you mention Indian Point?" In their familiarization flights over the New York area, Atta had mentioned the nuclear power plant as a potential target, but the other pilots were leery—the airspace over nuclear plants was more heavily restricted, so they were unable to do reconnaissance flights. The chances of getting shot down during the actual attacks would be increased

"Yes, I'll mention it. But I think he will not approve." Atta looked at them. "Soon, the target list will be set, and we'll move into the final phase."

He raised his glass of tea to the others and drank deeply.

2.10
LAWRENCE LIVERMORE

On the morning of July 10, Ellis was just finishing up his room service breakfast when there was a quiet knock at his door.

"Come in," he called. He knew the Secret Service agent posted outside his door had a keycard.

The door opened and the agent poked his head in. "Dr. Ellis, Dr. Marburger is here for you."

Ellis nodded and Marburger entered, panting.

"Don, you've got to get packed."

"Good," Ellis said. "I don't like this waiting around, John. Not one bit."

Marburger nodded. "I know, Ellis, I know."

"You asked me down here to hold more meetings with the committee, which we did, and then you said to hang around town and wait. That was three days ago, and I've been held up here, cooling my heels. With a babysitter, no less," he said, pointing at the door. "What's going on?"

John glanced at the door and shrugged. "It was just for your own protection. There are rumors going around. But I just heard from Andrew Card—the committee is finished. The president approved our recommendations and wants to meet. Now. After that, we're heading to Livermore."

"No, that's not going to work," Ellis said, thinking of the warehouse in Red Hook and his family. He needed to be nearby—

"It's okay," Marburger said. "You'll be back in a week. The president wants to discuss the committee's recommendations and the machine. They have already set up a secure facility and are starting to create components for the machine. He wants us out there to oversee the project. The president wants it done as soon possible, just in case."

Don thought for a second and nodded. "OK, but I need to get back soon—I have to be with my family on 9/11, just to make sure nothing goes wrong."

Marburger nodded. "Absolutely."

2.11
A Leak

One month later, on the morning of August 12, 2001, Andrew Card and several other White House staffers were in the White House Situation Room, seated around a big conference room table. Everyone in the room was quietly eating bagels and drinking coffee from the table set up on one end of the room. Card noticed that no one was talking.

Everyone stood when President Bush entered the room, but he waved them back down into their seats and began pacing around the table, his face an angry scowl.

"Just how the *hell* did this happen?" the president asked before he even sat down.

No one answered.

"Have you read this yet?" he asked rhetorically, holding up a copy of this morning's *Washington Post*. Of course, everyone had read it—it was the point of the meeting.

Andrew Card had noticed a change, a focused sense of urgency in the president, since learning about the impending terrorist attack and its devastating effect on the future United States. Card had also noticed a hardening in the president's demeanor—it was as if the event had already taken place in his mind, and now he was determined to make sure it didn't really happen. He'd been on edge, less likely to want to discuss policy or diplomacy with the Chinese or carry on lengthy conversations about trade policy or the environment.

President Bush only wanted to know how the investigation was progressing. And he wanted daily updates on the machine.

As they got closer and closer to the date of the attack, Card had seen the president's stress level ratcheting up, day by day.

Now, he was mad. They had a leak.

The president looked down the table at all of them, then plopped down in the chair and began reading. "Sources in the Bush Administration are reporting that a high-level anti-terrorist committee has been created to study possible indications of a major terrorist strike to take place in the next six to eight weeks. Sources would not confirm whether these strikes were to occur in the United States or abroad, or any other details..."

The president stopped, looking around the room. His eyes stopped on Fleischer.

"What is this crap?" Bush barked. "Who is leaking this?"

Fleischer shook his head. "I have no clue, sir. The Committee isn't meeting anymore. Our staff has been monitoring Dr. Ellis' data, matching it against daily events, but so far I don't think we've raised any flags."

The president's eyes widened, and Card slowly shook his head. Ari should have known not to wave a red flag in front of a bull.

The president shook the paper at Fleischer. "This is a flag! A pretty goddamn big one!"

"I'll look into it, sir," Card spoke up. "I don't know this Cassie O'Neil, but we'll put someone on her, track down her sources, if we can." There was no reason to let this get out of hand.

The president nodded. "OK, about the timeline and Ellis. What have we learned?"

"Well, unfortunately," Andrew said, looking down at the report in front of him, "we've learned that it could happen next month—in fact, looking at the signs, I'd have to say that it's likely. All the hijackers are in place, and we've found nothing that contradicts the timeline."

Bush shook his head. "What do you mean?"

"Well, we're on the terrorists and elements of their plot, obviously. But we've also been comparing current events with the historical timeline provided, and so far, everything is on track. We've got several months' worth of political, environmental, and entertainment news to track, and it's been dead on. Earthquakes, celebrity weddings, everything."

Bush nodded.

"We've had to restrict access to the pop culture and sports information—it's too accurate. I don't want it being misused."

"What about the terrorists?" Fleischer asked.

Card shot him a look and continued. "Two are in San Diego, where they finished flight training classes about two weeks ago. The rest are congregated in an area in Florida. We've confirmed that they've all purchased tickets under their own names for the flights in question on September 11."

President Bush slowly shook his head. "Jesus Christ. So, when will we move?"

Card looked at the president and the others around the table.

"Well, that's your call, sir. The closer we get to the actual events, the more accurate our information is—and as soon as we prevent something from happening, the information in our possession becomes useless."

Fleischer nodded. "But we prevent the loss of 21,000 lives."

"Right," Card answered. "I would suggest we move on September 9, seizing the men and their equipment, and then announce that we've stopped a major terrorist operation, one designed to destroy the Capitol and the World Trade Center. We could even use some of the pictures from Ellis to illustrate our point, though we'd have to call them 'artistic renderings' or something."

Bush pondered this for a long moment and then nodded.

"That's good. Move everything into place, then on the ninth, arrest them. Get all the information ready to go. And start the ball rolling on rounding up any other al Qaeda here in the United States."

The president smiled and turned to Fleisher. "Now, what do we do about bin Laden and the Taliban?"

Fleisher smiled. "I've got some ideas about that, sir."

2.12

A Change in Plans

A large group of men were crowded into the small living room in Florida. The leader Atta stood, speaking in Arabic.

"God is Great," Mohammed Atta said, beginning the meeting with the opening phrase preferred by practitioners of the Koran. "We are about to embark on a heroic quest, my friends. We will be making a statement to the entire world, and that statement will be that the Zionist infidels will not survive Allah's wrath on the world. Their ways may be tempting and full of earthly pleasures, but their way is corrupt."

The men around the table nodded, listening. It appeared they had heard this before, many times. Atta continued, both for the people in the room and for Allah above to hear.

"God is Great. We will take their planes, and we will kidnap hundreds of their citizens, bringing their economy to a standstill. The ransoms will fund a thousand mosques. Hundreds of their politicians and leaders will demand justice, but others will demand that payment be made. And we will demand an end to all funding to the Zionist state."

He paused, and one of the other men, a younger man, tentatively raised his hand.

"God is Great. We will break the infidels, brother Atta," the young man said, pausing. "Mohammed, will we execute the hostages?"

Some of the others hissed at the young man.

Atta nodded. "God is Great. Yes, we will make our demands known and then begin executing the hostages until our demands are met. We will take the hostages with us after the Zionists refuel the planes. We will fly to Europe and, from there, back to Saudi Arabia. There, the hostages will be bartered for more money. It is the only thing that the Zionists understand."

Atta looked around, but there were no more questions. He ended the meeting with a prayer, then watched as most of the men walked out into the sticky Florida night. Four of the nineteen men remained behind.

Atta looked at the others.

"We are ready, I see. Can we delay, as I mentioned?"

Another one of the four men spoke up, respectfully. "God is Great," Hani Hanjour, the fourth pilot, answered. "Yes, the training is over. We are ready. And the delay will allow us more time. Have we discovered the reason for the increased security?"

Atta shook his head, looking at the others.

"No, simply that they are running some kind of exercise or doing some additional training during the first weeks of September. I don't think we have been discovered."

"What about the newspaper article?" They had all read and discussed the *Post* article and how it seemed to mirror their own plan.

"We ignore it," Atta said quietly, "and delay the date of our action. Will that give the other two teams time to be in place?"

"Each team is already prepared and trained," Hanjour said. It is simply a matter of setting them in motion. They already know their targets."

Atta nodded thoughtfully. "Have the other teams been mentioned in any of the reports back to Kandahar?"

"No, Mohammed," Hanjour said. "The Zionists apparently have information about some of our activities—how they found out, we have no idea. One of our men may have been compromised, or some of our communications with Hamburg may have been intercepted. There were many pilgrims in and around the mosque in Hamburg—one of them may have been a plant. I thought it wise to not include any of the changes to the schedule. We should suspend activities and move the teams again, then strike."

Mohammed Atta nodded, a small smile on his face. "We will delay to the secondary date we previously discussed," Atta said. He did not want to say the exact date out loud—it was always prudent to act as if they were under surveillance and in case the home might contain listening devices. He looked around at the others.

"I will contact each of you with further instructions. If I don't, or can't, move forward with the plan. Can we do this, my friends?"

The others glanced at each other, nodding. The others had been recruited and informed that the planes would be hijacked and landed and that the passengers would be held for ransom. Only the four men in the room understood the true nature of their mission.

Marwan al Shehhi spoke up. "Yes, we can. The others must not know, though. They will balk at the sacrifice—some are too young and others too simple. Their cowardice may rear its head at the moment of victory."

"Then kill them, if you must," Atta said. "This plan will succeed, even if we have to recruit local replacements. There is no shortage of citizens disillusioned by this nation's Zionist policies. And its decadence. But we will succeed—six planes, six targets, six simultaneous statements about the frailty of this nation."

The others looked at him for a moment, and it was easy for them to understand why bin Laden had personally chosen Mohammed Atta to lead this assault—he was a dynamic man, an engaging speaker, with a deep understanding of the Koran and what it meant, both figuratively and literally.

After a long moment, the others began to file out the door into the humid Florida night. Atta said goodbye to each in the traditional Muslim way, with quiet words exchanged and heads bowed. As he closed the door, the cell phone in his pocket rang.

"Yes?"

A voice on the phone—it was Zahmid, one of the other team leaders. "God is Great. We are being watched."

"As are we," Atta answered. "We have updated the schedule and are moving to our alternate locations. You will be contacted," he said curtly, hanging up the phone.

He looked around the sparsely decorated kitchen of the Florida rental home and then went into the bedroom and began packing.

2.13
CAR WASH

Dr. Don Ellis was in his driveway, washing his car, the grey Volvo. Sarah and Tina emerged from the house, smiling and laughing. Sarah was fiddling in her purse, clearly surprised to see him in the driveway.

"Oh," she said, stopping. "I thought you left. We're heading out—I left you a note."

Ellis stopped and turned, nodding. "Just washing the car."

Sarah smiled. "Aren't you late for class?" At her feet, Tina was digging through her Powerpuff Girls backpack.

"No class today. It got cancelled—a bunch of students are in the city, working on the primary." It was Tuesday, September 11, and the City of New York was holding a primary to choose, among others, a candidate for Mayor. As was often the case, students from the university would help out at various election and polling locations in the city.

"Oh. Tina and I are heading into the city."

Ellis nodded. "Your lunch with Elaine?"

"Yup. She's got that new job and wants to show off her new office. We'll toodle around for a while downtown and then meet her for lunch. Back around 2."

"Cool. Have fun," he said, kissing her before going back to washing the car.

Tina jumped up, and he pretended to spray her with the hose.

"We're going into town!" she said. "The big buildings!"

Ellis looked at Sarah, and they shared a smile—for years, Tina had been begging them to take her up in the Empire State Building and the World Trade Center and any other tall building they saw. Ellis was convinced that she would be a pilot when she got older, or an architect.

"Have fun, honey," he said, hugging her to his leg before she scampered off and climbed into Sarah's Passat. He waved as the car drove away.

When the car was clean, Don went inside. He made himself breakfast, toast and eggs, and saw that Sarah had left out a few dishes, including the pan. He hated it when she left without tidying up after herself.

He flipped on the TV while he had breakfast.

On the screen, the North Tower burned. People were jumping to their deaths, and from the side of the screen, a second plane appeared, low and fast, like a missile, and it hit the South Tower with a massive crash, a fireball boiling out the opposite side. Impact debris and what looked like part of the plane showered down onto the streets of New York below...

"Dr. Raines?"

Don glanced up.

Stevens was standing in the doorway.

Don looked down—he was sitting in his office in the warehouse. He had been looking over some schematics, looking for improvements. What had made him start thinking about that day?

"Dr. Raines?"

Ellis shook his head. "Yes?"

"Oh, nothing, sir," Stevens said. He looked embarrassed. "It's just... you looked like you were asleep, but your eyes were open. And you looked upset."

Ellis shook his head again and looked down—his fists were clenched, the fingers white. He breathed out, slowly, and unclenched his fists, resting them on the desk on either side of the computer keyboard.

"Nope," Ellis said, smiling. "I'm fine. Thanks for checking."

Stevens nodded, the concern obvious on his face, and then disappeared, moving down the hallway.

Don looked up at the skylights that looked down on the warehouse—it was a bright, sunny day outside, but he couldn't shake the feeling that things were wrong. It felt like something had changed, something in the air, and Ellis had no idea what it was.

2.14

Dumpster

Carter and Fields, two FBI agents, sat in a late-model sedan on the morning of August 14. They were parked on a tree-lined street across from a small two-story apartment building in Fort Lauderdale. Palm trees swayed in the ocean breeze.

Carter sipped at a cup of Dunkin Donuts coffee as they watched cars come and go.

"So, how was your trip?" he asked the man next to him.

Fields, a black man with very short hair, nodded.

"Great, great. Went up to Charleston for a few days."

Carter nodded, sipping his coffee. His partner waited for a moment for a follow-up question but none came. He reached and took a red folder off the dashboard and began flipping through it.

"So," he asked, "Are we supposed to do anything here?" The information in the folder was very sparse—just a name and address and a notation to "locate and observe."

Carter shook his head. "Nope. Just observing. I love this kind of assignment—I'm getting paid to sit in a car and drink coffee. Is this a great country or what?"

Fields rolled his eyes—this was not a great duty for him. He'd rather be out in the field, chasing down—

Suddenly, he climbed from the car and started across the street.

"Hey!" Carter said, grabbing his keys and locking the door before running across the street to catch up with Fields. "What are you doing? We're supposed to stay back—"

Fields walked up to a dumpster behind the apartment building and stopped, pointing.

"OK," the black agent said. "What if I observe that there is no one in that apartment up there?"

"What?" Carter panted.

"Look—the trash bin. It's full of furniture. That means they're gone."

2.15

SITUATION ROOM

"They're all gone?" the president asked, incredulous.

The room was completely quiet. It was the morning of August 16.

Andrew Card nodded solemnly. "Not a sign of the hijackers in any of the three locations. They must've gotten word, somehow. Mohammad Atta and two of the other pilots, Hazmi and Hanjour, flew to Las Vegas on August 13. They were supposed to stay one day and return to Florida, but they're gone, along with all of their crews."

"Christ, this is a mess," Fleischer said.

Card continued. "Between the newspaper articles and the fact that they were being watched…obviously they have changed their plans. It is doubtful they will strike on 9/11. We have people looking for them, but—"

"It doesn't matter, now," Bush said angrily. "Our information is out of date. And without that, we have no idea when they'll strike. Get Dr. Ellis in here."

Two Secret Service agents escorted Ellis and Marburger into the Situation Room.

"Shit." the president said. "Now what do we do?"

Ellis looked confused.

"I'm not sure I understand—" Ellis began to ask.

"They've moved," Card said quietly. "The hijackers—they're all gone."

Ellis and Marburger looked at each other.

"Well," Ellis said, looking at the table. "That is bad. Very bad. Did our information get out?"

"It doesn't matter what happened," the president said angrily. "It appears that our FBI agents in Florida and Newark were a little too careless. They were seen by Atta and his people, who went to ground. Now, we're looking for them."

"They didn't know what was at stake. No one does," Ellis said quietly.

"Well, they're gone now," Card said. "We have people looking for them, but we can't be sure we'll find them."

"What should we do?" Marburger asked.

"We need to find them, immediately," Ellis said. "You guys know their plans as well as I do—you've read the reports. They will carry out the plan as instructed, just on a different date—they are not in contact with al Qaeda now. They've moved into the part of the plan where they're autonomous—they already have a list of approved targets from bin Laden, but they can adjust the dates and locations as they see fit. Now that they've gone to ground, I expect they will hit the same targets, or try to, within weeks of the original date. We must increase airport security at Newark, Boston, and Dulles, and plaster their pictures all over the news."

The rest of the room was looking at him—his foreknowledge was not only uncanny but also more than a little disturbing. Bush stared at Card and the others, tapping on the table in front of him.

"Well," the president began, leaning backwards. "I always said that it's better to have two plans than no plans. We are almost finished with the machine, correct?

Marburger and Ellis nodded. Silence in the room.

"Good. Move forward with increased security at the airports and try to stop them, should they decide to attack. I'm hoping, for one, that they got spooked. Marburger and Ellis, you need to finish the machine; that would give us the opportunity to use the machine to warn ourselves if necessary. We may have missed our opportunity here, and I'm not going to let that happen again. We'll complete our machine and begin testing it. If something happens, we'll go back and fix it. Until then, let's find these bastards."

2.16

ARMED

Dr. Donald Ellis was in a happier mood then he'd been in months. Lately, he'd been anxious as the date approached, but things were looking up.

It was the morning of September 11, 2001 but, so far, nothing tragic had occurred.

Don was still on edge, to be sure, but it was nearly 11:00 a.m., and there had been no attacks, no hijackings. He'd wanted to pinch himself. In fact, Don had been outside this morning at 8:46 a.m., the time when the first plane had struck the North Tower in his original timeline. But nothing had happened. He'd stayed outside until 9:15—well after the second plane was supposed to strike—but it turned out to be just another beautiful Tuesday morning.

For the first time in a long time, Don felt relaxed.

He stood back and observed the continuing construction on the new particle accelerator—it was red and very large, like the original one he'd left behind. This time he'd been able to build it again from scratch, using less polybenudium, which was expensive and difficult to source.

Ellis was sweaty—he'd just finished a workout in the small apartment that he'd set up in one corner of the warehouse for his own use. His doppelganger and his family were safe now—they were all out in California at Lawrence Livermore National Labs, where the younger Ellis was working with Marburger and the scientists to construct their machine. He wished them good luck—he'd intentionally left out a crucial subsystem in the schematics, so the machine would never work. He didn't need the Bush or future administrations possessing a working time machine. Nothing good could come of that.

Ellis thought about the younger Don and his family. Ellis found it very difficult to be around this version of Sarah and Tina without missing his—they'd met a few times, but it had been awkward. They were the same, and yet somehow he knew they weren't "his"—of course, he would do anything to keep them safe, as the younger Ellis would. But he'd been actively avoiding them, spending more and more time holed up in the warehouse, working on the machine.

Ellis watched as several interns worked to bolt the last particle accelerator arm to the support mast, ensuring a stable wave field. Terry was below them, working on the reactor containment box—last time, it had been as big as a van, but now it was smaller, the size of a refrigerator on its side. The confinement box channeled the battery power into the accelerator, which then created a rift in space and time. The machine looked almost complete now, tidier than last time. Wires and pipes ran in clean lines across the warehouse floor instead of feeding into the machine in a ropy mess.

The only components that would be larger in this timeline were the batteries. Ellis knew that the industrial storage batteries that he'd used on the earlier machine would not be available here, but he wasn't expecting to have to jury-rig together his own battery matrix to store up enough juice to power the machine. He had a whole team working on that problem—he could fire off the machine just using power from ConEd, but he preferred not to. Doing so would cause a massive power outage along the entire eastern seaboard, and he didn't want that kind of attention during the testing phase.

Of course, if he used it to leave this timeline, it didn't really matter—but then, if he was using the machine to exit this timeline, then he had failed.

Stevens walked up to him, smiling.

"Dr. Raines?"

Ellis nodded.

"Those—other items you ordered are here," Stevens added. Together, they walked past the machine and all the ancillary areas required to build it—battery area, machine shop to custom mill parts, and the massive computer lab. He had ended up needing three times as many computers in this timeline to handle the data processing requirements to focus the accelerator and make the machine work. It was too bad the machine had a limited amount of mass that it could project through time—if he ever left this timeline to build the machine farther back in the past, he would be smart and bring his own computers.

Ellis and Stevens walked out into the front of the warehouse, where the building was stacked high with wooden crates. Three serious-looking Italian men stood next to two new wooden crates.

Ellis walked up, greeting them warmly.

"Favurio, hello. Gentlemen," Ellis said, acknowledging the others.

Favurio, the leader of the group, stepped up and shook Ellis' hand.

"How you doin', Dr. Raines?"

"I've been better, but today has been good. Very good. And I have a feeling I'm about to get some good news. What do you have for me today, Favurio?"

One of the large men stepped over and removed the lid from one of the crates. Inside rested scores of automatic weapons and a large pile of ammunition. Ellis reached in and took one out, nodding at it.

"Excellent," he said. "AK-47s."

Favurio nodded. "Untraceable. And there are more in the other crate, along with those two special items you requested."

Don looked at him. "Really? You were able to find those for me?" He felt like a kid on Christmas morning.

Favurio smiled. "Yes, Dr. Raines. It wasn't that difficult," he said, glancing around at the other people in the room.

Ellis smiled and nodded to Stevens, who reached into his pocket. He saw the other Italians tense up and look at Favurio, who shook his head to wave them off. Stevens pulled out a large envelope, handing it to Favurio.

"I can't thank you enough," Ellis said to Favurio, speaking quietly. "There's a little extra in there for you and your families. And remember what I said—a friend of mine in the government says that some serious shit might be happening in the next few weeks. Take that money, take your friends, and go upstate—take a little holiday, okay?"

Favurio nodded slowly, lifting at the bulging envelope. "There's a lot in here."

Ellis nodded. "I know you have a big family," he said quietly. "Split it up as you see fit," he said.

Favurio nodded and thanked him again, and then he and his crew left. Terry walked up and joined Ellis and Stevens, who were looking at the weapons.

Terry whistled.

"Wow, we've got our own arsenal, now. Are we expecting an invasion?" Terry reached in and picked up a gun, then held it and made a face. "Say hello to my little friend!" he said in a horrible Cuban accent.

Ellis laughed out loud, something he rarely did. "Thanks, Scarface."

Terry lifted the gun, feeling its heft. "You know what to do with these, Mr. Raines?" Terry asked, smiling.

Ellis picked up a weapon and expertly popped out the magazine, emptied the chamber, and reloaded it in a matter of moments. He turned and smiled at Terry.

"Yup, I know what I'm doing," Ellis said. "I'm just being careful, Terry. I don't want anything to go wrong. Stevens, another thing—can you look into reinforcing those doors?"

Stevens nodded as he counted the guns and made a notation on a clipboard he was carrying. After a second, he stepped over to the second crate and removed the lid.

Terry whistled again when he saw what was in the second crate.

"Jesus. Well, it would take an army to stop us now, sir."

Ellis smiled. "That's the idea, Terry."

The rest of the day was uneventful—Ellis finished Stevens' catalogue of the contents of the new armory, then got some more work on his latest project, attempting to reduce one of the subsystems by 40% in size and weight. This particular subsystem had been identified as one of the largest, by volume, so reducing it in size would allow them to further reduce the size of the overall machine.

Around sunset, he again walked outside to watch the sun settle down onto the horizon.

As evening fell on New York City on the evening of September 11, 2001, the twin towers began to sparkle with lights. Ellis watched as they and other buildings around them came to life, the lights inside them coming on as the light faded.

Dr. Donald Ellis stood in the cool breeze for a long time, watching the skyline across the river. He'd done it. He'd really changed the past.

2.17

THE TRUTH AND A LIE

The younger Dr. Ellis was not having a pleasant day. In fact, he was a nervous wreck—things were not progressing as planned with the machine, and even though he'd been able to bring Sarah and Tina out with him on this last trip, the trepidation was running through him like electricity.

It was September 11.

He'd been dreading this day and, at the same time, awaiting it. After the older Ellis had visited him that first time in his living room, things had changed for him forever. He'd taken a sabbatical from the university and taken those stacks of money and proof from Ellis and moved into a new phase of his life, a phase that involved meeting with government people and trying to convince them of the reality of an event that had not yet happened. He had argued with the elder Dr. Ellis about the roles they were to play. Wouldn't the argument be infinitely more convincing coming from the Dr. Ellis who had actually seen it, the one from the other timeline?

But the elder Ellis had disagreed—he thought it was too important that they start construction on the machine immediately, in case they were unable to convince the government to intervene and build one of their own.

But now it was that fateful day, and Ellis had been unable to sleep at all.

"You okay?" Sarah asked from the bed. Tina wasn't in the other bedroom—she had started first grade at the local elementary school. She'd be taking classes there until they could all return to Jericho.

Don looked at her, happy. "Yes, I am. Listen, I know things are strange, with my sudden involvement in this work out here. But it will make sense today, I think. Just stay in the hotel and don't go out for any reason."

She looked at him with a strange expression. "Why? What's going to happen?"

Ellis shook his head and shrugged his shoulders. "It doesn't matter now—in about an hour, terrorists are going to strike this country. Unless they get caught—their pictures are all over every airport in the country—they will hijack planes and crash them into the Capitol building and Pentagon in Washington, D.C., and the World Trade Center buildings in New York. More than 21,000 people will be killed."

"How... how do you know?" she asked quietly, looking out the window.

"That's the crazy part—I don't know. But do you remember in the spring, when I took those three days off in April?"

She nodded.

"One day, when I got home, there was another version of me in the house."

Her eyes went wide. "What?"

"Yes. Another Dr. Ellis was there, waiting to talk to me. He knew about the attacks. He called them '9/11'—I remember he said it with such solemnity, like he was talking about Pearl Harbor. That was one of the things that convinced me he was telling the truth."

"What did he say?"

Ellis sat at the corner of the bed. "He talked about the attacks and how they would affect the nation. The Capitol in D.C., and the Trade Center in New York—hijackers are going to crash planes into them. The Pentagon, as well. And... and he said that you and Tina died. In the World Trade Center."

Sarah's eyes darkened and she sat up. She glanced at the closed door that led to Tina's bedroom in the large suite.

Don continued. "He said that... you died in the attacks. One plane crashed into each tower, and you were in the South Tower, visiting your friend Elaine."

"But she works at the university," Sarah said, confused. "She was trying to get a job with a firm in the Towers, but... does that mean she's in the tower? Has it been attacked?"

Ellis shook his head. "No. I just checked. There have been no attacks—it was supposed to happen this morning. Everything's fine, so far. And after... in the world he's from, Ellis said that after you and Tina died, he was lost without you. He said that he started work immediately on finishing the machine."

Sarah looked at him for a long moment. "The machine...you mean those schematics hanging on the wall of our basement? A time machine, one that really works?"

Ellis nodded, smiling. "I know. It's crazy—I've done a lot of preliminary work, but he finished it. It took him nine years, but he came back to warn us. And to save you and Tina. He gave me the blueprints and all the information about 9/11 to give to the government."

They were both quiet. He knew the next question, and he hated to lie to her, but there was no other option. No one could know about Red Hook—it was unfortunate that even he knew about it, but the older Dr. Ellis had taken that security risk. It allowed both Dr. Ellis' to work on two different things at the same time.

Sarah stood and walked to the windows—outside, the sky was still dark. Ellis glanced at the clock—the first plane would begin hitting in a few minutes.

"What happened to... the other you?" she asked.

"He died. I was talking to him, and he collapsed," Ellis lied, his voice low. He hated to do it, but no one could know. "He was bleeding from his nose and mouth. I took him downstairs, and he gave me CDs full of information, and he was explaining it all to me as I looked at it on the computer in the basement. He saw the plans for the machine on the wall and smiled, and then he died. Massive aneurysm."

She was quiet.

"I think that two people cannot exist in the same timeline—he knew this was going to happen," Ellis said. It was a work of fiction—as far as he could ascertain, there was no limit to the number of possibilities and permutations that could be brought about with the construction of an operating time machine.

"He knew he would die," Ellis said. "But for him, it was worth it." Ellis looked out the window with her for a long moment, and then he held her hand.

"If anything were to happen to you..."

"Don't worry about me," she said. "I think it's crazy that this is all happening because... of me and Tina. If we had survived that attack—"

He turned her around. "Don't think about it like that. You and Tina are fine, and we're out of harm's way. We're almost finished with the machine—"

"You're building it? A time machine? Here?" she turned, her eyes wide.

He nodded. "That's why we're out here—Dr. Marburger and I are supervising the construction of the machine. President Bush said—"

"You've met the president?"

Ellis smiled. "Several times."

"Cool," she smiled.

"The President said our job was to get the machine up and running in ten months—I didn't think it was possible, but with all the resources of the government at our disposal, we're halfway done. And to think it took the other Ellis nine years."

She nodded. "And the terrorists?"

Ellis turned and began to get dressed. "That's the president's job—he's got his people working on it."

Sarah started to tidy the bed but stopped.

"But didn't they already know who the people were? Surely I would have heard about it on the radio. Couldn't they just arrest them?"

He looked at her. "That's what I suggested, and that's what they should have done, but they decided to follow the terrorists and catch them in the planning, so that they would be able to prosecute."

Sarah shook her head. "That doesn't make any sense."

"Well, the only people who knew what was coming were the terrorists themselves and the few people in the government that I had talked to. Knowledge from the future can't get you a search warrant, and it certainly isn't admissible in a court of law, no matter how horrible the videos and pictures are."

"There are videos?"

Ellis nodded. "Yes, it's horrible. I'll never be able to get some of the images out of my head. The New York ones are the worst, because you... you and Tina were in the building."

"Oh. What happened in D.C.?"

"Two planes—one into the Capitol building. About half of Congress was killed. The other plane took out part of the Pentagon."

"My God," she said quietly.

"The Capitol dome collapsed. At the Pentagon—the plane came in low and hit the west side of the building. The initial damage was bad enough, but then the fires spread really fast. Ellis said it was the 1940s' construction materials, along with no sprinkler systems. Something like 2,600 people died. The military took months to recover, and in that time, small wars broke out worldwide. Ellis said that there was a palpable sense of vulnerability in the air, as if anything could happen at any moment. Bush's wife had been at the Capitol, meeting with members of Congress, and she was killed as well. Ellis said the chaos lasted for years afterward, with President Bush and then President Cheney launching preemptive strikes whenever any threat came up."

"Cheney? President Cheney?" she asked.

"Yes, evidently Bush had some kind of breakdown after 9/11. His wife Laura had been up on the Hill and died in the attack. Losing his wife was too much. He was leading the nation without any direction. Within six months of the attacks, the United States was involved in several wars around the world, invading Afghanistan and bombing parts of Iraq, Pakistan, and the Philippines. Because Congress had been incapacitated, nations around the world moved forward with invasions and bombings, assuming the U.S. was weak."

Sarah was quiet.

"President Bush was trying to knock out al Qaeda, the group behind the attacks on 9/11."

"Jesus."

He walked around the bed and reached into his bag, taking out an object, and handed it to her. "Here."

She looked down at the item—it was flat, a foot long and eight inches wide. It appeared to be made out of black glass, with only one button on the front. She flipped it over and saw the familiar logo.

"Apple?"

He nodded. "Yes, it's called an iPad—they'll come out with a phone first, in 2007, and then this in 2010." He pushed the button to turn it on, then slid his finger across the screen to unlock it. "It's all touch-controlled."

He let her play with it for a few minutes—every once in a while, she'd make a happy or surprised sound as she discovered something else interesting about the device.

"This is amazing," she said. "It's really from the future?"

"Yup," Ellis answered. "Dr. Ellis brought several back with him. He said the wireless connection had to be modified to use our speeds, which are about 1/20th of those the device was built for."

She nodded and continued tapping. Music started playing.

"Ellis said that in the future, Apple pretty much owns the music business—they have the iPod now, but in ten years they'll have this and a phone and five more generations of iPods. You can buy and download almost any song you want wirelessly."

Sarah smiled. "Cool."

He walked over and tapped at the device, and a song began to play.

"Recognize this?" he asked, setting the device down on the bed. He took her hands and started slowly dancing around the messy hotel room. She listened to the song and slowly smiled.

"Willie Nelson."

"Yup, it's 'Darkness on the Face of the Earth,'" he said.

"Our song, at our wedding."

He nodded, even though they were dancing. "Don't worry about today. Hopefully, it will be just like any other day. That's why they're working so hard to make sure nothing happens today, but with the terrorists disappearing, they're not sure—"

"Disappearing?" she asked, looking up at him sharply. "I thought they were under surveillance?"

"They were," Ellis agreed. "But then they found out they were being watched. They've all disappeared."

She looked at him, suddenly scared. The music continued.

"So, it could happen. It could happen today," she said, looking up at him.

He nodded slowly, holding her tighter. "Yes, it could. But I think they'll delay for a few weeks. They're scattered, and in hiding. Even with every law enforcement agency in the nation looking for them, they still haven't been found. I just have to hope that the FBI catches them before they can strike. Until then, we just have to stay safe and stay out of New York and Washington, okay?"

She nodded and began to sob quietly into his shoulder.

2.18
A Non-Event

A few hours later, Dr. Ellis was riding in a white van across the dusty expanse of Lawrence Livermore National Labs, a large group of identical buildings that stretched into the California desert. Established in 1952 as an offshoot of the University of California, it had quickly grown to encompass much of the nation's most advanced nuclear and security research. Some of the most advanced experiments in the nation were carried out on the one-square-mile site, as well as at Site 300, a 7,000-acre sister site fifteen miles southeast of the main lab site.

The van approached a large central building and slowed, stopping at a large door. Armed guards motioned a white van inside the massive building. Inside, the van moved across the cement flooring and stopped. Two armed guards pulled the doors open, and Ellis and Marburger climbed down out of the van. They moved across the building's expansive floor and approached a brightly lit area where dozens of people were working on a large machine. It vaguely resembled the original machine that the "deceased" Dr. Ellis had built in his Long Island building.

"Well, it was to be expected," Dr. Marburger said. "We dodged a bullet."

Ellis nodded. "I know. Still, to have nothing happen at all on this 9/11...I'm just worried. Having nothing happen seems even more ominous."

"I just wish the other Ellis had lived," Marburger said, nodding. "Maybe he would have more insight into alternate targets, or the hijacker's new timeline. Assuming they still go through with it," Marburger said.

"The FBI will find them," Ellis replied, avoiding the subject. They walked into the computer lab. Ellis turned on the TV in the room and switched it to the news, but it was remarkably ordinary. There was coverage of Hurricane Erin, which was threatening to hit Bermuda. The top story was Britney Spears' performance at the 2001 MTV Video Music

Awards show that had taken place a week before—evidently, dancing on a stage with a giant yellow snake could get a performer coverage on the nightly news, even a full week later.

Or maybe it was just an excuse to show the same tacky burlesque photos of a sultry Britney Spears dancing, over and over, with a large yellow python.

Ellis shook his head and walked out onto the main floor, eager to get back to work on the machine.

2.19
TESTING PHASE

Three weeks after the uneventful 9/11, the elder Dr. Ellis was standing in front of the big screen TV in the computer lab, watching the news, when Terry came in. Ellis had been watching the news relentlessly, waiting for something to happen.

"Dr. Raines?" Terry asked tentatively.

"What?" Ellis snapped.

"We're...we're starting the test now."

Ellis nodded, walking out of the lab, his eyes darting at the machine. He'd been in a good mood on 9/11, but as each day passed, Ellis grew more apprehensive. Several of the other technicians noticed his nervousness as they went through the testing process. The machine wasn't done yet, but they were making progress.

Terry tapped at a keyboard, sending signals to the machine to conduct another test. One of the other techs, a young woman named Trish, stood behind Terry, pointing at the screen and suggesting a change. She had been recruited from a local school and had turned out to be a natural leader and a gifted mathematician, despite her age—she was only 19. In fact, she'd picked up things so quickly that she was directing today's test, working the machine's controls with a practiced hand. "Are you OK, Dr. Raines?" she asked.

"Oh," he'd said, surprised. "I'm fine. It's just a big day."

She'd nodded. "The test is going well. I think the machine will be finished soon," she'd said as he stood over the control panel. She had an easy demeanor. Last week, she'd found him standing at the loading dock doors, staring out at the World Trade Center, but hadn't seemed surprised.

A year was enough time to finish construction of the machine, especially with a complete set of final blueprints and endless amounts of money. He'd already done all the hard work in the first timeline, and here, all he had to do was build it again. But the schedule had slipped as he'd been forced to use 2001 technology on parts of the machine. Now it was October, and they were just starting to run the field calibration tests. He wished the machine was finished.

Trish completed the power-up and calibration tests, showing him the results on the screen. Ellis nodded—they were getting closer, but they weren't there yet. By his estimation, they were still weeks away from being operational.

Ellis left the machine room and walked into the computer lab, getting a Red Bull from the small fridge on the counter. Stevens was seated on the black couch, watching the TV.

"Any news yet?" Ellis asked.

Stevens shook his head.

"What are we watching for?" Terry asked, walking in the room behind Ellis. Since 9/11, Ellis had asked Stevens to increase external and internal facility security. He'd also asked some of the senior staffers, like Terry and Stevens, to help him keep an eye on the news.

"You'll know it when you see it," Ellis said.

2.20
Exposé

Two months ago, *The Washington Post* had run a short series of articles on a high-level committee studying a potential terrorist threat.

In the months since that series of four articles had run, Cassie O'Neil had not let the story go. In fact, she'd continued looking, taking the fragments of a story and piecing them together.

The writer had clearly done her research. Now, she was naming names.

What ran in the October 30, 2001, edition of *The Washington Post* was a powerful piece of journalism based on months of research and independent sourcing—and more than a few confidential sources. The article was about a horrific, predicted terrorist attack thwarted in early September. Evidently, members of the Executive Branch, along with members of Congress and multiple police departments around the nation, had been working together to prevent this supposed attack.

The most intriguing part of the article described a detailed set of evidence that had been created and distributed to convey the seriousness of the supposed attack. The evidence of the future attack included mocked-up newspaper articles, lengthy "reports" on the event, and computer-generated photos and videos of the supposed attack, which was supposed to take place on September 11. Some agency of the government had evidently spent enormous sums of time and money and manpower to create the body of "evidence." It was all produced from the "after" point of view, as if the event had already happened.

Through several contacts, Cassie had managed to review some of the evidence, and she included in her article several pieces. The front page story included a very disturbing photograph of what appeared to be one of the buildings of the World Trade Center crumbling into dust. She went on to describe in her article other evidence that she had seen, including casualty lists, mock-ups of the front pages of actual newspapers, and a hefty book titled *The Congressional Report on the 9/11*

Attacks. She had even seen a hauntingly realistic video of what looked like a passenger plane crashing into one of the Twin Towers. The cost of that video alone had to be north of $400,000, Cassie speculated—the special effects used to produce it were frighteningly realistic. If one didn't know that the event hadn't occurred, it would be difficult to distinguish the video from real life.

After detailing the evidence, Cassie had gone on to summarize the reasons such a body of evidence would be created.

"Why go to all the time and expense to create such believable 'evidence,' unless it was to release to the American people as justification for ramping up security in the name of safety," the article concluded. "Yet the 'evidence' has not been released, and this reporter has learned that members of the Executive Branch and others are still investigating the supposed 'threat,' taking it very seriously."

She ended the *Post* article with a sobering thought. "The only other option to explain the existence of this 'evidence' and its incredible level of detail is unthinkable—that someone knew ahead of time that these attacks were to happen and, through incompetence, allowed the perpetrators to escape arrest and prosecution."

2.21

TRICK OR TREAT

Dr. Ellis drove through the streets of Red Hook on Halloween as the sun began to set, watching out for trick-or-treaters. He drove slowly—he'd made the mistake of driving through the residential part of town on his way to the warehouse, and now he was going to be late.

Not that it really mattered anymore—ever since September 11, the meetings with the president and his team had been happening less and less frequently. Bush was convinced that they had somehow managed to scare off the terrorists, but Ellis wasn't convinced. He hoped that the FBI and Bush and Marburger were right—they thought the teams of hijackers had fled the country, especially after last week's piece in *The Washington Post*. In response, Fleischer had used a little of the information from Ellis' files to construct an approximate timeline for the planned attack and released it to the public, causing consternation but no real fear in the hearts of the American people—to them, it was just another terrorist attack stopped, another crisis averted.

Ellis was worried that it was a crisis delayed.

The security guard waved him through the barbed wire fence. Dr. Ellis drove around the side of the warehouse, parking. For a moment, after he climbed from his car, he regarded the Twin Towers as they dominated the skyline—he understood completely why the elder Dr. Ellis had chosen this location for his project. What better empirical proof could one have as to the efficacy of their tampering with the timeline? Go look out a window. If the World Trade Center was there, then you'd succeeded.

He heard a heavy door open and turned to see the other Dr. Ellis. The man raised his hand and waved, walking out to greet him in the lot.

"Well, it's still there," the younger Ellis said, nodding at the World Trade Center. "At least nothing happened on 9/11."

"Yes," the elder Ellis smiled. "They have you to thank for that, I think. Either Bush scared them off, or those newspaper articles did. Either way, now we have more time to prepare, or intervene, if something happens."

The younger Ellis nodded as they turned and headed inside.

2.22
Photos

The reporter lowered her high-powered camera, her eyes wide.

Cassie was two hundred yards away, in a nearby parking lot. She'd been keeping an eye on the warehouse for several days now.

Her research had revealed the name of Dr. Donald Ellis—it had continued to pop up in the 'evidence' she had seen. The man was a professor at the University of New York, specializing in quantum mechanics. Lately, he'd been spending a lot of time in Washington, D.C., meeting with government officials.

She had spent time with her sources, discussing the evidence of the future attack. The sources hadn't understood the evidence, but they knew that it came from the White House: the president, Andrew Card, John Marburger, and others. One of the others was the mysterious Dr. Ellis, who appeared to have had nothing to do with the White House up until a few months ago.

Mike Foreman, her editor, had put her on the right track with his FBI contact, but it had been her confidential sources at the Pentagon that had really broken the story. The Pentagon employees, all mid- or low-level civilians working in the massive building, had seen or heard about an impending terrorist attack that the government was attempting to prevent. Members of the U.S. government received warnings of terrorist attacks all the time, and working in real time to prevent them was just another day at the office for the Pentagon brass and other bureaucracies. What made this threat different was the supposed evidence that was being distributed. It was meant to bring home just how genuine the threat was and what kind of affect it could have on the nation.

After learning Dr. Ellis lived in Jericho, New York, Cassie made a few phone calls and hired a local private detective to trail Dr. Ellis. In the two weeks since he was hired, the private detective followed him, learning that Dr. Ellis split his time between the Jericho house and a dilapidated-looking warehouse in Brooklyn.

Last week, she'd come up to Brooklyn and settled into a small rented apartment on Columbia Street, above a Thai restaurant, scouting locations related to Dr. Ellis and the warehouse during the day and writing copy at night.

She was in her car—she'd found a great spot up the street to observe the warehouse. So far, she'd been able to discover little about the warehouse. The private detective had reported that large shipments had been arriving at the facility regularly, but since she'd started tailing Ellis personally, he'd only been to the warehouse once or twice.

The reporter looked at her camera—she'd never really taken photos to accompany her stories, happy to stick with writing the words and let professional photogs dress up the article. But she'd borrowed one of the new Nikon D1s, hoping to follow Ellis and catch him meeting with members of the Bush administration. This digital camera stored pictures on a little hard drive and had one of those new LCD screens on the back that allowed for review of the photos. She pushed the buttons, flipping back through the pictures she had just taken.

She squinted at the last few pictures. It had not been a trick of the light, or her imagination, or too much grappa last night.

Dr. Ellis was talking to another person who looked exactly like him.

The other man looked older, and a little more muscled, and the hair was shorter, but they were otherwise identical. Did Ellis have a twin or an older brother? Cassie didn't think so, but she'd have to double-check. Any other explanation was, plainly, impossible.

2.23
PORTLAND, MAINE

On the morning of November 23, 2001, a United Airlines plane landed at the tiny airport located just north of Portland, Maine. The out-of-the-way airport sported several restaurants, ample parking, and the most lax security screening program of any airport on the eastern seaboard. The plane taxied to the terminal and parked. After a few moments, the passengers began unloading down a ramp onto the tarmac—the airport didn't have passenger ramps that connected to the airport building, so the passengers bundled up for the cold walk through the blustery wind.

Mohammed Atta appeared in the doorway of the plane and glanced around, looking at the airport tarmac and buildings beyond. Early snow covered part of the runway, but flights were still going in and out.

That had been one thing he had not counted on—the weather. He was from Egypt and had grown up in the warmth of Cairo. He'd visited other countries in the winter before, but he'd not realized just how cold it could get or how that cold could affect the airports. After the weather dropped below zero, airlines instituted a strict policy of de-icing their planes before takeoff, a procedure that could easily delay takeoff by a half hour or more.

The success of their plan was contingent on the planes being in the air at the same time—all of them needed to hit their respective targets within a one-hour period to achieve the maximum psychological effect.

Bin Laden had said, on several occasions, that the ultimate goal of the operation was not the taking of lives, but rather the effect their actions would have on the American psyche. Atta had argued that spreading out the hijackings and crashes would heighten the tension, but bin Laden had cautioned them that the U.S. authorities would step up airport security after a first incident. Getting his men through security all at once, and carrying out the attacks simultaneously, was the better solution.

It would terrorize Americans—and infuriate the American government—if several attacks happened at the same time. The nation would be paralyzed, unable to act, bin Laden had argued. They would feel "helpless and small," in bin Laden's words. And Atta was responsible for making those words come true.

Atta climbed down the steps of the plane, pulling his jacket tighter around him. An airport security guard at the bottom of the stairs glanced at the faces of the passengers as they disembarked. The guard took a long look at Atta and then waved him on to the terminal.

Atta hurried to catch up with the others.

2.24
BLACK FRIDAY

Tina was looking out the floor-to-ceiling glass windows.

The city was spread out below her like a play mat—the river to one side and the buildings and cars in a grid below, looking like tiny toys. She could see planes and helicopters buzzing across the sky. Smoke poured from the top of the other glittery metal tower, the one next door that looked just like the building she was in.

"Mommy, are those people OK?" she said, pointing, but her mom didn't answer. Sometimes, when Tina asked questions, her mom didn't answer right away. "There's more smoke now," turning to see her mother, who was talking with Mrs. Clausen. They were whispering, their voices low. She knew that grown-ups sometimes whispered, when they didn't want kids to hear what they were talking about.

Her mom and Mrs. Clausen both turned to Tina.

"Sure, honey," her mom answered. "They're working on evacuating those folks right now—it's a big fire, so they'll make sure everyone leaves."

Tina nodded, looking back at the smoke. She could see fire coming out of the sides of the building, between the thin metal pieces. She remembered that the buildings looked exactly the same.

"What about us?" Tina asked. "Should we leave?"

"We're not sure," her mom said. "We're waiting to find out."

Tina turned and got out her Powerpuff Girls backpack. She loved her backpack, carried it with her everywhere. On the floor by the windows, there were a bunch of brown boxes full of books and papers. Tina's mother had said that Mrs. Clausen had just gotten a job here in the Trade Center and was still moving in. Tina wondered what grown-ups used to decorate their offices—her dad's office at the university was pretty boring, all books and papers and nothing at to play with.

Behind her, she heard her mom and Mrs. Clausen talking.

"Anyway, it sounds pretty nice," her mother said to Mrs. Clausen, who was gathering up her purse. "And they're giving you a 401(k), too, which is nothing to sneeze at."

"And I'm getting lots of vacation time, too," Mrs. Clausen answered. She stepped to the window out into the hallway and looked at the other employees. "Much better than at Basics—there you had to work three years to get any vacation."

Tina was sitting on the floor by the windows, playing. In the distance, she saw another plane, a big one.

Her mother spoke up again. "Elaine, should we leave? I'd feel better if we left, with the fire next door."

Tina heard Mrs. Clausen start to speak, and then a loud voice came over some speakers in the hallway outside Mrs. Clausen's office.

"Please excuse this interruption, but the North Tower is being evacuated due to a fire on the top floors. As a precaution, the South Tower is also being evacuated at this time. Please proceed to the nearest stairway and begin an orderly descent to the ground floors, where emergency personnel will direct you away from the buildings."

Out the window, Tina watched as the plane starts to bank, headed toward the building.

"Sorry about the rotten luck," Mrs. Clausen said to both of them. "It's the first day I've had visitors and then there's a fire next door. I guess—"

Outside, the plane banks and approaches silently.

Tina pointed.

"Mommy. See that plane? It's getting bigger."

"Pick up your things, Tina," her mother said, turning to look. "we're leaving—"

Sarah turned to see that the plane was flying right at them. Tina turned to her mother, seeing a look of shock and horror on her mom's face.

A moment later, the plane smashed into the windows. There was nothing but fire and pain and destruction.

Ellis sat up.

He had been sleeping. He was splayed on the same black couch in his office. His heart was racing.

The nightmares were coming more often, now that 9/11 had come and gone. Ellis was just waiting for the other shoe to drop.

He stood, wavering, and walked to the break room for a cup of coffee. He was exhausted. Too many late nights, too many days out on the riverbank, staring at the Twin Towers…

Ellis had ended up spending the last few months holed up in the warehouse. But he had been out a few times, including a few trips downtown. He'd gotten up the courage to visit the Trade Center and had even enjoyed a quick lunch at the Windows on the World restaurant at the top of the South Tower.

"Enjoyed" probably wasn't the best word choice—he'd felt like a visitor from another planet, nervously glancing at the greeters and wait staff. They had no idea that they were supposed to be dead—they were all living on borrowed time, time that he had given them.

They had no idea that they should all be dead.

The staff didn't know that the space taken up by the restaurant should have been just another empty space in the sky, a cube of windy nothingness, high above an open pit filled with twisted steel and pulverized human remains.

It was strange, not seeing Ground Zero. There was no massive, fenced-off pit, where they were trying to reconstruct lower Manhattan's subway system. There were no chain link fences, covered with posters and hand-written memorials to all the people that had died. He was used to seeing the open pit in the ground and chain-link fences and hearing the scrape of metal on metal as volunteers removed massive chunks of steel, all the while hopelessly looking for survivors. Futilely searching the rubble for a body, any kind of physical object, to give a family comfort.

In July, he'd traveled by train—he would never fly in a plane again—to Washington, D.C., to visit the Capitol building and the Pentagon. One of his bogus sets of identification was as a defense contractor who worked for MacMillan Architecture, an actual firm in Los Angeles, so he'd been able to get a VIP tour of the Pentagon.

He'd walked the halls of the massive building with his young military escort, who had pointed out the 1940s-era construction techniques as if they were something to be proud of. It was all that Ellis could do to stop himself from pointing out that, without reinforced concrete and explosion-proof windows, the building was a sitting duck. Planes landing at National Airport (here in this timeline it was still called National and would not be renamed Reagan National Airport until 2005) banked right over the Pentagon. It had been just a matter of good fortune that a plane hadn't already accidentally crashed into the building. And with the 60-year-old building techniques and construction materials, if there ever were a crash, half of the place would burn. And the building's bold and unique shape made it even more identifiable from the air.

Ellis didn't have the heart to tell the escort that thousands would die because of the substandard sprinkler system. The boy had proudly told him that after the attack on Pearl Harbor, the War Department, the predecessor to the Department of Defense, had managed to build the massive structure in less than seven months. Ellis did not burst the kid's bubble—putting up the building so fast had been possible, because they'd slapped it together. Over the past 60 years, no one had ever gotten around to updating it—even though it represented the center of the United States' military power.

In another reality, half of it had gone up in flames.

Ellis glanced down at the papers he'd been looking at when he'd dozed off. It was Black Friday—he'd given everyone yesterday off for Thanksgiving, but now that the machine was almost done, he'd wanted people to work as much as they could before the Christmas break, when he was closing the warehouse for a week. Today, Ellis was reviewing an ongoing thorn in the side of the project—he and the other Ellis were working on tracking down *The Washington Post* reporter who had caused all the trouble, leaking the original story and then following it up with actual pieces of the real 9/11 evidence he had brought back from the future. She was a dogged reporter and had pieced things together with remarkable speed.

The White House had pulled together a report on her, and Ellis had been looking through it. The woman's picture showed her to be small and thin, with dark hair. The report used the word "tenacious" six times—evidently, she'd made her name in investigative journalism in Florida and Ohio. Now, it looked like she was digging into this story. If so, it would only be a matter of time before she figured out enough to expose their operations. He would need to talk to the younger Ellis soon—

Terry burst into the room.

"Mr. Raines!"

Ellis sat up.

"A plane—a plane crashed into the World Trade Center! It's all over the news!" Terry shouted, his face white.

Ellis felt his entire body drain of blood—it was like a shadow had passed over the sun. This world would never be the same. The downward spiral—

"No." Ellis said as he flipped on the TV.

The screen filled with the image of the North Tower of the World Trade Center, smoke streaming from a jagged whole near the top. He remembered—it was so familiar—but different somehow. The plane had hit lower on the North Tower.

"...and then smoke started coming out of the building," he heard the announcer say on the TV. Terry sat heavily on the couch next to him.

"Oh, Christ," Ellis said heavily, the tears coming instantly. "Not again."

He felt Terry turn and look at him, but he ignored it, looking at the screen. The building punctured by a jagged hole, broken girders like metal teeth in the opening...

Several other interns and technicians ran into the room. One of the young women was crying.

"They said it might be an accident," she said hopefully.

"It was no accident," Ellis said. "The Pentagon plane is coming soon and then the other tower."

Several people in the room looked at him strangely, but he had nothing to say. Stevens and several of the guards came into the room and watched the broadcast.

"What do you mean, a 'Pentagon plane?'" Terry asked. "And what you said earlier—you said 'not again.'"

Dr. Ellis started to answer, but on the TV, the announcer was interrupted by another reporter.

"Ted?" the other reporter broke in. "Ted, we're getting word of another plane crash."

"Here it comes," Ellis said, shaking his head. "Another plane has hit the Pentagon in D.C." All the work getting in with the Bush administration, all the warnings—it had all been for nothing. It was all happening, all over again. Technically, it was happening again, for the first time.

Terry looked at him but didn't say anything.

"Let's go to Kentucky," the reporter said.

Ellis stood suddenly, his brow furrowed. "Kentucky?"

On the screen, the scene switched to a massive stone building that looked like a maximum security prison, solidly built with multiple rows of tall fences surrounding it. Flames and smoke poured from the building, and plane debris was scattered about. On a pristine lawn nearby, an airplane engine smoldered. The news report was showing a helicopter shot of the burning building, and a massive column of smoke rose from a crater in the roof of the building.

Ellis was confused.

"What is that? Is that a prison?"

The others shushed him as the news report switched to a reporter on the ground near the building, burning in the background. He shouted to be heard over the wailing sirens.

"A large jet, possibly a 747, crashed minutes ago directly into the Federal Reserve building here at Fort Knox, Kentucky. At least 130 people were onboard the plane—it was evidently hijacked this morning from St. Louis. Treasury officials are not commenting yet on the nation's second-largest stockpile of gold and other valuables, which were stored in the National Gold Bullion Repository, more famously known as Fort Knox. We're being told that the repository holds about 148 million ounces of gold, so at $275 an ounce, the gold inside the burning building is worth somewhere north of $40 billion."

"This isn't right," Ellis said. "This didn't happen. Why would they be attacking Fort Knox?"

"Who?" Terry asked. "Who's attacking?"

"Al Qaeda. Agents of Osama bin Laden," Ellis snapped at him. "They've hijacked planes and are crashing them into structures."

Everyone in the room was listening to him.

"So," Terry said, "you're saying this is a terrorist attack?"

Ellis nodded, and the young woman burst into tears and ran from the room.

On the TV, the reporter resumed speaking.

"As you can see, the building was surrounded by large open areas and fencing to protect it from being robbed, but nothing could stop the massive airliner from crashing into the building. Officials say—"

The anchorman came back on, cutting him off.

"Brian, let me stop you. We're getting conflicting reports here in the newsroom that the plane crashes at the World Trade Center and Fort Knox may be deliberate acts, a coordinated terrorist attack, where unknown persons are using commercial planes as suicide weapons. We have just learned there are several planes unaccounted for in U.S. airspace. The FAA has announced that they are closing down all airspace over the United States, ordering every plane to land immediately."

Terry nodded. "Good. They need to get those planes down."

"It won't matter," Ellis said. "The hijackers are already in control of the planes by now—nothing can stop them—"

"We're getting another report of two more attacks, this time in D.C.," the reporter cut in again.

Ellis wanted to look away, but he couldn't.

The screen switched to a smoking Capitol building, the remnants of a large plane resting on the front steps of the huge building. Portions of the Capitol appeared to be on fire, and people streamed from the building, rubble everywhere. In the distance, the Pentagon was on fire.

"Oh my God," Terry said quietly. The others gasped, seeing the destruction. Several of them began to cry, hugging each other. Trish stood behind the couch, her face a mask of grief.

"It's… it's all the same," Ellis said, the color drained from his face. "No, it's worse this time, somehow."

A reporter began speaking on the TV, her face and hair streaked with black. Smoke billowed behind her. "Witnesses say that about ten minutes ago, two planes approached the D.C. area from the west. One plane turned and flew in low over the National Mall, barely missing the

Washington Monument before crashing to the ground in front of the Capitol building. It is impossible to estimate the number of casualties—"

"This can't be happening," Ellis said, and then suddenly remembered.

He bolted from the room, racing to the front of the warehouse, searching for the crates. Terry, Trish, and Stevens ran after him, and after he explained, they helped him find what he was looking for. Moments later he was running again, the object in his hand. Ellis ran, bursting out through the loading dock doors that faced the river and ran down to the edge of the water.

The North Tower of the World Trade Center was on fire.

"No!" Ellis screamed at the sight of the building afire. So much effort, so much work, lost. Wasted. The others raced up behind him. Ellis knelt by the edge of the water, unpacking the device.

"Mr. Blaine," Stevens shouted. "It's connected? The World Trade Center—"

"Will be destroyed," Ellis said. "The North Tower is on fire—it will collapse in less than an hour."

"Collapse?" Terry asked incredulously. "How could it collapse—?"

"The jet fuel," Ellis said. "The plane was out of Boston and heading cross-country with over 10,000 pounds of fuel on board. A full tank. It ignited, and right now it's burning through the floor supports, weakening the metal connections. The supports that attach the floors to the metal curtains will bend and give way, and the building will pancake all the way to the ground, each floor crushing the one below it. Everyone inside will die."

He set the bulky bag down on the grass and began unwrapping it.

"I've only made it worse," Ellis said, hurrying. "Somehow. I guess I gave them more time to plan, more time to get things in order and make this version of history somehow even worse."

Stevens bent to help Ellis take the items out of the bag—the pieces of a small, shoulder-launched surface-to-air missile. Ellis unwrapped the tube-like launcher, pulling off the plastic coating and uncapping both ends of the device, then held it out so Stevens could snap on the aiming apparatus on top. Trish and Terry unrolled three smaller tubes, these with pointed tips on one end and short, aerodynamic fins on the other. They waited until Ellis was ready, then loaded the barrel with a projectile.

Helicopters buzzed around the North Tower—Ellis knew that some of them would try to rescue people from the roof, but the terrible heat and wind would make it impossible for the helicopters to hover for more than a few seconds in place.

"It should come in from the southwest," Ellis said, pointing the surface-to-air missile into the air and watching the sky. "Help me watch for it!"

"Watch for what?" Terry shouted.

"The other plane! There's another plane, one that will hit the South Tower. It should come in from the southwest!"

A huge fireball erupted over the skyline.

Ellis turned—the South Tower had been hit. Fire and debris rained down on the streets below. Behind him, Terry screamed. Stevens stared at the fireball and the debris, falling on the buildings below the tower. Trish stood silent, her eyes wide, her hands at her mouth.

Ellis shook his head and started screaming at the fires and the burning buildings.

"No! Oh, Christ! Different flight path—they came in from the west, not the southwest! Why? Probably a different plane altogether," he yelled, looking at the burning buildings. "Maybe from a different airport." Ellis sank to his knees, dropping the shoulder launcher. "It... it doesn't matter. It doesn't matter anymore."

Ellis was helpless, powerless. He had done nothing.

No, that wasn't true. Somehow, he'd made things worse.

"I didn't fix anything," he said quietly, but the others didn't hear. They were too busy staring at the horror across the East River.

2.25
TEXAS
ELEMENTARY SCHOOL

President Bush was sitting in front of a group of small children in an elementary school in Houston—the teacher was reading a story to them, and he was listening and nodding along. He'd canceled on these students once before; the first visit had been scheduled to take place on 9/11, but the secret service and his staff had rescheduled it for security reasons—and out of an sense of superstition. They hadn't wanted to tempt fate by holding any events that day.

He'd rescheduled, and the elementary school had graciously accommodated his always-shifting schedule, bringing these students in for a special half-day—normally they would not be in school on the day after Thanksgiving.

President Bush was listening to the story, something about a whale, when the classroom door opened and Andrew Card, his chief of staff, came into the room.

Bush could tell from the look on Card's face that something had happened.

President Bush put his head down, hoping against hope that it wasn't an attack. Bush had seen the video from the other timeline, the one where his doppelganger was sitting in front of a group of similar children in a similar classroom when he's informed about the first events on 9/11. After watching the classroom video over and over, the president now felt a dreadful moment of déjà vu—this was a different school, with a different class, but the end result might be the same.

"Mr. President," Card said into his ear. "We're under attack."

Bush tried to not make that face that he'd seen in the photos, the one with his face all screwed up like he was eating a lemon.

But he couldn't help cursing.

"Son of a bitch." he said quietly. "What is happening?"

The teacher stopped reading, and she and the students looked up at him and Card.

President Bush stood, aware of the criticism he'd received in the other timeline for remaining in the classroom with the children for seven minutes before getting up and leaving. He could see the troubled looks on the kids' faces, but he needed to get out of here and go to work. At least this time, people wouldn't criticize him for just sitting there looking like an idiot.

Of course, this time they would probably criticize him for scaring a room full of kids.

He had an idea. "Mrs. Stevens, students, I apologize. I've just been informed that there is a critical shortage of ice cream and other treats in your cafeteria. Is this correct?" Bush asked.

The kids nodded, and the teacher smiled for a second.

"Well," Bush said, standing. "Maybe it's because none of the other students are here today, but I need to look into this immediately. You kids have a good day, and listen to Mrs. Stevens—she knows what she's talking about."

He nodded to the teacher, and then he and Card made their way out of the room. In the hallway, a contingent of Secret Service agents hurried him away. They passed a school administrator on the way out, and Bush thanked him for bringing the students in for a half-day. Outside, President Bush and the others climbed into a waiting car.

"What's happening?" The president shouted. "Did they attack?"

Andrew Card nodded, opening a report. "Six planes this time instead of four. The Capitol, the Pentagon, both buildings of the World Trade Center, Fort Knox, and the Mall of America."

"Holy shit."

Card nodded.

"We don't have any idea on the casualty estimates, but the emergency orders you set in place are working. We're headed to Air Force One now and we'll be in the air soon."

"Jesus, Mary, and Joseph," President Bush said, looking at the reports in front of him. "What about Laura?" he asked, his voice straying higher.

"She's fine," Card nodded. "She's in lockdown with Cheney right now, under the White House."

Bush visibly relaxed and began reading through the preliminary reports Card had handed him in the car. When they arrived and boarded Air Force One, which was already fueled and prepared to leave, the plane began taxiing. They were airborne before he was even to the briefing room. A wing of fighter jets escorted the plane, along with several other support aircraft. The plane banked and turned north, heading for an undisclosed location.

Minutes later, after they went through the initial reports, Bush and the others watched the news reports come in on the large TV in the conference room. The TV news was always going to be a little ahead of the vetted news that the president received through official channels.

The TV showed the Capitol on fire, smoke and fire billowing from the front of the building. What looked like the remains of a 747 covered the western steps of the Capitol, and large holes in the façade of the building indicated that portions of the plane had penetrated the building. The Capitol dome seemed undamaged. Fire trucks screamed through the streets as emergency vehicles congregated on the scene. Across the river, a column of smoke rose from the damaged Pentagon.

"I can't believe this is happening," the president said, looking at the table. Several members of his cabinet and staff were at the table, and large screens lined the walls. Other cabinet members attended the meeting via remote video link.

The president spoke. "This attack on our country must be halted."

The Director of the Department of Transportation spoke up from one of the screens. "We've already grounded all flights in U.S. airspace and are diverting all incoming international flights to airports in Canada. All flights are now on the ground or accounted for."

"Are there any missing flights or other potential hijacked planes?" Andrew Card asked.

"No," the FAA director said. "All planes in U.S. airspace are accounted for. The six planes that were hijacked were lost early on in the process, and visual or verbal contact has been made and verified with all other planes still aloft."

"They're continuing on to their destinations?" Ari Fleischer asked.

"Yes," the FAA director said. "I thought it would be best to not disrupt them—"

"Get all of those goddamned planes down now," the president ordered. "We have no idea if there are more. I don't care about inconvenience," he said sharply.

The president turned to one screen, which showed Don Rumsfeld, the Secretary of Defense.

"We have detected no other threats in the area or on any of our borders," Rumsfeld answered. "This appears to be a coordinated terrorist attack, not the work of a foreign government or power."

Bush sighed, looking around at everyone in attendance, then stood.

"OK, here goes. The information I am about to give you is going to sound hard to believe, but it comes from a very reliable source. The attacks today are the work of al Qaeda on orders from the terrorist mastermind Osama bin Laden. The lead hijacker, Mohammed Atta, flew the first plane into the North Tower of the World Trade Center."

There was silence around the table and on the video links.

"We have been working to prevent this attack for almost six months," the president continued. "We had some prior intel of the terrorists and where they might strike, but in trying to thwart those attacks, we appear to have given them more time to gather forces and carry off an even larger attack."

"This planned attack was to occur on September 11, 2001. We learned of this impending attack and did what we could to prevent it. One result of the original attack that I found particularly troubling was the essential crippling of the U.S. Congress, due to the serious loss of life in the Capitol. I, therefore, signed into law two months ago a provision that required all congressional members to designate or arrange for a list of three representative replacements who would be able to step into the congressperson's role until such time as a special election could be held to fill the post through the voting process."

The others looked at Bush and nodded.

"Because we had most Congress members designate an emergency backup appointee, the transfer of power has already started. They are to convene at Constitution Hall in Philadelphia this evening. Most of the backups and designees are on their way now or will attend the opening session via video link."

He waited for a few moments, and then continued, explaining exactly how they would proceed.

2.26

AFTERMATH

Laura Bush was fine. If there was anything President Bush had learned from the other timeline, it was that he needed to stay in control and not allow Cheney to push him out of office. He'd asked Laura to limit her number of visits to the Capitol building, just in case something happened.

Stationing surface-to-air missile batteries on the Capitol building had seemed like a crazy idea at the time—now, he looked prescient. The surface-to-air missiles had fired on the incoming jetliner, striking it midair. The plane had still crashed, but had been downed in front of the building, sliding into the western-facing steps and the front of the Capitol building. The plane had not crashed directly into the dome, which did not fall, so the damage to the building and the loss of life had been greatly reduced.

But fires and debris still killed many, including thirty-seven senators and representatives. Because of the backup plan put into place by Bush, their alternates had already been designated and got to work immediately, averting the constitutional crisis from the other timeline.

Things were worse in New York and at the Pentagon—the casualty numbers were roughly the same as in the original timeline. And the bottom line was that they had still been attacked, and by foreign terrorists. He was reading through a version of tonight's speech, working through the details, and wondered which direction to move in first. He knew the perpetrators, the exact location of their training camps, and all about their Taliban supporters. Thanks to the future intelligence, he even knew which future military operations he ordered would be the most successful. But things were different enough here, with the two-month delay, to warrant caution.

The Mall of America and Fort Knox—he hadn't anticipated additional attack locations. He hadn't counted on a backup set of targets, or additional teams of al Qaeda operatives in the country, or the additional eight weeks of planning time that he'd given them.

Now, he had to decide what to do.

Afghanistan—that was obvious. Bomb the camps, take out the Taliban, release all the information they had on al Qaeda.

Bush had already worked it out with the Joint Chiefs—forces were in movement within 48 hours of the attacks on 11/24, moving into theater and preparing for combat operations.

Tonight, they would begin bombing Afghanistan. It was the evening of December 7, 2001, and his speech tonight would open with a discussion of the sixtieth anniversary of the attack on Pearl Harbor. His speechwriter had conjured up a moving tribute to those soldiers and airmen who had died decades ago in the surprise attack. Bush would then announce the beginning of major combat operations. That was the military's signal to begin bombing runs from the ships already stationed off the coast of Afghanistan.

Ground troops would follow three days later, if all went according to plan. Bush had a line in tonight's speech about the Taliban giving up power and turning in their al Qaeda compatriots, but he didn't think it was likely to happen. In the other timeline, it had taken the nuclear annihilation of one of Afghanistan's major cities to break the will of the Taliban. In this version of history, Bush hoped to do it the old-fashioned way. He didn't relish the idea of a massive expanse of irradiated desert being named after him.

No, this time it would be bombs, ground troops, and a ruthless embargo of all ships into and out of Afghan ports. The Taliban would be pushed from power and the vacuum filled with an interim government, one more aligned with U.S. foreign policy.

But if he had to, he would back the Taliban and al Qaeda into the mountains and tunnels between Afghanistan and Pakistan. And if that happened, and there was a stalemate, then he might think about the nuclear option.

But the war in Iraq to follow—that concerned him. President Cheney, in the first timeline, had moved too quickly, moved to quash Hussein before doing his due diligence and without taking the proper time to prepare and build up sufficient forces. When the weapons of mass destruction had been unleashed on the invasion forces, the ground war had come to a halt.

Bush didn't want to repeat that.

2.27
AN OLDER TWIN

"What else do you have?" Foreman asked her over the phone.

Cassie shook her head. "Massive power usage, lots of equipment going in, and nothing coming out. If they were producing something, they're not sending it anywhere." She was exhausted from weeks of living on takeout food and staking out the warehouse and Ellis' home in Jericho around the clock. The floor of her rented apartment was covered with yellow notepads along with Thai takeout bags and dry cleaner bags.

"And with that level of power consumption," Cassie said, "they could be running an automobile factory inside."

"You can't get any closer?"

"No," Cassie answered. "He's got internal and external security. Plus, it looks like he's got the local Padrino and his crew on the payroll as well. I can drive by a few times a day, but between the barbed wire, security guards, and blacked-out windows, I'm getting nothing."

She heard Foreman grunt. "What about the guy's house?"

"In Jericho? Nothing there, either. Cute family."

"OK. And what about the older brother?"

Again, she shook her head. "Nope, he doesn't have an older brother. Or older cousins that would fit the description. Plus, the guy looked like a twin, an older twin."

"You can't have an 'older twin.'" Foreman said. "It's against the rules, in case you didn't know."

She smiled. "Yeah. I don't know any other way to explain the guy."

2.28

LIVERMORE

Dr. Ellis and Marburger were waiting at the conference room table in Lawrence Livermore National Laboratories (LLNL) on the day before Christmas, 2001, when the doors opened and President Bush entered, followed by Andrew Card, Secretary of Defense Rumsfeld, and at least a dozen Secret Service agents. The president sat, waving the security agents out.

"Gentlemen, thanks for coming," Card began, passing out a stack of paperwork.

"Look," President Bush said, "we're here to talk about what happened and what we can do about it. Dr. Ellis, what happened?"

Ellis swallowed and began speaking slowly.

"Obviously, our actions affected the timeline. In the original event, four planes were hijacked instead of six. The Fort Knox and Mall of America incidents didn't happen. Our actions in trying to prevent the attacks from happening in the first place only delayed them."

"That much is obvious," Rumsfeld said dryly.

"If we had not changed the timeline," Ellis continued, "things would have progressed exactly as they did originally. Four planes, four teams of hijackers."

Bush nodded. "But the extra security, and the FBI rummaging around, knocking over everything—"

Card shook his head. "This isn't about your suggestion. There was no way we were going to let the U.S. military run that investigation. You can't have the military on U.S. soil trying to find terrorists."

"At least we could've kept it quiet," Rumsfeld answered. "At least we know how to follow orders."

Card shook his head. It was an argument they had had many times before.

Bush looked at them both. "It doesn't matter now, anyway. The delay gave them enough time to work on their plan, expand it. And now things are worse and impossible to predict."

Ellis disagreed. "Prediction is what we do—we had all the information we needed to accurately predict the outcome of this. It should never have happened—"

"OK, this is what we're going to do," the president said curtly, ending the conversation. "We're going to send ourselves a warning—"

Ellis shook his head. "It won't work."

"Why not?"

"Well, for one, the machine isn't working correctly yet," Marburger said. "It's not operational."

Bush nodded. "We know that. But when it is—"

"It still won't work," Ellis said.

Rumsfeld leaned forward. "Cut the crap and speak your mind, Ellis."

"Because we won't believe the message when we receive it in the past," Ellis said. He stood and began to pace the room. "We hardly believed it this time and that was with reams of evidence. Why would we believe it next time?"

Bush was confused. "What?"

"What's changed that would make us believe another message from the future and take it seriously this time? I already gave you a message from the future, and we still allowed the attacks to happen."

"That wasn't really what happened," Andrew Card began, but Ellis cut him off.

"The president said that we should 'send a warning' back to ourselves. Based on our track record, I don't think it would work, even if the machine were operational."

The room grew quiet as Ellis walked back to his chair and sat down. It was a pointless discussion, as far as he was concerned.

2.29
INVASION PLANS

President Bush's war on Afghanistan was much more successful than President Cheney's had been in the original timeline. Ground forces, augmented by artillery bombardment from naval destroyers off the Afghan coast, quickly pushed the Taliban south, out of power and into hiding.

Soon, Bush had trapped the entire Afghan branch of al Qaeda in a series of tunnels along the Pakistani border. Then he deployed the final weapon in his arsenal. The battlefield nuke destroyed what the CIA had pinpointed as a massive series of tunnels and hiding places, plugging them up forever and killing anyone in the caves inside under thousands of tons of rock. The mountain passes and rough crags were irradiated, so even if anyone did somehow escape the blast that occurred, they would never escape the radiation.

Bush didn't go to the U.N. for permission to attack Iraq—it hadn't worked for Cheney—but he did stretch out the timeline. Over the next twelve months, Bush worked to build an international coalition of forces, motivated by Hussein's historical possession of weapons of mass destruction, to join the United States–led coalition. Bush also moved more forces into theatre before the official invasion of Iraq, which took place on 11/24/02, the one-year anniversary of the attacks. Bush waited until major combat operations were over in Afghanistan and every single soldier had returned before he invaded Iraq, not wanting to get caught up in two simultaneous wars.

As 2003 began, the war progressed quickly. Because of the aggressive aerial bombing from local bases and other locations a half a world away, Bush's invasion force avoided the challenge of Hussein's weapons of mass destruction. Bombing also wiped out most of the stores and production facilities in the first hours of the war, and U.S. and coalition forces moved quickly across the desert. They faced and defeated organized resistance from the Republican Guard, leaving Iraqi tanks littering the desert.

Retreating forces set fire to hundreds of oil wells, darkening the sky to impede invading troops, but Bush had anticipated that. In the earlier timeline, President Cheney had taken two full weeks to deploy the special firefighting and explosives battalions required to put out the smoky fires. This time, those special units had been staged in Kuwait and followed the invasion forces across the border, ready to quench the fires. In the first timeline, those fires had delayed Cheney's forces and allowed the Republican Guard to fall back into Baghdad, strengthening their defenses around the city.

This time, that didn't happen. Within weeks of the invasion, U.S. and coalition forces were in Baghdad. Worldwide, people watched on TV as Iraqi citizens, assisted by eager U.S. and coalition forces, began pulling down the massive statues of Saddam Hussein that littered the capital city. It was the Iraqis' "Berlin Wall" moment, and Bush was smart enough to not interrupt it with a useless speech.

And the Iraqi leader disappeared. Bush didn't know where to look for him, as Hussein had never been caught in Cheney's timeline, so he just instructed U.S. forces to search high and low for him. Until the dictator was caught and tried in Iraq by a court of his peers, the war in Iraq would never truly be over.

2.30
AL-HAZED AIRPORT

Sunlight glimmered off the large airplanes gathered around the state-of-the-art Jeddah International Airport. It was the morning of February 10, 2003, and the relentless heat of the desert made the tarmac of the airport appear to shimmer. It was a new airport, located just east of the sprawling city of Jeddah in western Saudi Arabia.

One of the large airplanes, a Boeing 747 decorated with a United Airlines logo, sat at a loading gate, glimmering with sunlight that bounced off the glass and stainless steel. Passengers were beginning to enter the plane through a glass boarding tunnel. On the tarmac below, the desert sun fell harshly as sand whipped across the concrete. Several men, dressed in traditional Arabian garb, worked beneath the plane, fueling it.

Other planes were unloading pilgrims from all over the world, arriving at the airport before beginning their ten-mile trek to Mecca, Islam's most revered site. Followers of the Koran were instructed to make the pilgrimage to Mecca at least once in their lives, but many millions of Muslims returned yearly for their opportunity to be closer to God, to commune with him on that most holy of holy sites, the Ka'aba.

At the airport coffee shop, Wade Tulinger sat quietly in a booth, his rolling luggage bag at his feet like a loyal dog. His pilot's cap sat on the table, next to the latte he'd been nursing for over a half hour. Wade desperately wanted a gin and tonic, but Saudi Arabia was a dry country. Alcohol, bars, nightclubs—all were illegal here. The pilot wondered what it would be like to live in a country where you couldn't even sit down with your friends and enjoy a nice cold beer.

Cindy always enjoyed a drink. She liked the fancy, girly ones. Lately, she'd been into Martinis, trying out different kinds whenever they went out for dinner. His flight schedule had made it difficult to get a weekend night out for them, and finding sitters for the kids had always been a problem.

He didn't have any of those problems any more. He missed those problems.

Wade pulled his wallet out and removed a small photo.

Behind him at the coffee bar, the barista called over to the pilot, but he was lost in thought, looking at the photo.

After a minute, he walked over and touched the pilot on the shoulder, making him jump.

"Sir?" the Middle Eastern man asked.

The pilot looked up from his coffee.

"Yes?"

The barista pointed at the loading area, where a United stewardess was waving at him, trying to get Wade's attention.

"You'll miss your flight," the barista said politely, smiling and pointing.

Wade looked at the stewardess and the passengers, lining up to board the plane. He tapped the hat on the table next to him.

"They're not going anywhere without me."

The pilot looked down and, for an awkward moment, the barista wasn't sure what else to say. After a moment, he turned away, shrugging at the United stewardess.

Wade finished his drink and looked at the picture resting on the table in front of him. It showed him with a smiling, happy woman and two laughing children. They appeared to be at a festival or fair—one of the kids was eating cotton candy.

After a long moment, the pilot picked up the photo and kissed it. He stood, grabbed the handle of his luggage bag, and headed for the gate and the nervous stewardess.

2.31
AIR SPACE

Aboard the 747, passengers and crew alike settled in for the two-hour flight to Cairo. Many of the passengers on the jet were traveling on to Europe after having enjoyed short vacations along the Red Sea—Jeddah was Saudi Arabia's largest port on the Red Sea and the second largest city in Saudi Arabia after the capital, Riyadh—and most visitors came for the beaches and the cosmopolitan environment. Jeddah was also the gateway city for most visiting pilgrims making their way to nearby Mecca.

In the cockpit, Wade Tulinger slowly banked the massive plane to the east, sunlight glinting off the water to the west. He was quickly working his way through the checklist of switches and buttons to flip after take-off. Keeping a massive 747 in the air was a complex operation.

Next to him, the copilot was of little help—he had a large knife sticking out of his chest. His eyes were blank, and blood was still pooling in his lap.

Wade reached into his pocket and took out the photo of his family and leaned forward, tucking into the instrument panel.

"I'm sorry, Cindy," he said to the picture. "But I can't get over it."

He turned, looking out the window at the desert.

"6,242 people died," he continued, talking to no one. "And the people who did it… it's their religion. It's so primitive. They're jealous of us, of our technology, of the way we live. No beer, in a whole country? Women forced to cover themselves from head to toe. And all these pilgrims, come to kiss a rock. A magical rock from space."

The pilot flipped more switches as the plane slowly turned.

"I couldn't help," the pilot said. "You, and the kids, and all those other people, just going about their day. It's not fair—"

Wade broke down, sobbing.

And the plane, fully loaded with fuel and passengers, continued to bank slowly to the east.

2.32
THE KA'ABA

From far above, the Temple of the Ka'aba was a stunning religious sight, even when the Hajj wasn't underway. The rest of the year, the Ka'aba was the holy site in Mecca where each Muslim turned to pray five times a day. Muslims showed their obeisance with their prayers, but it was also how they showed their love and respect for Mohammed and for their Islamic traditions. As they unrolled their prayer mats, wherever they were, and prayed, they were reminded of their unity, of a shared experience that brought them all together, no matter where they were in the world. Or off of the world, as had begun recently—Muslim astronauts still followed the procedure and, unrolling ornate prayer mats, pointed their bodies to Mecca.

During the annual Muslim pilgrimage to Mecca, known as the Hajj, tens of thousands of pilgrims crowded into the site every day—over the course of two weeks, nearly two million devout Muslims would find their way to the site.

Authorities stood by to manage the massive crowds, ensuring safe passage for pilgrims to and from the holy site. Even with security precautions and other methods in place, the Hajj had seen many stampedes of pilgrims and a few deaths. It was a challenge for the Saudi Arabian government to manage so many pilgrims over the two-week period.

To the outsider, the Temple of the Ka'aba might seem a strange place to worship—a sea of Muslim pilgrims, each dressed in a simple white shift, surrounded a sixty-by-sixty foot cube-shaped temple.

A massive black stone was embedded in the southeastern corner of the cube and surrounded by a large silver ring. The origin of the stone was a mystery, but there was no doubt that it was at least 4,000 years old and, according to the Koran, the prophet Mohammed had visited the Temple and kissed it. And in the intervening years, millions of pilgrims had jostled for a chance to touch or kiss the large black stone—the surface of the stone had been rubbed smooth by the touch of millions of worshipers. As part of the ritual, each person was to make seven revolutions, or circumlocutions, around the sacred stone.

On this day at the Temple of the Ka'aba, the peak day for the Hajj, seventy-four thousand Muslims were in attendance.

In the sky above, a 747, the tail of the plane emblazoned with the white and blue markings of United Airlines, banked suddenly and turned, screaming down out of the sky.

Ten thousand heads, bowed in prayer, turned upwards. Another ten thousand souls saw a massive airliner drop precipitously from the blue desert sky.

2.33
WHITE HOUSE SITUATION ROOM

The doors opened and an aide rushed in, speaking quietly to Rumsfeld and handing him a sheet of paper. President Bush and Andrew Card watched as the Secretary of Defense grimaced before waving the aide away.

"Well, things just got worse," Rumsfeld said.

"Worse?" Card asked.

They had been sitting in the conference room, going over the Iraq war and the military's efforts to find Saddam Hussein. In the original timeline, he had never been found, so they would get no help from that direction. It was up to Rumsfeld and his troops to kick down every door in Iraq to find the ousted leader before he could foment a rebellion. The war was essentially over, but Bush had wanted to make sure everything about their planned troop drawdown was planned, down to the tiniest level of detail.

"Yes," Rumsfeld said quietly. "It appears that someone decided to retaliate. An ex–Air Force pilot, a civilian working for United Airlines, just crashed his plane into the Hajj."

"No," Card, sitting next to them, stood, his eyes wide. The president simply shook his head.

Rumsfeld nodded, his eyes scanning the document.

"The 747 had been fully loaded with fuel. They were flying out of Saudi Arabia when the pilot barricaded himself in the cockpit and changed course. He hit the site dead on."

"This will unleash a religious war," the president said.

Andrew Card sat back in his chair. "My God."

Rumsfeld read on. "It appears that the plane came in vertically at maximum speed right into the crowd of pilgrims. Everything within three hundred feet of the impact zone was vaporized, including the temple and the Black Stone of the Ka'aba, Islam's most sacred relic."

He paused, looking at Bush and Card. Everyone knew what he was thinking. This would trigger a whole new level of worldwide conflict.

"Initial casualty estimates are somewhere between 30,000 and 40,000 worshippers," Rumsfeld continued. "Today was the peak day from pilgrimage."

"My God," Card said.

"Why would someone do that—" Bush began to ask.

"The Mall of America attack—" Rumsfeld interrupted. "The pilot lost his wife and kids."

"Damn it," Bush said, standing and planting both palms on the table in front of him. "This has to stop. We need to be ready. This changes everything. Now, no one will sit idly by and wait for orders from the Middle East—retaliation will come from all over the world. Donald, put all of our forces on high alert. I'll get started on a speech—I need to get in front of the American people. I need a speech on tolerance and religious freedom right now."

Bush turned to Andrew Card.

"And call Marburger and Ellis, and get that goddamned machine working. We need it now, more than ever."

2.34
JIHAD

Around the world, Muslim communities reeled.

Rocked by the loss of their most sacred and holy site, the calls began almost immediately for a religious Jihad, or holy war. And a worldwide collection of militant imams and clerics and Muslim leaders answered.

There were calls from within the Muslim community for peace, for restraint, but those calls fell on deaf ears.

And so the bombing began.

Although the number of Muslims in the States was small, the militants among them had been agitated in a way that could not be predicted. And others from around the world made their way to the shores of the United States, seeking revenge.

Suicide bombers began striking in public buildings, destroying churches and synagogues across the country. The attacks were random, and terrifying. Cathedrals were bombed, sometimes by suicide bombers and, in other cases, by devices that had been hidden inside the buildings and remotely detonated, often during mass. Boston's catholic community was particularly hard hit, with twelve catholic masses targeted with suicide bombers.

More disturbing than those attacks were the fires set at religious child care centers and schools. Dozens around the country were targeted. In Dayton, a catholic school and day care facility was bombed, and the attackers had gone the extra step of chaining all of the doors closed, trapping hundreds inside the burning structure.

It was a religious war, and not confined to the United States. Iran struck Israel, joined by a handful of other Muslim countries, in an attempt to take back the Holy Land and restore Muslim control over the remaining shrines mentioned in the Koran. Some commentators felt that, with the destruction of the Ka'aba, Islam needed a new holy site.

The Vatican was attacked by jacketed suicide bombers—if the Ka'aba fell, so should the Pope and the Vatican and Vatican City.

On February 15th, during Sunday mass at New York City's famous St. Bart's Cathedral, two suicide bombers, who had entered with the rest of the congregation, detonated nail- and C4-filled bombs inside. Almost three hundred people died in a matter of moments, shocking the city. On the same morning, two more suicide bombers struck the Crystal Cathedral in Los Angeles. The attacks had been coordinated.

A day later, during a live report from the local NBC affiliate, Muslims and anti-Muslims clashed, fighting in the streets as police tried to separate them. Moments later, shots rang out as some sprayed the street with gunfire, sending everyone, including the reporter and cameraman, scrambling for cover. One police official called the scene "chaotic," while the reporter, once she was back on the air, compared it to madness.

The following week, President Bush was to speak at a ceremony calling for peace at the National Cathedral in Washington, D.C. Security was at an all-time high—live reports showed the congregation filing through the metal detectors. The building was searched multiple times—the Secret Service and D.C. police forces were sweeping for devices and doing background checks on every person in attendance, including the senior religious leaders who would be holding the service.

To lighten the nation's somber mood, Bush himself even stepped through the metal detectors and made a face when they went off.

After words from two clergymen, Bush nodded and somberly stepped up to the podium. Just as his speech began, three hidden incendiary devices detonated inside the church.

One hundred and six people died, a low number considering the enclosed location and the number of devices that had been used. The injured numbered in the hundreds, including President Bush, who had dropped behind the podium and been protected from the nearest blast. His left hand and arm were broken—it remained in a cast and sling for months—and his right hand was severely burned.

Later, investigations showed that the bombs had been placed inside the heavy wooden pews. The sealed pews had been built to look exactly like the pews inside the cathedral and were switched out sometime, at least two weeks before the service, right under the noses of the D.C. Police.

2.35

A NEW SKYLINE

The new version of the New York skyline stood behind the warehouse. Dust rose from the pit at Ground Zero—even after a year, they were still carting away pieces of broken steel. The dust and ash thrown up by the construction workers blanketed lower Manhattan. Trucks piled high with broken steel beams and burned bricks streamed away from the hole in the ground and made their way to Staten Island and the waste repository, where scientists and investigators poured over each piece, looking for clues as to what happened.

Dr. Ellis could have told them—the World Trade Center had used centralized support beams to hold up the floors, but those support beams were covered with a substandard amount of fireproofing. Metal, heated by tens of thousands of gallons of jet fuel and the ample "kindling" provided by the contents of the building, began to strain and twist and stretch. Eventually, the floors above the twisting point lost their support and pancaked down onto the floors below.

It was a story he'd heard before. And he'd hoped to never hear it again.

But today, February 26, 2003, the world was smoldering again—the attack on the Hajj was another unforeseen consequence of the terrorist attacks here in the United States.

He'd seen the towers come and go, but they were always there in his mind, somehow. It was like the experiment involving Schrödinger's Cat, trapped in a box with a vial of poison equipped with a random release timer. This thought experiment argued that the cat was both alive and dead at the same time, because it was impossible to know for certain either way due to the randomness of the timer. The only way to know was to open the box.

For Dr. Ellis, the Twin Towers were his Schrödinger's Cat—they seemed there and not there at the same time, existing and not existing. The existence of the Twin Towers could only be confirmed with a look out the window. To him, the buildings forever existed in the shadowy nether realm of an atomic spark, quantum entangled, both there and not there.

On his few visits to the towers, he would walk through the halls and ride the elevators and eat in the restaurants, always feeling like he was moving through a dream world, wholly created out of his imagination. Behind him, Ellis heard the loading doors slide open.

"Mr. Raines?"

It was Stevens.

Don turned. "Yes?"

"It's Terry—he says he's ready."

Don glanced back at the skyline and followed Stevens back inside. It had been a stroke of genius, hiring a facilities manager this time around. Stevens had proven very useful, allowing Terry to manage the staff and freeing Don up to work with the other Dr. Ellis and other outside contacts. Stevens had also done a discreet job of beefing up their security—it amazed Ellis that he'd worked in the old warehouse for so many years before with just a skeleton crew of rent-a-cops without any problems or thefts of equipment.

His work was just too important.

As they headed inside, a group of helicopters flew low over the river, buzzing like bees returning to the hive. They skimmed the water and traveled up the East River. Three of the choppers had troops in the doors, ready to rappel out. For one horrible moment, Don thought they were coming for him and for the machine, but the helicopters continued onward, buzzing over the Brooklyn Bridge and disappearing from view.

Terry was underneath the primary accelerator chamber—in this version of the machine, the accelerator pointed downward to a taped-off area on the warehouse's concrete floor—soldering something to the bottom of the machine. Ellis had expanded the power consumption methodology on this version of the machine, which should allow for a larger mass to be projected back into time. He had done away with the table from which he had fallen in the first timeline—instead, anything inside the circle on the ground would go through the temporal fold. Several technicians stood watching—Trish was at the primary control panel, while others were making adjustments behind the machine. Blueprints for the machine covered part of the control panel.

They had finished primary construction months ago, and they were well into the testing phase now, with a score of successful experiments so far. Ellis had worked night and day—living in the warehouse had few perks, but twenty-four-hour access to the machine was one of them. He'd carried out several experiments on his own, refining the process and making sure to record any improvements.

"OK, that's good," Trish said as Stevens and Ellis walked up. Terry climbed out from under the machine and stood, pulling up his pants.

"Oh," Terry said. "There you guys are. We're ready," he said, nodding to Trish.

Ellis pointed at the soldering Terry had just finished. "What was that?"

"Oh, I added a camera pointed down onto the target area. Makes pinpointing the laser easier."

Ellis nodded—Terry was a gem. Maybe, he wouldn't have to kill him in this timeline, or any of these other people. But if Don needed to leave, the machine had to be destroyed. Leaving it operational was just too dangerous.

Don walked over and nodded at Trish. She was smart as a whip, with a real gift for engineering. He had no idea where Terry had found her and the other interns, but they were priceless. Don looked at the schematic draped over the control panel, making a notation on the sheet, and then turned and read the numbers that covered the computer monitor.

"Good. The power is higher," he said, tapping the monitor.

Trish spoke up. "It can still sustain the field, even with the larger event radius. We've also improved the flow-through by tweaking some of the settings on the accelerator actuator."

Ellis smiled at her. "You guys are good."

She smiled, and her face reddened.

Ellis looked up at Terry. "Looks like we're ready for another test. Can you save those latest changes?"

Terry nodded at one of the interns, who scurried off to the primary computer lab. Ellis smiled—it was good to see Terry using his resources efficiently.

Outside, Ellis heard a siren begin to wail. After a moment, he heard another and another.

"What's that?" Terry asked, looking around.

Ellis walked to the loading doors and stepped outside, and the others followed.

The warehouse next door was on fire.

"What the hell is this?" Ellis asked the others. They watched for a moment, and then Trish shrieked and pointed across the water. They followed her gaze.

"Part of the waterfront is on fire," she said.

Across the river, along the Jersey side, dozens of warehouses and buildings were ablaze—the horizon was darkened with smoke. The flames must've been two hundred feet high for them to be seen from Red Hook.

"Oh my God," Ellis said and turned, looking at the other warehouses on his side of the river.

Behind them, Stevens was shouting at them to come inside.

He directed everyone to the computer lab, where Terry was watching the TV. Behind him, one of the interns was finishing up, creating new CD versions of the schematics and placing them in a red CD case that always held the latest schematics and testing and experiment data.

"Sir? You better see this," Terry said quietly.

On the screen, massive numbers of rioters were moving through the streets of New York.

The CNN announcer came back on the screen.

"Again, these are live pictures from above New York City. The rioters have moved slowly through the city, setting fires and destroying cars as they went. We have unconfirmed reports of gunfire as police in riot gear have attempted to step in and stop the crowd, which appears to be making its way up the east side, traveling up 12th Avenue. We are also receiving reports of mass rioting, looting, and setting fires from several other large cities around the world, mostly in the western nations. A group has barricaded themselves inside the top of the Eiffel Tower, threatening to blow themselves up. We're also hearing—"

The power went out.

"Jesus," Terry said. "I'll get the backup generators running." The other interns ran off after him to help, all of them except Trish.

Ellis turned, shouting after Terry. "And check with security! Why didn't they come on automatically? I thought they were set up—"

"That was me," Trish said quietly. "It was my fault. We needed some of those components to increase the power output."

He looked at her but wasn't sure what to say. She reminded him of Sarah, the Sarah he'd met in college, the Sarah that had told him so many stories of her childhood in Texas.

"Oh, uh—that's fine," he stammered.

Trish shook her head. "No, it's not fine. I could have jeopardized everything for a sixteen percent increase in the primary power actuators."

Ellis looked at her.

"You know this machine as well as I do, don't you?"

She nodded. "I should."

Before he could ask her what she meant, the power snapped back on, and he turned the TV back on.

"Reports are coming in from all over the world with similar stories of Islamic riots. The destruction of the Ka'aba, their religion's most holy site, had sent the entire religion into a state of unorganized panic. Governments around the world are calling for calm."

Terry and the interns returned with two security guards.

"Mr. Stevens—there's a fire at the front gate!"

Ellis turned to Terry.

"You get the machine operational. Now."

Terry looked confused, but Trish nodded, somber.

Ellis grabbed his shoulders. "Terry! It might already be too late, if there's another power outage. Get the machine working right now!"

Ellis and Stevens ran after the guards to the front of the building and out into the parking lot.

The Red Hook area of lower Brooklyn was covered in a pall of smoke—it looked like entire blocks of buildings and warehouses were now on fire, far too many for a fire department to handle. Across the river, helicopters buzzed over New York City.

A large group of rioters were making their way down Van Brunt Street, firing their guns into the air and throwing Molotov cocktails through random windows. As he watched, he saw one of the mob shoot an unarmed man running through the streets. They had vehicles, too—trucks carrying more guns and a long row of taxis following behind. It looked like a long, yellow snake, dragging its way up the street.

In the middle of the street, a dark-haired woman was standing next to the open door of a car, taking pictures of the mass of rioters moving down the street. Ellis immediately recognized her—it was the *Post* reporter.

"Shit," Ellis said quietly.

The guard and one of the Italians came running over.

"They've gone ape-shit," the Italian said. "I've only got eight guys, but we can push this crowd away, if you want. It's going to get ugly, though, and draw a lot of attention."

Ellis knew what he meant—even if they saved the warehouse, the cops would be all over the scene. Assuming there were still cops out there.

But trying to explain away the machine was a lot easier than rebuilding it.

"Break out the guns," Ellis said to the group. "We have to protect the warehouse." He turned to Stevens. "And did you notice our other visitor? Escort her inside and bring her to me."

Ellis led the men inside and started handing out automatic weapons and grenades.

From outside, he heard the distinctive patter of gunfire.

"Keep your men under cover and open fire," he told the Italians. "And hand out the extra guns to the other guards."

Ellis ran back into the machine area—he saw the interns crawling all over the machine, removing safety equipment and plastic coverings. At the control panel, Terry and Trish were working feverishly at the controls.

Ellis turned and ran into the computer lab. He opened a large, locked safe that sat on the floor behind his desk. From inside, he took out a familiar-looking leather satchel, along with a squat, drum-like device.

2.36
Brooklyn Bridge

The Brooklyn Bridge had stood as a symbol of American can-do attitude for over a hundred years. Completed in 1883, the massive stone and metal structure connected Manhattan with Brooklyn, bridging the East River and allowing pedestrian and vehicular traffic into New York City. It took 13 years to sink the massive pilings and build the towers and decking, and it cost 27 men their lives, including the architect, German immigrant John Augustus Roebling. During the surveying phase of the project, his foot was crushed by an arriving ferry at the dock where he stood—his toes were amputated. The resulting tetanus infection killed him soon afterward.

The bridge was 85 feet wide, enough room for three lanes of vehicular traffic in each direction. Television helicopters were hovering over the bridge, and Ellis glanced at the TV to watch. It looked like people were shooting into other vehicles. In both directions, vans full of men had stopped on the bridge.

The announcer came on again, stating the obvious. "Again, it looks like they've blocked the bridge and are firing at cars as they approach. We've seen several drivers shot, and in one case, the victim was thrown over the side of the bridge into the river. He looked like he was still alive when they threw him over."

The scene changed to replay recorded footage. "Earlier, the gunmen were simply firing randomly at cars, but now traffic in both directions has been blocked by the vans and crashed vehicles. The gunmen used ladders atop the vans to climb up to the pedestrian bridge and continued firing on cars and pedestrians. The walkway is clear now of people, except for the gunmen."

The reporter was quiet for a moment as the helicopter zoomed in, and the camera clearly showed the gunmen firing at drivers trapped in blocked cars. Other drivers were jumping out of their cars and fleeing back to the Brooklyn and New York sides of the bridge.

"We assume that the police are on their way," the reporter continued. "But with the other riots and fires taking place in lower Manhattan—"

The helicopter jerked and appeared to spin away from the bridge, and for a moment, the camera showed only the shining surface of the East River, smoke drifting over it. After a moment, the helicopter righted itself.

"OK, yup, we're back on," the reporter said, panting. "Sorry about that, folks. It appears the gunmen in the white van were firing at us as well, so we're backing off."

The screen showed the bridge, this time from farther away. On top of the white van were several men, jumping up and down and waving AK-47s in the air. One of them squeezed off a few celebratory rounds.

"OK, I see the police coming," the reporter said, and the camera turned to the entrance ramp from Manhattan. "Actually, it's a SWAT team," the reporter added.

Ellis shook his head and looked away. He didn't have time for this— he needed to get his stuff together.

2.37
VISITOR'S PASS

"Where are we going?" Cassie screamed, but the man would not let go. He dragged her through the gate of the barbed wire fence that surrounded the warehouse. Behind them, rioters were firing indiscriminately at the buildings on either side of the street.

Cassie passed several men that she had seen before, hanging around the warehouse. Now, she understood they were security—they were armed and stationed behind the fences and crates and cars, protecting the front entrance of the warehouse. She was looking up at the front of the building when a window above her shattered.

She gripped her camera closer as the man led her up the steps and inside, and the sound of gunfire behind her lessened.

"I don't know if you can tell, but we've got a situation here," the man said, looking down at her.

She'd been outside the warehouse, taking photos, when her editor had phoned about the rioting. For some reason, Muslim anger had coalesced in the past twenty-four hours into palpable violence, and the epicenter was New York City and the surrounding boroughs. Foreman told her that armed groups of men were moving through the streets, setting fires and gunning down people.

She looked up at the tall man. "Who are you, again?"

"I'm Stevens, the facility manager."

She glanced around—they were in the front room of what looked like a doctor's office. There was a reception area and some low tables and chairs. There were even magazines out for people to read. On the wall behind the desk hung a huge "Blossom Investments" logo.

"OK, well, thanks," she said quietly.

"No problem," Stevens answered. "Why didn't you get in your car and leave? You saw them coming."

She nodded and held up the camera. "I wanted some more pictures."

He shook his head—he reminded her of Mike, her editor. He was always yelling at her for putting herself in dangerous situations. Of course, she argued, if she were a bleached blonde hottie, she wouldn't have to work so hard. Instead, she was brunette and plain, nothing flashy. And she was driven.

Stevens was looking at her.

"What?" she asked.

"Nothing. It's just… we've been keeping our eye on you for a while."

"What?"

Stevens smiled. "You've been hanging around, taking pictures. Dr. Ellis said to leave you alone, that it didn't matter. I thought your articles were very…interesting. Especially since I'm in charge of keeping this place quiet. How did you find out so much?"

She looked at him—he wasn't angry, just genuinely curious. "Well, I spend a lot of time in basements."

He made a face.

"I do a lot of research," she continued, smiling. "Public records, ownership records, things like that."

"Oh. Well, I need to take you to Dr. Ellis—he wants to talk to you. Come on."

2.38

THE OUTSIDER

Stevens walked in, followed by the mousy reporter. Ellis looked up and saw them standing there. Stevens was looking at him, but the reporter was still outside the office, looking up.

"Thanks, Stevens. Can you make sure the front of the building is secure?"

Stevens nodded and ran off.

Cassie wasn't looking at Ellis—she was staring out at the massive particle accelerator, which took up half of the floor of the warehouse. She lifted her camera to take a picture.

"I wouldn't do that, if I were you," Ellis said quietly. His bag and the small bomb were on his desk, ready to go.

She turned to him. "You're the older Ellis, right? The older brother?"

Ellis smiled and indicated the chair in front of his desk.

"Please, have a seat. Where are you from?"

He could tell she didn't want to turn her back on the massive, mysterious machine in the center of the warehouse. After a moment, she sat down.

"I'm Cassie O'Neil. But you know that."

Ellis nodded. "Tell me something about yourself, something only a few people know."

She was taken aback, both by the question and by his impertinence.

"Well, I don't know you that well, Dr. Ellis."

Ellis smiled and sat back. "But you want to know what's going on here, right?"

She nodded, biting her lip. "OK, I'll play along. Umm, oh, I know—my editor's a little bit crazy. I think it's because his cousin was killed in 1997."

Ellis had not expected that. He'd had Stevens look into her background, and combined with the information he'd gotten from the younger Ellis, her FBI report, he'd thought he knew Cassie O'Neal pretty well.

"Really?" Ellis asked.

She nodded. "Yeah, his cousin Abe lived in a little town in Virginia, a place called Liberty. A serial killer came through town and killed several people, including Abe and the woman he was seeing."

Ellis leaned forward.

Cassie nodded. "Sounds like a movie, right? My editor doesn't like to talk about it. It was all over the news at the time—do you remember the murderer with the white van? He was a collector, so he took trophies—"

Ellis nodded, glancing out at the sounds of shouting—several men ran through the warehouse, heading towards the doors. He stood and grabbed a few more things from one of the side tables and put it in the bag.

"I'm sorry to hear about your editor's cousin—though I don't remember the details. But your articles have caused quite a bit of trouble for me and others, more trouble than you know," Ellis said to her. "I was trying to make things better here, not worse."

She shook her head. "I don't understand."

"What would you say if I told you that the 'evidence' you saw of the attacks on 9/11 was not fabricated?" Ellis asked.

She didn't say anything.

"One of your early articles," Ellis continued, "said that the materials you had seen were 'remarkably realistic.' That wording gave me a laugh, I can tell you. But there was nothing remarkable about them. They were just real."

Cassie shook her head. "The government needed to justify increased security, so those photos and the video were fabricated."

"Which production company created the videos?" Ellis interrupted. "You're a great reporter—surely you tried to track down the special effects facility in Hollywood where they made the videos."

She looked at him, frowning.

Ellis continued. "You never found it, right? Never found who made the 'shockingly realistic' videos of the towers falling. And now they've fallen for real, thanks to you."

"That's not true. I was reporting on a secret committee—"

"That was me," Ellis said quietly. "The committee was me and several others folks from high up in the White House. But I started it with this."

He turned, reached up, and turned the monitor of his PC so that she could see it. On the screen, he was running the video of the Twin Towers falling. He watched her, watching the video. "That's the one you saw, right?"

Cassie nodded, glancing at him.

"Well," he continued, "I have dozens more, some of which I'm sure you haven't seen."

He clicked on the PC mouse. A string of videos came up on the monitor, and he flipped through them for her: the towers falling, the plane crashing into the South Tower, the Pentagon on fire. But there were differences: on one, the Capitol Dome collapsing on itself, something that hadn't happened in this timeline. On another, the acting Mayor of New York was speaking while a crawl ran at the bottom of the screen, saying Mayor Giuliani and most of the cities' leaders had been killed in a building collapse at 7 World Trade Center.

She looked at him.

"Those must be from 11/24. But why did you change the dates?" she asked. "And the Capitol collapse, and that bit about Giuliani, those things didn't happen."

Ellis shook his head.

"They did happen. Once."

He stood and picked up the bag.

"I didn't alter any of those—they came straight from CNN. See, in my world, these events took place on 9/11. That is the date that was burned into our brains. I came here, to this place, to try and stop it. Thanks to you, word got out."

She looked up at him.

"No, don't worry," he said, smiling. "I don't blame you—you're just the messenger. A tenacious one, at that, but just the messenger. Maybe one of these times I'll have to hire you away from the paper."

She looked confused.

Ellis sighed and leaned forward, handing her a small USB drive.

"It's all true—it happened like those videos, and on September 11, 2001. I saw it, recorded all the videos and pictures to create a mass of 'evidence' to prove it happened. You've seen a small portion of it. The rest is on there. I have to go."

Ellis walked out of the office.

2.39
Unforeseen Variables

Cassie followed Ellis as he walked out to the machine.

"What do you mean, it's all real?" Cassie asked again. "How could it have happened before?"

Ellis set his bag down next to the machine.

"What do you mean you 'came to this place' to stop it from happening?"

He turned and looked at her.

"I am from another time. After our 9/11, I came here, to this world. Your world. I gave all the information about 9/11 and the attacks to the government and prevented the attack, I thought. Turns out, I only delayed it."

Stevens ran into the room.

"Dr. Ellis! Something else is happening!"

Ellis looked at Cassie and followed Stevens into the computer room, where several members of the staff were again huddled around the TV.

"Apparently, these are suicides," the announcer was saying. They were showing a different bridge this time, a green one, but there were more men in white vans, shooting at anything that moved. "The drivers of some of these vehicles are jumping off of the bridge rather than being shot by the gunmen. Again, this is live from Los Angeles—the bridge runs from Los Angeles to Long Beach, a major route. These rioters are shooting the drivers of cars stopped there, just as in New York and a bridge in London." The announcer went quiet for a moment. "OK, I got it. Thanks. We're going to the U.N. building now in New York City."

The screen changed abruptly.

A female reporter was on the street next to the massive U.N. building. "Thanks, Mike. The police are telling us that a group of Muslim extremists has stormed the U.N. and is executing people. We're getting conflicting reports that representatives from Islamic nations were allowed to leave—in fact, we've seen a few speeding away in vehicles.

There have been no further details from the police or from the terrorists holed up inside the building. Earlier, we did see several helicopters full of soldiers rappel onto the roof."

Ellis knew that he should go, but he couldn't take his eyes off the TV. Stevens and the reporter were watching the news report, as well. Ellis wondered if anyone was working on the machine or guarding the building.

The woman reporter tapped at her ear. "OK, OK, I'm hearing something now. It sounds like a list of demands. Charlie, can we cut over to that? It's on the police broadcast band—"

Ellis heard the audio click over, and a different voice came over the speaker. On the screen, he could still see the reporter and the U.N. building looming above her.

"...without Allah. There can be no peace without Allah. And without Mecca and the most sacred of relics, Allah shall abandon his chosen people. I am the prophet, and I shall bathe all the lands in fire. There can be no world without Allah. There can be no peace without Allah..."

The woman reporter cut back in. "It's not a list of demands. In fact, it sounds more like a—"

The tall building behind her exploded.

An incredibly bright pulse of white light shot out from the middle floors of the U.N. building, followed by a massive blast of fire as the building was severed in half. The top portion of the building actually moved visibly upward as an orgy of fire washed toward the ground.

And then the screen went blank. A moment later, Ellis felt the ground tremble beneath his feet.

He turned and walked back into his office, retrieving the drum-like bomb. When he returned, Terry and Trish were back at the control panel.

"We're ready, Dr. Ellis," Trish said. Ellis went to the screen and tapped at the controls, double-checking the settings. One thing he would have to do, if he ever got the chance, was to improve the controls for the machine—it was hacked together and prone to unexpected failure.

Terry was looking like he would start panicking at any moment. "That was a nuclear bomb—terrorists just blew up the U.N."

They looked at each other and the other techs, who were gathered around the machine.

Ellis nodded.

"Look, we have to protect this machine," he told them. "I need each of you to run to the front of the building, grab a weapon, and hold off the mob. They'll try to burn down the warehouse, and if they do, we'll lose everything. Terry, Trish, I need you to stay."

The other technicians and interns nodded and then ran off.

Ellis turned to Terry and Trish.

"I have to go, now—I have to use the machine and go back and try to fix things again."

Terry looked confused, but Trish understood.

"Again?" Terry asked. "You've done this before."

Cassie looked up. "This... this is a time machine? You weren't kidding about coming here to fix things?"

Ellis pointed at the construct above them. "That's not the first one I built—the last one was bigger, if you can believe that. I did come back here to fix things. What a great job, huh?"

Trish came around the control panel and put her hand on his shoulder. "You did good."

Ellis looked at her.

Trish looked at Terry and smiled. "There were actually three machines—the one Dr. Ellis used to get here, this machine, and a third one, under construction right now at Lawrence Livermore."

Ellis stared at her—how could she know that? He'd known she was a talented technician—she had come up with many improvements to the systems, including an innovative power regulation component that made sure none of the extra stored energy was wasted. But this?

"Trish," Ellis said. "How do you know that?"

"Don't worry about it," she said, smiling. "And my name isn't Trish. It's Tina."

Tina? His Tina?

"I don't understand."

She smiled. "Actually, this already happened for me—this warehouse and everything inside it were destroyed by the 1/25 riots. This is another day that will be infamous. I remember—we were out in California. They didn't tell us anything at school—I was only seven at the time, but my parents showed me the news when I got home. These riots—they took place all over the world. This portion of Brooklyn was essentially leveled, and all of these warehouses were destroyed. We learned later that, before you and Terry could make it operational, this machine was destroyed and you were all killed."

They were all looking at her.

"But my father continued your work," Tina continued, nodding at Ellis. "He never gave up. He was convinced that he could fix things. He said that you had given him the means to complete the machine, but it took a lot longer without you. After years, he finally got the machine at Lawrence Livermore working."

Don looked at her, smiling. "The other me got it working. I'll be damned. And you came back to change things. You helped your father with the Livermore machine, didn't you?"

She nodded. "He always said I had a knack for numbers. Now, we need to get you out of here—you need to escape this timeline and try again. My father always said it had been your greatest desire, to find and save your family. So let's get you going. What are the coordinates?" she asked, reaching for the controls.

But before she could, Ellis grabbed her up, hugging her tightly.

"Thank you. Thank you for coming back and making this possible," Ellis said, tears in his eyes. "Without you—" he started to say.

Terry interrupted. "I don't care how many machines there are. This one's not ready. It's not been properly tested."

Trish and Ellis both gave him a look at the same moment.

Ellis nodded. "I've tested it when no one was here. It works. Besides, it's now or never." He pointed at the black drum. "You guys need to get out of here—that's a bomb. I need to destroy the machine."

Cassie stopped taking pictures. "You're leaving, again? Where will you go?"

Ellis smiled. "Farther back in the timeline. Each time I reenter the timeline, it creates a branch, like streams off a river. To get back to an unfettered timeline, I have to jump farther and farther back."

Cassie was scribbling it all down. "What will you do when you get there?"

"I'll try again," he said.

"Go, Dr. Ellis," Terry said. "We'll get you out of here, and then we'll leave the warehouse." Ellis saw him look at Tina and smile. "Oh, I'm not going to let anything happen to her," Terry said, taking Tina's hand. Terry looked at her for a moment, then smiled at Ellis. "Don't worry."

Ellis looked at the two of them and suddenly understood. In the last timeline he had killed Terry, shooting him in cold blood to eliminate any other knowledge of the machine. In this one, Terry was marrying a grown-up version of his daughter who had used a third machine—one still under construction in California—to come back and save him. His brain had trouble keeping up.

Shaking his head, Don walked to the center of the circle. He set down the leather duffel bag and the bomb.

"Do I need to set the timer?" Ellis asked Tina, indicating the bomb.

Tina shook her head.

"No, I'll do it. The fire will take care of the warehouse and machine, but they were able to retrieve some parts from the wreckage. We don't want that, so just to be sure this machine is completely destroyed, I'll set up the bomb when we leave."

Ellis nodded.

"OK, set it for 1994. August 31st. And thank you."

Terry watched as Tina typed the coordinates into the machine. After a second, she looked up.

"Don't worry about it. Dad," Tina said, a sad smile on her face.

Ellis looked up at her sharply. They looked at each other for a long moment—

People burst into the room, guns firing. Cassie jumped away from the machine, crawling behind one of the large batteries. Terry and Tina ducked down behind the table.

Ellis ducked down as the automatic weapon fire seemed to fill the warehouse. Near the doors that lead out to the front of the building, several Italians and guards had fallen back, using the doorway as cover and firing out into the reception area. That meant rioters were inside the warehouse.

Bullets bounced off the concrete around Ellis, and one struck in him the leg.

Terry stood to run to Ellis' aid, but he caught a bullet in the thick part of his shoulder and spun to the ground. Ellis could see his shirt turning red.

Tina shrieked—she had ducked behind the control panel but was up now. She pulled something from a pocket and fired a weapon, a strange bluish gun that Ellis didn't recognize. The gun made an odd coughing sound as she pulled the trigger. Ellis saw that, instead of bullets, the gun fired what looked like a small cloud of individual miniature projectiles. Like a shotgun blast of rock salt, but much more powerful, the cloud of mini-bullets knocked four of the attackers down.

Ellis lay on the ground, blood running down his leg. He ignored it and crawled to the center of the circle, pulling the duffel bag with him. Dragging the bag created a moist smear of blood on the concrete.

"Terry!" Tina yelled, aiming her gun at the doorway. "Terry, activate the machine."

He nodded, slowly pulling himself up from the ground. He struggled over to the controls. Ellis could see that he was bleeding freely.

"Ready?" Terry asked Ellis.

Ellis grimaced, nodding. "Yes!" he said, ignoring the pain in his bleeding leg. He looked at them both. "And thanks."

A window at the far end of the warehouse shattered and what looked like a glass bottle crashed to the floor of the warehouse, exploding. Gasoline and fire engulfed the far wall of the warehouse. Flames raced up the walls and licked at the batteries and junctions that powered the machine.

Tina ran around the control table and leaned down, hugging Ellis.

"Here," she said, shoving a white box into his hands. "Take care of yourself."

Another group of people broke into the room, and for a moment, Ellis thought all was lost. Then he saw it was more of his own people, the technicians and interns and what was left of the guards and Italians. It looked like they were falling back again, and in greater numbers. This would be their final stand.

More machine gun fire echoed through the room. He looked at Terry. "Now!" Ellis shouted.

Tina backed away from the painted circle on the ground as Terry slammed his bloody hand down on the big green button, leaving a scarlet handprint. He and Tina looked at the machine as it powered up, energy coursing through the apparatus. Ellis saw Cassie O'Neil snapping pictures of the machine in action, the firefight, and him, bleeding on the floor. She smiled weakly at him and continued taking pictures.

The lights in the room flickered as massive amounts of energy poured from storage batteries into the bulky machine.

Ellis sat in the middle of the circle of blue. He clutched the duffel bag and the white box to his chest.

Suddenly, there were the huge booming cracks, the sounds of ice twisting, shattering.

Ellis glanced up and saw that the room around him was beginning to fade. He saw Tina, his beautiful little girl. She smiled at him, then turned and stationed herself between her father and the doors. She had a machine gun now and was firing back into the smoke that was drifting in from the front rooms of the warehouse. Terry was manning the control panel, operating it with one arm, the other limp at his side. He was watching the temporal fold form around Don. It looked like he was trying to ignore everything going on around him.

The air cracked and Ellis turned to look at the group of people near the door. The security guards, two of the mob guys he had hired, and several from Trish's group of interns were holding off the rioters. He watched the casings from one intern's gun fall slowly to the ground, a metallic shower that bounced on the concrete. To Ellis, the bullet casings looked like they were moving in slow motion and—

PART THREE

3.1
MEDICAL ATTENTION

—suddenly he was sitting on the floor of an empty warehouse. The room swam around him, the floor tilting like a carnival ride. Ellis held onto the bag, gripping it tightly, until the room stopped spinning.

Slowly, he tried to stand. When he couldn't, he looked down and saw that the bullet had grazed his thigh—he was still bleeding. Some part of his mind noted that the blood on the concrete around him formed a perfect circle—everything, including the blood on the concrete, had traveled back with him. It looked like a halo in red.

He looked down at the box that Tina had thrown him—only moments and 12 years ago—and saw that it was a first aid kit.

Don smiled and looked around at the empty space and suddenly he felt the weight of it all on him. He realized that he was alone again, alone in this new place, with only the things he had brought with him. He didn't know if he had the energy to start over, to try again.

He looked up at the closed doors across the floor. Schrödinger's Cat was calling him.

Would they be there? Surely they would. But losing everyone like that in the last timeline, causing all those deaths—had it been worth it? He hadn't stopped the disaster—in fact, many more people had died. He was trying to make it better, not worse. Should he try again, or leave it alone and let it all happen?

Don didn't know what to do.

He looked down at this leg; he needed to tend to the wound before he bled to death. Ellis knew he also needed to figure out what he was going to do. But there was something he had to do first.

Ellis began crawling across the concrete floor. It hurt to move. Leaving his bag, Don slowly crept across the floor of the warehouse, leaving a long trail of smeared blood. Finally, he reached the loading doors.

He put his hands up to open them and stopped.

"What if it's not there?" he asked himself. His voice echoed in the empty building. Don wanted to know. He shook his head and pushed at the doors, which seemed heavier than they ever had been before. With a loud grunt, he pushed the doors open.

The sky was bright outside, impossibly bright. He squinted at the city. The World Trade Center was there.

No fires, no smoke. The buildings stood, shiny and proud in the summer air.

He glanced upriver and saw the U.N. building, still standing. Or standing all over again, depending on your perspective.

The streets were no longer filled with rioters, or never would be. A dark pall of smoke didn't hang over the city.

Dr. Donald Ellis leaned heavily against the open doorway, his spirit buoyed. He noticed he'd left bloody handprints on the doors.

The buildings were there, so everything had been worth it. But should he get involved again? Or should he just let things work themselves out? He could save the Ellis that was here, and build another machine, but that would take time and money. And in his frustration and his longing to solve a seemingly-unsolvable problem, Don wondered if it was even worth the trouble.

He looked around for the first aid kit. He'd dragged it across the floor with him without even realizing it. Ellis pulled it to him and opened it.

Inside, resting on a bed of bandages and tape, he found the weird bluish gun that Tina had been firing. He lifted it out and examined it—the gun was much heavier than it appeared. Beneath the gun was a hastily-scribbled Post-it note. It was similar to the ones he'd sent through time to himself. Now, he was getting a note from his grown-up daughter.

"Good luck Dad," was all it said.

He smiled. He had managed to save her, and their family, and it had ended up being the deciding factor in his ability to escape. She had been smart and pleasant, a joy to be around. At least he'd saved her.

Don set the note and gun on the concrete and began looking through the rest of the first aid kit. He got out the bandages and other items he would need to clean the wound and bandage his leg.

3.2
A BREAKFAST MEETING

Three years later, on the morning of January 23, 1997, President Clinton jogged through the early-morning streets of Washington, D.C. The weather was warmer than usual for late January, and Clinton took advantage of the sunshine to get out. It was his routine to run outside as much as he could during the warmer months, but winter weather usually forced him to run in the small White House gym.

It was nice to get out.

Of course, the Secret Service hated it—they went on and on about the security risks. Usually he had six or seven guys with him, but a few years ago the Secret Service had added two more agents on bicycles. Clinton hated all the hassle—he just wanted to run. It helped him think, and it got him out of the White House for a few precious minutes.

Today, he and the agents ran south out of the White House compound and west, through Foggy Bottom and down to the waterfront and Lincoln Memorial. He loved the memorials along the mall, incorporating them into his runs as often as possible.

Following him were five jogging Secret Service agents and a military aide. A block behind, a bullet-proof Chevy Suburban with blacked-out windows, another part of the presidential detail, followed to provide assistance or as an option for a quick evacuation—just in case.

Clinton continued up Independence Avenue and across the Kutz Bridge to the Washington Monument, surrounded by a ring of American flags. At 14th Street, he turned south, running past the new Holocaust Museum and past the Bureau of Engraving and Printing. There was a small crowd of tourists out front, lined up to take the ever-popular tour to see the nation's money being printed, and he waved at them—a few yelled and waved back when they realized who he was, and several of the tourists snapped hurried pictures.

The agents on their bicycles continued south on 14th, heading for the bridge over to the Jefferson Memorial, but Clinton turned suddenly and took D Street, heading east. The runners kept up with him, but the bikers were already across the bridge and would have to turn around.

Clinton smiled. He loved to keep these agents on their toes. Besides, his mood was buoyant—he'd just won reelection, something no sitting Democrat had done since F.D.R. Now, he was back from the campaign trail, working on his State of the Union address, to be given in two weeks.

And he was back to running regularly---and back to keeping these Secret Service guys on their toes.

Clinton suddenly remembered a great bakery in the area, east of the U.S. Mint. He tried to get down here at least once a month, but he'd not been able to visit since last summer. He remembered their excellent crullers.

The agents should be happy—at least he wasn't running to the McDonald's over on 13th Street and New York again. He loved the looks on the people's faces when he ran in there—it was always precious, that look of utter surprise. Often, William Jefferson Clinton felt like this is what a president was supposed to be doing, popping in on regular folks and seeing how they were doing. Presidents who stayed safely tucked away behind the fences at 1600 Pennsylvania Avenue—how were they supposed to know how people were really doing? Read it in some report, or hear about it fifth-hand from the Secretary of Commerce?

Clinton continued east on D Street, passing the huge buildings where tens of thousands of federal workers reported for duty every day. It was amazing to think just how much of the population of Washington, D.C., worked for the federal government. Turning south on 7th, he passed the HUD building and their strange collection of UFO-looking canopies that floated above the grassy seating areas and an entrance to the Metro. He turned east again, waving at the people he saw—two deliverymen gave him a wave. Taking a side alley, he made two more quick turns— he wasn't actually trying to lose the Secret Service agents, but it was fun to keep them guessing.

He sped up, jogging up 3rd Avenue, and finally saw the bakery up ahead. He ducked inside, knowing the agents would be along momentarily.

Once inside, Clinton saw, out of the corner of his eye, a man standing right next to the door, waiting just out of sight. Turning, Clinton saw the tall man move quickly, stepping to the door and flipping the deadbolt.

"You're a difficult person to get to, Mr. President," the man said, his hands at his sides, relaxed. One hand held a thick ring of keys.

Clinton smiled and glanced around—it appeared there was no one else in the bakery.

"That's all part of the plan, friend," the president said, nodded at the door behind him. "You know, you have about five seconds before those men begin shooting into that door."

The tall man nodded.

"You mix up your route daily—how did I know you were coming?" The man smiled and gently tossed the ring of keys to Clinton.

"Lucky guess," Clinton said, shrugging. "Or you happened to be here—maybe you're just taking advantage of an opportunity," Clinton said, his blue eyes never leaving the man.

"That's true," the tall man said, smiling. "In my line of work, it is all about taking advantage of opportunities."

Outside, the Secret Service agents arrived at the door and tried to open it. They found it locked and began pounding on it loudly.

The tall man slid away from the door, keeping an eye on the president. Clinton noted how calm the man seemed to be, even though the man was currently committing a felony and would soon be in the hands of furious Secret Service agents.

"What is your line of work, friend? Assassin?" the president asked, jingling the keys and stepping to the door.

"No, Mr. President," Ellis said quietly. "I know many things, but little about killing people. I know that you have that important trade mission on your schedule for tomorrow, and you're trying to choose a new Supreme Court justice."

The man waited a beat.

"And I know about Monica."

Clinton was sliding the key into the lock when he stopped.

"What?" the president asked.

"I know about Monica Lewinsky, Mr. President."

Clinton turned. The agents pounded again on the door, but he ignored it.

"Sorry, friend. Not sure what you're getting at—"

"You know who I'm talking about, Mr. President," the tall man said. "White House intern." he said slowly. "A close, close friend."

Clinton looked at him, ignoring the shouting agents outside.

"I know how you feel about her," the tall man said quietly. "You've had several dalliances with her over the past twenty months and you consider the affair to be over, but you'll reconnect with her later this year."

Clinton didn't know what to say. Everything with Monica was over—

"I also know that Impeachment proceedings will be brought against you," the tall man continued, sitting down in one of the empty booths. Clinton noticed that there was a small stack of papers on the booth table.

"After the scandal breaks next January, you'll be forced to lie and cover up the relationship, and it will be a cloud over the remainder of your presidency. After Impeachment charges are brought, you'll give grand jury testimony. The meaning of the word 'intern' will be changed forever. You'll beat the scandal and remain president."

The president was silent.

"I know many things, sir," the man in the booth said quietly. "I'm simply asking you for five minutes of your time. Or ten, if you find what I have to say interesting. I think you will. If not, the Secret Service can drag me away to wherever they take people who kidnap the president."

From outside, the agents shouted that they were going to open fire.

"Hold your fire!" the president yelled loudly. He turned, unlocking the door.

The Secret Service agents burst inside.

Several agents grabbed the seated man from the booth, pushing him to the dirty floor of the restaurant. The lead agent grabbed Clinton, roughly pushing him toward the door. Outside, a black Suburban raced up and squealed to a stop.

"Enough," Clinton shouted, pushing the agent off. "Stop it!"

Three agents were on top of the man, and another stood back, his gun trained on them.

From beneath the agents, Clinton heard the tall man calmly talking. "My name is Dr. Donald Ellis."

One of the agents was working to get his handcuffs out of his jogging shorts to cuff the man.

"Stop that!" Clinton yelled, pulling them off. "Get off of him," he said as the scuffle ended. He looked at the agents.

"Give us a few minutes, men. Someone scare us up some coffee— and a couple of those donuts," he said, nodding at the counter.

The agents looked around, confused.

Clinton smiled and slapped the lead agent hard on the back, then walked over and sat back down at the booth the man had earlier occupied. The man, rubbing his arms, followed, his limp noticeable.

"Thank you. I know many things, and I hope to help you." the man said, sitting. Clinton nodded, and, from the back of the bakery, Clinton heard a commotion—he turned to see that the agents had gone into the back and released the cook and a waitress. A waitress began shrieking as soon as she walked out from the back room.

"This man came in here and locked us in—that's him!" the waitress yelled, pointing at the man seated with Clinton. She started to walk over, but the agents held her back and began talking to her. After a moment, she calmed down.

"I know things, too, Dr. Ellis," Clinton said, looking at Ellis after the waitress left. "I know too many things. Nothing surprises me anymore. Except you, friend."

The waitress reappeared, bringing them coffee and a small plate of donuts.

"And I know you know many things, sir," Ellis said, adding cream and sugar to his coffee from the containers on the table. "That is true. But you don't know what I know. Did you ever see the TV show *Early Edition?*"

Clinton looked up at him, a donut halfway to his mouth.

"I don't think so."

"It was a science fiction show about a man who lived in Chicago," Ellis explained. "He was a normal person—except he got the *Chicago Sun-Times* a day early."

Ellis opened the folder on the table between them and tapped the newspaper on top of a stack of papers. The headline of the *USA Today* paper read, "Bush Beats Gore in Florida Showdown."

"On the TV show," Ellis began, tapping at the paper, "the man was always trying to do good, but he only had one day's notice, so it was difficult. The show mostly consisted of him catching children falling out of trees or preventing car accidents."

Clinton pulled the paper closer, looking at the date.

"It says it's from December 4, 2000."

"And I assure you, it's genuine," Ellis said, leaning forward. "Gore will be beaten in the 2000 election, but it will come down to Florida. Those electoral votes will be up in the air, and there will be a lot of discussion of recounts and hanging chads—those pieces of paper that come out of a tabulated vote."

"Is this real?" Clinton asked, tapping the paper.

Ellis nodded. "As real as the fact that you and Ms. Lewinsky will be exposed in the press. January, to be exact."

Clinton shook his head. "Everything is over between us. I ended it in March of last year, and now she works at the Pentagon."

Ellis nodded.

"I know. But you'll have two more encounters, and then she'll begin confiding in a friend at the Pentagon. What Monica doesn't know is that her friend will tape their conversations and turn them over to Ken Starr, who is running the Paula Jones case."

Clinton didn't even want to consider what might happen if the whole thing became public knowledge. What he did behind closed doors was his business....

"The scandal will cloud the remaining years of your presidency,"

Ellis began again, his voice low. "But worse, it will cast a pall over Gore's candidacy in the 2000 election. It will cost him the presidency. After January 1997 and the events that follow, the voters won't trust you. And, by association, they won't trust Mr. Gore."

Clinton shook his head, staring out the window. "It's too hard to believe, Dr. Ellis, if that's your real name. How could you possibly know this? Where did you get this paper?"

Ellis shook his head. "You wouldn't believe me, even if I told you. But my name is Dr. Donald Ellis, and I'm Dean of Physics at the University of New York. Or I used to be, some years back."

Clinton looked at him and saw a strange, sad smile on the man's face.

"Bush will make a strong showing in the polls," Ellis began again. "Though, at first, it will appear that McCain has enough support to make it interesting. Bush wins the nomination, and it's a close race. Too close—the Supreme Court eventually steps in and invalidates a last-minute recount petition by Gore's primary counsel. As the votes could not be legally recounted, Bush was declared the victor."

Clinton shook his head and sipped at his coffee. "No, it can't be. I… there is no way that my relationship with Monica could cause this, even if it were exposed…"

"It doesn't matter, anyway," Ellis said, shaking his head. "It's all trivial."

"Trivial?" Clinton said loudly, and the agents looked over—the president knew they were watching every movement from the table. "How is the outcome of an election trivial? It sounds like Bush's kid steals it from Al, all because of…"

"I'm saying that it doesn't matter, sir," Ellis interrupted. "I am not here to talk about the election of 2000 or Whitewater. I could care less about Monica and her constant need to give you gifts, like the tie. Hugo Boss, right?"

Clinton looked at him sharply.

Ellis leaned in.

"Mr. President, something horrible is going to happen. And you have the power to prevent it."

3.3

BROOKLYN

At a large warehouse on the Brooklyn waterfront, a young Dr. Donald Ellis looked up at machine. He wasn't sure what to make of it. The machine, and all of the ancillary production facilities that took up at least half of this warehouse in Red Hook, had gone from an abstraction to a reality in days.

He'd never have believed it, if he hadn't seen it with his own eyes.

Things in his life had been getting odd since two weeks ago when he'd received a strange invitation to lunch. Don had been quietly working in his office at the university, talking to his T.A. about grades and working diligently on the syllabus for next semester. There had been a quiet knock at the door, and a Mr. Stevens had entered the office and introduced himself, saying that a group of investors wanted to meet with Dr. Ellis over lunch to discuss monetizing some of his research.

Intrigued, Don had agreed. Following the man out to the faculty parking lot, Don had found a large limo waiting.

It had only gotten stranger from there.

The ride into town was odd—Mr. Stevens had refused to answer any of Don's questions. Expecting the car to continue into Manhattan, Don was surprised when it turned south into Brooklyn and stopped a few minutes later in front of what looked like an abandoned warehouse in a very shady-looking area of Brooklyn.

Of course, a closer look—and the armed guards—made it clear that the location wasn't abandoned.

Mr. Stevens had led him inside, waving the security guards away. Don had noticed the strange looks the guards had given him. He was whisked inside and down a hallway to a normal-looking conference room.

There was already a man in the room, seated at a table strewn with papers and drawings. Don noticed that the drawings looked like schematics. As Don reached to shake the seated man's hand, he realized that the man looked almost exactly like him. Older, sure, but the same...

"Hello, Dr. Ellis," the older man had said, a smile on his face.

Don shook his hand and, unsure of what else to do or say, sat down.

"You," he began, stammering. "Are you and I... related?"

The older man nodded, smiling. "Yup. We're more than related, I can assure you," the smiling man said. Don could tell he was enjoying this. "I'm you. In about fifteen years."

Don remembered nodding and stammering for a long minute, eventually saying something stupid. And then the older man had spent a solid hour peppering him with details only he could know about "their" shared history. It was bewildering.

Now, two weeks later, Don was spending a lot less time at the school and more here, getting up to speed on the machine. Don was still trying to get his head around it, of course—he thought it would take several more months before he got used to the idea of another version of himself driving around the streets of New York.

It was even crazier to think that they were building a time machine together.

Don hadn't been surprised by the concept, of course—he'd already done a lot of preliminary work in the field. Fourth-dimensional space theory was his specialty as was wave formation dynamics. The older Ellis had gone on to explain the role that quantum entanglement played in the machine, something that the younger Ellis had never considered, even though the concept had been around for years. Don was now spending every moment at the warehouse, pouring through the schematics and drawings, absorbing as much as he could of the machine's unique properties. Don was working with a guy named Terry and Mr. Stevens, the facilities manager, and he was helping out where he could, trying to get up to speed so as to be useful.

The schematics were leaps and bounds beyond the crude drawings that hung on the walls of his basement office in Jericho. Those hasty drawings were of a mythical, theoretical device—these drawings were of a final product, one that was quickly approaching completion. They had already begun testing the device.

But Don understood the reasons the machine had been built. He hoped that he would never again have to look at the videos and pictures and newspaper headlines of the 9/11/2001 event. It was almost more than a person could take, reading the horrible details of what could come to pass. Reading multiple versions of it somehow made it seem less real—it was impossible to imagine the first version, from Ellis' original timeline, with the destruction of the Capitol building and the loss of half of the U.S. Congress.

Reading though the accounts of that day had been bad enough, but listening to the older Dr. Ellis describe what was to come had been enough to convince Don that it was all very real. There was a disaster coming, one that would change this country and the world forever. Don would do whatever he could to prevent it.

Even now, the older version of him was in Washington, D.C., approaching the Clinton administration for the first time to provide information about future events.

"Don?"

He turned to see Stevens, the facility manager, walk up to him. Stevens and the others had taken it in stride to have another person working on the project that looked like and sounded like Dr. Ellis—in fact, they'd immediately started calling the younger man "Don" and the elder man "Dr. Ellis." Don thought it was because the older man commanded more respect.

Stevens had been working for Dr. Ellis since 1995 and had always called him "Dr. Ellis," so it was easiest. Evidently, Mr. Stevens and Terry had also worked for Dr. Ellis in the other timelines, though of course, they had no knowledge of that. It made Don's mind swim with the idea of alternate versions of everyone in the world.

Ellis had found Mr. Stevens in this timeline and hired him again to oversee staffing, logistics, and security for the facility.

"Yes?" Don said.

Stevens handed him a clipboard. "Dr. Ellis called and asked me to give these to you as soon as you arrived today—there's another scheduled test in about an hour, but he wanted you to work with Terry on the phasing equipment, if you could."

Don looked at the clipboard and nodded, feeling completely out of his element.

3.4
Donuts and Coffee

A dozen customers came and went in the time it took for the tall man to spin his story—Clinton knew the Secret Service agents were checking each one before they were even allowed into the bakery.

Clinton sat back, nodding slowly. The man across from him had just spent ten solid minutes spinning a fantastic story, and some part of Clinton prayed that it was all fiction. But parts of the story...

"Well, part of that makes sense," the president said quietly. "Osama bin Laden has been coalescing power for many years. First in Sudan and now Afghanistan. We think he was behind the Khobar Towers bombing last year. We've had the opportunity to take him out, on a few occasions, but didn't. Not enough evidence."

Ellis glanced around at the interior of the bakery.

"Yes, that will be a topic of discussion for many years to come."

"What will?" Clinton asked.

"Your apparent inaction," Ellis said. "It's in the congressional record—you had several opportunities to act and did not, especially after Khobar. Your apparent reticence allowed al Qaeda to continue growing, especially when shielded by the Taliban. Training camps, unrestricted movement, support. The 1995 Bojinka plot to blow up airliners in flight between Asia and the United States. The plans for 9/11/2001 are already on the drawing board, even now."

"And how do you know this?" Clinton asked, his eyes narrowing.

"Now that—that you wouldn't believe," Ellis said.

The president finished his third donut and smiled, brushing crumbs from his sweatshirt. He stood, nodding at Ellis.

"Come on," the president said, nodding to the agents.

The president walked over to the door but didn't forget to thank the folks that worked at the bakery. As he and Dr. Ellis walked outside and climbed into the black Suburban, President Clinton was reminded again of just how important it was to keep close to the people on the streets. If any of the stuff that Ellis was saying were to come true, Clinton would need as many friends—and supporters—as he could muster.

3.5
A NEW REACTOR

The machine sat in the middle of the concrete floor of the warehouse. Most of the rest of the space was taken up with battery packs and other mechanisms needed to power the device.

This version of the machine was notably smaller than the previous versions he had seen in pictures. They had all been constructed in the same warehouse, so the scale was easy to judge. Each time Dr. Ellis built the machine, it got smaller and more efficient. In this third version, the machine took up a smaller footprint—it was about the size of two semi trailers, side by side, in the middle of the concrete floor.

The particle accelerator, so massive before, now hung at a 45-degree angle above the target area, a large circle painted white on the concrete floor next to the machine. Ellis had found a way to utilize more efficient materials by bringing some advanced technology back with him. He'd patented a few materials and released them into the world through his shell corporations and, in turn, had used that money to advance materials science, in this timeline, by several decades, in a matter of months.

They were also implementing an alternate power source for this version. The last two machines had run off of massive storage batteries, which had drawn energy from the city's power grid over a period of weeks and then released the stored energy in one massive jolt. In the second timeline, power outages and fluctuations in the availability of power had almost doomed the project—it had only been by dumb luck that someone had been able to keep the power on.

For this version, the elder Dr. Ellis had spent ten months creating a miniaturized nuclear power plant to power the device. The tiny nuclear fission reactor, smaller than those in use on nuclear submarines, was years ahead of its time.

Actually, the idea of mini nuclear power plants had been around since the early 1950s, when scientists had envisioned using nuclear power to propel rockets into space. It had been theorized that if a nuclear reactor could be sized to meet the needs of a rocket, then the inexhaustible power source would make quick work of powering men to the moon and beyond.

Advancements in miniaturization had worked for electronics and other components of rockets, but creating a viable combustion chamber that could withstand the effects of nuclear fission turned out to be more difficult. The project, known as NERVA, was officially scrapped in the mid-60s.

Like in the other timelines, there were massive rows of industrial batteries, taking up a good portion of the other end of the warehouse, feeding power into the machine through massive cables strewn on the floor. Today they would power up the reactor and begin preliminary testing.

Don carried the clipboard over to Terry, who was standing next to the control station—it was smaller than before, only a desk with two monitors and a keyboard. All the switches and dials that had controlled various aspects of the earlier machines were now handled internally by the custom software that Terry and a group of programmers had spent a year writing.

The preliminary testing phase of the machine was almost complete, and now they were incorporating two new variables—the alternate nuclear power source and an alternate "setting" for the machine.

This secondary usage for the massive machine was something that the other machines had not been able to do—not only could this device project items in time, it also had the capability to move them through three-dimensional space. It was a time machine, and it was also the first operational teleporter.

Don could hardly believe it.

In fact, once they had been able to get a handle on the power-consumption issues, the teleporter aspects of the machine had been not been terribly difficult to work out. The physical location of the object or person could be "adjusted," but the timeframe adjustment was left at zero. A positive value moved the item "up" the time stream into the future and a negative value moved it "down," or backwards into the past. But a value of zero simply caused the item to dematerialize and rematerialize at the same moment, but in a different location, as determined by a new set of coordinates implemented in this iteration of the machine.

Incorporating these additional physical parameters had sent the code programmers back to the lab. They needed to come up with a fourth-dimensional descriptor to assist the machine in determining where to "place" the physical object in space-time. Terry and Don were testing a new iteration of the software today, along with using the nuclear plant for the first time to power the machine.

Now, they were brainstorming ways to monetize the teleportation aspect of the device without creating a time machine in every garage. The machines would be massive and insanely expensive when they went on the market—only large corporations and governments would be able to purchase them, and only entities with very deep pockets would be able to power the devices and use them to transport goods around the world. It would disrupt almost every business on the planet—when shipping became almost free and instantaneous, how would many industries react? Don was convinced that the first industry to go under would be the airlines, but the older Dr. Ellis wasn't convinced—he didn't think that many people would want their "molecules rearranged" in such a way.

Nothing was set in stone, but Don thought he had figured out a way to permanently disable that aspect of the machine's variations—the elder Dr. Ellis didn't like the idea at all. The country was full of tinkerers, and the man was convinced that someone would eventually figure out that moving items in three dimensions was pretty much the same as moving them in four.

"Terry," Don said. "We ready for the test?"

Terry looked up and smiled—the man looked older than his 28 years. Don had read about Terry in the other timelines, and he was always the same—goofy, playful, always quoting movies. It was amazing, thinking about different versions of this man running around in different versions of this warehouse, working on duplicates of the machine.

"Yup, Don," Terry said, nodding. "We ran that first test of the teleport function from batteries last week, but they couldn't put out enough power. It's stunning, the amount of power needed."

Don nodded.

"I'm glad the reactor's done," Terry said. "It's been humming along now for a month, putting out a steady power stream. We've been using it to augment the power coming from the city and for our internal systems," he said.

"Well, let's get started, then," Don said.

3.6
WHITE HOUSE COUNSEL MEETING

Three days later, on the morning of January 26, 1997, President Clinton called a meeting of some of his most important advisors. Vice President Gore sat on one of the couches across from Cheryl Mills. Clinton sat in a chair at one end, near the massive Resolute desk, used by so many other presidents before him.

Between them, on the floor, was the famous presidential seal embedded in the carpet of the Oval Office.

Dr. Ellis felt out of place on the couch next to Mills—he kept flipping through his papers as if to organize them better, but in reality, he didn't want to make eye contact with any of these folks. They had no idea their world was about to change.

And Ellis couldn't believe he was here—it had gone far better than he had ever hoped. The president had listened to what he had to say at that bakery and then had invited him back to the White House, where they had talked at length about many topics. Mostly 9/11 and the Lewinsky affair, but Clinton had been curious about other things as well. Now they were going to discuss the topic with some of his senior staff members and the VP.

The last person to enter the room had done so by wheelchair—it was Charles Ruff, a famous D.C. lawyer that had just joined the staff as White House Counsel, brought in after the previous Counsel had left the job. Previously, Ruff had been a Watergate special prosecutor and top Justice Department official before being selected to oversee an office that was dealing with several crises at once: ongoing inquiries into the Whitewater affair, the 1993 firing of the White House travel office staff, and the improper collection of FBI files. Recently, the White House had been dealing with questions about the White House's role in helping raise money for the Democratic National Committee.

The woman next to Ellis on the couch was Cheryl Mills, a young black woman and the Deputy White House Counsel under Ruff. Historically, the 33-year old attorney had worked behind the scenes, defending the first family's interests and keeping their secrets. She was famous for keeping as much information as possible from the press—and she was famous for her arguments with other staff members.

None of them knew why they were here.

Ellis knew the Lewinsky information wasn't public yet, but he also knew that the White House staff was well aware of the situation. In fact, Lewinsky had been moved to a new job at the Pentagon in April 1996, because staff members felt she was spending too much time with the president and that, if word got out, it would look bad and affect his chances for reelection on the November 1996 ballot.

"Thank you all for coming," Clinton said, smiling.

He was a cool customer—Ellis could see why people continued to put their faith and trust in him, even after the litany of scandals and problems that had come before. He was a fiercely honest person, of a sort—he told you what you needed to know, and no more, and drew the line at his personal life. Ellis had read several biographies on the man, even before his 2004 assassination—interest in the former president had peaked after he was killed. In most cases, the biographies all said the same thing—Clinton believed with every part of his being that the private lives of public figures were off limits and had nothing to do with what kind of job the person was doing.

"I'm not sure what I'm doing here," Ruff began in his slow, deliberate way. Confined to a wheelchair after a mysterious illness paralyzed his legs, he looked back and forth between the people seated at the two couches.

Clinton smiled.

"I invited all of you here to meet a new friend of mine," he said, indicating Ellis. "This is Dr. Donald Ellis, a theoretical physicist from New York. Can each of you introduce yourselves, please?" Clinton asked, looking around.

Ellis put up his hand. He felt like an idiot.

"Excuse me, sir," he said to the president. "That's not necessary. I know everyone."

The room was quiet for a moment, as they all looked at him.

Cheryl Mills leaned slightly forward."I'm sorry, but I don't know you."

Ellis smiled. "The president just introduced me."

She turned and looked at Clinton. "Well, can I ask in what capacity Dr. Ellis has been asked to join us? I expected we were to discuss private matters, which this man doesn't have any knowledge of—"

"I'm here to talk about the 2000 election and how Mr. Clinton's dalliance with Monica Lewinsky will torpedo Mr. Gore's chances of winning," Ellis said, nodding at the vice president, who had not spoken yet.

The room was silent.

"And I'm not sure why you're smiling, Mr. President," Ellis said quietly. "This scandal with Lewinsky, when exposed, will paralyze your presidency. I know you don't want that—you have plans, such as the Middle East accord, but people will laugh when you present new ideas. All they'll be able to think about, until you leave office, is the blue dress."

"What 'blue dress?'" Ruff asked.

Ellis looked around at them.

"Mr. Clinton carried on an affair with White House intern Monica Lewinsky from November 1995 to March 1996," Ellis said, speaking from memory. "In that period, they had seven encounters of a sexual nature."

Mills leaned forward, starting to interrupt him, but the president held up a hand for silence, then nodded at Ellis.

"Go on, Dr. Ellis."

"Ms. Lewinsky was transferred to a new position at the Pentagon last April, when members of the White House staff became concerned that her presence could become a campaign liability."

He looked around, but no one challenged him on the statement, so he continued.

"Beginning next month, if everything continues unchanged, Mr. Clinton will 'revisit' that relationship and have two more encounters with Lewinsky. One encounter will involve a certain activity, and Monica will be wearing a blue dress that will eventually end up in the possession of Whitewater and Paula Jones prosecutor Ken Starr. He will test the dress and get a positive match to the president's DNA."

Vice President Gore leaned forward.

"Bullshit."

"Who is this person?" Ruff asked the president, ignoring Ellis completely. "I'm sorry, but I thought this information was restricted to White House staff only." Cheryl Mills sat back in her chair, crossing her arms. "Does this mean we have a leak? How does he know these things—did you tell him these things? And I thought things were over with Lewinsky. This is crazy—I don't know where this information is coming from, but it's—"

"It's one hundred percent accurate, Ms. Mills," Ellis said, taking out a stack of papers. "I have access to knowledge that you do not. I know what's happened up to this point and, as hard as it may be for the people in this room to believe, I know what is going to happen."

Bill Clinton put his hands up, stopping the others from asking more questions.

"OK, Dr. Ellis. Tell us what happens this year and next."

Ellis looked at him and sighed, then continued.

"The Whitewater and Travel Office scandals will die down, but Ken Starr will continue to aggressively pursue the Paula Jones case, looking for more evidence of Mr. Clinton's improprieties." Ellis and the others glanced at the president, who shrugged.

"I know we've discussed this before," the president said forcefully, "but I still think what should matter is what I do in this office, as the Commander in Chief. What I or others do behind closed doors—what does that matter?"

Ruff shook her head.

"We've had this discussion, Bill," she said. "You know that wishing it doesn't make it true."

"And part of it did take place in this office," Ellis interrupted.

Clinton shot him a look. "You know what I mean. Not in this physical room, but in my capacity as the president. The actions I take as president, the policies I implement—those are the things that matter. Not what I choose to do with my personal time."

Gore shook his head. "It doesn't matter, Bill. People see it as a distraction from the issues you should be dealing with."

Ellis nodded, agreeing. "That's true. And it besmirches the office of the presidency."

The others looked at him.

Ellis continued. "One of the Impeachment Terms that will be brought against you in January 1999 alleges that your misleading statements and deceit undermined the office of the president."

"Impeachment?" Gore asked suddenly. "Who said anything about impeachment?"

Ellis began shuffling through the papers in front of him and pulled out small, stapled stack of papers.

"I know it's hard for you to believe, but I know what I'm talking about. Here, let me pass this around," Ellis said, handing the papers to Clinton.

The president looked at it for a long moment, flipping through each page, before handing it to Mills.

"My State of the Union speech."

Ellis nodded. "Yes, you'll deliver it on February 4. I particularly like the part at the end about the 'thousand days' to the new millennium."

Mills handed the speech to Gore, who looked up at the president.

"Is this your speech?" Gore asked him.

Clinton nodded and got up, grabbing a stack of typed pages from his desk and passing them around. "This is what I've been working on, so far. I've seen Dr. Ellis' copy—it's the final speech. I stopped working on mine, because his is perfect—it's exactly what I wanted to say."

"That's not possible," Ruff said, flipping through the pages.

Ellis nodded. "It's a copy of his speech. And yes, the president will be formally impeached. The proceedings will consume this presidency and the nation for the better part of three years. Most of the president's close friends, and quite a bit of his staff, will be required to testify," Ellis said, glancing around. "The two of you," Ellis said, indicating Ruff and Mills, "will make up the primary members of his defense team, along with Gregory Craig, David Kendall, and Dale Bumpers."

The others glanced at each other. Ellis could tell that Cheryl Mills, for one, wasn't buying a word of what he was saying. Her arms were crossed, and she was looking at Clinton as if she wanted to be excused.

He took out another sheaf of papers.

"Here are the Articles of Impeachment," he said, handing them to the president, who glanced at them and handed them to Ruff, who immediately began reading them out loud.

"Trial Memorandum of the U.S. House of Representatives. Now comes the U.S. House, by and through its duly authorized Managers, and respectfully submits to the U.S. Senate its Brief in connection with the Impeachment Trial of William Jefferson Clinton, President of the United States," Ruff read.

"It doesn't matter," Al Gore said quietly. "Anyone can put together some words that sound like what the U.S. House would write, if they were going to impeach someone—in fact, you could probably copy the words from the Andrew Johnson impeachment. Anyone can make this up," Gore said, his eyes on Ellis. "I want to know how this man knows. The Lewinsky issue was resolved, I thought."

"Yes, it was—I've had almost no contact with her since last April. But I had been thinking about contacting her again—"

"What?" Cheryl Mills said, sitting forward. "Haven't you learned your lesson?"

Clinton looked at her. "What I do is my business."

Gore shook his head. "Not if the rest of us pay the price. You've got staff members getting her jobs to keep her away from you. Wasn't she going to get a job at the U.N.? Bill, you need to end it, now."

"It's not that simple," Ellis said. "Lewinsky was told that she could come back to the White House after the election and that she could have any job she wanted. She won't go away easily. She will confide in a friend at the Pentagon, a Linda Tripp, who will clandestinely record their conversations. Those recordings, along with the blue dress that Tripp convinces Lewinsky not to have dry cleaned, will form the basis of the impeachment."

The room was quiet.

Clinton nodded after a long moment of quiet. "I have met with Dr. Ellis several times over the past few days to go over his information. Believe me, what he says is the truth. What we need to do is figure out what we're going to do—"

"What we're going to do?" Gore said angrily. "What 'we're going to do' is have you castrated."

Clinton looked at him and slowly, a smile broke out on his face.

"Very funny, Al."

"Actually, that's not a bad idea," Cheryl Mills said, not smiling. "You need to learn to control yourself, Mr. President. Is it worth it to have this Lewinsky matter dominate your agenda for your second term, if it ever gets out?"

"It will get out," Ellis said, passing around more papers—both were photocopies of articles from the front page of *The Washington Post*. "And I assure you, Mr. Gore, these items are real. I have the technology to fake articles from the *Post*, if I cared to, but these are accurate."

Clinton took the papers and passed them around again after a quick glance—Ellis remembered reading somewhere that he was a very fast reader.

"The first sheet is an article from the *Post* on January 19 of next year, covering the president's defense team. The second sheet is a series of articles, including one from January 8 on Mr. Ruff's appointment, then another on the White House response in July to the subpoena for Mr. Clinton to appear before Ken Starr. The last is Mr. Ruff's opening statement at the impeachment trial."

The sheets went around, and Ruff read through his statements, including the one that he would present on the floor of the Senate. The room was quiet for several minutes as he read through the entire transcript.

The vice president broke the silence.

"What is a 'Wikipedia'?" he asked Ellis, holding up one of the sheets and pointing to the logo printed in the bottom margin.

"It's a website on the Internet," Ellis said. "The Internet will explode in popularity over the next few years. Wikipedia is one of the companies that will spring up as information migrates to the Internet—it is an online repository of all human knowledge that anyone with computer access can read, add to, or change," Ellis answered, looking at the vice president.

"Really," Mr. Gore said, smiling. "And you say anyone can edit it? How do they keep the articles from being defaced, or keep false information from being placed in the article?"

Ellis smiled.

"Actually, it's a very clever system. Say you have an article that you're interested in, like fly fishing. You might read the article and that's it, or you might register with the site to make some changes and additions—it makes sense, actually, to have fly fishermen keep that particular article up-to-date and accurate. You could also subscribe to it and, thereby, be notified via electronic mail, or email, of any further changes and updates."

Gore nodded. "So someone comes along and puts bad information into the Internet website, and you fix it. What keeps it from getting into a circle of updates? And how does the website make any money?"

"Good questions," Ellis said. "Wikipedia would have a group of administrators that oversee the site but don't make content decisions—they would look at how long each user had been registered with the site, how much content they had added and changed, and if there were any complaints. Some controversial articles, such as ones on abortion, or the 2000 presidential election—" he glanced at Clinton, then back to Gore— "can be 'locked' to prevent future changes or defacement. And because so many people use the site regularly, the website sells advertising in the margins."

Ruff put his hand up after reading the entire speech.

"OK, that was odd. Mr. President, if the facts we are discussing were to come to light, and I was asked to represent you in front of an impeachment hearing, that document I just read would be exactly what I would say. There are even references in there that I don't know off the top of my head, but I'm sure they're accurate—clearly I researched the speech before presenting it."

"Researched it? What do you mean you researched it?" Gore said angrily. "You haven't given it yet or maybe never will. This is all crazy," Gore said, shaking his head and standing, walking to the windows and looking out.

"No," Ellis said quietly. "You losing the 2000 election to George W. Bush because of this scandal, that's not crazy. It's true—I was there."

Gore turned to look at Ellis. Now, they were all looking at him.

"I remember that night," Ellis continued. "Watching the news, watching the returns coming in. Everyone thought it was a done deal when you lost Arkansas, and then—"

"I lost Arkansas?" Gore asked, incredulous. "Bill's home state?"

Ellis nodded.

"People had years to stew on this scandal and the others that came before. You get lumped in with the 'Clinton White House' and the 'shovel crew,' the nickname for Clinton staffers who spent all their time working to keep more scandals from coming out. But you lose Arkansas, and then it looks like you'll win Florida and take the election. Instead, it gets hung up in a statewide, county-by-county recount of every vote."

Ellis got out the *USA Today* that he'd shown Mr. Clinton on the morning at the bakery and passed it around.

"Hanging chads—do you know what those are?" Ellis asked the room. No one responded. "Those are the little pieces of paper that are punched out of a paper ballot. Sometimes, they don't get punched enough to fall out and remain attached to the ballot. Attorneys for Mr. Bush and Mr. Gore will spend days arguing about hanging chads, about what counts as a real vote and what does not. There will be a lot of discussion about absentee ballots and disenfranchised voters, and it will go on for almost a week, until the U.S. Supreme Court refuses to hear arguments on the recount. As Bush seemed to be the winner in Florida, his brother, the governor, and the Florida Secretary of State declared George W. Bush the victor and therefore the winner of the election."

The room was quiet.

"What seemed like a victory was actually a very negative thing," Ellis continued. "Many people thought that Bush stole the election, and the controversy followed him through his short term in office, weakening him. And the office."

Clinton watched the others in the room and nodded, making a decision.

"OK, here's what we're going to do," Clinton said. "I've read in the information from Dr. Ellis that two more incidents are supposed to take place between Ms. Lewinsky and myself in February and March of this year. I'm here to promise that those will not happen—especially the famous blue dress incident."

The others in the room, all except for Dr. Ellis, nodded.

"Next, let's put together some options and meet again in one week to see how best to get a handle on Lewinsky and this Linda Tripp person— from what I've read, our activities are over for a while before Monica decides to confide in her friend Tripp. It is she who, on the advice of a book agent, records the conversations that later end up as the primary evidence against me."

Ellis nods. "That's right. And Monica's need for revenge. If you can figure out a way to let her down easily, it would go a long way toward preventing the impeachment."

Clinton nodded, jotting something down on a pad of paper.

Ruff nods. "OK, that seems like a prudent course. The Whitewater stuff is running its course, and David Kendall has a good handle on all of that. I don't know where this DNC fundraising thing is going to go. The key here is to get in front of the matter, find out who might talk, and then convince them to keep it zipped up. As for Monica—Bill, that is the most important part. No further contact, especially anything—" he looked around, uncomfortable "—that could be traced back to you. You must smooth things over with her, and then avoid all further contact."

Clinton nodded and stood.

"Excellent—let's move forward on this immediately. And believe me, I want to see this problem solved as quietly and quickly as you both do. Thank you for coming," Clinton said to Ruff and Mills. "Can we get together again tomorrow and figure out how to proceed?"

Ruff and Cheryl nodded and turned to leave—she opened the door and held it open as he wheeled past her, already deep in discussion with her.

Vice President Gore walked around the couch as if to leave—he'd still been standing over by the windows, looking out at the Washington Monument—but Clinton put up a hand and then pointed at the couch.

"OK," Clinton said, looking at Gore, "now we can get on with the real reason we met."

Gore looked at Clinton, then glanced at Ellis.

"What do you mean?"

"My weakened presidency doesn't just cost you the election," Clinton said quietly, his usual jovial manner gone in a heartbeat. Ellis noticed that the president had kept it light while his Counsel was in the room, but now he'd turned serious.

"Something bad is going to happen, Al. Very bad. And Bush in the White House just makes it worse. We need to make sure you're the president, and that you're ready to deal with the situation."

Gore looked at Ellis. "What's going to happen?"

Ellis reached into his stack of papers and took out a small file.

"September 11, 2001, will start out just like any other day..." Ellis began, taking out the pictures and handing them to Gore.

3.7
A Reporter

Cassandra O'Neil sat at her desk, reading through a stack of reports and taking notes on a small yellow pad. Her desk was surrounded by dozens of others, and hers was a complete mess. A stack of books was piled up precariously on one edge, threatening to fall at any moment and block the aisle between her desk and the next one.

She was staring at a pile of papers, trying to decide where to start. The Clinton administration had certainly kept the press hopping, with one scandal after another, and it made Cassie suddenly wish she had a mole on the inside, someone to leak out an occasional lead. It was very difficult to cultivate those types of contacts, which was why reporters and journalists didn't like to share their sources.

She'd been toying with the idea of doing an overview of all the scandals that had taken place so far, but wondered if it was just beating a dead horse. She wanted to go back and dig more into the plane crash that killed Commerce Secretary Ron Brown and 34 others in Croatia last year and see if she could tie it to technology transfers to China. She thought there might be a series in it, or at least two good columns, but others she'd pitched the idea to said it had already been done to death.

Cassie decided to pitch it to her new editor—he'd only been brought on a few weeks back, but they were getting along great, so far. Of course that would change soon, if she didn't start bringing him some ideas of her own instead of waiting around for story assignments.

She set the report down and stood, knocking over another small pile of books on the floor next to her chair. She stepped over them and was walking to the editor's room, when she passed Billy, the mailroom clerk.

"Ms. O'Neil?" the boy said.

She turned. "Yup? Oh, hi, Billy. Just call me Cassie, OK? It's fine. I promise."

He looked at her blankly—he was wearing enormous glasses that looked like the bottom of Coke bottles—and then nodded, grateful.

She'd told him a dozen times in her two years here, and it still hadn't stuck.

"Thanks, Ms. Cassie. Doing anything for Christmas?" he said, smiling. It was mid–December, and most people were taking off for holiday plans, but Cassie shook her head.

She looked down at his cart. "What do you got for me?"

He turned and handed her a thick manila envelope, already opened. It looked stuffed full of papers.

"Don't worry," Billy said, smiling. "It's been checked. Some very strange stuff in there. The pictures are scary."

She nodded and took the envelope as Billy turned and walked away, continuing to deliver mail to the other desks. Cassie knew that the mail room routinely opened suspicious packages, and this qualified.

On the front was written "For Cassandra O'Neil's Eyes Only!" in big bold handwriting. That was a big red flag, right there.

The full mailing address of *The Washington Post* below it—no matter how crazy the rest of the envelope was, the wackos always got the newspaper's address perfect. Why go to all the trouble to spill out all your craziness and then send it to the wrong address? Every reporter in the bullpen probably got two or three hundred wacky pieces of mail a year—they jokingly referred to it as "fan mail." Cassie pitied the folks that wrote about anything even slightly mysterious, like UFOs or Bigfoot—they got easily ten times as much crazy mail.

As for a return address on the thick envelope, it said only "New York City, New York." The postmark read December 12, 1997, just a few days ago.

Cassie reached in and pulled the items out of the envelope.

It was a stack of papers in a manila folder. On the cover was scribbled a short note.

"Cassie, you don't know me, but we met once. You told me about your editor, Mike Foreman. You told me over drinks the story of how his cousin Abe was murdered in a small town in Virginia this September. You said it was a serial killer, and then you laughed and said it sounded made up, like a movie."

A chill ran up her back.

She didn't know Mike Foreman that well—he'd only just arrived, really—and knew nothing about a story like that.

Biting her lip, she set the envelope down on her desk and walked down the hallway. She stood outside his office for a long couple of minutes before knocking.

"Come in," he said from inside.

Cassie entered the office—it had a great view of downtown, with the

Capitol and Library of Congress peeking out above the trees.

"Hi, Mike," she said. "I was going to run a story idea past you, but I wanted to ask you a question first."

Mike nodded and indicated the only open seat in the office—every other surface was covered with either newspapers or open boxes, still filled with papers and books.

"Sure. What's up?"

"I just heard a strange story about you, and I wondered if it might be true," she said.

He looked up at her—she had his full attention.

"What?" he asked quietly.

Cassie looked out the window. "Do…do you have a cousin named Abe?"

Mike looked at her for a moment and then turned, looking at his computer monitor. "Yes, I did. He passed away."

He was not looking at her, so she leaned forward, one hand on the desk.

"Did he die recently, just a couple of months ago?"

Mike turned and looked at her. "Congratulations, Ms. O'Neil. You've cracked the case. Yup, that's my cousin—he was killed this pastSeptember in Virginia."

Cassie stammered. "Oh, Mike, I wasn't trying to pry or…"

"No, pry away. Yes, it was that serial killer with the white van," Mike said. He was staring at her, almost challenging her to ask him another question about it.

Cassie decided to let it go. She knew enough about it now to prove that the person who had sent the envelope knew what they were talking about—in fact, they knew more than she did.

She stood to leave. "I'm sorry, Mike. I didn't mean to…"

"How did you find out?" Mike asked. "We share the same last name, but—"

"I got a tip," Cassie said, shaking her head. "It's not important. And really, I didn't mean to pry. It's none of my business."

Mike's shoulders sagged as he looked back down at his desk. "I'd appreciate it if you keep this to yourself."

"Of course."

"It's just…his death really affected me, for some reason," Mike said. "It was just so out-of-the-blue. And then I needed to leave where I was and get a new job—that's why I'm here."

Cassie nodded. "And we're happy to have you. You're a great editor."

Mike nodded and smiled. "Ok, stop kissing ass. What's this story idea?"

She spent the next few minutes pitching her idea on the Croatian plane crash, and he approved her moving forward. After that, she stood to leave.

"Cassie, one more thing."

She turned. "Yes?"

"I'll tell you the whole story sometime, I promise," he said. "I just need more time to process it all."

She nodded and left, pulling the door shut behind her and letting out a big sigh on the way back to her desk.

When she got back to her desk, she read through the note again just to be sure. That was all the note said; she turned it over, but the back was blank. She flipped the folder open.

The first page was a photograph of the World Trade Center in New York City.

The massive building was in the process of collapsing to the ground.

Cassie recognized the building immediately—she'd been to New York enough times to have been up in the buildings. The photograph showed the second tower, behind the first, but there was a blackened, jagged scar near the top of the building, and a fire burned out of control. It looked like something had crashed into the side.

Cassie sat down at her desk and began poring through the contents of the manila folder. There were so many photos, and so many questions—each photo was more terrifying than the last.

On the last photo was a short note:

"Meet me at the Starbucks at the corner of K and Elm, 2:00 p.m., Friday the 22nd. I have much more information."

3.8
TELEPORTATION TRIALS

Testing of the Red Hook machine continued throughout 1997 and for the next two years. They worked hard to finalize the process and worked through the variations—time travel upstream and downstream, retrieval of items from the time stream, and simple teleportation of items without a change in the time variable. It started out slowly, with failure after failure, until they were able to perfect the energy levels required. Taking what the elder Dr. Ellis knew about the machine, and adding in some new ideas from the younger Dr. Ellis and a few recorded ideas from "Trish," Ellis' grown daughter from the last timeline, they were able to increase the machine's output and make teleportation attempts possible—and repeatable.

They improved the machine between the elder Ellis' frequent trips to Washington, D.C., and other locations to meet with representatives of the Clinton administration.

In Red Hook, portions of the machine were constantly being improved, to the point where the machine would sometimes be out of commission for a week or two as a subsystem was swapped out with a smaller, more efficient replacement. Each time, the machine would undergo testing to ensure it worked as well as before, or better.

By the fall of 1999, the Ellises were engaged in a debate—how best to monetize the teleportation aspect of the machine without letting the time travel variant out into the wild. Teleportation would revolutionize the world—communications, travel, shipping, manufacturing, healthcare—almost every aspect of human existence would be changed. Even if the machine was the size of two large tractor trailers and would retail for something north of 530 million dollars.

The Ellis's argued about how to reveal their machine to the world, what impact it would have, and how they would determine who purchased the first machines. It was an ongoing debate, without resolution. Often Stevens and Cassie O'Neal, their new communications coordinator, got involved in the conversations as well. Cassie had been brought aboard Power Blossom in a part-time capacity to help market and publicize the company's advancements in materials and battery technology. She still remained a reporter at *The Washington Post*, where Dr. Ellis had found her and brought her into the fold on the machine and its planned and potential uses.

"You know, the military will take it first, as soon as they get wind of it," Cassie argued at one of their discussions in late 1999. "They'll call it National Security and take it for use only by them and the federal government."

The elder Ellis nodded. "I know. We have this amazing breakthrough, one that could revolutionize humanity, and we can't move forward with it."

The younger Ellis agreed. "Right. We have to control it."

"It doesn't matter," the elder Ellis replied. "The whole point of this is to ensure that 9/11 doesn't happen and that you and your family and the hundreds of other families impacted on that day are protected. Getting into the teleportation business is a side issue, at best, and, at worst, a distraction from our real mission."

The younger Ellis shook his head. "I disagree. We've moved beyond that issue, I think. My family is safe, and we're well aware of what's coming. It's been pounded into my brain, and my wife and Tina know enough of the situation to avoid the World Trade Center for the next twenty years. I don't think I could get them to go in there if I had to."

Stevens nodded. "Same goes for most of the crew—they've all heard the stories. No one is going anywhere near the downtown area anymore."

"Good."

"And you said the president is on board," the younger Ellis continued. "You said he managed to avoid the scandal that brought him down in the other timeline. That never happened, and the other details never came out, so he's in charge, with no impeachment issues. Gore will win, and with his foreknowledge, rounding up the 9/11 perpetrators shouldn't be a problem."

"But it wasn't a problem last time either, and it still happened," the elder Dr. Ellis said. "All I'm saying is, why can't we wait until after 9/11 comes and goes? Hopefully, nothing will happen, and we can take the machine public."

Stevens and Cassie nodded their approval.

The younger Ellis glanced at them and then agreed. "OK, that makes sense. But I think we should start working on a retail version now. And this machine should be moved to a more secure location. Just look at what happened last time!"

The elder Ellis nodded.

"This machine is our insurance policy," the younger man said, gesturing at the machine. "It exists as a second chance for this timeline—if anything were to go wrong, we or someone we instruct could use the machine to go back and do a reset. It wouldn't fix this timeline, but it would give others a chance to move forward. It just seems stupid to have our insurance policy located 10 miles from downtown New York City. Regardless of what happens with al Qaeda, a population center like downtown Manhattan will always be a target."

"Where would you move it?" Stevens asked. "That would be a major operation."

"I don't know," the younger Ellis said. "Somewhere on the East Coast. You could put it in the middle of nowhere, Nevada or Kansas, but as soon as the feds detect the reactor, they're going to know something is up. You could put it in a Navy town, like Newport News or Groton."

"And Stevens, it won't be as big a task as you think," the elder Ellis said. "The machine will have to be disassembled and physically moved, of course, but most of the other equipment, machinery and interior items in the warehouse, we can simply teleport to the new location."

Stevens nodded, smiling. "I hadn't thought of that."

"You need to be located near an operating nuclear power source," Cassie said. "Or near an operating nuclear power station, like Indian Point."

The elder Ellis shook his head.

"That just introduces another problem—any incident, like Three Mile Island or Fukushima would irradiate the area and make the machine inaccessible for a hundred years."

"Fukushima?" the younger Ellis asked.

"Oh, sorry. In spring 2011 a Japanese earthquake and a massive tidal wave decimates central Japan, and the tidal wave inundates the four reactors at the Fukushima power station, located on the coast. It goes into meltdown—takes them months to get the reaction under control, mostly by dumping in seawater, which gets contaminated. After that, there's a major debate about nuclear power, especially from plants that are built right on the ocean."

The younger Ellis nodded. "That makes sense, but I think it's too dangerous to let the government locate the machine. You said that after 9/11, the government started scanning large urban areas with helicopter-mounted radiation detectors?"

"Yup," the elder Ellis said.

"OK, let me look into moving the machine," the younger Ellis said. "Send me your input, and I'll come up with a short list of alternate locations. And you think about how we're going to sell the teleporter."

The older Ellis smiled. "I tell you, if we could figure that out, we'd have more money than Midas himself."

Stevens leaned forward. "I have a question—if we can teleport, why can't we just take care of 9/11 ourselves? Couldn't we just locate Atta and the other hijackers and teleport them out into the middle of the ocean? Or into a jail?"

"Well," the younger Ellis smiled. "That's one way to prevent 9/11."

"Or strand them on an island," Cassie added. "No one would even know, and it would take a while before al Qaeda replaced them."

Ellis smiled. "That's not a bad idea. Maybe there'll be a smoke monster on the island with them, like the crash survivors from Flight 815. That would be funny."

The younger Ellis made a face. "Huh? What's a smoke monster?"

"*Lost.* The TV show," the elder Ellis said. The others were just looking at him. "The show with the creepy island and John Locke and the smoke monster? That hasn't started up yet?"

No one seemed to know what he was talking about.

"Wow," the elder Ellis said, glancing out the window. "It seemed like that show was on for a long time."

3.9
ELECTION NIGHT

"And how does it look?"

Ellis turned—it was President Clinton. He looked a lot happier than he had three years ago, when Ellis and the White House staff had worked so diligently to keep the Lewinsky scandal from surfacing. Clinton had gone on to sign several pieces of important legislation, including a historic expansion of healthcare coverage for less fortunate Americans. It was amazing what one scandal could destroy or derail—and it was amazing how removing one speed bump like the Lewinsky scandal could smooth out a president's legacy.

But Ellis had happily worked to change history—Clinton had also taken the al Qaeda threat more seriously and had, in the last year, bombed their Afghan and Philippine training camps on four occasions. Ellis didn't know if it would be enough to shut down al Qaeda, but at least this President Clinton was doing something about the real problem, instead of getting caught up in another pointless scandal.

Ellis thought Clinton must have come down from the residence to the Situation Room, located in the basement of the West Wing of the White House. Don knew that Bill loved all the TVs, of which there were seven—up in the White House residence, there were only two. Or maybe he had just gotten lonely. Hillary was out on the campaign trail, trying to help get out the Gore voters in the final push over the top.

Ellis had been watching the early returns come in from the East Coast—the 2000 election was well under way. None of the networks had made any predictions yet on who might win, but polling had Gore well ahead of Bush coming out of the debates, and he'd never looked back. Ellis smiled—it was odd how he was now an accepted, de facto member of the White House staff. He had a badge and everything. He half expected them to offer a reserved parking space soon.

Of course, Clinton and Gore owed him.

Clinton would now go down in the record books as the U.S. president who finally made peace in the Middle East a reality, working out tensions between Israel and every other country in the region, save Iran. His presidential legacy now was a historic peace plan, instead of a stained blue dress, five more years of jokes, and being blamed for 9/11.

And Gore—well, Gore would have been famous anyway, but more for his work on climate change. Now, he would be President Gore and potentially lead the country during one of its most challenging episodes. That was assuming they couldn't stop 9/11.

After what happened last time, Ellis wasn't 100 percent sure it could be prevented.

"Good, Mr. President," Ellis said, nodding at the TVs. "Gore's looking good. I'm sure things will go well."

Clinton smiled. "Go well? You saved my presidency, friend."

"Thank you, sir," Ellis smiled. "I'm glad I was able to help out."

Clinton smiled and looked at Ellis. "Modest, as usual. You fixed everything. I can't…I don't even want to imagine what might have happened."

"I don't have to imagine," Ellis said, his eyes on the TV. "This has all happened for me before."

Clinton nodded, looking at the returns. They stood quietly together for a long moment before Clinton spoke again.

"It disturbed me, greatly, hearing how I would die," the president said quietly.

Ellis looked at him and nodded slowly. Obviously the president had been reading through some of the materials Ellis had given him.

"The biographer was wrong. You were just the target of all that frustration, all that loss. Many people blamed you for not targeting bin Laden more in Afghanistan, but the experts at the time said…"

"Screw the experts," Clinton said. "I wanted a legacy, not to go down in history as the most incompetent fool ever to hold the office."

Ellis turned back to the TV. "And this time you have. You ended things with Lewinsky and made sure that those last two incidents never happened, the ones that really would have cooked your goose. And you got Lewinsky and Linda Tripp nice assignments on opposite ends of the country, where they could never meet and conspire to bring down a presidency."

Out of the corner of his eye, Ellis saw the president nod.

"Excellent ideas, all of those," Clinton said. "You have a knack for this sort of thing, don't you? You should be a politician."

Ellis shook his head. "No, that's the difference. A scientist admits that he doesn't understand, then seeks to understand. A politician is categorically incapable of admitting that he doesn't know something—he would rather B.S. an answer than admit he doesn't know."

Clinton didn't say anything.

"Present company exempted, of course," Ellis added.

"So, you're saying we're all actors? Politicians are just faking it?" Clinton asked.

"In a way," Ellis said. "A scientist must admit not knowing, so that he is free to seek the answer. How can one look for the truth, when he's convinced himself he already knows it?"

Clinton nodded soberly and said nothing.

On the screen, the CNN announcer mentioned that recent exit polling out of Arkansas put Gore ahead by six points.

"Didn't he lose Arkansas last time?" Clinton asked with a mischievous little smile.

"You know he did," Ellis said. "I just hope things continue to go our way. And I hope we can prevent al Qaeda from acting. Gore should be able to shut them down, when they start to put the plan into action."

"He looked great coming out of the debates," the president said again.

Ellis nodded. "Well, he had the entire transcripts of the previous versions to study. I would hope he did great, considering he cheated," Ellis said, raising his glass.

Several hours later, NBC called the state of Florida for Gore, and the election was over.

3.10
A New President

Ellis spent the first few months of the Gore presidency slowly extricating himself from the White House. He'd passed along all the information he had, and now it was up them to implement it. Some of the staffers came to him with questions about the future, but not nearly as many as had during the Clinton presidency. Gore's White House had a different feel than the Clinton regime, much more sober and directed. President Gore threw himself into his new position, so he didn't really notice Ellis backing off from the daily meetings and strategy sessions that had become the norm under Clinton.

Besides, Ellis had things to do. He was working more closely with his counterparts in Red Hook, working with the younger Ellis to perfect the machine. But Dr. Ellis had a good feeling about Gore—the man seemed to take all of the 9/11 information very seriously, considering the track record that Ellis had spent years building for the Clinton White House. Every quake and other natural disaster, predicted weeks ahead of time.

But Gore was more cautious, more reserved. Where Clinton had frightened Ellis by sending FBI agents to watch the 9/11 suspects, Gore was considering sending covert members of the military. Ellis liked the plan, but he had learned from the last timeline—if anything went wrong, he'd be the first to get blamed.

Several weeks into the new presidency, Gore called him in for a meeting. Ellis had been making excuses, explaining that he was traveling a lot, when in fact he had been at the warehouse, working with the other Ellis and his team on finishing the machine.

Ellis was waiting in his office when Gore came in and sat down.

This president was more formal than Clinton, yet he preferred to hold meetings outside of the Oval Office. Gore explained that he had become so disheartened by what he'd learned that had taken place in there, he had disliked the Oval Office ever since. Now, few meetings were held there.

"Dr. Ellis," Gore said, sitting down.

"Mr. President. Sorry about the meeting delays—I've been traveling."

He nodded. "You've been traveling a lot."

"Yes, I'm still trying to research more about al Qaeda's activities," Ellis lied. "I know how they operated in the original timeline, but I went to Munich to verify their activities."

Gore nodded. "So we know their plans, and we know their time-table," the president said. "When should we move forward?"

Ellis pointed at the files in front of them.

"Last time, President Bush started with standard surveillance, working from the playbook. The hijackers realized they were being watched."

Gore shook his head. "That sounds strange, now, hearing you say 'President Bush.'"

"Well, he was the president, and everything went to hell. You have to promise me that you'll keep things quiet this time."

"Because once we deviate from the plan, we won't know what's coming."

"Exactly."

Gore nodded. "We've done the hard work already. I have the military in charge this time, and they're using covert ops to observe the targets. So far, none of them have deviated from the plan."

"Good."

"Yes, that's very good," Gore agreed. He handed Ellis a timetable that showed where all of the 9/11 actors were located, with a grayed-out area of the table showing when they were scheduled to move into action.

"We've suspended *posse comitatus*," the president continued. "We're operating with three teams on the ground, tracking the terrorists. We've also put into place as many precautions as we can: succession plans for Congress and staff, surface-to-air missile emplacements on top of the Capitol building, Pentagon, and White House, and beefed up aerial security around Fort Knox. We're working to reduce occupancy in the World Trade Center buildings. And the Mall of America is undergoing an extensive 'renovation' and is closed to the public for the foreseeable future."

Ellis nodded, looking at the printout. Atta and the others were still in Florida, and three of the pilots were finishing their flight training, one in Florida and the other two in Pennsylvania. Nothing appeared to be deviating from the original timeline.

"This is excellent news, sir," Ellis answered, handing the sheet back.

Gore nodded. "So, why do you still look so concerned?" he asked as he put the sheet back in the folder and set it on Ellis' desk.

Ellis glanced up at the calendar—it read May 2001. "It's just—so many things can go wrong, and it all can fall apart so quickly. And it takes almost nothing—an overzealous cop, or a flat tire, or a mislabeled file. Last time, it was a couple of FBI agents and a *Washington Post* reporter. I've seen how this happens—one minute, things are under control, and everyone is confident. In the next minute, the towers have fallen, and we're all in a conference room somewhere screaming at each other."

"It's OK," Gore said. "I know what you mean. I'm keeping this project very close to the vest. Most of the new White House staffers don't know anything about it, or who you are, or why you have an office in the Old Executive Building."

"Good," Ellis said, looking around. "Actually, I knew this office before I ever came in here—it was to be John Marburger's, President Bush's Science Advisor. I bought him coffee once, at that Starbucks on K and 16th. I introduced myself and gave him a little insight as to what was coming, and we came back here. I spent a lot of time in this office, long before you and I ever met, sir."

Gore looked around at the room, as if seeing it for the first time. "But that would have been about now, right? May 2001? So where is he now?"

"No idea. He was good, though, and helped us get through some tough times," Ellis said, remembering back. It seemed like years ago—in fact, it was years ago, before 11/24 and the Mall of America and the Hajj. It seemed like an elaborate story instead of real life. He remembered the mob attacking the warehouse and the suicide bomber hitting the U.N.

"Yes," Ellis said, after a quiet moment. "It was bad there for a while. But now we have a chance to do it right. Just keep those military guys under control and don't wait too long. Believe me, stopping them is more important than catching them in the act."

3.11
TEA

In Fort Lauderdale, Florida, on the evening of July 6, three men were seated around a small table in a dining room. Middle Eastern music played quietly in the background. They were eating flatbread and hummus and sipping hot tea and discussing a series of plane trips they had recently taken—each had been able to successfully conceal a small, metal box cutter on them and had made it onto their flights with no difficulty.

The three men had been taking intensive flight training over the past six months and were talking about the relative difficulties of flying large passenger jets when a phone on the wall in the kitchen rang.

One man stood, answering the phone.

"This is Atta," he said in Arabic.

After a long pause, he replied back into the phone.

"God is Great. This is excellent. Thank you. Praise be to Allah."

Atta walked back over to the table and sat down, regarding the others. They remained silent for a long moment, before one of them, Marwan al Shehhi, spoke up.

"Is that the news we've been waiting for?"

Atta nodded. "Yes, my brothers."

The third man, Ziad Jarrah, nodded and smiled.

"The other teams have passed through Canadian customs without incident. God is Great. We are now in the final stages."

Groups of other Saudi Arabians were entering the country—each pilot had a team of people under him. "Are we to help get them settled?" Shehhi asked.

Atta nodded. "I'll be traveling in a few days to Madrid, so you'll need to get them settled. Get them new IDs, and the younger men seem to enjoy going to the gym. Don't let them get too settled into American life."

Shehhi nodded. "Madrid?"

"Yes, to meet Binalshibh. I'm sure he'll pass along the final instructions."

Jarrah spoke up. "I agree with you—I think the Capitol would be a better target. Why does bin Laden want to strike the White House?"

Atta shook his head and ate. "I'm not sure. He prefers it, so it shall be."

"Will you mention Indian Point?" In their familiarization flights over the New York area, Atta had mentioned the nuclear power plant as a potential target, but the other pilots were leery—the airspace over nuclear plants was more heavily restricted, so they were unable to do reconnaissance flights. The chances of getting shot down during the actual attacks would be increased.

"Yes, I'll mention it. But I think he will not approve." Atta looked at them. "Soon, the target list will be set, and we'll move into the final phase."

He raised his glass of tea to the others and smiled, drinking deeply.

3.12
ANOTHER SEPTEMBER 11

On the morning of September 11, 2001, the elder Dr. Don Ellis arose early from his bed. His well-appointed apartment at the warehouse was built in the high rafters. He'd had it constructed as high up as he could, and it had floor-to-ceiling windows that looked out on Manhattan. On this early morning, he stood and watched at the window. He hoped that nothing would happen on that day, but he couldn't be sure.

That was the problem with the past—it was all laid out in front of him, but once anything was changed, it became a Rubik's Cube, difficult to solve and unpredictable. Every change in the timeline spawned another dozen permutations. Any changes created layers upon layers of unseen variables.

Just a few days ago, he'd received a message: President Gore had lost track of the hijackers.

Even after all the warnings, all the reminders from Ellis about secrecy, the military had still been seen. The hijackers had disappeared and so far hadn't followed any of their former plans. There was no way to know if they had simply picked new planes and new airports. Maybe they were out there right now, looking out of the windows of passenger jets sitting on runways in Ohio and Texas and Maryland, waiting for the planes to taxi out and take to the skies.

Ellis didn't know what to do anymore.

Gore and he had met several more times over the summer of 2001, and Ellis had made suggestions about tightening up airline security, placing phone taps on suspected terrorists, shutting down the flight training schools. But the suggestions had fallen on deaf ears—Gore was more than happy to pursue the known hijackers, but he was leery about impinging on Americans' rights. The president had increased airport security but had chosen to not implement all of the suggested changes, fixes that might have stopped the attacks.

"But I don't want to treat the American public like criminals," the president had argued. Ellis had brought in a stripped-down version of President Bush's "Patriot Act" which, in this timeline, would probably never be needed. But many of the provisions contained therein were workable and useful, and Ellis had expected the suggestions to be quickly adopted.

Instead, Gore had balked at almost all of them.

"And what about these wiretaps?" the president had said at the time, indicating that portion of Ellis' proposal. "The FBI and the Justice Department would be allowed to have continuous wiretaps on suspects' phone and Internet conversations with almost no judicial oversight beyond an initial approval. Doesn't that seem like it could invite misuse?"

Ellis shook his head—he didn't want to argue civil rights with the sitting president.

"Mr. Gore, I'm saying that these methods were used successfully to prevent further attacks after 9/11. Presidents Bush and Cheney both, in different timelines, used the scope of the three Patriot Acts to ensure that no more attacks took place. These rules and regulations work, Mr. President."

Gore nodded, but Ellis could see that further discussion was futile. The new president was concerned about things that Ellis could afford to ignore. Gore hadn't seen the towers fall. This man sitting across the desk from Ellis had not seen the TV coverage of the radioactive wasteland that had been Houston, Texas, or watched the U.N. building explode.

Gore had an objectivity that Ellis had lost long ago. And, in the long run, it didn't really matter what Ellis thought—Gore was in charge, setting the tone.

He also had his own agenda—just weeks after entering office, he had moved forward with a "Green Initiative," made up of several different pieces of legislation that would increase domestic oil production and nuclear power, while decreasing American dependence on foreign oil. Ellis had to credit the man—it was a bold plan. The president had pored over all the information Ellis had provided from the two other futures and reached one conclusion: the United States had to wean itself off of foreign oil to secure its economic independence and remove the giant anvil that hung over the country's head—oil prices.

The initiative included building forty new nuclear power plants over the next ten years, funded by a carbon cap-and-trade system of taxes on industry. The power plants were already in the design phase, and ground would soon be broken to add a third reactor at a power station outside of Atlanta.

Manufacturers and industry leaders had, of course, balked at the cap-and-trade system, calling it a "Gore-ing" of American industrial might, but Gore had provided an interesting provision in the legislation to encourage widespread adoption: the traded "carbon" credits could be cashed in at a later date for free power from the nuclear plants, once they came online.

Ellis had been impressed by the audacity of the plan—Gore was taking a different tack to solve the long-term problem. But Ellis wasn't sure if it would work—besides, he was more worried about the short-term.

And today was 9/11. The terrorists were missing, and Ellis was on edge, waiting to see what, if anything, would happen.

He climbed from bed and walked to the window. It was already almost 9:00, and the towers were fine—if events were repeating exactly as they had gone before, the first plane would have already impacted the North Tower. He'd been awake since 5:00 a.m., listening for far-away sirens.

Ellis turned and did what he did first every morning—he flipped on the TV and tuned it to CNN. While he watched, he pulled clothes from the small closet and got dressed.

He missed his LCD flat screen, the one that hung on the wall of the family room of his old house, the one he rarely visited now. That TV had been huge, a 55-inch Hitachi LCD he'd picked up in January 2008 at an after-Christmas sale at Best Buy. Here, they didn't have LCDs yet—the first flat screens were just starting to come out, but they were plasmas, expensive and prone to burn-in that could ruin the screen. The best he could do was one of those old projection screens, the ones in the huge cabinets that stood out 18 inches from the wall.

And they didn't have high-definition TV yet, either—to his eyes everything looked grainy. He had enjoyed watching his news and *24* and *Fringe* in hi-def. In this timeline, *24* was supposed to premier its first episode in the fall, and he wondered how it would be received in this world. In his timeline, the nation had been reeling from the terrorist attacks and needed to fight back, even on the TV shows. Jack Bauer had been a salve for the nation's wounds, fighting terrorists with fierce determination and the occasional beheading.

In this timeline, *Lost* and *Fringe* were still years away from being on TV. J.J. Abrams was still working on *Felicity,* and *Alias* was set to premier in a couple of weeks on September 30. Ellis wished there was a way for him to bet on the outcome of the shows that he'd enjoyed years ago. For him, all the things that had taken place on *Alias*—the adventures of Sydney Bristow and the red matter and the connections with ancient history—it was all a memory.

And in this timeline, for many of his shows and movies, the screenwriters had yet to put pen to paper. He wondered, could he get hired in

Hollywood with all his great "ideas?"

And how had Ellis affected things? Would Gore as president change pop culture? Surely Hollywood would embrace President Gore more than they had President Bush—he remembered in his timeline, how Alec Baldwin had threatened to move to Canada if Bush won the 2000 election. Surely things would smooth out, but would they be the same? Had he already changed too much? He wondered idly which movies he remembered would get made in this timeline and which ones would not. Michael Moore's proudly anti-Bush film *Fahrenheit 9/11* would never be produced in this timeline, making Ellis the only person in this reality who had ever seen it.

Sometimes, he wondered if the changes he made behind the scenes could cause any problems. So far, in two different timelines, he'd arrived and immediately begun setting up shell companies and investment accounts. He had access to all the financial information for the next fifteen years, so it wasn't difficult to predict stock prices.

The difficult thing to do was to not make too much or to draw too much attention to himself. He used several different companies to do his investing and several different corporations to hide his money. He employed the same accounting firm from California, a group of people he had never met but who were in charge of making sure he paid the minimum in taxes and maximized his returns.

Ellis had made a few bad bets as well—it looked too suspicious if all of his holdings skyrocketed in value, but he always knew when to cut his losses before things went south. And his losses were dwarfed by his gains.

But was he taking money out of the system that should have gone to other people?

He didn't think so—that was one of the market's strengths, the liquidity. His buying stocks didn't necessarily mean someone else didn't get that stock; more likely, it meant that they would pay a penny or two more for their shares. Ellis had been diligent, and if any stock deviated too far from the "historical" data, he would slowly move out of the position, no matter how lucrative it had been. He didn't want to do anything to upset the market.

Of course, if someone were to get really curious, they could trace all the money back to him. But it was all under a fake social security number anyway, one of several that he'd brought back from the future.

Ellis finished dressing and walked out of the small room that he used for an apartment. No one was in—he'd given Terry and the others the day off; in fact, he'd sent them all to Atlantic City for a much-deserved mini-vacation. They had no idea why—where he was from, today was a national holiday, a day of mourning. Ellis didn't want them downtown, either, if there were to be an attack.

He walked over to the machine. It was beautiful.

And small, compared to his earlier machines. This one was compact, sturdy. Much smaller than even his last machine, but that came from building and rebuilding and rebuilding—Ellis had long ago figured out how the machine operated, so now, with each iteration, it was just about making it smaller, more compact, more efficient, without affecting performance.

All the recent tests had gone well, and with the ideas and plans he had jotted down, this should be the most powerful machine ever. He'd been working on it for seven years, ever since he'd arrived in the timeline. The teleportation aspect of the machine made it even more powerful, but it hadn't added any size to the apparatus—in fact, if he ever had to build it again, he thought he just might be able to make it portable.

He smiled and tapped on the computer panel, inputting a series of coordinates, and then stepped into the center of the white disc painted on the floor beneath the accelerator. He strapped on the bulky arm controls—it looked like half of a cast for a broken arm, but instead of being covered with doodles and good wishes, this large glove was interwoven with several dials and a large control pad.

Dr. Ellis tapped at the pad, and immediately the machine fired up. The room filled with the sound of cracking ice, and he felt the room begin to spin. As many times as he tested this machine, he never quite got used to it—

The warehouse faded out of reality, replaced with a dense group of trees.

As the world solidified around him, he fell slightly—a quarter inch, straight down onto the grass beneath his feet. He looked around at the cemetery—no one had seen him. And that was a good thing.

Ellis looked at the control glove—everything looked fine. A small monitor showed the machine status: "Awaiting Return Request."

There were two major problems with teleportation: the ground beneath your feet and other people.

Terry had worked out the other issue with teleportation, which had been a doozy to fix—appearing somewhere where there was already something else, like a tree or a car. The coordinates entered into the targeting computer told the machine where to move his pattern, but it took some tweaking with the software to make sure he wasn't fused with an object. Terry had finally figured out the trick—an instantaneous pre-teleportation phase testing, which scanned ahead of the incoming object to ensure there was nothing "in the way" when the teleported person or object arrived. The phase testing automatically adjusted horizontal or vertical positioning on its own, with no operator guidance, trying different locations within a few feet of the desired coordinates that were "unblocked."

But it didn't help with the ground beneath. Local fluctuations in elevation, ground height, paved and unpaved roads, and buildings with multiple floors made it very difficult to predetermine the vertical positioning of the object or person. To prevent accidents, the machine did two things—the phase testing also scanned the ground out ten feet in each direction of the optimal arrival location and extrapolated the height of the surface, and then it added a quarter inch, just as a safety precaution.

There was no way to know if any witnesses would be around, which is why they tried to materialize test subjects in forests or inside small rooms—it made the likelihood of encountering witnesses less likely.

But no matter how many times he did this, Ellis was always worried that he would be spotted.

Ellis stepped from the small stand of trees and made his way into the quiet cemetery. The sun was just coming up, and there was no one else out yet, but he still walked quickly over to where he needed to go.

The ground was empty here, but he knew it well. The headstones weren't here—in fact, in this timeline, they never would be. But Ellis remembered the graves of his wife and daughter as if they stood before him. He knelt, touching empty air where, in some other universe, the cold marble headstones stood, their names carved in the side. On some other hillside like this one, another him stooped over their graves, weeping.

Ellis knelt for a long time, wondering what had happened to them. They weren't here, but the Sarah and Tina that lived in this timeline were not his—he had not been there at this Tina's birth or been able to spend much time with Sarah. He longed for her great stories, but any time he spent at the Ellis home in Jericho was just awkward. They all treated him like a strange uncle. His past was different from theirs, his future radically altered. They spoke stiffly around him.

Dr. Donald Ellis wondered exactly how old he really was. Ellis still celebrated his birthdays on August 31, just as he had always done, and had just celebrated another one two weeks before. But it wasn't as simple as it had once been. He'd been born in 1968 and it was 2001, so by normal reckoning that made him chronologically 33, the same age as the Ellis who lived in this world, the one who had invited him to Thanksgiving dinner last year.

But Ellis had done the math, counting up the number of August 31s that he had experienced, and this past week was his 53rd. Looping through time, reliving the same years over and over, it could make things difficult to follow.

Like the music, or TV, or the movies. He found himself craving particular songs by artists whose bands hadn't even been formed yet. Coldplay had been a favorite, but they had only released "Parachutes" last year—"The Scientist" and "Clocks" and "Warning Sign" only existed on Ellis' iPad, for now, and possibly had begun gestating in the mind of Chris Martin, their lead singer. They would be released on the 2005 album, *A Rush of Blood to the Head*. Ellis knew the music would come in a few years, and he still missed it. Martin would meet Gwyneth Paltrow backstage next year at a concert, and they would marry in 2003. Their daughter, Apple, would be born in 2004.

It was disconcerting, sometimes, the extent of his knowledge. But acting on the knowledge had the dangerous side effect of changing the outcome. What if he conspired to meet Chris Martin backstage at that 2002 concert and somehow prevented his meeting with the Hollywood starlet? Would he and his band still go on to write the music Ellis remembered? If not, then those songs would exist only in his memory and on the iPad in his safe.

He'd brought some stuff back with him, but not a lot—there hadn't been room on the iPad to bring the *Lord of the Rings* trilogy or *Iron Man*. Really there had only been room for *Inception* and a smattering of *Seinfeld* and *Modern Family* episodes.

Ellis flipped on the TV again. It seemed like so much of his time lately was spent watching, like those bald Observers on *Fringe*. But, on this September 11, nothing happened.

3.13
HOLIDAY PLANS

Gore released his cap-and-trade system in October 2001. On the news, the Dow Jones Industrial Average lost almost 9 percent of its value, one of the largest one-day declines in history. The fact that the market fell as far as it did told astute market watchers two things.

First, the cap-and-trade system was a "harbinger of doom" for U.S. industries still clinging to old ways. American companies that designed and produced heavy industrial goods, along with the companies that transported, marketed, or supported them, were looking at a sea change—a government-mandated tax of at least thirty percent on top of their other production costs and taxes.

American competition took another body blow—after unions, and taxes, and tariffs, and a host of other costs, the American companies simply could not compete with the prices of items made in other nations. The cap-and-trade systems, which were quickly labeled "Gore-nomics," would signal the death knell for American manufacturing and other heavy industries.

The second things that astute market watchers took away from the massive drop in the Dow was that the legislation was likely to pass Congress and be signed into law—the market was already baking that information into their valuations of stocks.

Caterpillar and Rio Tinto and a dozen other companies that were involved in or supported heavy manufacturing were hammered on that first day after the new initiatives had been announced. For a week straight, the market continued to drop. It was well into its sixth straight day of major losses when Dr. Ellis was escorted into the Oval Office to meet with the president.

Gore was sitting on one of the couches that flanked the large seal on the floor in the middle of the room. One thing Ellis had noticed was that the seal was always changing—each president redecorated the office to his own personal style, and that included the massive presidential seal that took up the majority of the rug that spanned the middle of the room. Couches and low tables were aligned on the rug as the president preferred, but Ellis always wondered why they, the presidents, went to all the trouble to get new rugs made. He guessed it had something to do with making their mark on the office.

"Dr. Ellis," Gore said, standing and taking his hand. He sat back down and indicated the TV, which he'd been watching. "What do you think about the market?"

Ellis sat, glancing up at the TV. "I don't really follow finance that much," he lied, looking back to the president, who was still staring at the TV. Ellis and his corporation had betted big that the cap-and-trade system would send the market into a tailspin, and they had profited handsomely from it.

"Well, I don't know what to make of it," Gore said, shaking his head. "I'm trying to put us on a new path toward a more independent future."

Ellis nodded. "It's tough medicine. But a lot of folks are just looking at the short term."

Gore nodded, agreeing. "So, September 11, right?" The president sat back, smiling. "Bet you were glad when nothing happened that morning."

Ellis leaned forward and helped himself to a cup of coffee from the tray on the table in front of them. Silence hung awkwardly between them as he poured, and then he sat back and sipped.

"You guys always have the best coffee here," Ellis said. "Bush's kitchen made their coffee a little differently. Have you ever had Chicory coffee?"

The president shook his head.

"Chicory? Nope, I've never had that."

"It's a southern thing," Ellis nodded, setting his coffee down. "I'm surprised you haven't had it, being from Tennessee. Anyway, chicory is a plant, and you can dry and grind it just like coffee beans. In some places in the south, a cup of coffee is really half coffee beans, half chicory. It gives it a unique flavor."

They looked at each other for a long moment, neither wanting to speak. Ellis sipped again at his coffee.

"My point is things change," Ellis said. "You and Bush did things differently but ended up with the same result. Bush spooked the terrorists with too much surveillance, and the attacks happened on Black Friday, November 24. Now that the terrorists have disappeared, your team needs to be working doubly hard to find them. We're not out of the woods yet," Ellis added.

"I agree. Finding the terrorists, before they can act, is the first priority of this administration—"

"I doubt that," Ellis said quietly.

"What do you mean?" Gore asked, his eyes narrowing.

Ellis pointed a finger at the financial news broadcast on the TV. "Knocking the market on its ass with your cap-and-trade system is clearly the first priority. And it's taking your focus off 9/11."

"There was no 9/11. There will be no 9/11," the president countered.

"But there may be," Ellis answered. "I don't know when it will come, or from what direction, but as long as Atta and his team are in the country, they will continue to plan this attack until they can carry it out. Your team, and you, should be spending all day, every day, looking for these people. If you don't, the country will be brought to its knees, sooner or later."

Gore shook his head.

"We're doing everything we can, Dr. Ellis," the president said. "The terrorists are on every watch list and on the radar of every police officer in the nation. They will be caught, I guarantee."

Ellis held his tongue.

"And my cap-and-trade system is not my only focus," Gore continued. "Though it has been taking up a lot of my time. But I'm trying to fix the long-term problems that cause al Qaeda and other groups to send teams of terrorists to this and other countries in the first place."

Ellis wasn't sure what to say.

Gore stood and began pacing. "We, as a nation, need to get out of the Middle East, now that there is a relative peace. Our policies do no good, and we wouldn't be bogged down in their affairs, if it weren't for oil. Look at Africa—a hundred countries, and we're not in there, supporting one nation over another, befriending, bombing, supporting, rejecting. We don't meddle in Africa, and that's a good thing—those nations should be free to follow their own destinies. And, in the same way, I think the Middle East needs to set its own course."

"Without our involvement," Ellis added.

"Right," Gore said. "Our support of regimes that provide us with natural resources has retarded the growth of the region, making the fight a one-sided affair. Nations that agree with us and sell us oil get better toys, more tanks, more money, and those that don't get bombed. I'm telling you, every time we bomb another country in the Middle East, we create a hundred new terrorists."

The president stood by the TV and watched the ticker of stock prices run along the bottom of the screen for a moment—all the numbers were in red.

"I, for one, think it's a noble plan," Ellis said. "Reducing our dependence on foreign oil is a great idea. I just don't want you taking your focus off the goal here, which is catching Atta and the others. I need you to remember—they're out there right now, plotting and planning. They don't care about your future plans for diplomacy in the Middle East."

Gore nodded and walked back over to the twin couches that flanked the seal on the carpet between them. "You said there were two reasons you didn't like the plan," Gore asked, sitting.

Ellis nodded. "Yes, there are. The second reason is a little...intangible, but serious, nonetheless. You've made a big change, sir, taking the country in a new direction with the cap-and-trade system. And, as you know, any big changes can reduce the reliability of my foreknowledge of what's coming."

"You think this new legislation could affect Atta and the others, somehow?"

"I don't know," Ellis said, sitting back. "Probably not. But any major changes to the timeline make it harder for us to predict what's going to happen. Just look at the market—your actions are affecting Americans in very basic ways today, with lost money. Businesses will close, people will lose their jobs. Other businesses will thrive, ones that can take advantage of the new regulatory environment. When things change, it introduces additional unpredictability. And the system can only handle so much of that. What if events skew off into a new direction, one that we can't foresee?"

3.14
BLACK FRIDAY

"Can anyone say 'anti-climactic'?"

The elder Ellis looked at his younger self and smiled.

"Excitement is overrated, believe me. I can only cross my fingers and hope that 9/11 or 11/24, or whatever it might be called in this timeline, doesn't happen."

The Ellises and Stevens and Cassie were sitting at the conference room table off the main computer lab in the warehouse in Red Hook. It was the evening of 11/24/2001 and the day had come and gone with no attack.

Cassie pushed today's front page of *The Washington Post* across the table—her article was running, front and center. It predicted a large attack on Black Friday. "Well, let's just say that my editor's opinion of me has declined significantly in the last 24 hours. I'm suddenly glad that's not my only means of employment," she said, looking at the others.

The elder Ellis looked at her. "If you have trouble imagining what the event will look like, why don't you go back through my photos again?"

"That's not what I mean," Cassie said. "I'm just saying that I can't keep running predictions about an event without something happening. And every day we get farther from 9/11, your information gets less and less accurate, right?"

The younger Ellis nodded. "That's right. The economy's in a different place than it was in the prior timeline, and there have been layoffs and plant closings that we couldn't predict. That, in turn, has affected people's lives. That shooting at the Ford plant last week, that didn't happen in the last version of events, right?"

Cassie nodded. "No, that was new. Labor relations are being strained in all the Rust Belt industries."

After a while, the elder Ellis spoke. "As time passes, things will move farther and farther away from what I know," he said quietly. "Gore is making changes in the economy, and with the terrorists gone to ground, it's anyone's guess what will happen next. They could still attack."

The younger Ellis leaned forward.

"Is that why we're using the Faraday every night now?"

A new protocol, established over the last few months, was to wheel all the sensitive, portable electronics related to the machine into a large metal cage. Known as a Faraday cage, the metal-screened enclosure protected items inside it from external electrical fields and electromagnetic radiation. The military used them to protect sensitive equipment from EMPs, or electromagnetic pulses, which sometimes accompanied nuclear detonations.

"Yes," the elder Ellis said. "The computer lab walls were converted over in 1998, so the entire room serves as a cage. The electronics on the machine are built to be far sturdier, but the computer and some of the more sensitive equipment need to be protected." Ellis looked around, but no one challenged him on it, so he continued. "Stevens, do you have anything?"

Ellis' loyal employee in at least two different timelines shook his head. "No sign of Atta or his people. None of the PIs or security firms we engaged was able to find any of them."

Cassie shook her head as well. "None of my people have heard anything either. I've checked in with several FBI offices nationwide—they're still looking, of course, but there are no leads."

Stevens looked at the elder Ellis. "It's possible they've called the whole thing off and returned to Saudi Arabia."

The elder Ellis shook his head. "They haven't called it off."

"It's possible," Cassie said. "Bin Laden may have called them back to Afghanistan to work up new options, or maybe they've been arrested or killed. Accidents happen."

"Not all of them. And not Mohammed Atta—he's committed," the elder Ellis said.

Stevens spoke. "I know we tabled the idea of moving the machine, but I think we should still be discussing it."

The elder Ellis shook his head. "No, I don't want to risk it. The machine would be out of commission for at least two weeks. Anything could happen."

"I think it needs to be moved," the younger Ellis spoke up. "I know in the last timeline there were two machines, but here, we only have one. It's our insurance policy—if anything happened to it, we could theoretically build another one, but it would take time. And if anything happened to you"—he looked at the elder Ellis—"it would significantly hamper our efforts, even with everything written down and recorded and saved in four different locations. I think the machine is too important to be left here, within sight of the 9/11 and 11/24 attacks. We need to dismantle the machine and move it to a more secure location."

Cassie chimed in. "And if we move it, it will make it harder for the government to find. The reactor gives off a lot of signature energy—one low pass by one of those NEST helicopters, and they'll know we're here."

"And co-locating it with a source of nuclear power will allow us to mask our reactor's power signature," Stevens continued. "And, in the case of an emergency, serve as a backup generator for the machine." Stevens had his own mini police force to protect the space around and above the machine, but if the U.S. military showed up, it would be a mismatched fight. But the guard force could probably take control of a co-located power source like a nuclear reactor, if needed, to temporarily power the machine.

The group had talked about this before, on many occasions, and it seemed all the kinks had been worked out of the system. Now, they were just waiting for the go-ahead from the de facto leader of their little band.

The elder Ellis was staring at the back of the loading doors, out on the main floor. He couldn't see the twin towers, but they were in that direction. The others at the table knew what he was staring at, what he was reliving, and they remained silent.

After a long moment of quiet, he nodded his head.

3.15
A Sliver of Darkness

It was the afternoon of Christmas 2001, and President Gore was sitting in the Oval Office. He had the Baltimore NFL game on and was preparing his speech for tonight's live holiday broadcast, when his chief of staff and a group of Secret Service agents burst into the room.

"It's a terrorist attack—someone crashed a passenger jet into one of the towers of the World Trade Center in New York," the man said, his eyes wide with the knowledge that Gore and he had discussed only days before.

"Mr. President, come with us," the lead agent said brusquely. "There may be an attack imminent."

Another agent gathered the items on Gore's desk and stuffed them into a bag. Outside the door, he heard other members of his staff hurriedly gathering their items as they were escorted from the area.

Gore grabbed the man's arm. "Are we under attack?"

The agent shook his head. "Not sure, sir. We just got a scramble order—we're taking you to Andrews. The vice president is in the building, so he'll be heading down to the bunker." In another part of the White House, President Gore heard a siren begin to keen.

Gore nodded. "OK, get the staff to safety."

His chief of staff nodded as the agents took Gore out the doors and into the Rose Garden. Just across the expansive lawn, a helicopter adorned with the presidential seal was setting down onto the green grass.

Gore's press secretary ran up to him as he crossed the lawn, handing him a folder.

"That's all we have so far, sir. We'll confer after we're in the air."

Gore nodded and climbed into the chopper. He saw three F-16 fighter jets streak over the city, racing westward. He glanced up and saw that the U.S. Capitol dome was fine—at least that hadn't happened yet.

"Get me onto the frequency with those fighters," Gore said as he sat in the chopper and pulled on the headset handed to him by the pilot.

The pilot gave him a thumbs-up as the door was slammed shut from the outside. He saw the other Secret Service agents scramble across the lawn and back into the building—he hoped they were able to get everyone else out. His wife, Tipper, and the girls were on vacation in Arizona, so they were safe. He'd been sending Tipper and the girls on a lot of vacations lately—and none of them to New York. Tipper had finally started asking about the frequency of the trips, but Al had dodged her questions.

Two other choppers with identical markings lifted up from the lawn and hovered at treetop level—there would soon be three helicopters heading to Andrews, reducing the chances of his being shot down.

The president adjusted his headset and heard clicking as the frequencies changed.

"Delta Foxtrot," a voice said, "the scrambled fighters are forming a perimeter defense around the city. Over."

"Roger that, base," the pilot said over the radio. "Any intel yet?"

"Negative, nothing," the first voice said—it was D.C. airspace control. Located at Washington National Airport, the air traffic controllers for the airport liaised with the ATC operators at Andrews Air Force Base to keep the airspace over the Capitol region clear of all unauthorized air traffic.

Gore flipped through the reports in the folder—one plane into the Trade Center, several other planes unaccounted for. The situation was unfolding quickly. Nothing so far about the Pentagon. He glanced westward and saw the massive building and imagined it on fire, smoke pouring out of a gaping hole in the western side of the structure. The smoke would rise and blanket the river, and then the Capitol—

The president tapped at the microphone connected to the headset.

"D.C. control, this is POTUS."

"POTUS, this is D.C. control. We read you loud and clear sir."

"Listen carefully—all efforts are to be made to intercept any planes headed for the Capitol building or the White House. Are there any unaccounted for aircraft on such a course, airman?"

There was a long silence. Gore saw the other helicopters keeping formation with his.

"No, nothing sir."

"Good," the president said, relieved. "Where were those three jets going?"

"Heading west to check out a plane—it's not responding to radio hails. It's traveling southeasterly. Just crossing into Maryland from Pennsylvania."

"OK," the president said. "Keep me in the loop on that plane.

Anything else unaccounted for?"

"Several more civilian planes."

"I'm almost to Andrews, and I'll meet with the FAA soon. We'll be shutting down nationwide air traffic soon, but go ahead and land all the D.C.-area planes right away."

The pilot in the seat in front of him waved and pointed down—they were already almost to Andrews. The pilot was going to land as close to the massive Air Force One as possible.

Gore nodded and looked back at the files. "D.C. control, this is POTUS. There might be a second plane vectoring from the west into the South Tower of the Trade Center. Do you have any reports of a second plane—"

A flash of light bloomed from below the helicopter. A sliver of darkness raced up into the air.

"Missile! Surface to air missile!" the pilot shouted. He jerked the helicopter sharply to the side, throwing the president against the window. For a moment, Gore was staring straight down through the glass at the tarmac and trees below him.

The helicopter next to the president's exploded in a fiery flower, spraying pieces of the helicopter out in all directions. Burning shrapnel banged against the airframe next to the president's head, and one of the cockpit windows shattered. Smoke poured from the underside of the president's helicopter as it began to spin lazily from the sky. Gore saw pieces of the other helicopter raining down onto the concrete expanse of the tarmac below—the runway was lined by a high barbed wire fence on all sides that separated the base from the dense forest beyond.

The pilot struggled to keep the helicopter airborne, but the best he could manage was a wide, flat spin. The shrapnel from the other chopper had punctured hydraulic control lines on the underside of the helicopter, and it was coming in hard. As the helicopter smashed to the ground, the landing struts underneath collapsed, splaying outward.

Gore was dazed—it felt like everything was moving in slow motion.

He slowly reached up and pulled the headphones free as smoke filled the cockpit. His left leg was hurting, and his head was throbbing. He waved at the smoke, but it wouldn't clear.

The pilot was pushing at the cockpit door, trying to get it open. Gore saw that the copilot wasn't moving at all. The president leaned forward to shake the copilot's arm—the man's head turned to one side, and Gore saw a long piece of helicopter blade sticking out of the man's face. His dead eyes were wide open.

Suddenly, the door next to the president was wrenched open, and hands reached through the smoke to the president. Someone managed to undo his seat belt. A Secret Service agent he did not recognize pulled him from the helicopter and picked him up, throwing him over his shoulder.

Gore's leg sang out in pain as the agent raced away from the wreck. In a moment of clarity, Gore saw that fire was running up the man's legs, but the man ignored it.

Fifty feet away from the downed helicopter, the agent stopped running. He put Gore down and slapped at his pant legs, putting out the fire. Trying to stand and putting weight on his leg, Gore cringed and bit his lip.

In a moment, the agent was carrying him again, running for the bulky 747 marked AIR FORCE ONE that sat on the tarmac a hundred yards away. Gore saw two large black SUVs racing toward them from the plane, with armed Secret Service personnel hanging on the sides.

From the trees near the base fence line, Gore heard automatic weapon fire, and he felt the agent pull him down to the ground, putting himself between the president and the trees. He glanced over his shoulder and saw American soldiers moving toward the fenced area south of the runway.

The terrorists must have fired a surface-to-air missile at his helicopter as they were coming in to land. That meant the terrorists had more teams than they had in the previous timelines, or that in this timeline they were targeting him directly. They'd never done that before, he thought, and that could mean they had more teams in the country. Gore could see American soldiers firing into the woods, and then return weapon fire from somewhere in the trees—

"Sir, get down!" the agent said. Behind him, near the tree line, Gore heard a loud hissing sound, like a snake.

Another missile shot up into the air, chasing after the third chopper that had been marked with the presidential seal. As Gore watched, the missile spun in the air like a cat and targeted the helicopter, which tried to spin out of the way at the last moment. The missile found its mark, and the helicopter exploded in a massive fireball, raining debris down onto the runway.

"Jesus!" the man shouted as the helicopter exploded behind them. Gore realized that the man wasn't a Secret Service agent—he was the pilot from his helicopter. Gore also saw for the first time that the pilot had his sidearm out and was ready to defend them, if needed.

"Thank you," Gore said weakly, tasting blood in his mouth. He reached up with one hand and felt at his forehead. It was slick, and his hair was wet.

"Don't do that, sir," the pilot said. "They'll get you all patched up on the plane," he said, indicating the massive plane still a good distance away.

As Gore turned to look, he saw the SUVs arrive, parking between the fallen president and the firefight taking place at the edge of the tarmac. Hands roughly grabbed Gore up and bundled him inside the other SUV, and within twenty seconds, the car had reached the bottom steps of the stairway that led up to the plane. Four Secret Service agents helped him from the vehicle, and several more agents formed a circle around the base of the staircase, weapons out.

"OK, here we go," the lead agent shouted, and the four of them dragged the president up the stairs.

"My leg, I'm not sure..." Gore said, his eyes feeling heavy, and then the world swam into darkness.

3.16
AIR FORCE ONE

Gore woke to the sounds of a heart monitor.

He sat up slowly and realized that he was in the small infirmary on Air Force One. His head felt strange—solid and heavy.

"Doctor?"

The woman turned and smiled.

"Glad you're awake, sir. I'm Doctor Rory. You had a pretty bad laceration on your head from the crash—it looked like there was some glass in the wound as well. Debris from the other helicopter must have come through the window and struck you in the head. It's fine—it wasn't a serious wound. You've also broken your left leg, probably from the landing. You're all fixed up now."

"Good," he answered. "Can I get some water?"

She nodded and called outside of the small room. In a moment, Gore's chief of staff entered, handing him a bottle of water.

"You said the leg was broken?" Gore asked the doctor. "But it didn't hurt that bad."

"Adrenalin," the doctor answered. "It's amazing—it masks the pain. You're all splinted up now, and the head wound looks fine."

His chief of staff nodded. "Good. The meeting's already started—you up for it?"

The available members of the cabinet were videoconferencing. Gore nodded and climbed from the bed.

Out in the hallway, he saw several armed soldiers between the infirmary and the larger press area, which was full of support staff and White House staff—there hadn't been time to get the press onto Air Force One. Gore leaned on his crutch and gingerly made his way aft to the primary conference room.

The screens were lit up, and several people were arrayed around the table. Vice President Joe Lieberman's face took up one whole screen.

"There you are," the Defense Secretary said from his screen. "Good to see you, sir."

Gore nodded as the other members of his cabinet applauded lightly and wished him well. The president sat down heavily in a chair that an airman held out for him, leaning his crutch against the table.

"No big deal—the helicopter got shot down, we crashed, I cut my head and broke my leg."

The room grew quiet as the president spoke, and he wondered if they were all thinking the same thing. Not only was this a coordinated attack, but the terrorists had anticipated his evacuation to Andrews Air Force Base and Air Force One and had set up a group of soldiers with automatic weapons and surface-to-air missiles, in an attempt to take him out as he fled to safety.

"So what do we know so far?"

The vice president cleared his throat—it sounded remarkably clear, considering he was in the Presidential Emergency Operations Center (PEOC) under the East Wing of the White House. "Well, it appears to have happened nearly as predicted, but three months later. There is still one plane in the air, unaccounted for, but we think it will be heading toward the White House or Capitol building."

Gore nodded. "Yes, it was over Maryland when I was landing. What happened to it? And what about the second World Trade Center plane?"

"There was only one World Trade Center plane, so far," Lieberman said, and on another monitor the scene from New York appeared. One of the Trade Center buildings was on fire, but the South Tower was undamaged. "While you were in the air, a plane crashed into the Pentagon—a large part of it is on fire."

President Gore looked at the monitors and noticed someone was missing. "Where are the Joint Chiefs?"

"The video link into and out of the Pentagon appears to be down," Lieberman said, looking at Gore. "They were on with us when the plane struck—it apparently hit the outer ring, western side, away from the river and the offices of the senior military staff. The broadcast center is under the innermost ring, so they should be broadcasting. They were on the air with us for a while, but then the connection was broken, so they've got people working on it now."

Gore nodded. "OK, so only one Trade Center building and the Pentagon—that makes two planes unaccounted for. What else do we know? Any planes in the vicinity of D.C., or Minnesota, or Fort Knox?"

Some of the other cabinet members looked at him strangely, and he remembered that they were not all familiar with what he was talking about.

Lieberman seemed equally surprised. "No other planes, sir."

"OK," Gore answered. "We need to ground all FAA air traffic immediately, in case there are other planes. Make sure there's nothing in the airspace around Fort Knox or the Mall of America in Minnesota."

On one of the other screens, the static disappeared, and a man in a military uniform appeared. His hair was disheveled.

"Mr. President. Good to see you, sir."

Gore nodded. "You too, Anderson. What do you have for me?"

The chairman of the Joint Chiefs straightened his uniform. "The situation here is under control—the fires are out, but they did burn a portion of the building. The plane impacted the southwest side of the outermost ring, near the helicopter pad."

The others nodded.

"Reports are that it was a Boeing 757, but others are saying it was a missile. We're working to confirm—"

"Oh, no," Gore heard someone say and looked at the other monitors. Lieberman was holding up his hand, his face as white as a sheet.

"I'm sorry to interrupt," Lieberman said, his face ashen. "I'm just getting the information now, sir, about that missing plane over Maryland. It apparently has crashed in downtown Baltimore. The jets scrambled and forced the plane to turn, and the hijackers crashed it into the harbor area, near the football stadium. There was a football game going on at the time in the Baltimore stadium, a Ravens game. I haven't gotten any more information than that, sir."

The room went quiet.

"OK," Gore said after a long moment. "The FAA has my orders—land every plane in U.S. airspace. All international flights approaching the United States need to be diverted and landed at non-sensitive airports or military bases, if necessary. I want every plane down, now. Scrambled jets are to force any planes down that don't comply with the mandatory FAA grounding."

Lieberman nodded, then looked up at the screen. "What if they don't land voluntarily? If it looks like the hijackers plan to crash into a target, are the jets authorized to shoot them down?"

Gore sat back. This was one of those decisions he hated making. Such a loss of life…

"No, don't shoot any planes down. Just force them down. We have to protect the Capitol and any other major facilities or population centers, but I'm not going to make it worse by shooting down a plane full of innocent civilians."

The Pentagon spokesman spoke up. "Are you sure, sir?"

Gore nodded. "Yes, I don't want to make this situation even worse."

"But there may be more casualties."

"I know, but I'm not killing innocent Americans."

3.17
THE PATRIOT ACT

In the months that followed the Christmas Day attacks, the nation reeled at the loss of life in the four coordinated terrorist attacks. The lone Trade Center tower stood as a testament to its fallen compatriot, and the destruction at the Pentagon was more extensive than previously estimated. But it was the images of devastation and loss of life at the destroyed Baltimore Ravens stadium that became the primary image identified with the attacks.

Spirits and the American psyche were buoyed when it was discovered that the passengers on the Baltimore plane had fought back—family members of the passengers had been able to speak to some of the passengers before the plane went down. Between the phone conversations and the knowledge that F-16s were chasing their aircraft, the passengers had decided to act. They'd coordinated their efforts and launched a counterattack on the hijackers, who were evidently all in the cockpit. The heroic passengers of United flight 93 had evidently not been able to breach the cockpit doors in time. The pilot, having been forced away from downtown D.C. by fighter jets, had crashed the plane into what must have been a pre-chosen secondary target, killing tens of thousands.

But President Gore had remained calmly in control of the nation throughout the crisis, a steady hand at the wheel. Dr. Donald Ellis noted, along with many other people around the world, that President Gore seemed less inclined to go to war than other wartime presidents in the nation's history. Ellis couldn't help but compare Gore to the other presidents he had known before, and Ellis quickly realized that he had made a serious mistake in attempting to predict Gore's behavior.

Gore took his time, gathering information about al Qaeda and the Taliban, not using any of the foreknowledge available to him or information about the other timelines to construct his case. The CIA and FBI gathered independent data over the next three months as the United States recovered from the staggering body blow inflicted upon it by a loosely-organized cabal of international terrorists. And the president was a diplomat, enjoying the goodwill that poured in from the rest of the world over the horrible Christmas attacks.

In January 2002, Gore and Lieberman personally went in front of the assembled U.N. Security Council with information about the attacks. They showed that agents of al Qaeda had carried out the attacks and that the Afghanistan-based Taliban had provided them with safe haven. After a week of deliberations, the Security Council voted to allow the United States to invade Afghanistan.

Also in January 2002, President Gore was agonizing over the passage of the Patriot Act. He knew that in the original timeline it had been passed into law in October 2001, six weeks after their attacks, but there were so many provisions in the Act that he was categorically opposed to. He met with Lieberman on several occasions to work out the final details.

During one conference, they had been discussing the section on surveillance. "I still think we should improve airline safety," Lieberman stated again as they worked through the pile of papers on the conference room table between them.

Gore looked up at him.

"Personal liberty and freedom. We mustn't forget that this country was established on personal freedoms. I'm reluctant to expand the reach of wiretaps, and I've seen what can happen with the indefinite detentions. You read those Guantanamo Bay and Abu Ghraib reports."

Lieberman nodded. "Disturbing to read about, even though none of that really happened. At least, not yet."

"It's not going to happen," Gore said. "Not on my watch."

Lieberman nodded, conceding the point. "But I still think we should increase border security, and I think upgrading the TSA with more scanners and inspectors is necessary."

Gore shook his head. "I don't think more airport security is the answer. It's intrusive, it's unnecessary, and it treats each airline passenger as a potential terrorist. At the very least, it would make the people suspicious of their government. I won't restrict flights or rework airline safety measures—I think it violates citizen's personal rights."

Lieberman shook his head but held his tongue. Gore was the president, and he set the agenda. This version of the Patriot Act would leave out many of the provisions of the "original" bill that Lieberman had studied in depth. He just hoped that the U.S. government didn't regret not flexing those additional powers.

3.18

AFGHANISTAN

The war in Afghanistan began shortly thereafter, and Gore threw the weight of the entire U.S. military behind it. Many, including Dr. Ellis, expected him to simply throw a few dozen missiles at the country, but Gore surprised many by sending ground forces into the country.

The Taliban was defeated quickly, and Gore made the tactical decision to not build bases or establish any kind of military presence in Afghanistan. He'd read about his "predecessors" in the other timelines—they had become bogged down in lengthy, Vietnam-style wars that would last a decade, cost half a trillion dollars, and have no real or lasting impact on the world's geopolitical scene.

So Gore made his intentions known—he would invade, bring down the Taliban, put into place a temporary government, and then ask the U.N. peacemakers to step in and do the heavy lifting when it came to "nation-building," a word that sounded promising to Gore but, in accounts from the other timelines, often became a synonym for intractable wars with no concrete resolution.

But on Iraq, Gore overplayed his hand. He repeated the actions he'd taken to convince the U.N. to sanction the Afghan invasion, but in this case, he met a wall of opposition. When he presented proof of the existence of weapons of mass destruction in Iraq and lobbied the U.N. for sanctions, the first step to bringing the nation down, he found fewer sympathetic ears. International sympathies were running out, and Gore couldn't count on the world to support every American action.

In the previous timeline, President Bush had used the bully pulpit and the military might of the most powerful nation on Earth to convince the world that the Taliban and Saddam Hussein needed to be removed.

But Gore seemed reluctant to force the will of the American people on the rest of the world—it was as if he had decided that free will and the right for a country to determine its own destiny were of the ultimate importance. In many speeches, he came across as begging the world to help America deal with the threat in Iraq. In the eyes of some, President Al Gore was not an international leader, but a simpering salesman, cajoling the world to "do the right thing" and join his coalition of forces.

April and May 2002 came and went, and President Gore was no closer to invading Iraq. He knew it needed to be done, that the Hussein threat would not simply go away, but he couldn't bring himself to break from the world and unilaterally invade without the tacit approval of the U.N.

Gore was convinced that he could sanction and embarrass Saddam Hussein into giving up his position, but it was not to happen. Slowly, he lost his influence with the rest of the world.

Nations began to look away from the United States for direction, for advice. They stopped looking to the U.S. or the U.N. for permission to invade neighbors or run skirmishes along borders or seize boats on international waters.

Pulling out of Afghanistan didn't help the situation, either.

Gore had assumed that routing the Taliban would be seen as a positive, and he had assumed that a new, moderate government would quickly form. But the nation, mired in two thousand years of invasions and infighting and tribal warfare, could not suddenly put in place a working government. The pullout of American forces on the last day of March 2002 had caused a massive power vacuum, and it was quickly filled by drug lords, Pakistanis with dreams of expanding their nation's footprint, and a hundred low-level Taliban officials who had gone to ground and avoided capture by the Americans.

Within days, Afghanistan was embroiled in a bloody civil war.

It played out on the evening news, and every day, America's failures seemed more obvious. What had seemed like a good idea—wipe out the Taliban, then allow the nation to self-determine its next course of action—had been woefully naïve.

The nations of the world began to doubt the United States—doubt its military might and its resolve to defeat evil around the world. There was talk that the United States would simply abandon its aggressive verbal campaign against Saddam Hussein and the current government in Iraq.

And, soon after, people and governments began to doubt the resolve of the Americans in supporting and protecting their best friend in the Middle East: Israel.

In late May, when Iran began to threaten the sovereignty of Israel, Gore could not bring himself to make the hard decisions.

It began with Israel making unscheduled and completely illegal fly-overs of several locations in western Iran. To reach those locations, Israel had to overfly portions of Iraq, but carefully circumvented Saddam Hussein's extensive anti-aircraft batteries. Iran had recently begun claiming they had reached the ability to process and create their own nuclear fuel. Israel couldn't afford to let those centrifuges get operational, so they began covert flyovers to assess Iran's nuclear capability. Israel had plenty of satellite access due to their close ties with the West, but low-altitude flyovers allowed them to do radiation counts from heights as low as 2,000 feet above the suspected facilities. By lowering sensitive Geiger counters from tow lines, the planes were able to establish baseline radioactive levels in and around the facilities and to pinpoint the locations of Iran's "research institutes."

These flights over two hostile nations were inherently dangerous. Israel carried out over a hundred before they had an incident. On June 20, 2002, one of the planes lost hydraulic pressure and crashed, breaking apart on impact. The pilot, Ganei Omer, parachuted to safety but was promptly captured by Iranian officials.

From the wreckage of the plane (the towed radiation detection equipment had survived the crash) and the coerced confessions of the 22-year-old pilot, Iran proved that Israel was violating its airspace. Israel also flew over Iraqi and Iranian airspace on three more occasions as they worked to rescue the pilot.

On the last unsuccessful rescue sortie, on June 24, an Israeli Air Force plane shot down three Iranian planes. The Iranian planes were older and slower, and one of the three happened to crash into a hospital, damaging the building and causing even more deaths.

It was at this point that Gore made a critical mistake—he spoke out against Israel.

After private consultations with Israeli leaders, he went on the record at a White House press conference as saying that Israel had been "out of line" in violating international law by flying illegal reconnaissance missions over Iran.

Perhaps it was fear that motivated Gore, or perhaps his memories of that horrible Christmas day and the helicopter crash. His limp was still noticeable, and a cast was still on. The president hobbled to the podium, looking weak. He felt weak as well; weak, un-presidential, indecisive.

But it didn't seem to matter—there was nothing that he could do to go back and fix the Christmas attacks. Even with years of forewarning, he hadn't been able to prevent them. With the foreknowledge, he had been able to mitigate the disaster somewhat—after Gore and the FBI had lost track of the hijackers, it had seemed prudent to assume that the Trade Center was still a target, and the number of people in the buildings had been reduced to a minimum. Because of this, portions of the North Tower of the World Trade Center had been empty on the day of the attacks. And because the hijackers had decided to only attack one of the World Trade Center buildings, the South Tower was spared and still stood in New York City.

The government had also carried out some of the same preparations at the Pentagon—it had been impossible to evacuate the whole building for the last six months of 2001, but they had reduced staffing down to a bare minimum, spreading out the remaining employees throughout the building to reduce casualties. The Pentagon had also been holding very regular evacuation training sessions, and surface-to-air missiles had been deployed on the roof, although they were not ready in time for the attacks.

The attack on the Capitol had been averted completely, but only out of sheer luck—because of increased traffic at the Newark airport, the plane destined to strike the Capitol or White House had been delayed by almost a half hour, giving planes on the ground time to scramble. The pilots of the hijacked plane had diverted to what must have been a secondary target, killing almost 19,000 at the Ravens Stadium in downtown Baltimore.

But still—they had been attacked. Gore hated that, and he hated the fact that Israel was provoking the already unstable regime in Iran into more action. Wasn't there enough going on already?

So, in the press conference, in a moment of indecisiveness, he had spoken the words that would precipitate an international crisis: "I don't agree with Israel when they say they are just protecting their assets. It was a violation of international law to fly over those other countries. The flyovers of Iran's facilities were unjustified and illegal and must end immediately."

3.19
A FLAMING SWORD

Two days later, a man stood on a raised platform in front of a crowd of hundreds that seemed to pack every corner of the large chamber. Rows and rows of chairs arced in half-circles around him as he spoke, giving the chamber the look of a theater.

"We now begin the confrontation," the leader of Iran began, speaking slowly and carefully to allow the translators to do their work. "We will now move to begin the removal of Zionism from the region, and soon, the entire world will thank us for our efforts, for our sacrifices, and for our courage."

"They will recognize the strength of our conviction and will tremble at the power of our weapons. But, in the end, they will thank us for bringing about the end of a troubled and troubling regime that forces its will on others through any means necessary: false promises, imaginary and counterfeit negotiations, decades of illegal spying, a staggering history of violence, and now the immoral and unjustified unleashing of their military planes and spies on a search for trumped-up lies." He spoke quietly, each word freighted with four decades of hatred.

"Israel will pay for their spying, for their lies on the national stage. And as all of you are aware, even their great puppet, the United States, has condemned their actions to the world. We concur with the words of president of the United States, Mr. Al Gore—'the flyovers were unjustified and illegal.' But, my friends, the elected senators and representatives of our great nation, I have good news. Their bombing runs and spying pilots and mighty explosions were interesting to see on the television news. But it was all for nothing."

As the room went silent, the leader of Iran turned and pointed to a large television screen behind him. An image appeared, showing what looked like pipes and machinery underground; on one of the pipes was painted a large sword. Above the pipes, a hole opened up in the roof, a perfect circle with blue sky beyond, and the audience gasped—they realized that they were looking up, from inside an underground silo. The pipes and machinery were actually an underground launch tube.

The screen flickered for a moment, went green, and then switched to a different camera, this one above ground. The nose cone of the rocket began to slowly rise out of the hole. The back of the lid that had covered the missile silo was clearly painted with the international Red Cross symbol.

"We developed these missiles last year," the leader of Iran continued. "Using secret underground laboratories the Zionists could not discover, not if they searched the deserts of Iran for a thousand years. In those facilities, we have perfected our weapons. We have reached into the forge and fashioned our new sword. Now, praise be to Allah! We will use our swords and strike at their hearts." The leader of Iran shouted, his arms in the air, victorious. "We shall drive the Zionists from our midst and, at the same time, teach the hulking monster of the West a valuable lesson in humility."

The smoke and fire were coming faster now, shooting out of the hole on all sides. Finally, the rocket began to move, up and out of the silo. It climbed on a column of fire and smoke, arcing up into the sky, heading west.

In the distance, six more rockets lifted off from the ground and chased after their leader.

"Our flaming sword will strike at their hearts," the leader said, but no eyes turned to look at him on the podium. They all watched the cloud trails rise slowly up into the sky.

3.20

PALMACHIM

The Palmachim Air Force Base, located in central Israel near the ancient coastal city of Yavne, housed the primary rocket testing grounds of the Israeli Defense Forces. Tucked away on one side of the air base, men and women also monitored Israeli airspace for intruders. The base served as the primary testing facility for the Israeli Space Agency. There was a nuclear research facility, the Soreq Nuclear Research Center, and a small nuclear reactor, built to take advantage of the base's relative isolation.

In the dark facility, all eyes were on the TV monitors showing CNN, which was carrying the live speech from the leader of Iran. Many of the men and women in the room were palpably nervous.

When the screen began to show what looked like Iranian missile launches, the soldiers, including Station Chief Gan Sorek, raced back to their stations.

"I have six launch detections, sir," a young woman spoke up.

Gan was looking at his monitors as well. "I see them. Scramble fighters."

Gan turned to another man seated next to him.

"Hanan, can you set up a track? We need to know exactly where these are going," Gan said.

The man nodded. "Surely. I will let you know when the track is done."

The Station Chief nodded and stood, walking over to another person, who was holding out a black phone for him.

"Yes, this is Gan Sorek at IAF Palmachim. We've confirmed the incoming missiles and are calculating the paths now."

"Sir!"

He turned and looked at another young man—they seemed to get younger by the year. Gan handed the phone back and ran over to his monitor, where the young man was pointing at a cloud.

"Sir, it looks like another swarm. These are smaller missiles or rockets—probably Katyushas. It looks like they're coming out of Syria."

Gan nodded. "A coordinated attack. Inform the Air Force and let the missile defenses know that the big missiles from Iran are the priority. Tell them to not waste their interceptors on the little ones."

The young man nodded.

Gan walked back over to his station. He tapped at the computer keyboard with his one hand—he had lost his left arm in the Six-Day War. He signaled the computer to transfer his screen to the main screen, a large color display that hung on the wall at the front of the room.

On the screen, Gan could see the seven incoming missiles, crossing into Iraq. They were fast and big, and that scared Gan. Scared him and pleased him at the same time—they were big enough to carry nukes, but that meant they were also big enough for the Arrows to shoot down. They needed big targets but could be confused by little ones, which was probably why operatives in Syria were releasing a fusillade of smaller rockets to confuse the interceptors.

As he watched, another cloud of small rockets appeared to lift off from southern Jordan. This new cloud was going almost due north—they could pass over the Dead Sea and strike populated areas in the south, like Hebron and Jerusalem.

"Sir, another cloud of rockets from Jordan—"

"I see them," he said.

A coordinated attack meant that the Israeli Defense Force (IDF) members manning the Arrow systems, deployed throughout the nation, would have to carefully target the larger Iranian missiles, since the smaller rockets would act like chaff to draw off the interceptors. The Arrow 2 system, developed and produced by the Israelis and Americans, was good at shooting down larger incoming missiles. It followed on the successes of the Arrow 1 system, which had been deployed in 1986 during the height of President Reagan's Strategic Defense Initiative. The United States had essentially used Israel as a proving ground for many innovative anti-rocket and anti-missile technologies. Gan had even heard that the new version, the Arrow 2 Block 2, would be able to shoot down missiles in outer space, but those wouldn't come online until 2003.

Hanan turned to Gan.

"Sir, I've got the tracks."

Gan looked up at the main screen and spoke loudly so that everyone could hear.

"OK, three at Jerusalem, one each at Haifa, Tel Aviv, Ashdod, and Be'er Sheva. Assuming they're Shahab-2 missiles and not something new, then they are single warhead and have an affective range of 500 kilometers, so they should easily reach their targets. We need to get countermeasures up, as well as any jamming we can initiate."

Gan knew that the word Shahab meant "meteor" in Farsi, but, to him, the streaks on his screen looked more like comets.

Over the next few minutes, the men and women were bent over their keyboards and talking into their headsets, coordinating the IDF response to the incoming missile and rocket attack.

"Fighters are in the air, sir," one of the technicians said.

"Good. Direct them to the missiles and see if they can shoot them down."

"Sir," a woman soldier spoke up. "I'm on the line with the southern command—they have selectively launched all of their interceptors, but the missile made it through. It seems the other rockets were flying lower to the ground, and the interceptors locked on them instead," the woman said grimly. She gripped her headset as she listened, and her face changed to shock. "They're reporting a detonation in Be'er Sheva, sir. A mushroom cloud."

Gan shook his head and looked down at his hand, not sure what to do next. He felt the shock run over him, like water poured from a bucket. It was cold. He felt like he had in the hospital, when they had told him they would have to take his arm.

For a solid twenty seconds, the room was completely silent.

"Yes!" one of the others finally said, breaking the silence. He pointed at the screen.

One of the missile tracks was gone. As Gan watched, two more disappeared.

"Is that the eastern defense group?" he asked the young man, who nodded.

"Yes, sir. They've shot down all three of the missiles headed to Jerusalem!"

The technicians whooped and cheered, but Gan was watching the clouds of smaller rockets coming in from Syria and Jordan. As he watched, dozens of smaller circles blossomed on the map as the rockets found their marks in towns like Ofakim and Kseifa and Arad in the south. Those would be equivalent to artillery shells, capable of destroying a factory or a small block of homes, but in great numbers, they could do real damage. And they were forced to completely ignore them due to the larger Iranian missile threat.

"What's left?" Gan asked. "It looks like the one headed for Haifa and two more for Tel Aviv and Ashdod. Those two were traveling close together—their targets are only miles apart."

Hanan spoke up.

"Gan, what about the surface-to-air missiles? Could we get assistance from the ships in port in Haifa and Tel Aviv?"

Gan nodded. "Yes, they may be crewed. Get on it."

He turned back to the other technicians. "What's Central Command's status? Are all the interceptors gone?"

One of the technicians tapped at his headset. "They fired a full spread and are working to reload now. They're going to aim for the two southern missiles—they've entered Israeli airspace and are over Jerusalem now. Central is waiting until they're over a less populated area."

"OK, OK," Gan said, waving his hand.

Hanan whooped and Gan looked up—the missile headed toward Haifa had disappeared.

"A surface-to-air battery on one of the ships in the harbor," Hanan shouted, smiling.

The next few minutes were tense as they waited and watched the screen. In the meantime, more Syrian rockets rained down on the unprotected cities in the north. Finally, another swarm of anti-missile ordinance was launched.

On screen, one of the missiles bloomed and winked out of existence. It was impossible to tell which one—the tracks were identical. At the last second, the remaining missile veered slightly to the north, and Tel Aviv, the nation's second-largest city, was reduced to a radioactive cloud of rubble and glass.

3.21
PHONE CALL

Over the next twenty-four hours, the situation in the Middle East went from tenuous to all-out war.

In Washington, Gore learned about the nuclear attacks on Tel Aviv and Be'er Sheva but made no move to retaliate. He was unsure of how to proceed. He felt that Israel had gone too far in their covert surveillance of Iran's nuclear program, but that was all moot now. Gore called Ariel Sharon, the Prime Minister, to offer his condolences.

"Thank you, Mr. President," the Prime Minister answered coldly.

Gore sat back. "Ariel, what have you learned so far?"

There was silence on the other end. Finally, he answered. "At least 200,000 dead, initially. And the radiation clouds are growing and spreading, so the casualty numbers will grow."

"I'm sorry, Ariel. I don't know what to do—" Gore answered, trying to be supportive, but the Prime Minister cut him off.

"Here's what you do, Mr. Gore. You support your friends. You don't make statements that embolden rogue nations."

Gore was taken aback. He wasn't sure what to say, and he wasn't used to hearing other heads of state speak to him like this.

"Ariel, the American people support—"

"Mr. President, can we be honest for a moment? I don't think you like us, or like what the Israeli government has been doing of late. But is that a good enough reason to throw away sixty years of friendship and cooperation? We're the only moderate nation in the region, and your only ally."

Gore nodded. "You're right, Ariel. We support you—I support you. What can we do to help?"

"Thank you, Mr. President, but I have to go now. If you would like to assist the nation of Israel, arrange for medical and disaster teams in Tel Aviv and Be'er Sheva. Both are coastal cities, so you have permission to make landings and assist us."

"We can do that, Ariel. We'll get our forces underway immediately," Gore answered.

The Prime Minister spoke up. "Oh, and one more thing. Make sure none of your military units are downwind from Tehran."

The line went dead.

Gore knew what that last statement meant, but he didn't want to think about it. Israel had the right to defend itself, but Gore was also worried about the effects of nuclear war. Even a limited local conflict could plunge the world into nuclear winter.

3.22
RETALIATION

Israel's retaliation was swift and fierce.

Four hours after the loss of two of its five largest cities, nuclear missiles from Israel destroyed Tehran. Missiles also destroyed Iran's three other largest cities. Fighter jets and bombers sped across Iraqi airspace, taking out surface-to-air missile batteries and anti-aircraft guns in that country, before proceeding into Iran. Bombs fell heavily on Iran's launch facilities and nuclear research facilities.

No matter what would follow, the Israelis wanted to make sure that Iran could not strike back with more Shahab-2 missiles.

With the destruction of Iran's nuclear facilities, including a small operational reactor, radioactive materials were released into the air as the nuclear processing facilities were destroyed. The clouds grew, spreading north and westward, contaminating the cities of Amol and Babol and Sari, killing thousands. The clouds continued north and west, drifting out over the Caspian Sea and then over sparsely populated regions of Turkmenistan and eastern Uzbekistan.

Bombing runs continued, but Iraq came to the aid of their previous enemy and began actively intercepting Israeli planes in Iraqi airspace. Several Israeli planes were shot down, and Israel decided to take out all of the Iraqi surface-to-air missile and anti-air sites.

The first bombs began to fall over Iraq on June 30.

With the attacks on Iran and Iraq, Syria and Jordan and Lebanon began to prepare for war. Troops began massing on the borders, and low-level rocket attacks began to shower onto Israel from contested areas in the north and east. Palestinians in the occupied territories began fighting back, killing "settlers" and taking their land and vehicles to continue the fight.

Iraq's Air Force began bombing sorties over Israel—the first waves of planes were shredded by Israel's technologically superior surface-to-air missile systems and anti-aircraft batteries, but with much of the Israeli

Air Force engaged in interdiction duties in Iran, homeland defense suffered. Iraq had only a few old, Soviet-era bombers, but saved them for the third and fourth sorties, and one of the bombers scored a direct hit on Jerusalem. Iraq had no nuclear capabilities, but the Jerusalem bomb had been rigged to release a hastily produced batch of Sarin gas upon detonation.

Syrian and Jordanian troops begin shelling Israel, and President Gore continued to only observe and deliberate. He was reluctant to involve American forces in what he considered to be a regional conflict. He couldn't bring himself to commit forces for anything other than humanitarian and cleanup efforts.

American troops returning from Afghanistan were diverted to ships off of the coast of Israel. Other than shelling the advancing Jordanian and Syrian forces, the U.S. military did nothing to stop the invasion. Instead, they followed instructions from their Commander in Chief and continued with hundreds of small craft and helicopter sorties to and from shore, recovering victims of the nuclear attacks and taking them aboard American ships for treatment.

But leaders in the region did not fail to notice that, without the immediate support of the United States, Israel was a sitting duck.

On July 2, Iraqi forces made it across the Jordanian border and also crossed the Israeli border, joining in the fight. As the sun set on that day, Israel was fighting back, but they were being overrun by the combined forces of several countries, and the citizens of Israel were fighting with trained soldiers, engaged in house-to-house combat, warring fiercely to defend their homes.

Still, the American president waited.

Finally, on the evening of July 2, 2002, he went on TV and announced America's intentions to defend the defenseless Israel. Iraq, Jordan, and Syria were ordered to withdraw all troops from Israeli territory, or an attack would come.

3.23
LAST DAY AT RED HOOK

July 4th, the American holiday, began in 2002 like any other morning. By the end of the day, a not-insignificant portion of the American populace would be dead or dying.

The elder Dr. Donald Ellis, of course, had no way of knowing this. His knowledge of the other timelines he had experienced was useless—too many changes had been made, and events had skewed off on a completely different, unpredictable tangent.

But he wasn't blind, and he had more experience in international geopolitics than most people. The unrest in the Middle East, coupled with President Gore's reluctance to openly support Israel, had pushed the region into war. And now he, like the rest of the nation and the world beyond, were waiting to hear the president's primetime speech tonight, which would hopefully outline a path towards peace. But with Israel back on its heels and more Middle Eastern nations' forces pouring into Jerusalem and Haifa, Ellis didn't think that Israel would survive.

He and Stevens were busy at the Red Hook warehouse, boxing up the final components of the machine. Most of the rest of the machine had already arrived at its new location, where the younger Dr. Ellis, Terry, Cassie O'Neal, and a group of technicians were working to reassemble it. The new location was near the Indian Point Energy Center, a nuclear power plant located on the Hudson about eighty miles north of New York City.

They'd selected a location that was still convenient to New York City. And Ellis had learned his lesson—after all those troubles with power lines and the batteries in the last timeline, he'd needed a new power source that he could rely on.

Security would be better, and the location was certainly less populated, the elder Ellis thought as the final truck pulled out. He and Stevens walked out and locked up. Ellis had been in Red Hook for so long, it didn't seem right to see the place empty. He glanced across the river and saw the South Tower, standing there by itself—in this timeline, that plane had been intercepted before it could get to New York. The pilot had instead crashed the plane into Baltimore's M&T Bank Stadium, home stadium to the Baltimore Ravens NFL team, and the latest death toll for that attack was up to 22,000. The team of hijackers for the fourth plane had evidently been used instead for the failed attempt on the president's life at Andrews Air Force Base.

Ellis always wondered what had happened to the other two teams—in the second timeline, there had been six planes hijacked, but in this one, three planes and the assassination team had been activated. Did that mean at least two teams of sleeper agents were still out there?

"Looks strange, doesn't it?" Stevens asked as they climbed into the car.

Ellis nodded and got in to drive. They pulled away, following the boxy white van that carried the final shipment of components—they were down to parts and components that could fit in a box van, instead of the flatbed trucks they'd used before to move the larger machine sections.

They had used the machine itself to transport much of the interior furnishings from the Red Hook warehouse to the new one. Computers, machine shop components, the contents of the office and Ellis' apartment—teleportation worked so well, they'd moved much of the warehouse's contents in just a few hours.

Ellis had gone through a few times—it was mind-boggling to be standing on the pad in Red Hook and then instantly be sixty miles away in Buchanan, New York. Of course, he was traveling between two warehouses, so the scenery wasn't that great, but the process still amazed him.

But the actual machine could not transport itself, and therefore it had to be disassembled and carried, piece by piece, to Indian Point.

Ellis often mused about the possibility of having two machines. If he had, could he transport one with the other? Could he move the machines around *ad infinitum*, making the physical locations of the machines moot? If machine A could be counted on to move machine B out of harm's way, and vice versa, then it would take a coordinated attack on both at the same time to disable them.

Or what if he could transport rock from the interior of a mountain, hollowing it out, and then transport one machine inside it? His mind raced at the possibilities for safe locations for the machines—the middle of the Amazon Rainforest, the bottom of the ocean, the far side of the moon? Each one introduced logistical problems, but none were insurmountable. As long as he had the unlimited power of the mini-reactor,

Ellis knew there were possibilities too numerous to grasp.

If worst came to worst, he could even hide the machines in time. Could he use one machine to transport another back in time? How would that impact the timeline?

It was about two hours to Buchanan with traffic, Ellis thought, so they should get there before noon. Once they arrived at Indian Point, it would take only a day or two to integrate the parts and get the machine back up and running.

Ellis didn't like having the machine taken apart. He felt like his life insurance policy had lapsed, and he was dragging his feet before he signed the next one. There was no safety net now, and nothing could be done until the machine was reassembled.

3.24
TWELVE MEN

Twelve Middle Eastern men boarded three different commercial passenger jets on the morning of July 4, 2002, and took their seats in the first-class cabins, waiting for takeoff.

Seven of the twelve men appeared on a no-fly list of known or suspected al Qaeda members that was regularly published and updated by persons at the CIA who tracked al Qaeda. Unfortunately, those provisions in the Patriot Act that required information sharing between agencies and the FAA and TSA had been taken out of the version passed by Congress and signed by the president. Gore had felt that keeping the information secret was more important than sharing it—even among responsible agencies.

But an up-to-date, comprehensive no-fly list might have flagged two of the men for additional checks. And enhanced screenings would possibly have located the small box cutters that each one carried.

Perhaps more layers of security would have done nothing. In fact, Mohammed Atta, the leader of the Christmas attacks, was, by chance, selected for additional screening and pulled out of line at Bangor Airport on that morning, but the cursory inspection he received was a joke.

The planes were all airborne at about the same time—the flights had been selected carefully. And on these planes, the cockpit doors had not been strengthened. Another provision of improving airline security had been that the airlines were "encouraged" to implement certain safety improvements, along with strengthening various physical aspects of the planes themselves, including reinforced cockpit and entry/exit doors, viewports in cockpit doors. The airlines had also been encouraged to install backup ventilation systems for the cockpit, separate from the rest of the plane, and better communications systems between the flight deck and other airline personnel on board. The government also suggested that airlines install complicated and expensive "chaff" systems to prevent incoming missiles from striking a plane. The government also strongly recommended the airlines hire, at their own expense, air marshals to fly on random planes to bolster security.

But because of the additional expenses and the fact that these were simply suggestions from the federal government, instead of mandates, most of the major airlines ignored them. It was the thinking among many airline executives that they had already had their disaster, so the chances of another attack, involving multiple hijacked planes, were close to zero.

Shortly after takeoff, the terrorists made their coordinated assaults on the cockpits of their planes.

In all three cases, within just minutes, the planes were under their control. On the flight out of Los Angeles, the pilot lay bleeding to death in a seat in first class, while on the St. Louis plane, the passengers and flight crew were herded to the back of the plane.

Based on what happened during the Christmas attacks, the al Qaeda teams understood that they would not be able to control the passengers. During the Christmas attacks, passengers had been told that the terrorists had a bomb on board and that they would be landing soon. The passengers had no idea that the planes themselves had been turned into guided missiles, aimed at critical U.S. targets.

But subsequent hijacked passengers might assume they were racing toward the same fate and fight back.

In the cockpit of the plane that had recently taken off from Newark Airport, the new pilot toggled a few switches that controlled the cabin air mixture and air pressure. He reduced the cabin pressure and pulled on the pilot's emergency oxygen mask, which was stowed next to the pilot's seat. Next to him, another hijacker did the same with the copilot's silver oxygen tank and mask. The pilot also flipped another switch, disabling the emergency oxygen masks in the main cabin.

In the cabin, passengers suddenly felt short of breath, exhausted, and weak. It was immediately clear what was happening—by lowering the cabin pressure and reducing their oxygen supply, the pilot was putting the passengers in a state of hypoxia. One by one, the passengers and flight crew passed out.

On the passenger plane that had been crashed into the Baltimore Ravens' stadium, the passengers had revolted, trying to retake control of the plane. But on this flight, there would be no on-board resistance.

3.25
ROAD TRIP

They were making their way out of the city, just passing Woodlawn Cemetery north of the Bronx, when the first reports of plane hijackings came on the radio. Stevens reached to turn the radio up as the elder Ellis craned his neck, looking for planes in the sky.

"We know at least two planes have been hijacked," the reporter was saying. "There have been no calls or demands from the hijackers, but the primary concern seems to be that the planes will be used as missiles to strike at sensitive targets. Fighter jets have scrambled and are patrolling over Washington, D.C., and New York."

"Christ, not again," Stevens said, his voice low.

Ellis had his eyes back on the road again.

"I knew it was a bad idea to disassemble the machine. We've got no recourse, if something really bad happens."

Stevens nodded. "Let's just get to Buchanan. Maybe they're trying again for the Trade Center or the president."

Ellis nodded. "I wonder where Gore is."

3.26
ALERT

President Gore was forty-five feet under the White House, in the hardened Presidential Emergency Operation Center, a bunker constructed beneath the East Wing by President Kennedy after the debacle at the Bay of Pigs, which was thought to be exacerbated by a lack of real-time information and communications between the White House and teams in the field. The bunker was designed to correct that problem.

"Three planes?" Gore asked.

"It looks like it, sir," Chairman Anderson of the Joint Chiefs spoke from one of the large television screens. "We've only got the three unaccounted for, and fighters are searching for them now."

Sandy Berger, Gore's National Security Advisor, spoke up, pointing at a document. "We're still operating under the no-shoot-down policy that you instituted during the Christmas attacks. Do you want to update that?"

Gore leaned back and looked at Berger. "Why, do you think I should?"

"Yes, clearly," Berger said. "If the fighters can find these planes and shoot them down, it's a no-brainer," he said, before looking up and quickly adding "sir."

"I don't think it's a no-brainer—I'm not comfortable shooting down planes full of innocent civilians."

Berger sighed. He decided to drop the subject for the moment.

"OK," Anderson said on the screen. "We've got something. A pair of F-16s out of Scott Air Force Base is shadowing a commercial jet that has dropped to 10,000 feet. I'm working to get video now."

"Why would they reduce altitude?" Berger asked. He knew that most commercial airlines flew at between 30,000 and 35,000 feet for the bulk of the flight.

"Not sure, sir," Anderson answered, even though Gore had been talking to Berger and the others gathered in the Operations Center. "OK, I'm getting F-22 nose cone video."

3.27
CHICAGO PLANE

With the cabin doors open, it was a lot harder for the terrorists to keep their balance. Wind howled through the plane, gusting and knocking them off their feet. Two of the hijackers were still in the cockpit, flying the plane, but two more were working in the back, wearing portable oxygen masks.

On the floor of the cabin lay the passengers and flight crew. A few of them still moved listlessly. One burly man had even managed to stand up and take a very weak swing at one of the hijackers.

He'd been the first one out.

Now, they worked together, carrying passengers, one by one, to the open door of the plane and, after a second, tossing them out into the wind.

After throwing out the final passenger, one of the hijackers remained at the open door, fighting the wind to peer outside at the fighter jets that were flanking the plane. Just in case they were looking, he waved.

3.28
Nose Cone Video

"What are they throwing out?" Gore asked, leaning forward. They were watching grainy, black-and-white video, streaming live from the nose cone of one of the F-22s.

"People," Anderson said simply over the video link.

The room went silent.

"Passengers," Berger said. "Innocent passengers are dying, sir. We need to shoot down this plane. There's no telling—"

"Where is it going?" Gore shouted. "What's the flight path? It looks like they're going north, to Chicago. Maybe the Sears Tower? And someone draft up a shoot-down order. Now!"

The others at the table scrambled to find papers as Anderson turned back to the screen.

"We're not sure, sir, but it looks like Chicago."

Gore shook his head and looked at the screen. On the grainy video, he saw a hijacker lean slightly out the open airplane door, look at the fighter jet following him. In a surreal moment, Gore saw the hijacker wave at the camera.

3.29
OVER LOS ANGELES

The plane over Los Angeles didn't have far to go, so the hijackers dispensed with the plan to throw the passengers from the plane—instead, they had simply lowered the cabin pressure and temperature, until the passengers and flight crew passed out. The plane was flying low—and three of the four hijackers were pulling on parachutes.

"Is he going to be okay?" one of them asked, nodding at the cockpit.

"Yes, I think so," another answered. "He is committed, but he also knows that someone must live to tell the tale. Between the three of us, at least one should avoid capture. They will be welcomed in New Mecca as a conquering hero."

The others smiled and then each, in turn, walked to the door. Fighting the winds that buffeted them, the men jumped.

From the cockpit, the remaining hijacker scanned the ground beneath him for landmarks. He knew he needed to get to the coast, but he was looking for the highway, Interstate 5, to follow. It would go south and approach the coast, jagging southeast and hugging the water. He tipped the plane and followed the road over San Clemente and then began his descent. He could see below him the twin domes of the San Onofre Nuclear Generating Station. Perched on the side of highway, the station was just feet from the ocean.

He aimed the plane's nose at the crisscrossing lattice of pipes and metal tubes between the two domes. From above, the rounded tops almost looked like the glittering domes of the Muhammad Ali Mosque in Cairo.

"Allah Akbar," the man said quietly as the ground rushed up toward him. He held the control column as steady as he could, even as his heart pounded in his chest.

3.30
SHOOT IT DOWN

"They're terrorists," Sandy Berger answered.

"I know. I just don't see why they are throwing people out of the planes. It serves no logical purpose," Gore answered.

"It doesn't matter—they're trying to scare us."

"Well, let's see if we can keep that out of the press," Berger said, watching the screen.

Anderson came on the screen from the Pentagon.

"They've struck, sir. A nuclear power station, one located south of Los Angeles. San Onofre, between L.A. and San Diego."

"Oh, no," Gore said, bewildered.

"Jesus," Berger said quietly, sitting back.

Gore stood. "Not a nuclear power plant. The radiation will kill thousands, tens of thousands." He looked around at the others in the room. "It could cause a nuclear winter, wipe out all plant life..."

Berger spoke up. "Anderson, it's more important than ever to find that missing plane."

"Byron Nuclear Power Station," one of the other people in the situation room said, looking up. She apparently hadn't thought she was talking that loudly and now, the room fell silent.

"What was that?" Berger asked, looking at her.

The young woman stammered. "I was just looking at the flight path of the St. Louis plane. If they were going to Chicago, it would have turned. But there's a nuclear power station in Byron, about two hundred miles west of Chicago."

Gore turned and looked at the plane—the fighters were still following it. He swallowed, hard.

"Anderson," the president said.

Anderson looked up, and the two men made eye contact via view screen, even though the president was safely sequestered under the White House and Anderson was in a similar bunker, buried deep under the innermost ring of the Pentagon.

"Yes, sir?"

"Shoot down that plane. On my orders—I'm signing the order now," Gore said, and grabbed the hastily-prepared memo on the table in front of him, signing it and holding it up for the camera.

"Yes, sir."

Over the next thirty seconds, all eyes were on the black and white screen as the F-16s backed off, lining up directly behind the large tail fin of the passenger jet. On a signal that no one in the Situation Room could hear, both fighters fired sidewinder missiles.

They both struck.

The back third of the plane erupted in a cloud of fire and metal and smoke. The plane immediately tilted upward, as it had lost most of the weight behind the wings, and then tipped over, slowly, lazily spinning through the sky until it impacted a cornfield some two hundred miles south of its intended target.

3.31

ON THE ROAD

"To confirm, a nuclear power plant south of Los Angeles has been struck by a hijacked passenger plane," the announcer said on the radio.

Stevens was on his cell phone, trying to contact the younger Dr. Ellis or Terry or any of the other people working at the new warehouse. It was located about a mile and a half north of the power plant at Indian Point. After hearing the terrorists seemed to be targeting nuclear plants, Stevens had started dialing.

The elder Ellis was speeding up, changing lanes to get in front of the big white box van he'd been following. He honked and motioned for the driver to pull over, and the man turned and worked his way across the three lanes of Interstate 87. Ellis pulled his car off the road as well and got out to go speak to the driver.

"What's going on?" the driver asked.

"You been listening to the radio?" Ellis asked.

"Nope."

"More terrorist attacks, one in Los Angeles." Ellis said.

"Oh, Christ," the driver said.

"We don't need to have all of us out on the streets—you take my car and head home, okay? I'll drive the van."

The driver nodded, and they exchanged keys as Stevens walked up.

"I called Terry, but he wasn't at the warehouse," Stevens said. "He went out to get lunch. He's on his way back to clear the place out."

Ellis nodded. "OK, I'll keep calling Ellis until he picks up. But we don't all need to go to Buchanan. You guys head home. Stevens, I'll call you when I get there. You can come up when this is all over."

"You sure?" Stevens asked.

Ellis nodded and climbed up into the van. With a wave, he pulled the van out onto the highway and continued north. Within minutes, he'd exited I-87 and was heading north on the Saw Mill River Road, toward Buchanan. He kept trying the younger Dr. Ellis' number, but he wasn't picking up.

3.32
BUCHANAN, NEW YORK

Just north of the expansive Indian Point Nuclear Station in Buchanan was a small group of buildings next to the river. One of these was the new warehouse, and inside, the younger Ellis was racing against time. He cursed and answered his phone, which had been ringing off the hook.

"Yup?"

It was his voice on the other end. Deeper and a little gruffer, but his voice, nonetheless. He never got used to that.

"You need to get out of there now," the elder Ellis said.

"I know," the younger Ellis answered. "We heard on the radio; terrorists hit a nuclear power station near Los Angeles. I'm just putting the last of the sensitive materials in the Faraday." He had been locking up precious components in the new metal cage. As he talked on the phone, he pulled the door closed and spun the large wheel lock to make sure it was secure.

"Yup," the elder Ellis answered. "I just heard that they shot down another plane—that one was headed for a nuclear station outside of Chicago. That just leaves the East Coast."

"You think they could hit Indian Point?"

"Not sure," the elder voice said. "But get out of there, anyway. It's the closest one to New York City."

"OK, will do," Ellis said.

"Be safe," the older version of him said and hung up.

The younger Ellis ran through the offices, making sure everyone else had gotten out. He glanced over his shoulder and out the office window—this space had formerly been used by Interstate Battery System as a loading station. It wasn't as big as the Red Hook warehouse, but it would do. And it was located within a mile of Indian Point which, up until a few minutes ago, had seemed like a great idea. Out of the office window, he could see Lent's Cove and two other large warehouses that sat along the waterfront. Indian Point was a mile south, along the Hudson.

He ran through a system of hallways and out onto the main floor, where the machine sat, almost finished. The elder Ellis had the remaining pieces in his truck—it was just bad timing that they hadn't already finished reassembling the machine. There was a loading dock around back, on the side that faced the river, and Terry and several other men were still unloading supplies and extra components from the last truck.

"Almost done?" Ellis asked as he ran up.

Terry nodded. "That's it. The truck is leaving—go ahead and close the gate," he said to another man, who slapped at a control on the wall. A heavy metal shutter-like gate began lowering from the ceiling, and Ellis saw the truck disappear.

"We need to leave, now," Ellis said. "They shot down another plane—it was trying to hit another nuclear power plant, this one near Chicago."

Terry looked up, his eyes wide. "Are they trying to hit Indian Point?"

Ellis shrugged. "No one knows, but let's clear out."

Terry nodded and gathered up the other men. Running, they all returned up the hallway and came out of the building next to the office. There was a circular drive in front of the building, a concrete planter filled with bushes and flowers. Most of the men ran down the drive and climbed into their cars, driving away. Ellis waited until Terry and Cassie came outside, then locked up behind them. They talked as they jogged to their car—they had driven up together.

"Is that everything?" he asked them.

Cassie nodded. "It's all secure. The plans are all locked up."

"I put the reactor on the lowest setting," Terry said as they opened the car doors. "It won't need any maintenance for at least a month, and then only to empty the baffles—"

Behind them, in the sky, Ellis heard something that sounded like a train. He turned and looked up.

A plane was coming in, streaking through the sky like a meteor.

Dr. Donald Ellis turned and saw Terry staring up at the plane as well. They only had a moment or two to recognize that the plane was a commercial jet and that it was coming straight down out of the sky. A moment later, the plane impacted into the horizon a mile south of their location, sending up a massive explosion. A wave of heat and radiation swept over the world, engulfing everything in flames.

3.33

EVACUATION

On the evening of July 4, the governor of Connecticut appeared on CNN and ordered the population of his entire state to flee northward, over the border and into Massachusetts, as the radioactive cloud began to grow and spread slowly eastward. The 80,000 residents of Danbury, Connecticut, the closest large city east of Indian Point, immediately began exiting the city as the radioactive cloud drifted across the New York/Connecticut border.

The exclusion zone began as a 400-square-mile area centered on the Indian Point reactor, but as the prevailing winds began to move the cloud, the plume of fallout affected a larger and larger area. Meteorologists examined the prevailing wind patterns and determined that the cloud, while spreading daily, would move almost due west, sparing the New York City metropolis area only 50 miles to the south. But Danbury and Norwalk and Bridgeport and New Haven, Connecticut, were doomed.

The highways were jammed almost immediately. The governor of Connecticut called in his National Guard to assist in the evacuations, but the rule of law began to break down quickly. People without transportation stole vehicles to make their way north and out of the way of the cloud. A bank in Milford was robbed by opportunistic thieves. One man in Trumbull shot his family and then turned the gun on himself. In Fairfield and Westport, there were reports of unexplained explosions.

In Groton, civilians were transported away from the areas in immediate danger by boats as naval personnel prepared to evacuate the base—classified materials had to be moved or destroyed, and several research and development projects in partial stages of completion had to be destroyed. Some were hurriedly transferred to a large military barge, taken out into the middle of Groton Harbor and sunk.

As the radioactive cloud bloomed eastward, in coastal cities like Greenwich and Stratford, boats full of fleeing citizens raced across the Sound to the relative safety of Long Island. In some Connecticut harbors, every boat had left its home port, in many cases, not piloted by the rightful owner.

3.34
MELTDOWN

He sat alone in the Oval Office, at his desk, but the president's thoughts were far away.

They were with the rescue teams, and the meteorologists, and the climatologists. His thoughts were with the gaggle of scientists trying to figure out exactly how much of the United States was no longer fit for human habitation. President Gore sat, thumbing through papers on his desk, and was unable to focus on any of them.

The desk he sat at was the famous Resolute Desk, built from the timbers of the 1850 British warship HMS *Resolute*. It was one of a matching pair of desks, the twin sitting in Buckingham Palace in London. The desk President Gore sat at had been a gift from Queen Victoria to President Rutherford B. Hayes in 1880.

But Gore didn't feel much like a president any more. He'd allowed a second attack on his homeland. This morning, the day after the July 4th attacks, he'd asked the Surgeon General for a casualty count. The shaken physician wasn't even able to hazard a guess.

Most of the immediate deaths had been in the towns of Buchanan, New York, and San Clemente, California. The scientists said that the planes, impacting and destroying the containment structures at both plants, had sent vast amounts of radioactive materials into the air.

And these twin radioactive clouds, slowly growing and spreading, would determine the final tally. Gore was powerless to affect the weather, and they had lost San Juan Capistrano in California, along with Mission Viejo and Dana Point and Oceanside and Camp Pendleton. The so-called "Western Cloud" was now moving south over the border with Mexico, slowly irradiating San Diego and Tijuana. Anyone trapped on the highways and roads, leading out of the killing zones, would be dead soon.

In the east, it was worse.

The Indian Point Energy Center had been located on the Hudson about 40 miles north of New York City. Casualty estimates were 100 percent in the immediate area of the meltdown, which occurred only minutes after the plane destroyed all of the containment systems surrounding the radioactive core.

Immediately, evacuation procedures were started. New York State, east of the Hudson, was evacuated northward to Albany, but initial casualty estimates were already at 8,000 people just in the Buchanan–Peekskill–Yorktown Heights area. Anyone who was still able fled southward to White Plains and other locations closer to New York City.

White Plains General received a massive influx of radiated patients with high levels of exposure to fallout, manifesting in extreme fevers, headaches, vomiting, and diarrhea. Mortality rates in patients with a dosage of more than 3,000 radians (rads) were 100 percent within two days of exposure. In comparison, natural radiation in the environment exposed a person to about .026 rads over the course of a year, depending on elevation. A dental x-ray exposure was .005 rads, and a whole-body CAT scan provided an exposure of about 1 rad.

The acute radiation poisoning that resulted from exposure killed in the same way a nuclear weapon would have. Thermal burns and beta and gamma burns accounted for the majority of casualties, along with fallout and long-term exposure to the radioactive elements in the environment.

Smaller doses of radioactivity could be treated with blood transfusions and antibiotics, though both were in disastrously short supply. But long-term exposure to radioactive elements, such as those that were coating every building and tree and surface in eastern New York State, would soon cause an unprecedented epidemic of low blood cell counts, neurological problems, and cancers.

3.35
EVACUATE NEW YORK CITY

On the evening of July 5, President Gore ordered the immediate evacuation of New York City, along with Rhode Island, Long Island, and the northern half of New Jersey.

It was a laughable request, of course—a city the size of New York would take two or three weeks to empty—but it got people moving. The roads leading south out of the metropolitan area were immediately jammed but were kept moving by armed National Guardsmen in Humvees and on motorcycles. The collective citizenry of New York, carrying whatever they could stuff into their Toyotas and Volvos, flowed steadily southward into New Jersey and Philadelphia. Over the next three days, massive tent cities were constructed by FEMA in the parks inland from Atlantic City and Ocean City and Toms River, and the former residents of New York City settled into a new, and unfamiliar, routine.

As the "Eastern Cloud" moved eastward, it passed over Norwalk and Bridgeport and Milford and out over Long Island Sound, hugging the Connecticut coastline. Behind the cloud, military personnel and scientists in radiation suits, staged in Stony Point and West Haverstraw, New Jersey, moved across the Hudson into Indian Point, measuring the environmental radiation levels.

And over the next few days, as the cloud moved off the eastern seaboard and out into the Atlantic, the real scope of the devastation became clear: a fifty by one hundred and twenty mile zone, some 6,000 square miles, had been rendered uninhabitable for the next 100 years. This Exclusion Zone, which included most of Connecticut, the southern half of Rhode Island, and the eastern third of Long Island, would be cordoned off from the rest of the nation.

Bordering the Exclusion Zone on all sides was a large strip of land, an area of "heightened exposure" that could, potentially, be decontaminated over time for future use. This Border Zone, which included White Plains and Stamford to the south and Providence and most of Massachusetts south of Boston, including Martha's Vineyard, were to be off limits for civilians until sections could be decontaminated enough for future use.

Once the immediate evacuations were completed and the affected zones were established, life slowly began to return to something approaching normal. Two months after moving to the massive tent cities of southern New Jersey, the government began to allow the population of New York to slowly migrate back into the city. Many people never returned—they feared the radiation levels from the small amount of fallout that reached the city. Others decided that living in such a visible location was no longer for them.

Some enjoyed their new lives in southern New Jersey and decided to purchase homes and stay for good.

President Gore appeared on the television as often as possible as the weeks passed into months, assuring Americans that they would recover from this horrible attack that had scarred the nation and rendered a slice of the country permanently uninhabitable. But commentators remarked on how drawn and tired the president looked and how much he had appeared to age in the months since the Christmas attacks and the helicopter crash.

In public, Gore was a stoic, resolute figure. In private, he was anything but. He felt enormous guilt for not being able to prevent the 9/11-style attacks on Christmas, even when aided with reams of foreknowledge.

3.36

PIERMONT, NEW JERSEY

He sat in the living room, unable to move. He had never felt more like giving up.

The other Dr. Ellis, the young one with the family that was a copy of his. And Terry. And Cassie, whom he'd talked into leaving her job at the *Post*. They were all dead now—dead because of him. And untold hundreds of thousands more, dead in southern California and Connecticut and Tijuana and Long Island. His old town of Jericho had been evacuated. And in the confusion, he'd been unable to find the Sarah and Tina from this timeline—they could be dead as well, or caught up in the panicked evacuation of New York City and Long Island.

Dr. Don Ellis sat in the rented house and flipped through the art books again. He'd been in a horrible place since the attacks seven weeks ago, but looking at the art books in this dingy home had cheered him up.

There were several Warhol paintings reproduced in the book that intrigued him—for a short time, they distracted his fevered mind from thinking about Terry and Cassie and the other Ellis at that warehouse in Buchanan. Had they seen it coming? Or had they been inside when it happened and not known what was happening?

Ellis shook his head and looked at the biography of the painter. He'd never been a fan of Warhol—all of the works he'd seen seemed to smack of crass commercialization. But there were several in this book that were interesting—the man certainly had a talent for creating interesting works. Ellis had seen the Marilyn Monroes and Campbell's soup cans, just like everyone else, but these were new to him. They were a series of paintings from late in Warhol's life, including some interesting abstracts such as *Camouflage* and *Rorschach* and an oversized take on the Last Supper. His favorite was a swirly, Jackson Pollack–style painting, made to look like multicolored yarn.

But the thing that struck Ellis most about the Warhol book was a quote from the man, "They always say that time changes things, but you actually have to change them yourself."

That quote could have been the story of Ellis' life. He had felt chills when he'd read that, and a second quote from Warhol, "Sometimes the little times you don't think are anything while they're happening turn out to be what marks a whole period of your life." After reading that, he'd gotten Sarah's note out again and stared at it for a long time. Ellis was determined to hold onto the memory of that morning until his last breath.

Ellis closed the Warhol book and stood, going to the large window that looked out onto the river.

His new boat was almost ready to go.

His leg was throbbing from moving too many boxes and carrying too much stuff out to the truck. He knew to rest it between trips, but he just wanted to get this part done and be on to the next.

Dr. Donald Ellis shook his head and went back to work, carrying boxes. He worked steadily, focused and driven. He was covered with sweat as he loaded the truck with gear, a bulky helmet, and his black duffel bag, the one that had already seen two other universes. Tonight, it was packed with everything he could carry, in preparation for this clandestine river trip.

Dr. Ellis had escaped death by not being at the new warehouse in Buchanan, but the other Dr. Ellis and Terry and all the other technicians had perished. The machine was nearly complete—if he was going to escape this timeline, he needed to get to the machine and set things right.

After loading the truck, he sat down to rest his leg and watched a little of the late news. It wasn't good—more news from the Exclusion Zones and riots in the tent cities in New Jersey. He scanned the crowds shown on the TV, looking for Sarah and Tina, but didn't see anyone he knew. Almost everyone he knew in this timeline was dead.

He hadn't spoken to President Gore since the July 4th attacks. There wasn't really much to say. Obviously, al Qaeda had three more teams in the country and had used them to target nuclear power plants. Reduced security at the airports had made it possible—but if he were to speak to Gore about it, the conversation would quickly have devolved into a shouting match about which one of them was more to blame.

Ellis didn't need that kind of aggravation, and besides, the president was busy.

He flipped off the TV and had a quick meal—it was nearly 2:00 a.m., and he was just killing time, waiting to leave. He had more coffee and read through the Warhol and other art books again while he ate—the woman that owned this cabin clearly was interested in art. The walls were crammed with dozens of paintings and framed art of varying levels of quality.

Finishing up, Don left the cabin and locked it behind him—he wouldn't be coming back—and drove his new red truck down to the harbor.

The town of Piermont, near the Border Zone, was almost completely abandoned, but Ellis had kept everything above board, paying rent, buying the new truck, and renting the boat from one of the remaining townspeople. Tonight, he parked at the harbor and worked alone, steadily loading the last of the boxes and machine parts onto the small boat.

It was late August, approaching his birthday, but he wasn't thinking about cake or presents.

In the seven weeks since the attack, the military had shut down all traffic into and out of the Exclusion Zone. Armed guards blocked all the roads and checkpoints into the Border Zones as well. Cleanup efforts were underway for the towns in the Border Zone that could be salvaged, but the decontamination work was time consuming and labor intensive. Helicopters and aircraft were constantly overhead, dropping loads of sodium chloride on "hotspots," radioactive patches of fallout, attempting to soak up as much as possible and sequester the dangerous, ash-like material before it could wash into rivers or seep into the groundwater.

After the Indian River attack, Ellis had exited the highway and immediately driven back to the warehouse in Brooklyn, stopping only to visit several pharmacies to purchase bulk amounts of potassium iodide—he knew, once the fallout rumors began, there would be a run on the tablets, which blocked radiation poisoning. He'd unlocked the warehouse doors and pulled the van inside, then sat in the parked van for a half hour, his hands shaking. If only he had left the machine here, everything would be fine. Instead, the only hope for fixing the timeline was now at the center of a military-sponsored quarantine zone. And it had been dosed with lethal levels of radiation.

Ellis had spent weeks trying to figure out the best way to get the missing machine parts up to the new warehouse, where the time machine had been nearly completely reassembled. If they had completed the machine, he could have remotely triggered the machine and been teleported to the warehouse.

After that, he would've needed only a moment or two to reset the machine and exit this timeline, one that had started out with such promise but had, somehow, spiraled into hell.

Ellis knew that the entire Indian Point and Buchanan area had been heavily irradiated—even a few minutes' exposure to the central detonation area would be deadly. He'd been pondering the levels of contamination and decided that if he could keep his exposure to a minimum, it might still be possible.

Doing a little research, he'd learned that boat traffic was being blocked near the Tappan Zee Bridge, but it might be possible to skirt the line and make his way upriver. Since he'd learned that, he'd spent the last two weeks recovering the machine parts and transporting them and himself to Piermont, New Jersey, a city on the Hudson, south of the Tappan Zee and about forty miles south of Indian Point. He'd rented a house and a boat—neither the home or boat owners were around, and he worked through a local agent—and began preparing for his upriver cruise.

He would only have one shot at this, so he needed to make it count.

Ellis had brought guns from the old warehouse, and food, just in case. He couldn't imagine getting stuck at the new warehouse for long—his exposure levels would be lethal within hours, at most, even with the medical precautions he was taking.

He was dosing himself with potassium iodide—the iodide blocked radiation poisoning by filling the thyroid with iodide, keeping it from absorbing radioactive iodide from the environment. He was taking the recommended dosage, which was 130 mg every 24 hours, and had been for a week or so—he knew that potassium iodide didn't build up in the system or offer any additional protection, but it just seemed like a good idea. He also had enough supplies to dose him for two months.

And there was other protection. An underground economy had sprung up near the Border Zones that dealt in radiation medications and protective outerwear. He'd bought two specially-made outfits that looked, to the untrained eye, like oddly-constructed suits of armor.

Lead was particularly good at shielding the body against radiation—in fact, a sheet only .4 inches thick cut radiation exposure in half. Local craftspeople had begun venturing into the Border Zones wearing outfits made of durable, stretchy fabric lined by plates of lead across the chest, legs, arms, and back. The leaded suits, or "metal suits," as they were being called, were topped by a metallic helmet, made of thicker lead, and included heavy-duty gloves and boots.

Beneath the suit, he'd worn thick jeans and three shirts. It worked, and he could move in it, but he wondered how much he could realistically do in so many uncomfortable layers. And the outfit made him feel like Iron Man—he'd walked around with that characteristic "clunkiness" from the movie which, for everyone else, wouldn't be out for another six years.

Finally, early on the morning of August 26, he was ready. The boat was loaded, and he had as much protection as he could gather.

3.37
Tappan Zee Bridge

There were few lights on in Piermont's T&R Marina. It was nearly 3:00 a.m., when Ellis started the boat engines and eased quietly from the pier. He hoped to be to the warehouse by sunrise, in three hours, but there was no telling what he might run into.

Piermont was a nice little town—even as an outsider, he'd been welcomed. His money hadn't hurt and getting a boat had been no trouble—it wasn't huge, but it would do. It had come with a nice slip near the pier in the marina.

Over the past few days and nights, he'd taken the boat out for little excursions, finding out where the military patrolled. The river patrols and Naval and Coast Guard cutters that blocked upriver access were based out of a marina just upriver from the Tappan Zee Bridge in Tarrytown, New York. In fact, Tarrytown and Sleepy Hollow served as the primary military checkpoints for all points north on the Hudson, and anyone heading into the Border or Exclusion Zones had to pass through there.

Ellis moved up the river, hugging the western shore. He had a radar sounder and was moving as slow as the boat would go and as close to the shore as possible. Last night, he'd disconnected all the external lights, so now the only light on the entire boat was the eerie red glow of the map light.

There were dozens of short docks and boat slips that jutted out into the water, so whenever a patrol boat would pass, he'd pull over and stop next to one of them. To the unpracticed eye, his boat appeared to belong—it wasn't moving, it showed no lights, and it was next to a dock. It was, for all rights, invisible.

He was also checking the detailed Google map on his trusty iPad, scrolling the map as he traveled very slowly upriver. It was his last iPad from the original timeline, and he'd taken special care of it. He hoped the radiation wouldn't affect it—most electronics were susceptible to elevated radiation levels.

Almost an hour later, he had reached the Tappan Zee Bridge. This was taking a lot longer than he'd planned. Near the New York side, the bridge was a traditional suspension bridge, hundreds of feet above the water, but on his side, near the Jersey shore, the "bridge" was more of a causeway, suspended twenty feet above the river by small caissons with wooden piles. His boat couldn't negotiate under the low causeway, so he was forced to turn east out into deeper and deeper water, following the bridge until he could turn and ease under the roadway.

There was a close call as a Coast Guard cutter, motoring quickly up the river toward the bridge, looked like it was heading directly at him, but it turned and passed under the tallest part of the Tappan Zee. After about ten minutes, the pilings under the causeway opened up, and Ellis scooted through, turning immediately west and skirting the bridge again until he reached the shoreline.

The next two hours of the trip were uneventful—he drove the boat so slowly that, at times, it appeared to be sitting still in the dark water. He passed a collection of four large buildings as he left the Tappan Zee Bridge behind, and an ornate house topped with Spanish tile. He continued north, watching across the Hudson at Tarrytown and Sleepy Hollow—they were lit up with skylights. He could see larger boats in the harbor and Humvees and light tanks and school buses surrounded by troops and tents. High above the harbor stood a newly erected guard tower.

North, along the Jersey side, he passed Nyack, taking care to skirt the marina, and North Nyack and Hook Mountain, where the river turned sharply to the west. The faint smudge of sunrise brightened the sky to his east, and he knew he had to hurry—his boat would be much more obvious on the water in daylight. After another five miles upriver, he passed Haverstraw, then Stony Point and the deep quarry at Tomkins Cove.

His Geiger counter had started ticking at Haverstraw.

Ellis tried to ignore it, but he tied up the boat long enough to change into his Iron Man getup. After stripping down, he slapped a radiation badge on his bare chest and pulled on jeans, two shirts, and a thick sweater.

Next, he dressed in the metal suit—he felt like a kid trapped inside a science fiction robot, but it would save his life, he hoped. Or at least prolong it long enough. He carefully went over each seal with his bare hands, checking to make sure all of the metal pieces overlapped correctly, and then he tugged on the thick gloves and stepped into the lead boots. He felt like an idiot, and in the metal helmet he couldn't see much, but it was better than dying.

Over everything, he put on an oversized military-grade radiation suit and the oversized mask, which further blocked his vision. The black Nuclear, Biological, Chemical (NBC) suit was designed to further protect the wearer from contamination. The particular suit he'd purchased was made of impermeable rubber and included an air filter. On the outside of the suit, he slapped another badge.

He flicked off the Geiger counter to save the battery and started up the boat again, continuing north away from the quarry. The sun had risen while he'd been getting dressed, and now, in the light of morning, he felt exposed. Driving the boat was much more difficult now—he could hardly see out of the metal helmet, and the thick, double layer of gloves made it hard to grip the wheel and adjust the throttle.

It seemed impossible, but he managed to go even slower, the boat winding, hugging the Jersey shoreline, staying as close to the trees as possible. Soon, the Indian Point Power Plant, or what was left of it, came into view as he worked his way around the curve in the river. He began to relax a little—he was less worried about being caught now, as there wasn't another living soul around for at least five miles in any direction. The highest levels of contamination would be near the cores, where the plane had impacted the reactors and reactor containment structures. He just hoped that the levels were lower at the warehouse, or he wouldn't survive the eleven hours of work he'd estimated would be required to get the machine running.

Don put the thought out of his mind and searched the opposite shore for Lent's Cove.

A half hour later, he found it. He continued upriver as the morning sun approached and, when the river turned sharply to the west again, he tacked northeast.

Here, the Hudson was about 1,500 feet across, so he was soon approaching another causeway bridge on the New York shore. The sun began to peak over the horizon as he turned the boat east, skirting the bridge and following it into Peekskill, then south along the abandoned buildings and boats to Charles Point Pier Park and, finally, Lent's Cove.

Ellis took it slowly—there were wrecked boats from the destroyed marina blocking the cove, with empty masts pointing from the water like angry fingers. Closer to the New York shoreline, large pieces of metal jutted up out of the water. It boggled the mind, but he assumed they were parts of the power plant, a half-mile to the southwest, blown free in the impact and explosion.

Seeing the wreckage in the water, he was suddenly glad it was daylight. Navigating this mess at night would have been suicide.

He guided the boat up the narrow waterway, seeing the warehouse off to his left. He was relieved to see that it still looked intact. Don turned the small craft into a shallow area that bordered the parking lot and circular drive in front of the warehouse, shutting off on the throttle as the boat bumped onto the sandy shore.

Carrying the black satchel, Ellis climbed onto the railing and used the branches of a tree to pull himself up onto the bank, where he could see the circular driveway and parking lot in front of the warehouse. There were still several cars in the parking lot, and he noticed that they looked scorched, as did the trees that flanked either side of the main doors into the building. As he walked, he left tracks as he trudged through the thick layer of fine, ashy powder that covered the ground like dirty snow.

Don turned on the Geiger counter and watched as the needle spun around to indicate what should be a lethal dose of radiation. He needed to get inside—the contamination levels inside the structure should be noticeably lower.

The offices were in the southern part of the building, next to the circle, so he walked up to the front doors, fishing his keys out. It was unnecessary—the doors were open, propped open by a log.

He stepped over it and tried the switch, but there was no power. The emergency lighting was also out. He pulled out a flashlight and flicked it on.

The hallway was full of bodies.

Ellis stepped back and almost tripped over the body that held the door open—the body he had stepped over, mistaking it for a log. They were all technicians and employees of his, but their radiation burns rendered them unrecognizable. Carefully, he moved the body in the doorway and pulled the glass doors shut, locking them behind him.

Don made his way through the office area—each body looked less burned than the one before, so he assumed that those inside had been irradiated and the ones farther outside burned. They were all equally dead. There had only been about ten people working here, along with Cassie and Terry and the younger Ellis, none of whom he'd found. He walked through the office portion of the building and then out into the main warehouse.

The machine was intact.

It was a moment that he was anticipating, but it still sent a cascade of relief washing through him. It wasn't damaged, and the roof had held—lately, he'd been trying to think through every single contingency, and the one that scared him the most was the idea that the roof had caved in. Not only might the machine have been damaged, but the roof and walls blocked the ambient radioactivity outside. If the interior of the building had been exposed, it would have greatly shortened the amount of time he had.

He walked over and ran his gloved hands over the machine—it looked just like it had in Red Hook. Nothing seemed out of the ordinary, apart from the fact that the computer terminal and a few other key components were missing. The machine was only missing two sets of components—the sensitive computer equipment in the Faraday, which he would replace first, and the last few pieces that rested in the hold of his boat. He should be able to get it running, if he could survive the exposure.

First, he needed to check his exposure.

Don turned and went back into the computer lab—this room had been built much like a large Faraday cage. Everything inside appeared to be intact. Better still, the thick metallic walls would make this room the safest in the warehouse.

He pulled off his external radiation sticker and held it up.

It was black. That meant that an unprotected person would have received a lethal dose. He stripped off the metal suit and reached inside his shirt to check the sticker on his bare skin—it was blue. Green was fine, blue was exposure that could cause harm, red was full exposure, purple was extreme exposure, and black was death. Apparently, the ridiculous metal suit had helped.

Now, he had roughly ten to twelve hours of work. He looked at his watch—it was nearly 11 a.m., so he had until between 10 p.m. and midnight tonight to finish. The boat trip had taken five hours longer than he'd expected, increasing his exposure. The eleven-hour window had just been a guess—now, he wasn't sure how long it would be before the symptoms started in.

Don needed to start with the computer equipment in the Faraday cage. After that, he needed to get the machine parts from the boat, but all he wanted to do was rest. He wanted nothing more than to curl up on the couch in the computer lab and sleep. He was so tired—

Don shook his head and stood. He walked to the end of the computer lab and found the small refrigerator and pulled it open. The contents were no longer cold, but there were several cans of Red Bull inside. He wasn't sure if they were safe or not, but he shook his head and pulled one out and downed it, the sickly-sweet drink helping push off the edges of exhaustion.

He just needed to keep moving and get the job done.

3.38
SUPPLIES AND PARTS

Six hours later, Dr. Donald Ellis lugged the last box of parts inside—he'd put a plank of wood from the shore out onto the boat, so unloading had gone faster than he'd planned.

He had to thank the mysterious computer techie who'd stocked that mini-fridge—Ellis had brought along a few energy drinks in his supplies, but finding that small fridge had helped. He planned to drink only from the less-contaminated supplies he'd brought with him from now on, but it was nice to know those drinks were there as a backup. Don wasn't sure who had put them there, but he said a quiet thank you and moved on.

Don set the box down and locked the doors behind him. He'd only been outside four times since his arrival this morning, but each time he'd gone outside he'd applied a new radiation badge, and they had all turned black. Spreading out his exposure would hopefully give his body and the potassium iodine a chance to deal with the radiation he was absorbing. He also avoided stepping in the snowy blanket of fallout that covered the ground outside. From the Geiger readings, it was obvious that being outside for more than just a few minutes would have a permanent affect, so he'd paced himself.

First, he'd gotten the sensitive electronics from the Faraday cage and reinserted them into the machine—if those electronics were damaged or destroyed, the machine would be inoperable, and there would be no use in lugging in the remaining parts. But the Faraday cage had worked well, absorbing the environmental radiation, and the electronics appeared to be in good working order. He ran preliminary diagnostics on the machine, testing the pieces of equipment, which the other Ellis had locked away in the final minutes of his life, and verifying that the computers systems were operational. Don had also powered up the mini-reactor to purify and purge the air inside the warehouse.

Next, he'd dressed in the metal suit and retrieved a load of items from the boat. Back inside, he'd taken off some pieces of the more bulky metal suit, so that he could work. He'd emptied the parts out onto the worktable and put them into the machine, one component at a time. After the first two trips, he'd brought in and installed most of the missing machine parts.

On his third trip outside, Ellis had found the other him.

The younger version of him was sitting in one of the cars outside—Don had determined that the blackening on the cars and grounds and trees must have come from an initial explosion of high thermal intensity, flash cooking everything within a mile or two of the reactor. The other Dr. Ellis had been sitting inside his car, along with Terry and Cassie. Their skin had been mottled by the radiation exposure, but he recognized them, nonetheless. He didn't know what to do or how to feel anything other than incredible guilt. There wasn't anything to do, so he left them there and went inside.

The third trip to the boat had been for the last box of machine components. Once he was back inside, he'd removed the NBC suit and the metal helmet and leather gloves—he couldn't work in them. As he'd spread the components from the box out on the table and begun installing them, he'd noticed the first red lesions on the back of his hands. They looked like blisters.

Don had known they were coming, but he'd hoped it would be longer before the slow, low-level "burn" of the environmental radiation began to affect him. He needed to hurry. The patch he wore on his skin, under all the layers, showed his true dosage, and it had gone from blue to red in the last hour. Next would be purple, then black.

He brushed at his forehead with the back of one hand, and he realized how much he'd been sweating. Was that good? Was it helping purge the toxins or getting rid of good water, which he would soon replace with contaminated water? The back of his hands felt scratchy and mottled. He ignored it and snapped the missing components into place, hurrying to tighten the screws. Finally, he was done.

He caught a reflection of his face in a shiny portion of the machine and saw that his face was reddening and beginning to break out in the same blister-like pustules that now covered his arms and legs.

Don had started a systems diagnostic before he pulled the heavy metal helmet on one more time and went outside. The fourth and last trip to the boat was for the two small boxes of supplies he'd brought—water, some protein bars, and the rest of his potassium iodide.

All of the food he'd brought with him had been irradiated, but the radiation levels were far lower than in food and drinks from the fallout zone. Ellis tried not to think about it and hoped his body could handle it. Just to be safe, he ate as little as possible—a couple of protein bars, another Red Bull, and some bottled water, along with a triple dose of potassium iodine. He thought about setting up some kind of water purification system to take water from the river—it was coming from upstream and therefore less contaminated—but he decided against it. Hopefully, he wouldn't be here that long.

He was packing up his foodstuffs and the water and waiting on the diagnostic to finish. It seemed to be taking longer than it should have. He glanced at his watch—it read 6:00 p.m. He was at seven hours of exposure, since he had arrived, not counting what exposure he had received on the river. But the machine was done. Once the diagnostics came back clean, he'd be able to leave.

Don went into the office and began gathering his bags. Most of his books and things were still packed up in the boxes they'd used for transport, and all the furniture was pushed over into one corner, awaiting his arrival to set up the new office.

Everything he needed was in the large safe. As he'd done last time, he'd bring a large leather bag full of equipment, the printed and CD versions of the plans for the machine, and everything else he would need to start over. He wondered if he even needed the plans anymore—he probably could recite them from memory.

He wished, beyond anything, that he could use the machine to transport itself back in time. Terry had had a vision for the ultimate device—shrinking the existing machine down to the point where it was self-contained. It would be a true time machine, instead of a time tunneler or time projector, because it moved itself through time along with the operator.

Ellis shook his head—the prospect of starting over from scratch was so depressing—he wasn't sure if he could do it or not. He dreaded the idea of raising funds again, recruiting others, and rebuilding the machine over again in a new timeline. He shook his head as he stuffed wads of cash and a large bag of diamonds into the leather bag. Asking other people to help had been a bad idea—he'd proven that, over and over again. Informing the governments had caused nothing but problems.

Next time, he'd do it himself. He'd arrange for Mohammed Atta and his clowns to be caught, or he'd take care of them himself. He'd figure something out.

Into the bags, he stuffed everything he would need—identification, money, and jewels to be sold to raise startup funds, the machine plans, the last iPad from his original timeline, contact lenses, his wallet with the note from Sarah, the gun from Tina/Trish, and a few other items he had collected in the different timelines.

The gun from the future Tina had been an anomaly—he'd spent months working on it with a group of dedicated techs back in 1996, trying to figure out how it worked. They'd managed to partially disassemble it before they realized that it didn't use bullets—this gun's ammunition was liquid metal. Specifically, mercury, but any liquid would work. There was an intake valve in the base of the handle, and when the gun was placed in a vat of any liquid, the gun drew the liquid up into a chamber. When the gun was fired, small droplets of the liquid were accelerated to incredible speeds and expelled from the barrel—how the liquid was accelerated was still a mystery, as was the weapon's power source.

It was, essentially, a super-powered water gun—in some of the experiments, droplets of ordinary water had penetrated an inch of steel when fired from the odd blue pistol. Any liquid worked, but mercury seemed to have the most stopping power, so that's what he had loaded it with. He carried an ample supply of extra mercury as well.

Putting the gun in his bag, it was hard to believe he was leaving it all behind again, starting over. He felt like he was abandoning these people, but he needed to move on. He had to set things right, no matter how many tries it took.

He was starting to think that it might not be worth it—he could never save his Sarah and Tina. They were gone, lost somewhere in time. These other Sarahs and Tinas that he had met, in this timeline and the last, they weren't the real ones. Copies, doppelgangers, ghosts. He'd spent time with them, befriended them in awkward ways that made their relationships feel strained and artificial. Even when he'd sat those other Tinas on his lap and told them fantastic stories, it didn't feel real or right. And the quiet dinners with the Ellis family had always felt strained, especially when he would ask the Sarah at the table to tell him the stories he missed so dearly of her childhood in Texas. The stories were the same, and the voice was the same, but, somehow, it was all too forced and unreal. Instead of having dinner with his family, it felt like he'd been watching a recording of that dinner. There was a distance between them, somehow trivial and vast at the same time.

As he packed up the leather bag and carried it back into the warehouse, Don couldn't help wondering if he would ever see his wife and child again.

He set his bag down next to the control PC. The diagnostics routine was finally over—and it showed two components missing, both in the primary firing chamber.

"Shit."

Don turned and began searching for them.

3.39

FLYOVER

The Harrier flew low over the location again.

"Nope, I'm sure. There are fresh tracks in the ash, and a few lights are on. Like I said, I saw someone down there, in an NBC suit," the pilot said into his headset. "It's a big warehouse, next to the Hudson. Maybe a quarter-mile upriver from the power plant."

The pilot, a young man from the Texas panhandle, had flown more sorties in the past week than in the rest of his career, criss-crossing the Exclusion Zone, looking for anything unusual. He'd flown over this area, near the power plant on many occasions, and he was pretty sure he would have noticed those lights on the exterior of the large warehouse. None of the other buildings in the area had power—few inside the Exclusion Zone did, after this long, and none of the others had regained power—he was sure.

"Are you getting any readings? Is it survivors?"

He shook his head—there weren't any survivors. Didn't base understand that yet? They were up here flying thirty missions a day, looking for survivors, but they'd found none—no people, no animals, nothing. Everything was dead—anyone or anything alive in the Exclusion Zone had come in after the attacks—and died immediately.

The buildings and cities and forests and fields were already lost, and nothing could heal the region except for time. It would be at least a hundred years before the area could be safely inhabited, and even then, the new residents would have to be inoculated against the higher radiation levels.

"No, I don't think it's a sign of survivors. The warehouse looks like it's on emergency power or something."

"It's probably running on generators," the base controller said. "They just had a shit-ton of gasoline stored up. It'll run out soon, and then—"

"Wait a sec," the pilot interrupted. As his plane flew through the sky, it trailed a towed radioactive array, or TRA, to measure radiation levels in the Exclusion Zone. But he was getting a strange reading.

After a few long seconds, he tapped the communications button on his flight stick again.

"OK, this makes no sense. I'm getting high readings on the towed array—it's picking up active generation of radioactive energy. It doesn't appear to be from the background environment or the fallout."

Base was quiet for a minute.

"OK, gotcha," she finally said. "We've tagged the location for a helicopter flyover. Thanks, pilot—continue your grid."

The pilot acknowledged base and glanced one more time down at the warehouse, perched on the edge of the river. All the evidence pointed to a self-contained building with its own independent, nuclear power source. The array of Geiger counters and other detectors that he was dragging through the air an eighth of a mile behind his plane had sampled the air and could find no other explanation.

3.40
Diagnostics Complete

Halfway through the installation of the missing two components, Don's nose began to bleed.

He felt a tickle and set his tools down to remove the helmet and outer cover, and by the time his head was free, the blood was flowing freely. He found a rag and stuffed it up his nose, and then the other nostril began to leak as well.

"Crap."

He turned and inserted the last two pieces, snapping a cover in place over them. Something was still nagging at him, something he needed to do…

Don looked up at the lights.

Slowly, it dawned on him. With the reactor operating, any lights on the exterior of the warehouse would be glowing. Would anyone notice? He knew that the military was operating flights over the Zone, but he didn't think it would matter.

He put the helmet under his arm and walked back over to the controls, restarting the diagnostics. His nose had stopped bleeding, so he pulled the rags free and looked around, trying to think what else he needed to do. His leather bag was ready to go, sitting on the floor in the painted circle. As soon as the machine diagnostic came back clean, he was gone.

The reactor was running, and he had plenty of power. The building was doing fine—low-level lights, electric fences, motion detectors, cameras. If anyone came around, he would know.

3.41

HELICOPTER

At the Tarrytown Air Station, about twenty miles south of the ruins of the Indian River Nuclear Power Plant, a helicopter lifted off from a small field, jammed with much more equipment than it was designed to support.

Inside, the two pilots and four soldiers were covered head-to-toe in NBC suits, black rubber against the black of the interior of the helicopter. Both side doors of the Huey were open, and the soldiers were tying off, attaching the rappel lines they would use to drop to the ground to the overhead base plates.

In the west, the sun was dropping quickly toward the distant horizon.

Sorties of this type were dangerous enough without exposure to fallout and environmental radiation. The rubber NBC suits were necessary, but they made it much more difficult to deploy and "fast rope" down to the ground, which was likewise contaminated. They were losing daylight, so the pilot pushed his throttle to the maximum and turned north. Night missions were rare and dangerous—at night, the lack of power made it more difficult for the pilot to navigate and hard for the deploying soldiers to judge the distance to the ground. Some of the fast-rope soldiers had invented a new trick in the past few days—they dropped light sticks down to the ground before rappelling to get an idea of when to slow their descent.

3.42
Dilemma

Don waited for the diagnostics to end. They were taking forever, but there was nothing he could do. Staring at the PC didn't help—the machine was just making sure everything was in order.

His nose started bleeding again.

Don reached up, flipping back the NBC hood and lifting the heavy metal helmet off his head, setting it down on the table next to the keyboard. As he flipped the helmet over, a hunk of his hair fell to the ground.

Don looked down at it and cursed as more blood poured from his nose. Walking back to his office, he found some tissues and balled one up, stuffing some up each nostril. At least the bleeding stopped.

He heard a low, throbbing sound.

Don knew immediately what the sound was and ran to the loading doors for a peak outside.

A helicopter was approaching from the south.

He shook his head—he was ready to go, and he didn't need this. Soldiers and guns and curious members of the U.S. military.

He walked back over to the machine and made it almost all the way to the control PC, when his left leg locked up, and he tumbled heavily to the ground. There was a sudden, intense pain in his leg, like the worst cramp of his life, and the leg stiffened inside the metal suit.

Don rolled on the ground and banged on the leg with his gloved hands, but nothing happened. He couldn't reach inside to his leg and couldn't massage the knee or anything. The leg stayed ramrod straight, pulsating with pain, and Don could do nothing but lay on the ground in agony.

Outside, he heard the helicopter engines slow as they circled the warehouse. Someone must have seen the emergency lights, or maybe they'd spotted the boat from the air.

After another few moments, the pain in his leg passed, and he was able to stand. Wobbly, he staggered to the control PC.

The diagnostic had come back clean. He was ready.

But he didn't have time to set up. If he left, right now, they would find the machine. He needed more time to set up the explosive device and wipe all the computers. It was a horrible choice—stay here and set up the explosives and maybe get caught by the soldiers and go to jail forever or leave this timeline and give the U.S. government a fully operational time machine? God only knew what they would do with it.

Don needed to stop them before he could leave. Pulling off his gloves, he tapped at the keyboard.

He'd never tried this before, but they had done a few experiments. The computer could track him well enough, and it should work. Don was going to use the machine to teleport him into the air above the warehouse, then retrieve him after two seconds. He would be falling, but the machine would be able to compensate for that and retrieve him. He hoped.

It was either that or attempt to "grab" the helicopter in midair with the teleporter and send the whole aircraft somewhere else in the world.

Don pulled on his heavy gear and activated the machine. He pulled out the blue gun from the duffel bag and checked the gauge—it was fully loaded. He hated the idea of hurting more people, but there was no way to avoid it.

Kicking the leather satchel clear, Don stood in the middle of the circle painted on the ground and waited as the machine powered up. The lights inside the warehouse flickered. The sound of ice, cracking loudly, filled the room, and then—

—he was in the air above the warehouse.

Don had set the height at 1,000 feet with a five-second delay. In those seconds, Don saw several things.

He saw the warehouse below him, and the boat and river beyond, and the western glow of the horizon. He saw a few exterior lights on the warehouse. Dim as they were, they were very noticeable as the only lights for a mile in any direction. And he saw a helicopter approaching, black against the darkening sky. He could hear the rotors chopping at the air.

Don spun as he began to fall, and aimed the blue gun at the helicopter.

The gun made its odd coughing sound, and Ellis watched the gun fire its cloud of individual miniature projectiles. The cloud of mini-bullets fanned out as it approached the hovering helicopter, and then he was—

—back in the warehouse.

3.43
DEMON

"No, it was a man, I think!" the pilot shouted.

They had been approaching the warehouse, looking for a good landing place, when the copilot had noticed a flash of light off to his side. He'd turned, thinking it was a bird, and then shouted—it looked like a black demon, hanging in the sky. The demon turned and pointed something at the helicopter, and the pilot reacted instinctively, turning sharply and putting the bottom of the helicopter between his soldiers and whatever that thing was floating in the air. The pilot felt the helicopter buck as it felt like several waves of projectiles hit the underside of the copter—sparks flashed up as some of the projectiles burst through the floorboard, and immediately he began to lose control of the aircraft. The pilot glanced over at his copilot, but the man was dead.

The pilot leaned on the stick and looked for an open spot on the ground. It would be a hard landing.

3.44
A New Plan

Ellis was back in the warehouse, sitting on the floor in the painted circle. He'd collapsed as soon as he'd returned.

He'd lost sight in his left eye.

Outside, he heard the helicopter's engines whining, struggling to keep the bird in the air. He hadn't wanted to fire on them, but he had no choice. Now, they would be busy for a few minutes, and he needed to get out of here.

He blinked and struggled to his feet. His leg tightened up again, threatening to cramp. He slapped at the leg of his metal suit, willing his leg to cooperate.

Walking to his office, he retrieved the bomb from the safe. Carrying it back, he stumbled, catching himself before he fell. The radiation was setting in—he could feel his insides quivering. Ellis put the bomb down between the control PC and the machine and set the timer for 1:00:00. After a moment's hesitation, he started it. At least now, if he died, the machine would be destroyed.

His plan had been simple: jump back into the past again. But that wouldn't work now—he was far too sick. He'd arrive in the warehouse in Red Hook and die within minutes on that cold concrete floor of radiation poisoning.

He could teleport to a hospital, but he wasn't sure if his condition was treatable with present-day medical technology.

That was it, he realized in a sudden moment of clarity.

He would die if he stayed here or went into the past. He needed to go somewhere where he could be successfully treated, somewhere where they could cure him.

He needed to go into the future.

It made sense—in this timeline, they were dealing with radiation exposure over vast populations, both in the United States and in the Middle East. Some of the fallout cloud was supposed to travel all the way to Europe and Asia, and the Israeli cloud had been expected to expose millions to low levels of radioactivity throughout the Middle East and Asia. If anybody was going to be good at treating radiation poisoning, it would be these people, and their descendents.

Outside, he heard the helicopter crash. It sounded incredibly close. The sound of the engines and rotors spinning was cut off and followed by an explosion and then nothing but sudden silence.

His leg began cramping again, and Don made up his mind. He leaned over and began doing rough calculations on the computer in front of him, trying to not look at the blisters and oozing pustules on the backs of his hands.

Don scanned a geographic database and found the coordinates for the University of Washington Medical Center in Seattle—the city had great universities, schools, and industry. The city had not been affected by any of the nuclear attacks, so it was as good a guess as any. Hopefully, global warming hadn't swamped the city. And hopefully, the university still had a good hospital—and offered universal, no-questions-asked healthcare.

Ellis set the machine to auto-retrieve him from the same location in 30 days, returning him to this date and time plus one minute. Ellis was also taking the glove, but he'd seen enough time travel movies to know that things never went as planned. If he had the glove, he could tell the machine to retrieve him, but it also made sense to have the machine auto-retrieve him, in case something went wrong.

If not, the machine would be destroyed one hour from now. If it tried to retrieve him and nothing came back, then the machine would be destroyed. It was too dangerous, leaving an operating time machine behind.

He grabbed up his leather satchel, putting the little blue gun inside as well—who knew if people were nice in the future.

The machine powered up, humming loudly, and as he stepped into the circle, he suddenly felt like vomiting. The feeling was overwhelming. He ignored it and pulled the NBC hood over his metal suit and saw with the one eye that was working that the air began to waver around him. He heard the cracking of ice, louder than ever before, and then a strange series of pops—that was different. Maybe the radiation was affecting the internal systems. He should have run another diagnostic before using the machine again. He glanced back at the bomb and—

3.45
Splash Down

The helicopter splashed down in a low body of water, coming to rest near the shore in about five feet of water. The pilot hadn't really had time to plan the landing. He'd taken his bearings and factored in the uncontrollable spinning of the fuselage and tried to land the chopper as close to the shore as possible.

He pulled himself free of the helicopter and checked the others, but they were all dead. Two of the soldiers had been thrown free in the air and were nowhere to be found. Working free his handgun from inside the NBC suit, he grabbed the side of a small boat that was tied up to a tree and used it to pull himself up onto the shore.

"Base, this is 11-Charlie."

He tried several times but got nothing but static. It had been the same with the helicopter's radio. Comms rarely worked on the ground in the Exclusion Zone.

He climbed down between two trees and out into a parking lot, his pistol out. There was a circular drive in front of what looked like some offices, attached to a large warehouse. The light from several external lights showed a trail of heavy footprints leading up to the doors. He followed them and made his way to the door and pulled, but it was locked. He used the butt of his gun and broke the glass and entered—inside, it looked like ordinary offices, except for the bodies lining the hallways.

The pilot made his way down the hallway—it looked like a company was just moving in. There were lots of boxes, most of them still sealed, and everywhere was the "Power Blossom, LLC" logo, slapped on walls and boxes and computer towers. There were no pictures on the walls.

The pilot worked his way through the offices and then passed carefully through a set of double doors out into a massive warehouse.

He wasn't sure what to expect—maybe some big trucks, or a set of large machines for building cars or sorting mail. Once, when he was a kid, his school class had toured a box plant, where they made big cardboard boxes—there had been machinery for making the cardboard, rolling it out, and then cutting it into different sizes.

This looked nothing like that.

It looked like some sort of futuristic power generation device, or a massive CAT scan machine. There was scaffolding surrounding the machine, with innumerable pipes and wires leading to and away from it. Off to one side, he saw a large object that looked like a generator—it had a handle and wheels, so that it could be easily transported—but it made no sound and was filled with a weird blue glow. Large cables ran between it and the hulking machine next to it.

The pilot walked over to what looked like a computer console—the display was filled with numbers. It looked like it was scanning for something, but for what, he couldn't guess.

On the ground next to the machine was something he did recognize—an explosive device. As the pilot watched, a digital readout on top appeared to be counting down to zero—right now, it read 0:52:45.

Unsure of what else to do, he reached up and touched the ABORT button on the top the device, and the countdown stopped.

3.46

In a Park

—the world changed into something else, something bright and wonderful.

He was standing in a beautiful green park, looking at an odd sculpture of what looked like a person. Actually, he wasn't standing—the teleportation had left him levitating about a half-inch above the grass, and he'd fallen straight down, stumbling to the grass.

He looked up and saw a river behind him and more of the city of Seattle beyond. The sunlight hurt his eyes, and he put his hands up to shield him from the sun when he saw the back of his hands—they looked like the skin was starting to break apart. It was horrible.

As he stripped out of the metal suit, Don looked down at the ground, trying to burn the location of this six-foot-wide circle into his mind. He had 30 days to get treatment—the machine would auto retrieve him once and only once—and get back to this exact location, or he would be trapped here in the future forever.

Leaving the suit, he bent down and dug at the grass, burying one of the metal gloves in the exact spot where he'd appeared. He then stood and turned and walked to the sculpture, counting paces and using a pen to write it all down on the skin of his forearm. He turned and looked at the teleport location, memorizing it in relation to the sculpture and grass and river beyond.

When he was done, he walked across the expansive grass park, toward the tall buildings on the other side of the lawn. His leg cramped up twice, and he stopped to rub the muscles. The skin on his hands burned.

The building was large, beautiful, and covered with large sheets of incredibly clear glass. Don, feeling weak and dehydrated, looked up at the building with the one eye that was still working and hoped it was what hospitals looked like in the future.

3.47
Back From Seattle

—Dr. Donald Ellis materialized again in the circle painted on the floor, carrying his black leather bag, the blue gun in his hand.

He stood tall and looked happy, and all of the signs of radiation sickness were gone. The backs of his hands were completely healed. He also looked years younger—his face seemed brighter, more animated.

The first thing Don noticed was the man.

He was bent over, covering his ears, his gun forgotten. He was dressed in black, in one of those hideous radiation suits that Don had almost forgotten about.

Don lifted the blue gun.

"Don't move," he said.

The man stood and looked at him. He looked like a pilot from the markings on the flight suit that Don could see underneath the NBC suit. Don kept his gun on the man and glanced around—the machine, the control PC, even the bomb on the ground, right where he had left it a month ago. On the bomb, the countdown had been stopped.

"What is all this?" the pilot spoke up.

"It's a backup cycle, an insurance policy," Don said, smiling. "Let's just say when things go square, I can use this to make everything shiny again."

The pilot looked confused. "Shiny?"

Don nodded. "Sorry. I can make things better. My vernac is a little off. So, what should I do with you?" Don asked. "You can't stop me from going, but I need to destroy this machine after I've gone. That's why the explosive device was on a timer. But I don't want to hurt you, or anyone else."

"You killed my crew," the pilot said, nodding out the doors. "How did you appear in mid-air like that?"

Don smiled. "It's complicated, but believe me, I'm not here to hurt you, or anyone. Actually, I've been trying to help. None of this," he said, indicating the warehouse and the world around them, "is my fault."

Don could see the pilot wasn't buying it.

Ellis had an idea. "OK. Step into the circle, please," he said, indicating the circular area on the ground beneath the machine.

"No," the pilot looked at him.

Don pointed with the gun.

"I'm not going to hurt you. In fact, I'll help—if you could go anywhere in the world, where would you go?"

The pilot looked confused.

Don nodded at the machine above them. "It's a teleporter. That's how I appeared up in the air. Wow, I'd forgotten about that. It must've looked strange, me just blimping in the air."

The pilot didn't seem to know how to answer.

Don shook his head. "Wow. That was a long time ago. Anyway, where do you want to go? I need you out of the way, but I don't want to hurt you."

The pilot didn't speak but walked slowly over to the machine, standing in the circle.

"OK, well, I'll pick, then," Don said, smiling. He felt so much better, it was hard to remember what he'd felt like the last time he was here. He was also grateful to know that, no matter how long he chose to linger in this irradiated timeline, he would be fine. The medical treatments and inoculations he'd received would ensure his future health for years to come.

"How about Disney World?" Ellis asked. "I love that place. Have they finished Villains Park yet?"

The pilot didn't seem to indicate any interest in answering, so Ellis tapped in the coordinates and pressed the big green button.

The sounds of ice shattering and cracking filled the warehouse with deafening sound. It was clearly louder than ever before, and Don wondered if the machine was being affected by the radiation. He remembered being worried about that last time, just before he'd left.

In a moment, the machine cycled up, and the pilot, his eyes wide, was bathed in an ethereal blue light and winked out of existence.

"There, that's better," Don said to himself, looking around. "Oh, what am I thinking? They haven't even started on the Villains Park yet. Good thing I sent him to that lake in Epcot instead."

He'd thought about killing the pilot—it would have been easy to set the coordinates and have the man appear in the middle of the Pacific Ocean, a thousand miles from the nearest island. Or send him a thousand feet underground—the machine safeties were easy to override. But Ellis didn't think it would matter, one person knowing about the machine.

It would be destroyed moments after Ellis left, anyway. And the warehouse was well inside the Exclusion Zone, so any machine wreckage removed from the site after it was destroyed, would be heavily irradiated, making it more difficult to examine and reverse engineer.

Don looked down at the backs of his hands and smiled, remembering how they had looked when he'd arrived at that strange looking hospital in Seattle.

Don tapped at a what looked like a freckle on the back of his left hand. The skin on his left forearm faded away, replaced with an embedded, skin-computer readout. The colors were amazing, deep and true and stunning for something that was only a few microns deep and essentially painted onto the surface of his skin by a powerful computer chip.

Actually, Don had no idea exactly how the "skinputer" worked; he just knew that everyone had them in the future. They were something akin to a digital tattoo—he still had the layer of skin there, but the "screen" existed just under the level of the epidermis. He tapped at the interface that appeared with the fingers of his right hand, swiping the image. Don smiled at the collection of pictures that wheeled across the implanted viewing surface. After a moment, he tapped at the freckle again, and the skin on the back of his forearm reappeared, making his arm appear completely normal.

The whole thing ran on body heat and an implanted "chip" the size of a piece of rice, painlessly embedded in one of the knuckles of his left pinkie.

Ellis stood and checked on the bomb—it had been stopped at 0:52:45. He had plenty of time, but he didn't feel like taking any chances. There was the off-chance that the pilot had not been alone or that he could somehow communicate with his superiors and clue them in to the warehouse, so he changed the bomb timer to read "0:02:00" and then went around to the computer that controlled the machine. He tapped at the computer on the table one last time, marveling at the primitive interface he'd forgotten. He triple-checked the coordinates in space and time, and then grabbed the leather satchel, started the bomb timer, and stepped into the circle.

Don was going back to August 31, 1991. It just seemed like a good day—he'd chalk up yet another arbitrary birthday and give himself an even ten years to prevent 9/11 from happening.

And this time, he'd do it all himself—trusting the government to do anything was like herding cats. No matter how much time and knowledge you had, there were always going to be ones that got away. No, this time he'd figure out a way to fix things without showing himself. He'd make sure the Ellis of that timeline didn't lose his family, of course, but

Don knew that his priority would be to mitigate the outcome of the 9/11 disaster, not compound the problem or make it worse.

If he'd learned anything, it was that things could always get worse.

The air swirled around him. He reached into his pocket and took out a small round ball that glowed blue, then put it back, smiling. The air crackled with reactor energy as the machine spun up, and the sound of ice cracking filled the new warehouse. Ellis glanced up at the machine and smiled as the world—

PART FOUR

4.1

MAYTAG

—spun out of existence and back. The warehouse wavered around him, and, for a moment, he could see both warehouses—one in Buchanan, New York, in 2003 that was partially taken up with a massive machine and support equipment, the other a warehouse in Red Hook in 1991, nearly the same size, but completely filled with other machines and equipment.

Both warehouses shared a moment of uneasy coexistence, and then everything inside the Buchanan warehouse faded from view, leaving Ellis standing on a cold concrete floor.

He'd appeared in a dark, narrow area between two large trucks in the process of being loaded—men on forklifts were driving up ramps into the backs of the trucks, loading large cardboard boxes. In this era, the warehouse was operated by Maytag, and Ellis saw boxes labeled "Refrigerator" and "Washing Machine." Unaffected by changes in the timeline, Maytag would consolidate, and this warehouse operation would be closed in 1993, and the building would sit empty until Ellis came along to lease it.

Ellis smiled and waited, and a few seconds passed before a loud whistle blew, indicating lunchtime. He started slowly across the floor of the warehouse, weaving in and out of the trucks and machines as the other employees began filing out to take their lunches on the waterfront. Ellis grabbed a Maytag hat and pulled it on, down over his eyes, and walked to the sliding warehouse doors that fronted the loading docks that pointed toward the river. It was amazing, what a person could get used to.

Ellis put his hand on the doors and wondered, just for a moment, what he would do if the towers weren't there? What if only one tower stood? There was only way to be sure.

"You going out, man?"

Ellis turned and saw a big man in coveralls standing behind him. Don nodded and turned back, pushing open the doors.

Don felt a childish sense of relief at seeing them. There stood the towers of the World Trade Center, dwarfing everything else in lower Manhattan. They gleamed in the sunlight on yet another birthday.

Some part of his mind had convinced him that the towers were like him—both there and not there. He'd seen them come and go, appear and reappear, fall again and again. Every time he saw them anew, it was like a dream.

Don walked out onto the grassy lawn between the warehouse and the river—many of the men had come out here as well to take their lunches, sitting on wooden picnic tables provided by the company. He remembered these tables and benches—worn, broken-down versions of them had lurked behind the warehouse in each of the other timelines. Now they looked new, painted, and fresh.

After a moment, he looked up again at the towers. They stood against the blue sky, tall and proud. But maybe they had to fall. Maybe no matter what he did, they would fall.

Perhaps it was simply destined.

A ludicrous argument, coming from someone with a time machine. But perhaps, for some reason, those two hulking buildings weren't supposed to survive the winter of 2001.

A fatalistic attitude, he knew, but all evidence seemed to indicate that 9/11 was supposed to happen, or would happen, always. It seemed like a simmering pot—no matter what Ellis did, the pot would boil over at some point. It might be sooner, or later, or with different actors, or on a different stage, but the play always ended the same.

Ellis shouldered his leather bags and began working his way toward an exit. Large barbed-wire fences circled the building, and he wasn't sure that the gates wouldn't be guarded. And his bags were literally filled with treasure—and too heavy to get away with, if he had to run.

Don thought that he could work to save as many people as possible. He didn't think he could stop it from happening, but maybe he could mitigate the damage. Or maybe he could try finding Atta and the others—once he had a new machine, he could teleport in and out of locations, appearing and disappearing at will. Maybe he could take out the al Qaeda leadership.

Or maybe it had to happen. If so, he could work to save as many people as possible but allow it to happen. He hated the idea of playing God, being the one to decide who would live and who would die.

As he walked past the men enjoying their lunches and their conversations, he realized that none of them knew what was coming. Of course, it was ten years away, but it was coming. It was inevitable. And warning them probably wouldn't help.

He approached the gate and timed it to walk through the barbed-wire fence as the burly guard was speaking to a group of men around the gate. Ellis scooted quietly through and started up the street lined with warehouses, moving away, happy to be unseen.

Don was on his own.

4.2

PRESENTS AND OPPORTUNITIES

Dr. Beth Higgins walked back into her shared offices after her 1:00 p.m. lecture, flipping through the essay books that had just been submitted by her students. Sometimes, she was stunned at the complete lack of effort some of these kids put into their schoolwork. A semester, or four years of semesters, at the University of New York was expensive—you'd think the kids would want their money's worth. Of course, it wasn't their money that was paying for school in the first place, so it probably didn't matter. Maybe that was the problem.

She walked into her office, but before she'd even set her things down, her secretary Wendy came in from the outer office. "He's back!" she said, her glasses hanging from the strap around her neck.

"Dr. Ellis?" Beth asked, smiling.

Wendy nodded and disappeared.

Dr. Higgins set her things down and rooted through her bookcase, finding the wrapped present and the card that went with it, and looked into Don's office. The room was full—the offices here weren't very big, but it was still a good turnout.

"And she's cute?" one professor was asking Ellis as Beth scooted around a group of secretaries in the door and worked her way around to an open spot near Don's desk.

Dr. Ellis smiled, embarrassed.

"She's adorable," he said, passing around pictures, and holding one up. "And smart, too—she's already trying to roll over. That's good, right?" he asked, looking at the women in the room for validation.

Beth finally spoke up.

"I bet she's a smarty, judging by her parents. Here," she said, handing him the gift.

Don looked at her and smiled. "Oh, you didn't need to…" he began.

Beth cut him off. "Wendy wouldn't let me forget, are you kidding?"

Ellis unwrapped the gift, a small pink ceramic shoe. On the side was written, "Tina Marie Ellis, born August 18, 1995."

He looked up at her and smiled.

"Thanks, Beth."

The next ten minutes were filled with more presents and hugs, as the faculty of his department welcomed Dr. Ellis back from two weeks of paternity leave. Soon, the room emptied out, leaving only Beth, Wendy, and Don, who looked stunned at the outpouring of friendship.

"Wow," he said, moving the presents from his chair and sitting down. "They must've really missed me," he said, smiling.

"No, not really," Wendy teased as she left the room. "It's just been a slow two weeks with you out."

He nodded and looked at his desk, which was piled with an accumulation of papers, mail, university notices, and new textbooks to review.

"So, did I miss anything?" he asked, glancing up at Beth, who had settled into his comfiest chair.

"No, not much," she said, not looking at him. "Anderson thinks that he's made some kind of breakthrough on string theory."

"Again?" Ellis asked, smiling.

Beth nodded.

"Yeah, again. He's doing another paper on it. And Wilkins got invited to something next year, a ten-years-later thing in Chernobyl. Well, not in Chernobyl, but you know what I mean."

"I hope not in Chernobyl," Ellis answered, smiling. "He'll come back glowing in the dark. What's this?" he asked, holding up a thick envelope marked "Grant Opportunity."

"Oh, we all got those," Beth answered. "It's from the Dean—he's encouraging professors to help out MacMillan Enterprises. You know MacMillanSoft? They're branching out into physics, supposedly. They're paying lots of money for advanced work."

"Why? Who are they?" Ellis asked.

She shrugged. "Not sure, but they pay well, and you can still publish. They want first dibs on commercialization opportunities, but you keep the rights to anything you develop. It's a good deal—I finally wrote up that dark matter theory I was talking about, and they paid $8,000. I finally got that new car."

Beth watched as Ellis pulled open his envelope and skimmed the first few pages.

"So, everything is good with Tina?" she asked.

"Yes, she's perfect," Ellis said. "I can't believe how fast she's growing." Don tapped on the grant application. "It says here that they're interested in funding work on four-dimensional mechanism theory."

Beth nodded, impressed. "That's right up your alley. If you can work that whole mess out, you'd win the Sakurai Prize, no doubt."

Ellis set the thick envelope down.

"Beth, I haven't even asked. I'm sorry—how are you doing?"

She looked down for a moment, then back at Don. "Good. I'm good. He's moved out completely now. I got the keys back, finally."

Don nodded, frowning. "So the counseling didn't work out?" he asked.

Beth shook her head.

"No. I didn't think it really would, but…" she trailed off, not wanting to talk about it. She stood, composing herself, and took his hands. "Anyway, never mind that. Today is about you, and Sarah, and little Tina," Beth said, smiling. "You're so lucky, Don. Hold onto them both, okay?"

Ellis nodded and smiled as Beth turned and left. She hurried back to her office and almost got the door closed before she started crying.

4.3
A DINNER

"Tina!"

Don hated shouting, but it seemed no one could hear him unless he was shouting. Now that Tina was four, it seemed like he spent an inordinate amount of time raising his voice to be heard.

After a long moment that made him want to roll his eyes, he finally heard a "Coming, Daddy!" from the far end of the house.

Ellis looked around—the living room was a complete mess. Toys were everywhere; the TV was on with no one watching it. For some reason, there was a half-eaten bologna sandwich sitting on the arm of the couch.

Tina ran around the corner from the hallway and up to Don, smiling. "Yes, Daddy?"

He pointed at the room. "Bethany will be here any minute, and that room is a wreck. You need to clean it up, or I'll tell Bethany no hairdos."

Tina put her hands on her hips, a move that she knew almost always reduced her father to smiles. "No problem, Daddy. And I like the hairdos—Bethany knows all the good ways to fix my hair. And they last a long time."

Don nodded. "And what's with the sandwich?"

She turned and looked at it, then back to him. "I was hungry."

"Not hungry enough to eat it all?"

Tina shook her head. "I didn't want to spoil my apple-tite. Bethany is going to get pizza—she always does."

He nodded, smiling. "OK, well, clean it up. And it's 'appetite,' not 'apple-tite.'"

"OK," she said, smiling, and scooted off.

Outside, the limousine honked again.

"Sarah?" he called again, straightening his tie. He was nervous, and the limousine that the university had sent for them was making him even more nervous.

"I'm coming," his wife called from upstairs. At the same moment, the doorbell rang, and Tina squealed as only a four-year old girl could and ran for the door, throwing it open.

"BETHANY!"

The teenager smiled and picked up Tina, hugging her. "Sorry I'm late, Dr. Ellis. I've got it from here—just go," the young woman said. She lugged a large purse that seemed to be brimming with textbooks and papers.

Don nodded. "It's fine," he lied. "We just finished getting ready." He walked over and held the door open, waving at the limo driver again. It was the first time he'd ever ridden in a limo, and he was a little overwhelmed.

"Just put her down whenever you want," Don heard his wife saying from behind him, and he turned to look at her.

She was a vision, her hair up off her neck and tied back with a little barrette. She was wearing a slinky black dress that he'd never seen before—he suddenly realized that she'd bought a special dress for this event, and that made him smile. He felt like an idiot in his rented tux, but all eyes would be on her anyway, so it wouldn't matter.

"So," she asked, smiling. "What do you think?"

"You look amazing!" Tina yelled, running over to hug her, but Sarah was looking at Don. He smiled.

"I think they'll give you the prize, looking like that," he said.

Sarah picked up her clutch and walked past him, out to the limo. Don nodded at Bethany.

"Call us if there is a problem, right?"

Bethany nodded. "Go! I've never ridden in a limo before—you must be excited!"

Don walked out to the car and climbed in the door that the driver was holding open for him. The door closed solidly behind him as he slid in next to Sarah.

"Nervous?" she asked him.

He nodded. "I've got my speech ready," he said, tapping his chest. There was a small stack of cards in his breast pocket. Don leaned back against the seat as the car drove away from their house.

They drove in silence for a few minutes, just looking out the window and enjoying the quiet. One thing he'd noticed about having a child was just how quiet silence sounded—it was like a blanket that smothered everything. Sometimes he liked the quiet, and sometimes he didn't.

Sarah helped herself to the stocked bar and mixed up a couple of quick cocktails, handing one to him.

"Now, this is the life," she said, sipping at the drink. "You should win this prize every year."

He downed the cocktail in one gulp—it was sweet, like he liked them—and handed her back the empty glass.

"I think I'd run out of speeches."

She looked at the glass, her eyes wide.

"Are you okay? I've never seen you drink like that."

Don tapped his chest. "Just nervous, I guess," he said, looking out the window again. He was dreading the speech, dreading being up there in front of people. He hated speeches—listening to them or giving them—and always empathized with the people speaking.

He rubbed his palms together—he was starting to sweat. And it was warmer in the limo, suddenly—or was that the alcohol?

"Look," Sarah said, sliding closer to him. "You'll do fine. It's a bunch of scientist types, and your research has pushed forward the field. They want to hear what you have to say," she said quietly. "Do you think Mr. MacMillan will be there?"

Don shook his head. The owner of MacMillan Enterprises rarely attended social events, even if they were for prestigious prizes won by scientists on his payroll.

"That's too bad," she said. "What kind of name is Teague?"

He looked at her. "Irish. And are you nuts? Having him there would make it twenty times worse."

She nodded. "I know—I just wanted to meet him. First those grants that helped you to accelerate your research, and then that thing last year, remember? His software department was working on that oral history of Texas and wanted recordings of all my dorky Texas stories."

"Yeah, that was interesting," he said. "It's a technology company—why would they need those stories?"

"Oh, he wrote me back and explained," she answered.

"What? You never told me that."

"Yes, I did. He signed it 'Teague,' remember? You've just forgotten," she said, smiling. She took his head in her hands. "Sometimes, I think you're too smart for your own good. They were putting out their new operation system, and they wanted a non-threatening way to teach people to use the voice-recognition system. They had a user read the stories, and the software listened and learned the individual's voice patterns. It's cool, knowing that Aunt Ginny and Mom and Uncle Peter—that all their stories are out there, floating around the world."

Don nodded.

"Which was his favorite? Did he say?"

Sarah nodded. "Yup, the one about Uncle Peter and the rattlesnake hunt."

"I don't remember that one."

"Of course you do," she said, slapping him playfully on the leg. "It was the one with the wagon, and Uncle Pete was driving it into town. They were having a really hot summer, and Uncle Pete was just back from El Paso. They needed supplies…"

Don sat back and enjoyed the story, which flowed into another and another. He didn't notice crossing over the bridges or anything else until they arrived at the Ritz-Carlton.

4.4

On a Clear Morning

"I can drive," Don said quietly as he and Sarah walked out of the house.

Sarah shook her head.

"No, let me. It's gonna be warm soon—I'll put the top down." She loved her new convertible and had been offering to drive everywhere they went for the whole summer. Don loved it.

He nodded and carried the sleeping Tina to the Passat, holding her until Sarah opened the car and pushed the button that folded down the white fabric cover. Don put her down gently in the back and carefully strapped her in, trying to not wake her.

"I wonder why he wants to meet so early." Don mused, shaking his head. The sun was just coming up over the eastern horizon. "I feel like we should be leaving for the airport—we never go anywhere this early unless Disney World and Mickey Mouse are involved."

Sarah nodded as they climbed in and started off.

"I want to know why he insisted on meeting me. And Tina," she said. "Maybe he's dying and needs to find some heirs!"

He made a face. "Well, maybe he remembered your stories," he ribbed her as they climbed in. The legend of her stories had grown over the past three years, and the royalty checks paid to them by MacMillan Enterprises certainly hadn't hurt. They'd paid for the new convertible, among other things. If they weren't already living in the best school district around, they would have moved out of Jericho last year. As it was, they were taking more vacations, spending more time together.

Next year, the extra money would go towards a beach house they'd been eyeing in Costa Rica.

"Hey, those stories are making us rich," she said for what had to be the hundredth time. "And I love sending money back to the panhandle—everyone really appreciates it."

They got on the Long Island Expressway and headed west—the

headquarters for MacMillan Enterprises was out in Montauk, a small town on the eastern end of Long Island. To make the 8:00 a.m. meeting, they had to leave just after 6:00.

Sarah knew how Don was in the morning, so she swung the Passat through a McDonald's drive-thru for coffee and an egg sandwich, and then pulled onto 495 and headed east.

"You were right," Don said, sipping at his coffee. "This is better. It's like having a driver everywhere I go."

She smiled. "I love this car. I've always wanted a convertible."

He pulled out the paper and glanced at the front page—there was a primary downtown today, and classes at the university were cancelled.

"Who do you think will win for mayor?" he asked her.

She shook her head. "I don't know. I like Giuliani—it's too bad he's leaving. Crime is really down."

They drove on, taking in the sights. It was a Tuesday morning in mid-September, and the weather was absolutely perfect—the sky was a solid blue, with no clouds.

An hour later, they were passing through the quaint village of Montauk, looking for their turn. Don had only been to the headquarters building a couple of times, but they'd always flown him and the other scientists in and out by helicopter. This was the first time he was arriving by car.

"Take Montauk Point State Parkway," he said, reading from the back of the appointment card. Then south on Ranch Road."

They turned off of 27 onto a dirt road, which was labeled "Ranch."

"Is this right?" Sarah asked, craning her head to look back at the main road. "They can't be located on a dirt road."

Don shrugged, looking down the road, but trees cut off the view a quarter mile away. "I don't know—this says 495, then Captain Daniel Roe Highway south to 27 east until Lake Montauk, then south on Ranch Road. It's a half-mile—just drive."

She shrugged, and they started down the dirt road. There was a large farm on their left, which advertised itself as the oldest cattle ranch in the United States, and a line of trees to their right. They skirted the farm and continued south. The farm ended, and the trees edged both sides, threatening to close off the way.

"This can't be right…" she said again.

They wound through thick forest for another quarter mile and then came out onto an expansive, manicured lawn. A long, circular drive curled around in front of a large white house that overlooked the ocean beyond. On either side of the circle were more outbuildings, including a large garage and what looked like three smaller homes to the north.

In the center of the circular drive was a helicopter pad next to a large fountain.

"Wow," Sarah said.

"Is this a farm?" Tina said sleepily from the back seat—he hadn't heard her wake up.

"No, this isn't a farm. Well, I guess it is, sort of," Don said, recognizing the residence as Sarah took the curve and stopped in front of it.

"I wish we lived here," Tina said. "Do they have horses?"

"I don't know, hon," he said. "They didn't have horses the last time I was here." She'd been getting dangerously close lately to being completely obsessed with horses.

A man stepped from the front door of the home and approached, opening the car door for Don and Tina.

"Hi, I'm Mr. Stevens—I work for Mr. MacMillan. He's expecting you both. Just leave your car here, if you please."

Don glanced at Sarah, who was making her "wow, now I'm impressed" face, and they followed Mr. Stevens into the foyer of the home. Don called Tina over, who had immediately bolted across the driveway and was dipping her hands in the fountain.

It was a very large space, done in a simple craftsman style. Don held the door open until Tina came in. There were two large fireplaces on opposite ends of the room—and above the closest fireplace hung a painting that Don recognized. He turned to Mr. Stevens.

"Is that a Warhol?"

Stevens looked up at a large, screen-printed painting of Elvis that hung over the fireplace. At the bottom was scrawled the signature of the artist. As Don looked around the room, he saw several more paintings and prints—they all appeared to be signed by the iconic white-haired artist.

"Yes, it is," he answered. "Mr. MacMillan became interested in Mr. Warhol a few years ago and began collecting some of his works. In fact, that's why he bought this estate, which was previously owned by Mr. Warhol. The artist would have friends and acquaintances out here during the summers. That was one feature that drew Mr. MacMillan to the location, and when it became available, he purchased it. There are several other Warhols scattered around the grounds."

Don nodded, but Sarah had another question to ask. "Wait, I've heard of this place. Is this the Church estate?"

Mr. Stevens nodded. "Yes, it is—it was owned by a friend of Warhol's, but it became available. Mr. MacMillan stays here when he's not in Colorado, and this building and the others serve as the East Coast headquarters for the company."

Sarah and Don nodded as the front doors opened, and a young woman, decked from head to toe in garish horseback riding gear, came into the room.

"Ah, Ms. Jane, there you are," Stevens said to the young woman.

He turned to them. "Dr. and Mrs. Ellis, would your daughter be interested in a riding lesson? Ms. Jane is an experienced instructor."

Jane smiled at them. "We've got a great little pony, just her size. Buttercup."

Tina squealed and started jumping up and down.

"Buttercup, Mommy! Buttercup! Just like the Powerpuff girls!"

Sarah shushed her. She glanced at Don and nodded.

"Ah... yes, that will be fine," Sarah answered. "Tina, be very careful, and listen to Jane, okay?"

"I will, Mom!" she said.

"We'll just do some very basic stuff—don't worry," Jane said, flashing a dazzling smile. "She'll be fine."

In a moment, they were gone.

Mr. Stevens leaned closer. "I'm sorry about surprising you with that, but Mr. MacMillan thought she might enjoy a riding lesson more than staying in the house for your meeting."

Don nodded, agreeing.

"This way, then," Mr. Stevens said, and they were off, moving through the house. Mr. Stevens pointed out a few things along the way—Teague MacMillan was known for collecting Irish objects of interest, so Don was not surprised to see several suits of armor, large tapestries, and other Celtic items adorning the rooms. The floor was made up of huge old flagstones, giving the interior a very rustic feel. Lastly, they came into an office. One end was taken up with a large desk and a smattering of chairs, and the other half of the room was filled with a massive pool table.

"This is Mr. MacMillan's office. Please have a seat—he will be right with you," Mr. Stevens said, an odd smile on his face as he closed the doors behind him, leaving them alone.

"OK," Don said to the closed doors.

Sarah walked around the room. "This is weird, right? How did they know that Tina likes horses?"

Don walked over to the pool table and ran his hand over the velvet surface. "I think every six-year-old girl likes horses, right?"

Sarah nodded at the space above the desk. "Is that another Warhol?" It was a painting he didn't know, a swirling mass of colors. She walked around the desk and read the plaque below the illuminated painting. "Yup, it's a Warhol. It's called *Yarn*—I don't remember this one."

Behind her, Don racked up the pool balls and got down a cue. "Game, while we wait?"

She turned and shook her head. "You should leave that alone, Don. I'm sure he'll be along any moment."

Don smiled and lined up the cue ball, striking it firmly. The rack of balls broke apart, and the balls scattered, a few running the length of the smooth table. He sank the 2 ball and another solid on the break.

"I love pool," he said to no one in particular. "I haven't played in a long time, but I'd forgotten how much I enjoyed it. Maybe it's the physics of the balls," he said, holding out the cue to her. He remembered enjoying the game immensely in college, but somewhere along the line, he'd given it up. He wondered why.

Sarah shook her head and glanced at the back of the door.

"Don't worry about Mr. MacMillan," Don said, lining up his next shot. "I'm sure he'll be along any time now—"

He was lining up to hit the green 6 ball when he noticed the ball was vibrating. It began to travel on its own, rolling slightly. The other balls also began to shake.

Don turned to look at his wife and say something and then the room began to change color—the air started to take on a bluish tinge, and he heard a keening, like a distant siren and—

4.5

Pyramids

—Don and Sarah were suddenly somewhere else. The room that they had been standing in was gone.

"Holy shit," he heard Sarah say from behind him.

Don was just trying to get his legs steady—he put his hand out to steady himself and touched a wall, warm to the touch. It looked like stucco, and his hand cast a dark shadow in the daylight. He had been in one place and now he was in another. Don turned slowly to see if Sarah was okay. She was the same distance away as she had been in MacMillan's office, but now they were outside, and it was sunny and suddenly very warm. They appeared to be standing on a dusty roof.

Don saw that he was still holding the pool cue.

Sarah came over to him, unsteady, and put one hand on his shoulder. She was looking into the distance and pointing.

"Don. Look."

He followed her finger. There was a maze of other rooftops, a mishmash of buildings crowded together, baking in the hot sun. And he saw the pyramids beyond, hazy in the warmth of the day.

They were in Egypt.

"What?" He dropped the pool cue and looked at Sarah. "How… what happened?"

She shook her head. "I don't know. But I think we're in Cairo—those are the pyramids. And there's the Sphinx!"

Don didn't know what to think. They stood together for a few minutes on a small Cairo rooftop, taking in the sights and the smells and the heat of the day. He could hear children playing, laughing, and shouting in a language he did not know. There was a smell of cooking meat coming from a nearby home—the food smelled foreign, rich, and hearty, with spices he couldn't place.

"This doesn't make any sense," Sarah said. "We can't both be dreaming or hallucinating…"

He felt a low rumble this time to accompany the slight change in the air.

"It's happening. Again," Sarah said.

He nodded and looked around, trying to take everything in. Suddenly, he realized that Tina was thousands of miles away. He saw another subtle, bluish glow envelop them, like a ghostly cloud. He took her hand in his and heard the call of a distant siren and—

4.6

RENDEZVOUS

—the world flashed again.

This time Don knew it was happening and tried to pay more attention. He wanted to get a better sense of what was happening in those few scant seconds during the event. There was a definitive moment of transference, and of the surging of power, as they switched locations. For a moment that seemed both lengthy and instantaneous, he could see the Sarah and the rooftop and the pyramids around him and, at the same time, something else, something green and leafy behind them.

The desert was suddenly gone; they were on a trail through some woods. Beneath their feet was the crushed gravel that led uphill into some trees.

"Wow," Sarah said, leaning on a tree. "OK, that is strange. Are you seeing this, too?"

Don was starting to get an inkling about what was going on.

"Yes, we're in a forest. Come on," he said, starting unsteadily up the trail. He was glad to hear Sarah following him quietly.

They crunched up the gravel walkway—the gravel was interspersed with larger, well-worn stones and wound through some trees, coming out into a clearing. Off to his left, there were several large wooden buildings. It was very early morning here, with a low fog clinging to the ground, and the air was crisp and cool. To their right and farther up the hill was a platform and on it, he was surprised to see, there was a small crowd of people. They were tourists, snapping photos of something up and to their right.

Don and Sarah walked up onto the platform and turned to look.

Mount Rushmore.

The sun was just coming up, shining the thin yellow light of early morning on the granite faces. He heard someone gasp as the sunlight broke over the faces.

It was beautiful.

"Oh, geez," Sarah said, finding a wooden bench to sit down on.

Don turned and looked at Sarah—she had her head in her hands, ignoring the other tourists around her. Quickly, he sat down next to her and leaned in.

"We're being teleported," he said quietly to his wife.

She turned and looked at him.

"What?"

"We're being teleported to different locations. It's actually an extension of the work I've been doing, the work MacMillan has been funding," Don continued, his voice low and urgent. "You know the plans in the basement, on the wall? They're plans for a machine that could, theoretically, transmit objects through time or space."

Sarah shook her head.

"I know, it sounds crazy," Don said. "But it makes sense. And MacMillan is always asking me for more information, more details, and more theories about how to do this type of matter transference. Don't you see?" he asked Sarah, not bothering to keep his voice down. "They've invented a teleporter. And they're showing it off."

"I don't know," Sarah said, looking up at the carved heads of the presidents. "Wouldn't people know? Wouldn't something like that be, like, the biggest discovery ever made?"

An older gentleman carrying a camera turned and smiled at them. He'd been snapping pictures with the other tourists. At first glance, he looked a lot like Don Ellis.

"You're quite right, Sarah," the old man said, smiling. "We will release it to the public as soon as they're ready. But for now, we're keeping it under our hats."

Don and Sarah stared at the man, their mouths open. They shared a long moment of silence.

"Oh, sorry," the older man said, smiling. He took off his hat and shook Don's hand. "Teague MacMillan, at your service."

They didn't speak.

Teague glanced at his watch and the smile vanished from his lined face.

"Oh, my, is it that late? We have to go," he said and started down the path, back toward where Don and Sarah had materialized.

Unsure of what else to do, they followed. As soon as they were out of sight of the tourists, Teague stopped and waited for Don and Sarah. When they stopped, Teague rolled up the left sleeve of his shirt.

Don saw something there that didn't make sense.

The old man's arm was there, and the skin that covered his arm was there as well. But the arm also looked like it was covered with paint, or some kind of luminous, flickering tattoo. The swirling colors slowed and began to take shape, and Ellis understood intuitively that it was a display of some sort. It resolved into a black keyboard, along with several smaller "windows" that held readouts of their own—displaying information and a clock that read 8:22.

"It's a skinputer—neat, huh?" Teague said, holding it up for them to read. It was like a skin-based monitor, but the words and numbers were crystal clear. Teague smiled and jabbed at the glowing green button on the skinputer that read ACTIVATE.

The world began to shimmer and vibrate again.

"Here we go," Teague said, smiling.

The world wavered again, and Don saw that Teague was looking back up the walkway, making sure no one saw them.

"So," Don began to say, "this is your secret, your company's ability to teleport objects. Is it based—"

4.7
CLIFFSIDE

"—on my research?" Don finished the sentence 1,900 miles away.

They were standing on a cliff-side platform with a railing all around it, looking out at the ocean.

Don turned and saw the big house in Montauk behind them.

"I don't know if I'm getting used to this or not," Sarah said, and Teague took her hand to steady her.

"It gets better. I've been doing it for a while now," he said, and then turned and started for the house. "We need to hurry."

The three walked up a crushed stone path and saw the house and a fenced area to the west. Tina was there, riding on a small horse, and Jane was right next to her, running, with one hand on Tina's back. Before she could see them, Don and Sarah and Teague passed through a door, back inside the house.

Mr. Stevens was waiting for them.

"Has it started yet?" Teague asked.

Mr. Stevens shook his head.

"Good, good." Teague turned to Don and Sarah. "We're going to teleport again—hang on."

He jabbed at his arm, and the world swam again. Don closed his eyes this time, and it was better—he didn't have to see the bleeding together of two worlds. After the keening sound passed, he opened his eyes.

They were in a conference room.

"Where are we now?" Sarah asked, exasperated.

Teague indicated the chairs and sat.

"We're still in Montauk, about one hundred and fifty feet beneath the mansion. It was a natural cave, but we hollowed it out and made offices and other larger rooms. It's bomb-proof and inaccessible from above."

"Unless you have a teleporter," Don added.

Teague looked at him, and Don thought there was something very familiar about the man.

"Correct. Well, there are a couple of emergency exits, but yes, it's essentially sealed away from the world above."

"OK, so is the machine based on my research?"

Teague smiled. "Yes and no. Both at the same time, actually, if you can get your mind around it. But we're not here to talk about the machine. I needed you to understand that I possess that level of technology—it will make understanding what comes next easier."

Sarah and Don looked at him.

"What are we here to talk about? Why am I here?" Sarah asked.

"Look, some very bad things are going to happen today," Teague said, looking at his arm. Don saw that he was checking the time again. "In a few minutes, the United States will be attacked by terrorists, who will succeed in many of the things they are attempting to do—and fail in others."

"How do you know this?" Don asked.

Teague looked at him. "Don't worry, Tiger. You'll know in a moment."

Don was taken aback.

"Tiger. That's what my mom used to call me when I was young."

Teague reached up and took off his glasses and then tugged at his hairline, pulling off a grey wig. For a moment, Don didn't know what he was doing, but then the old man set the wig and glasses down and reached up, pulling off the fake mustache and beard.

"My mom used to call me Tiger, as well," the man said.

"Oh my God," Sarah said, standing, her hand at her mouth. "Don... Don! He's you!"

Don looked across the table at his double—it was remarkable. With the beard and wig gone, the man across the table could be his twin, just a decade older.

"Yes, it's true," Teague MacMillan said. "I'm Dr. Donald Ellis."

Don was speechless. "How?"

Teague smiled. "Well, I came back in time. It's the easiest way to explain it, really. I'm you, just an older, different version of you." Teague looked down at the mask and glasses. "I know it's crazy, but it's the truth."

The older man turned to Sarah. "That is your Don," he said, pointing at the younger man. "I'm from another timeline."

She looked back and forth between them and, after a minute, seemed to calm.

"And you... you've been teleporting us around the world?" she asked.

The older man nodded. "It was faster than explaining—it should have immediately removed any doubts about my ability to move objects and people through time and space."

Don nodded at the older man. "It was... an affective introduction."

"Good," the older man said. "I have traveled to several different timelines, and today you'll learn why I have used it. I'll tell you the whole story soon, but suffice it to say that something horrible is going to happen today, and I came back to stop it. It happened in my timeline, as well," Teague said, looking at Sarah. He was quiet for a moment. "Things went horribly, horribly wrong," he said, then looked back at Don. "So I spent ten years finishing our machine and went back to stop it."

Sarah looked confused. "But it's still happening?"

"I've tried to stop it, over and over, and it never worked. This time, I'm trying to—well, mitigate it, I guess. It will still be a terrible tragedy, I believe, but not as bad as it could have been. I'll answer all of your questions—all I ask is that you save your judgments until the end, okay?"

Don looked at Sarah and then back to Teague, nodding.

"Good," Teague said, standing. "Follow me—things are about to start, and I need to be ready to react, in case my plans don't work out."

4.8
CONTROL ROOM

They walked along a white hallway. There were many rooms in the underground space, and although it was constructed in what formerly was a cave, Don had seen no exposed walls or creepy stalactites. He could be in any office building in the country.

"I came to this timeline in 1991," Teague was saying. "I've been to other timelines, as well, trying to stop this event, but it always happens, in some form. I don't know why. I came back to 1991 with the machine plans and information about the future, and set about rebuilding my empire again."

"What do you mean?" Sarah asked.

"I've been through four timelines, including my original. In each, I've had to raise funds and build the machine, over and over. I've gotten pretty good at it, I think. In the last version, we figured out how to incorporate a teleporter function. We were getting ready to go public with the information, but there were more terrorist attacks."

"More?" Don asked. "I thought you stopped them?"

"No," Teague shook his head. "I never have. I've delayed them, twice, by giving critical information to the government. They used it to influence events, reduce the chances of the terrorist attacks happening, but they ended up only delaying the attacks. In both cases, the final outcome was much worse than in my original timeline."

They rounded a corner and entered a very large room that immediately reminded Don of mission control at a NASA launch. The front wall of the large room was lined with large screens. A group of men and women sat at a variety of computer terminals.

"OK, here we go," Teague said loudly, taking up a spot right in the middle of the room.

On one screen, Don saw the World Trade Center in downtown New York City. It looked like one of the towers was on fire.

"Oh my God," Sarah said, her hand to her mouth.

Teague nodded. "Yes, it's begun. Cassie, when did that happen?"

A woman seated at a computer terminal turned. "Right on time, Teague. It came in low, and from the north, and struck at 8:46. Floors 93-99 are involved in the fire."

"You knew this plane was going to crash into the building?" Don asked sharply.

Teague turned to him.

"I tried, okay? I got one of the attackers arrested—well, I didn't, but I knew where he was taking flight training lessons and arranged for several tips to be called in on him and some of the other hijackers. They were already looking at him, Zacarias Moussaoui. He was arrested in August, but the rest are carrying out their plan, now."

"But if you could catch one—" Sarah began, but Teague cut her off.

"I can't catch any of them. I know where they are, and where they're going, but I'm not the cops. I decided to let it happen—what happens today is part of American history, or will be. It will change many lives—who am I to say that it shouldn't happen? There will be four planes hijacked by terrorists—"

"So why get involved at all?" Don said.

Teague looked at Sarah again. "I... I had to."

Don looked at Teague. "Did something... happen to Sarah? In your original timeline, something happened, right?" he asked, feeling the skin on the back of his neck stand up. If anything ever happened to her, he wasn't sure what lengths he would go to—

Teague nodded. "She and Tina. They died in the World Trade Center," he said and turned away.

No one said anything for a long moment—they all looked at the monitors.

"That was the first plane, at 8:46," Teague finally said, pointing at the screen. "Another plane will hit the South Tower at around 9:03," he said, glancing at Sarah. "You and Tina were there, visiting a friend. You... died there. And many more were killed—both towers will burn and collapse within the hour."

Don shook his head. "It can't be..."

"A third plane will hit the Pentagon, in Washington, D.C.," the old man said, looking at Don. "The nation will reel from the coordinated attack. The fourth plane will target the Capitol building, causing the most damage of all. The government, for all intents and purposes, will cease to operate for several weeks. Half of Congress will be killed, along with much of the Senate. And the president's wife."

Sarah sat down at a table, shaking her head. Don didn't know what to do, so he walked around Teague and put his hands on her shoulders.

She was sobbing quietly.

"It changes the world," Teague said, looking at the monitor—on the screen, smoke poured from a jagged wound near the top of the North Tower. "The attacks today will change everything. President Bush and, later, President Cheney, will move aggressively against al Qaeda, the terrorist organization behind today's attacks. Without Congress to stop them, they take the nation to war and wipe out al Qaeda and their supporters."

"Good," Don said. "We should bomb them off the map."

Teague shook his head. "There are supposed to be checks and balances—the president answers to us and to Congress. He can't run off, willy-nilly, starting wars. I've seen where that leads."

The young woman spoke up again. "Mr. MacMillan? The networks are starting to cover the event. It's on all the major channels now, and the morning news shows have all been interrupted. They are broadcasting the video."

Teague nodded. "Does anyone have Flight 175 yet?"

One of the other technicians spoke up. "No, but I'm monitoring FAA and Air Traffic Control channels. They're discussing a possible hijacking of another plane," the man said.

Teague looked up at the clock and turned to the screens. "Here comes the second plane—that's United 175."

Don and Sarah turned to watch—on the screens, CNN and NBC anchors were talking as a second plane appeared at the edge of the screen, low and fast, like a missile. Don heard one of the announcers say, "What is that plane?" and then the plane impacted the South Tower with a massive explosion, a fireball roiling out the opposite side. Impact debris and what looked like part of the plane showered down onto the streets of New York below.

"Oh my God," Sarah said, her eyes wet.

"Now people will know that it's a terrorist attack," Teague said. "Military planes will be scrambled, and the FAA will begin to ground national and international flights." Teague looked up at a large display board, and Don noticed, for the first time, an outline of the events that would occur today and their exact time.

It said the Pentagon plane would be hitting in thirty minutes.

"Why can't we warn them?" Don asked. "Why can't we just call in a bomb threat to the building, or the portion of the building that will be hit—you must know where it will hit, right?"

Teague shook his head. "It would be too suspicious—it would prove later that someone had foreknowledge of the event."

"But you do!"

"No, I don't," Teague said. "I know what happened in the other time-lines, and I think I know what will happen. But I'm not sure. And I've made a lot of changes, changes that, hopefully, will save as many lives as possible."

"That's bullshit," Sarah said. She'd found some tissues somewhere and was dabbing at her eyes. "Who said you could pick who lives and who dies? You're not God."

"No, I'm not," Teague said. "But I have information that no one else has. I'm going to try and mitigate this event, fix it so that as few people as possible die. For example, your friend Elaine Clausen received an excellent job offer several months ago, right? I arranged for that, or she would be working in the south tower right now."

Sarah shook her head but said nothing.

"Look," Teague said. "What would you do?"

"I'd stop it!" Sarah shouted, pointing at the monitors. "People are dying, innocent people."

Teague nodded. "Yes, and I've tried to stop it, over and over. It never works."

"Then you have to keep trying," she said quietly.

The room was quiet for several minutes. Teague and the technicians monitored the FAA communications frequencies and listened in on local air traffic control. Other technicians were monitoring the networks, occasionally shouting something to Teague.

"Were we able to delay Flight 93?" he asked at one point, and a technician nodded before answering.

"Delays on the ground, congested runways. They were 40 minutes late getting away," the man said.

"Good," Teague said. "We can work with that."

Don was watching the monitor and counting down the seconds. "The Pentagon. Your timeline says that a plane will hit there soon."

Teague turned, and they all saw nothing—there was no live coverage of the plane hitting the Pentagon. Moments later, the screen switched to a live feed, showing smoke rising up from the headquarters of the U.S. military.

"The plane struck the Wedge One, on the western side of the building," Teague said, smiling and sitting down. He seemed very relieved. "Good, good."

"Good?" Sarah asked, incredulous. She stood and walked over to Teague, standing over him. "How can that possibly be good news? People will die—thousands of people!"

Don noticed the Cassie woman and several other MacMillan employees look up at the screaming woman. Stevens peeled himself away from a computer monitor and started walking over, but Teague waved him away.

"That is why," Teague said to Sarah, pointing at a huge schematic of the Pentagon on the wall. He stood and walked over to the plans, which were emblazoned with the logo for MacMillan Architecture, a subsidiary of his corporation.

"See this area?" Teague said, pointing at the plans. "This is Wedge One, and it's been reinforced against just this kind of attack. Strengthened materials, retrofitted and upgraded fireproofing, and new, high-pressure sprinkler systems. The original windows were replaced with two-inch thick, blast-resistant glass. Those new systems were installed just over the last six months and finished two weeks ago. If the plane had to strike anywhere in the building, that's the best possible place. And it hit right in the middle, where I'd hoped."

"How do you know that?" Don asked.

Teague smiled. "We won the contract. I've been petitioning the military for years, scaring them with tales of missile attacks and how the outdated, 1940s-style construction would crumble under a real terrorist attack. After the attack on the Murrah Federal Building in Oklahoma City, the Pentagon got serious. We won the contract in 1998 and have been strengthening portions of the Pentagon ever since. They call the individual pieces of the Pentagon wedges, and we started with Wedge One."

"Which you knew would be attacked."

Teague nodded. "Of course, that's where they've hit before. Not before, but in other timelines. I could only hope that the plane's trajectory would be close."

Sarah looked up. "I can't believe you, hoping that it hits—"

"I'm not hoping, Sarah," he said, and in his frustration Teague's voice sounded almost exactly like Don's. "But it's going to happen—face it. There is no way to prevent it. Believe me, I've tried. And 20,000 people work in the Pentagon every day. In my timeline, nearly 3,000 people died as the fires swept through the building. But I've done what I can to help, to reduce the number of casualties—"

"You talk about them like they're just numbers," Don said quietly. He was looking at the television coverage of the Pentagon, a wide plume of smoke coming off the building and drifting over Washington, D.C. "Statistics to be weighed and measured."

Teague turned to him. "No, each number is another family torn apart by today's events. We need to minimize those numbers. They're not empty statistics. Each is a father that won't see his kids graduate or a mother whose loss will destroy a family."

It was quiet for a few minutes. Teague walked around and talked with Stevens and the other technicians in the room.

"What do you think?" Don asked Sarah.

She shook her head. "It's all too much to take in. I can't even think of all of those people, trapped in those towers. To even imagine being in the South Tower when the plane hit—it's all just too much."

Don nodded. "Yeah. I'm starting to understand why he wanted us to come out and meet with him today—it was his way of keeping us safe, I think."

Sarah looked over at Teague as he walked up to join them.

"The FAA just shut down U.S. airspace," Teague said. "They'll be landing or forcing down every plane over the continental U.S."

"What about the World Trade Center?" Sarah asked, nodding at the other monitors, where both towers burned. "What did you do to mitigate the number of deaths?"

Teague looked at the screens, and Don could see the pain on his face. "That is where the most of the casualties will happen, or at least they did in the other timelines. Do you remember the 1993 terrorist attacks on the WTC? Terrorists blew up a van in the parking structure under one of the towers, trying to knock it over?"

Don and Sarah both nodded.

"Again, MacMillan Architecture won the contract for the cleanup after the attacks. We upgraded their egress system—new, wider staircases, larger signs, faster evacuation routes, and improved ventilation systems. And we instituted weekly fire drills to teach residents of the building how to get out, quickly and safely."

"What about above the fires?" Sarah was looking at the monitors, which showed both buildings on fire.

Teague shook his head. "It will be difficult for those people to escape. I don't want to think about it. Those people in each building above the crash sites are likely trapped, unless they can get to a passable stairwell and out of the building."

"You said the buildings will collapse," Sarah said.

Teague nodded. "Each will burn for about an hour and then fall. Hopefully, everyone below the crash sites will be out by then. The South Tower will go first, in just a few minutes."

Teague turned and tapped at a computer, pulling up a plot of an airplane and some audio on the large central screen.

"OK, this is the plane I'm worried about."

Don and Sarah looked up at the screen, where Teague was pointing.

"The fourth plane," Don said.

"Yes. It has one less hijacker on board, thanks to Zacarias Moussaoui getting nabbed by the FBI last month. And, due to a few things this morning, the flight was delayed by over an hour. And it's a different plane."

"What do you mean?" Sarah asked.

"The original plane didn't carry air phones, but this one does. It was hijacked over Ohio—air traffic controllers in Cleveland heard it being hijacked at about the same time as the Pentagon crash. Right now, it's flying straight toward D.C. In my timeline, it crashed into the Capitol. The New York and Pentagon crashes were disasters, certainly, but it was the destruction of the Capitol building and the virtual decapitation of the U.S. Congress that had the largest effect on the nation. In another timeline, the plane was chased by fighters and diverted to a secondary target, crashing into an NFL game at the football stadium in downtown Baltimore. I doubt the stadium is on the target list this time—there's not a game going on. Go ahead, Stevens."

Mr. Stevens was at another terminal and tapped at the computer station.

"What's he doing?" Sarah asked.

"He's calling to get a wrong number—a bunch of wrong numbers. He's instructing the computer to call all the cell phones of all the passengers on the flight, Flight 93, and then hang up. It should clue them in that their phones are operational, even in flight. A few of them will call loved ones and find out what's happening in New York and D.C."

"Will that help?" Don asked.

"I'm not sure," Teague answered. "In my timeline, all of this happened simultaneously. All of the flights took off at nearly the same time and crashed within a half-hour of each other. I am hoping that, by delaying that flight, the passengers will find out what's happening to the other hijacked planes and take action. Commandeer the plane, or revive the pilot, or crash it."

Don shook his head. "You don't care if they live or die—"

"Those people on the plane are dead, either way," Teague answered. "If I hadn't intervened, the hijackers would have already crashed it into the Capitol. By delaying the plane, I might have given the passengers a chance to fight back."

"A chance," Sarah said. "Another chance to change things but still die."

"There's nothing I can do," Teague said. "There are two people on board, other than the flight crew and the hijackers, who have the training to land the plane. If the passengers can get control of the plane, they have a good chance of surviving—"

"You have a teleporter—get those people off that plane, before they die!" Sarah said, standing. "Who cares if the information gets out? You could save those people."

Teague shook his head. "I'm sorry, but I can't do that. And I've done everything I can to save as many people as possible. I've arranged for the planes to be flying with many fewer passengers than average, but this event has to happen, or worse things will follow. Delay only makes it worse, and the attacks will force the government to finally face up to some of the decisions they've been making. The government, for the first time, will get serious about al Qaeda and other terrorist organizations. They'll wipe out the Taliban."

Behind them, Cassie yelled out and pointed at the monitors, which showed the South Tower collapsing. The floors fell, one on top of another, pancaking down to the ground and throwing up a dust plume two hundred feet high. The dust and pulverized rock cloud washed through the streets of lower Manhattan.

Several of the technicians had their heads down, unable to watch. Behind Teague and Don, Sarah sat at a table, crying.

Don nodded. "So, why are we here?"

Teague turned—he clearly hadn't been expecting that question.

"You're not too sure of this plan of yours," Don asked, "or you wouldn't have gotten us out of danger. Were you worried that something else might require our presence downtown this morning? You wanted us out of the area. And you had us bring Tina, just in case."

Teague nodded. "You don't understand—I saved your family. If you could imagine—"

"I can," Don said, and took Teague's hand. "Thank you."

The older man nodded.

Sarah stood and came over as well, standing behind Don. She was quiet for a long moment, and then finally looked up at Teague. "Yes, thank you. I might not agree with how you're handling this, but I don't know how to thank you for saving Tina. And me, I guess."

Teague nodded. "It's fine. And you're right—this may not be the best solution, but it's better than any others I've tried."

Sarah nodded.

"Oh, and thank you so much for those stories," he said quietly.

She looked at him.

"I miss her so much," Teague said, looking at Sarah. "My Sarah. You're like a reflection of her, another facet of the same jewel. You are her and not her. But having those stories, recorded in her voice, your voice, it was like I could hear her again. Thank you."

She nodded, her eyes wet again. She glanced up at the monitors. "You know, I'm kind of done watching all of this—can I see Tina now? I just want to walk outside and look at the sky and hold my girl."

Teague nodded, smiling.

"Absolutely."

He tapped at the skinputer, and Don watched as his wife began to fade—she gave him a wave and was gone.

"Thank you, Teague," Don said again. "So, when you got back to 1991 and starting setting all this up, why didn't you use your name—our name?"

"Too confusing, old boy," Teague said. "I wanted a new identity and one that wouldn't impact you. You know how we've always been fascinated with our Irish background?"

Don nodded.

"I had some genealogy work done. MacMillan is in our family tree, as was a gent named Teague. I adopted them for my own use and built MacMillan Enterprises and several other ancillary businesses. Speaking of that, I'd like to talk to you, when this is all over. I have a position in mind for you."

Don nodded and smiled. "I'd like that," he said.

They stood together for a few long minutes, looking at the screens, before Don spoke up again.

"So, now what?"

"I'm waiting to see what happens with that fourth plane," Teague said. The news stations were replaying the collapse of the South Tower, again and again.

"How many will die?" Don asked quietly.

Teague shook his head. "I don't know. In my original timeline, 21,502 people died during these attacks. Of course, in my timeline they hadn't implemented the improved safety and evacuation systems that resulted from the 1993 World Trade Center bombing. Plus, there's a primary this time, so hopefully many people stopped off to vote."

Don looked at him. "Don't tell me—you got the primary moved?"

"No, nothing like that," Teague said. "But in my timeline it had been delayed—something with the ballots and counting signatures, I think. Anyway, this time I made sure nothing delayed it."

Don smiled and nodded. "Nice."

The two versions of Dr. Donald Ellis watched the screens and monitors and listened to the news together for the next hour. The news reported that the U.N. building in New York and the Sears Tower in Chicago were being evacuated.

At 10:28, the North Tower fell, collapsing upon itself in the same manner as the South Tower. For a few seconds after the tower fell, a forty-story tall spire of structural support column stood, defying gravity for moments before collapsing.

The passengers of Flight 93 evidently got word about what was going on with the other planes. At 10:37, the Associated Press began reporting a plane crash in rural Pennsylvania. The speculation was that it was Flight 93 quickly turned to confirmation. The passengers had fought back, in some capacity, and brought down the plane.

"Now what?" Don asked as they sat. "Is that it?"

Teague nodded. "Yes. There will be a thousand rumors flying around about other planes and other groups of hijackers that were foiled by the FAA, forcing all the planes to land. Urban legends will be spun about other hijacking teams that exit their landed planes and disappear."

"Urban legends and conspiracy theories, no doubt," Don said.

Teague nodded. "In New York, Giuliani will step up and lead, I hope. He seems like a good wartime leader—in my timeline, he was killed in the collapse of WTC 7."

Don nodded.

"He seems like a sturdy one—the city will need him to get through."

"And then the U.S. should begin combat operations against the Taliban in Afghanistan," Teague continued. "Bush, hopefully, will have his head about him, this time. Last time, losing Laura pushed him over the edge. Cheney had him declared unfit."

"What about us?" Don asked.

Teague turned and looked at him. "You and your family will be fine. And you'll come to work for me, I hope. Let me show you."

Teague walked back out into the hallway, turning. Don followed him, and they reached a door that required Teague's handprint. "Your handprint would work just as well," the old man said with a smile and pushed open the large door.

Beyond the door was a massive space, a carved-out chamber big enough to hold ten buildings the size of the mansion. The ceiling was dotted with stalactites—the roof of the chamber was obviously part of the original cave.

But Don was looking at the floor of the chamber.

In the middle of the chamber sat a large machine that looked like the ones in his drawings. A large central core, pointing downward, an open area in the middle like a CAT scanner, and miles of piping, wiring, and tubing. It was either a particle accelerator or a—

"Time machine," Don said quietly.

Teague smiled and patted Don on the back.

"Yup, that was the first one, started when I arrived in 1991. I've built so many of them that I can practically do it in my sleep, but I was constrained by 1991-era equipment and electronics. Had to 'invent' a few new materials and electronic components along the way, and that's how MacMillan Enterprises got going, and MacMillan Software, and Mac-Millan Materials, and all the other companies."

"You said 'the first one,'" Don said.

"Yes." Teague kept walking. Near the large machine was a row of identical eighteen wheelers, each parked side by side in the cavern. There were seven. Each said WAL-MART on the side—they were apparently delivery trucks for the retail behemoth.

"These are the portable ones," Teague said. "We resized them and built them inside these trucks, so we could take them on the road without anyone knowing. We're working on some smaller versions, now—I'd love to get one down to a backpack size, someday. And they all have teleport capability, as well, so they can move each other, if needed. We've got more machines, in other locations, but I wanted to show you these first. And to offer you a job—I'm going to need help in the future."

Don looked at the trucks—they looked exactly like the eighteen wheelers he saw every day on the highway. He thought about portable time machines and a job offer, out of the blue. "You're joking me."

Teague smiled. "No, I'm not. I'll need your help."

Don nodded. "I'll have to talk to Sarah."

"Of course," Teague said. "Didn't your Tina say that when she was little, around two? 'You're joking me?'"

Don thought about it for a moment and realized that the old man was right—Tina had picked that phrase up from somewhere. He remembered that she had repeated it often, always at the cutest possible times.

"Yeah, I forgot about that," Don said, smiling.

Teague looked at Don looked for a long moment and then smiled.

"Never forget, Don," Teague said, his eyes sparkling. "I've learned that it's all precious, like water through your hands. Hold on to every bit of it you can."

EPILOGUE

"—and their technology was incredible," Teague MacMillan said, smiling.

They were enjoying a small reception in a beautiful restaurant downtown. The event outside had already started, and most of the guests at the reception had already been called out.

Since that day ten years ago, when Don and Sarah and Tina had taken a trip to Teague's Montauk headquarters, Don had wondered about the skinputer. Even after all the incredible things that he'd been told and seen, Don had always wondered about that particular piece of technology. It just didn't seem possible within the range of times Teague had talked about.

"You were in Seattle?"

Teague nodded.

"Near the University of Washington Hospital. Of course, it wasn't called that anymore—it was named after a President Roslin, whoever that was, or will be. Anyway, they had a triage booth in the main lobby—it was like an old phone booth, but it scanned me, and immediately I was being wheeled to the appropriate ward."

"Wheeled?" Don asked, sipping from his cup of coffee. He was a bear in the morning if he didn't get his coffee. "I'm surprised the gurneys didn't float."

"Yeah, right? I still wonder what happened to my jetpack and flying car," Teague said, smiling. "Anyway, the burns and radiation poisoning were treated in minutes. Gone, just like that. And I was inoculated against future exposure."

"Magic," Don said, smiling. "Just like Asimov said."

"Clarke, you mean."

Don smiled. "What?"

"Arthur C. Clarke," Teague answered. "He said that any sufficiently advanced technology would look like magic to the unskilled user. You said Asimov."

"Ah, that's right."

Teague looked at him across the table. "You still don't believe me?"

Don shook his head. "You went sixty years into the future for medical treatment and came back cured, with a computer implanted in your skin and some kind of glowing blue power source?"

"Well, when you say it all together like that, it sounds crazy."

Don smiled. "So how did you get the skinputer?"

Teague leaned forward and sipped his coffee. "Well, this is funny. They fixed me up, right, and then they wanted payment."

"This I gotta hear. They use money in the future?"

"So I don't have a clue what to do, and the payment guy, or whatever he was called there, leans over and taps my arm, trying to turn on my skinputer. I'd seen others using theirs, so I knew what he was doing, and I guess he could use it for payment, like an electronic wallet. I said that mine had been damaged by the radiation burns. The guy reaches into his desk and pulls out a little nozzle-looking thingy and jabs my pinkie knuckle. I SEE the little thingy go in—it didn't hurt—and then the skin on my arm just starts changing. It was like a tattoo, but under the skin, and a hundred times more colorful. And it boots up, and guess what it says?"

Don had no clue. "What?"

"It says 'Microsoft.' Can you believe that?"

Don smiled. "I need to buy more stock, I think. We should corner that market with MacMillanSoft as soon as it starts coming around. So, what happened after the guy wanted payment?"

"Well, the skinputer booted up, and then it blanked out, like it had no information on me or my identity, so he took me to what would be the equivalent of their library and left me there. He gave me a bill—not a paper bill, but it was on some kind of clear material. I spent days in that library, downloading everything I could into the skinputer."

Don sipped at his coffee and saw a man approaching their table. He had the nervous look of an underpaid underling.

"Excuse me, sirs, but we'll be ready for you in a moment. Would you follow me?"

Don Ellis and Teague MacMillan stood, putting their cloth napkins on the table, and followed the young man.

"Paid," Don asked. "You said you paid for a newer unit?"

Teague smiled. "I was there for 30 days, remember. I was only gone from the warehouse in Buchanan for moments, but I was in Seattle for long enough to pick up a little of the dialect. I also sold a few of the 'ancient' items I had with me. The most popular item, by far, was the iPad."

"You had one of those?" Don asked.

"From my original timeline. Anyway, that fetched a pretty penny, as it was a still working antique and loaded with all the original applications. The guy at their—well, I guess it was like a pawn shop or consignment store—took the iPad and handled it very gingerly, like it was from King Tut's tomb. He said he was going to sell it to a museum."

The young man led them to a set of doors, where they stopped.

"And with the money, you bought…" Don asked.

"A new skinputer. And the fusion core. And I went back and paid the hospital bill."

Don turned and looked at him.

"Fusion core?"

Teague nodded. "Yup. We've back-engineered what we could from it, but it's still years beyond our technology. But we'll get there," he said, smiling. "Or you will, more accurately."

The doors opened, and Teague and Don followed the young man out onto the dais, where dozens of other dignitaries were seated, including the mayor of New York City and several borough presidents. Arrayed in front of them, standing and filling every inch of Ground Zero and the new 9/11 memorial, was an audience of thousands—citizens, residents, people who had lost family members on 9/11, and anyone else who could crowd into the space.

Towering above them was the first thirty floors of the new Freedom Tower. It was being built on the same site as the World Trade Center. And below the podium, in between the two halves of the audience, one of the two new memorial pools sat, filled with gurgling water that ran down into the subterranean museum that would open in early 2012.

"Teague MacMillan and Dr. Donald Ellis of MacMillan Enterprises," someone said over the loudspeakers. "MacMillan Enterprises oversaw construction of the 9/11 Memorial," the voice said. The crowd applauded as Teague waved to the crowd and followed Don to their seats.

After they were seated, Don leaned over. "So they sell fusion generators in the future? Like in a 7-11?"

Teague looked at him as other dignitaries were introduced. "No, but the guy who bought the iPad knew he was getting a great deal. I had no use for the future currency, so I traded him for the core and the skinputer upgrade. I think he made out pretty good—I did read somewhere that those fusion cores were used to power lots of small things. I doubt they were as common as batteries, but they certainly weren't expensive."

Don nodded and sat back. After a few minutes, the loudspeaker introduced the president of the United States, who stepped up to the podium from somewhere that Don couldn't see. Teleprompters rose up out of the stage, and Obama asked for a moment of silence for the victims in the first plane to strike the World Trade Center. After a few moments, he began to speak.

"Our nation rose to this great challenge. We were tested, but we rose to the call. In this fateful place, ten years ago today, there was only tragedy and loss, death, and mourning. But we persevered, and the struggle continued…"

The speech continued, but Don wasn't paying much attention—he was looking in the crowd. Finally, he spotted Sarah. Tina was standing next to her, now sixteen and almost as tall as her mother. The twins, Dylan and Abigail, were clinging to their mother, who smiled at Don and made her "this is crazy" face.

"You took my advice," Teague said quietly, looking at Don's family.

Don nodded. "Live in the now, right?"

Teague smiled, looking around.

"This is a nice timeline—things turned out well."

"I think so," Don answered. "You did good."

After the speech, Ellis and Teague walked down into the crowd. Over the past ten years, Teague had been actively grooming Ellis to take over the company, so Don received almost as many congratulations and handshakes as the company founder. People seemed to really like the memorial, with the twin pools in the footprints of the fallen towers. The water fell away into darkness, an element that Don thought gave the memorial a haunting feel.

They finally made their way through the crowd to Sarah and the kids.

Tina hugged the older man.

"Hi, Uncle Teague," she said, smiling. The other kids grabbed one leg each and hugged the man they knew only as their father's brother. Teague picked up the smaller kids, in turn, and gave them pecks on the cheek. Then he smiled at Don and leaned over to whisper in his ear.

"You're a lucky man, Don."

Don heard the sadness in his voice and looked at Teague for a long moment.

Teague was looking at Sarah and Tina and spoke, his voice low.

"I tried to save my timeline," Teague said. "But that was impossible, I think. It had already happened, and now I'm the only one who remembers that world." He looked at the other people around them in the plaza. "It's still there, somewhere, but inaccessible, like a distant planet."

Don looked at him and nodded—Teague and he had talked about this often. Don had his wife and family, and Teague didn't spend much time with them. It was just too painful—to him, they were like copies of his family. Or ghosts.

"This is your family, not mine," Teague said. "They are exact copies, mirror images, but not the same. And I could save a thousand Sarahs, and it would never be the same."

Teague fished out his wallet and removed a laminated scrap of paper that Don had never seen before. Carefully, he held it up for Don to read. The paper was wrinkled and yellow, sealed inside the plastic, but he recognized his wife's handwriting immediately:

> *Gone into the city to visit Elaine at the Trade Center. Be back for lunch. Tina was excited, so I took her too.*
>
> > *Love you,*
> > *Sarah*

Teague turned to leave.

"Where are you going?" Ellis asked him. "Are you riding back with us?"

Teague glanced up at the podium, where the president had spoken and then up at the unfinished Freedom Tower.

"Enjoy your life, Don. Cherish your family. Live in the moment, do the things you want to do. You deserve it, and I wish you the best. But this isn't where I belong. We both know that."

Teague looked up at the skyscraper under construction, then turned to look at Don. Teague opened his coat, and Don saw the edge of one of their new prototype backpack machines—they were still in the testing phase, but they allowed a person to travel through time and space.

"She's out there, somewhere," Teague said, looking deep into Don's eyes. "They both are—I know it. Maybe if I go all the way back to the original timeline, then immediately forward without changing anything, I can save her. I don't know. I just have to figure out how to find her."

Don hesitated and then finally nodded in agreement.

Teague smiled and began tapping at his left forearm. Instead of the sounds of ice shattering, these smaller machines only emitted a low, dull rumble, like distant thunder. Teague looked back up at Don and smiled.

"Good luck," Don said as Teague MacMillan quickly and silently faded out of existence.

In the busy crowd, no one noticed.

Don turned and put his arm around Sarah. She smiled and looked for Teague and saw that he was gone.

"Where did he go?" she asked, her face close to Don's.

Don leaned in and kissed his wife.

"He's gone. I don't think he'll be back—he's gone to look for her. For them."

AFTERWORD

In researching this book, I read everything I could get my hands on about 9/11/2001 and the events leading up to that day. Of course, like everyone else who was alive, I remember that day—I had actually taken the whole week off from my job at Computer Sciences Corporation to get some writing done. I was working on my first book, *Black Bird*, and gearing up for a productive Tuesday morning when I started getting calls from my family and people at work to turn on the TV. I watched, along with everyone else, as it dawned on us what was happening—at first, people assumed the first plane into the North Tower was nothing more than a horrible accident. As the day progressed, it became obvious that we were under attack.

I remember waiting to hear about more attacks—I was relieved when they announced on the news that the FAA had grounded all flights over the United States. At one point, I remember them reporting that an additional seven or eight planes were "missing" and unaccounted for, raising the specter of more attacks.

The thing I remember most vividly from that day was the fact that I wanted to talk to my family and my friends. The events of that day drew our nation together and helped people better appreciate the miracle of life.

Inevitably, as part of my research, I became immersed in most of the popular conspiracy theories surrounding the events of 9/11. One cannot research the event without running up against a huge group of people—writers, filmmakers, videographers, and bloggers—who are convinced that the "official story" is filled with too many coincidences and leaves many important questions unanswered.

After my research, I am convinced that there was no overall conspiracy carried out on 9/11, other than that of the terrorists, working together to carry out the attacks. I do not believe that the U.S. government had any knowledge of the attacks ahead of time or that the government was, in any way, involved in planning or carrying out the attacks.

My basis for this supposition is not that the idea sits outside the realm of possibility. I am sure something like this could be planned and carried out, but I do not think that was the case on 9/11, for one simple reason: Too many people would have to be in on the conspiracy. Thousands of government officials, airline company employees, air traffic controllers, military personnel, first responders, and medical personnel would have had to have been in on it, and no one has come forward, in over ten years, to say they know the truth.

That does not change the fact that, in several cases, there are strange coincidences or discrepancies between the fabric of the story and common sense. In the course of the book, I have used fiction to answer some of these questions, explaining them by having Dr. Ellis have enough foreknowledge to intervene in very specific ways to reduce the number of casualties. If you are interested in reading about other 9/11 conspiracy theories or urban legends in general, try www.snopes.com as a good jumping-off point. They do a great job of summarizing most of the relevant issues.

But as for the real-life events that took place on 9/11, who is to say that we have heard the whole truth? Maybe we have not heard the whole story of 9/11, and maybe we never will.

The Pet Goat

President Bush's visit to a second-grade classroom in Florida has raised a bevy of questions around the timing and handling of the situation by the president, Secret Service, and others involved. Many in the conspiracy press have questioned the president's behavior, pointing to a timeline where, it appears to some, the president is unconcerned about the worst terrorist attack on the United States. Here is the established timeline for the president's visit to the second grade class in Sarasota, Florida, on that fateful morning.

8:48   CNN and other news stations begin live reports, covering the events in New York City, beginning with the first plane crash. (Video footage of this crash would not surface until much later in the day.)

9:00   Bush's motorcade arrives at the school.

9:03   Bush sits down with the class and begins a pre-planned, twenty-minute visit and photo opportunity with the students.

9:08   Bush is told of the second plane going into the World
        Trade Center. He reacts calmly and remains in the
        room, listening to the students read *The Pet Goat*.

9:10   The president asks the students several questions,
        smiling and chatting and unrushed. He also answers
        questions from the students and poses for a picture
        with the teacher.

9:16   Bush leaves the classroom.

9:29   President Bush makes a live television address.

9:55   Air Force One takes off from Florida.

The timeline, established by several sources, raises a few questions.
Some conspiracies assume the government's complicity in the attacks
(and some even assume that the government carried out the attacks
themselves) and point to the relaxed tone of the elementary school visit
as proof that the president was not threatened, because the government
already knew about the attacks.

Why would the Secret Service allow the scheduled school visit to
happen, if the country was evidently under attack? The Secret Service
must not have been fully aware of the extent of the hijackings. Clearly,
they did not perceive a threat against the president, even though there
were planes unaccounted for, and the president's visit to the school had
been highly publicized and was, by at least one account, being broadcast
live on local TV.

Why did the president linger for an extra eleven minutes after being
informed of the second attack? My feeling is that he was making a con-
scious effort to stay calm and not alarm the students or faculty.

Bush stated that, while waiting to go into the classroom and meet
with the students, he was watching a TV and saw the first plane hit the
North Tower. Critics point out that he could not have seen the first plane
strike, because that video evidence did not appear until much later on
the same day. If he had seen the first plane strike, then it is a video or
recording that no one else has seen in the past ten years or the government was somehow involved, and an agency of the government was
recording the events. Therefore, he must be talking about the second
plane strike—but if that is the case, then why did Andrew Card enter the
classroom several minutes later, and what did he tell the president? And
if the president was aware of the first and second plane strikes on the
World Trade Center, why did he linger at the school?

Doesn't the president remaining in the elementary school endanger the very lives of the students and the 2,000 other students and faculty in the building? Another question raised about this delay points out that the president stated that he did not want to alarm the students. If the president and Secret Service were truly concerned about the students, surely it would be better to leave the school, making it less of target. For safety's sake, the students could also have been evacuated from the school—at the time, no one was sure how many planes had actually been hijacked.

World Trade Center and Building 7

In my fiction, I have architects working for MacMillan retrofit and improve safety and evacuation procedures from the World Trade Center by winning the post-1993 attacks contracts, allowing many more people to be quickly and safely evacuated from the buildings in the time between the plane strikes and the collapse. In fact, there is no evidence that systems were upgraded.

Why weren't there more casualties at the World Trade Center? By a series of happy accidents, there were only 20,000 people working in the towers when the planes struck. Had the attacks happened later in the day, there would have been upwards of 50,000 employees working in the towers. Because the planes struck very early in the day, many people had not arrived at work yet, and there were few shoppers in the expansive mall at the World Trade Center under the towers. And a primary was being held that day, so many people had stopped to vote on the way to work.

What knocked down WTC Building 7? Building 7 of the World Trade Center was a 47-story steel-framed skyscraper located over 350 feet away from the North Tower. The official NIST reports say that WTC 7 fell after being severely damaged by portions of the North Tower that fell onto Building 7. *The 9/11 Commission Report* stated that raging fires inside WTC 7 caused it to collapse at 5:20 p.m., several hours after the North and South Towers collapsed. When the building fell straight down in what looked like a controlled demolition, neither of the buildings on either side of it were damaged. A state-of-the-art Emergency Command Center for the City of New York was located on the twenty-third floor, yet the mayor chose to set up a makeshift, temporary command center at street level.

Did someone order the building destroyed? One of the most curious aspects of the WTC 7 story is a comment made by the building owner, Larry Silverstein. During a PBS documentary titled *America Rebuilds,* which aired originally in September 2002, he recounts what happened:

"I remember getting a call from the fire department commander, telling me that they were not sure they were going to be able to contain the fire, and I said, 'We've had such terrible loss of life. Maybe the smartest thing to do is pull it.' And they made the decision to pull, and we watched the building collapse."

I am not sure how else to interpret this other than the building was in fact "pulled," the industry term for a controlled and intentional demolition. Although it normally takes weeks of planning to carry out a controlled demolition, I suppose it is possible to assume that the FDNY was able to bring down the building, but it takes a huge leap of faith.

Hardened Pentagon

By most accounts, there were about 20,000 people working in the Pentagon when Flight 175 struck.

Why weren't there more casualties at the Pentagon? By an amazing coincidence, the Pentagon had indeed been undergoing the series of structural upgrades described in the book. Amazingly, the hijacked airliner struck Wedge One, the only portion of the Pentagon that had been upgraded with reinforced concrete, new blast-proof windows, and improved construction techniques. The construction techniques used in the rest of the building dated to World War II, and if the plane had struck anywhere else in the building, casualties would have been much higher. As it was, only 125 Pentagon employees were killed that day.

This coincidence, for me, is the most curious. I can explain away much of the other conspiracy theories as dumb luck or happenstance, but this coincidence is simply hard to accept. It was after I learned about this particular coincidence that I began toying with the idea of writing a book about alternate 9/11 scenarios.

Flight 93

Flight 93 was delayed for forty-one minutes on the ground at Newark Airport—for my part, I explain this to be a deliberate act of Dr. Ellis to throw off the hijackers' coordinated schedule and, hopefully, give the passengers time to fight back.

What delayed Flight 93's departure from Newark Airport? In real life, the delay gave the passengers on the plane time to learn about the other hijackings and attacks that had taken place in New York and Washington. The passengers learned that, instead of being taken hostage to be freed later, they were in fact on a flying suicide bomb. It was up to them to stop the hijackers and wrest control of the plane from them to prevent another disaster. There is no official account of why the plane was delayed so long—the other flights all took off within minutes of each other, allowing them to strike their targets in a coordinated fashion.

Because Flight 93 was delayed, it gave the passengers time to find out what was going on and to decide to fight back. If the flight had not been delayed, it would have found its target at nearly the same time as the other plane struck the Pentagon.

Was Flight 93 shot down? One conspiracy theory states that the plane was shot down by an F-16 fighter jet. This theory grew out of several eyewitness accounts from observers on the ground in Pennsylvania that reported seeing a second, fighter-jet-like craft. Other critics point to the sounds from the recorded phone conversations and commentaries from the passengers: many spoke of hearing loud crashes and thumps, and, at one point, the plane apparently lost cabin pressure. One passenger said that they "had lost an engine" and could no longer hear the engine noise. F-16s typically carry Sidewinder heat-seeking missiles, so a missile or rocket launched from a U.S. military plane, chasing the plane, would have likely struck the plane's engine, the hottest part of the plane.

So why shoot the plane down, if the passengers were making a coordinated, concerted effort to take back the plane? There were at least two people with flying experience on board. Critics argue that, if the U.S. government was complicit with the hijackers (or their masters), shooting down the plane kills the hijackers along with the passengers. One critic stated that the passenger rebellion was an unforeseen circumstance, altering the plan.

I am not sure what to think—for a long time, I assumed that the plane had been shot down and the "heroes of Flight 93" story was just a cover for the hard truth that, faced with a terrible choice, Bush and Cheney had concluded that it was necessary to take the plane down with a missile.

Reduced Passenger Counts on the Hijacked Planes

There were four planes hijacked that morning, and in each case, the planes had oddly low occupancy rates. For example, Flight 93 had a capacity of 182 passengers but flew that morning with 26 passengers and the 4 hijackers, a 16.5 percent occupancy rate. The plane with the highest occupancy was Flight 11, which was just over 50 percent full. The aggregate occupancy, or "load factor," as it is referred to in the airline industry, of the four combined flights was 31 percent.

Why were passenger counts artificially low that day? In some cases, they were not artificially low. Flight 11 had a normal load factor of 39 percent on Tuesday morning flights, so it was actually busier than usual on 9/11. The Commission found no ticketing, passenger occupancy, or financial evidence to indicate that the hijackers or anyone else involved purchased additional seats (beyond the ones they actually used) to limit the number of passengers they would need to control during the operation.

One theory proposed was that the hijackers may have purposefully bought tickets on sparsely-populated planes to reduce the chances of the flight being full and the hijackers being bumped. It would have also made it much easier for the hijackers to control the plane if there were fewer passengers aboard.

Insider Stock Trading Prior to 9/11

This is a popular and often-mentioned legend surrounding 9/11. In the days between September 6 and September 10, interest in United Airlines puts increased 900 percent and American Airlines puts increased 600 percent. *Puts* are a common financial instrument used by traders to bet against a company's stock—purchasers of puts expect the stock to tumble. Put buyers, in effect, "borrow" shares of the stock and sell them on the open market. Then they wait and purchase those same shares back, at a later date, and return them to the entity from which they were borrowed.

This scenario was even mentioned in *Casino Royale*, the Daniel Craig-James Bond film released in 2006, and used to underscore a plot point in that film about speculators crashing a prototype plane and, having bet against the company that was building the prototype, making a killing as the company's stock tanked.

Did this really happen? The SEC, shortly after the attacks, investigated the unprecedented levels of shorting going on in the two companies' shares. The New York Stock Exchange was closed for four days, starting on 9/11, and when it reopened on September 17, shares of United Airlines fell from $30.82 to $17.50. Similarly, American Airlines shares fell from $29.70 to $18 in one day.

The 9/11 Commission Report stated that the SEC and FBI investigations provided answers for this buying anomaly. Ninety-five percent of the United Airlines puts purchased on September 6 were purchased by a single U.S.-based institutional investor, as part of an investment strategy that also included buying 115,000 shares of American Airlines stock. The suspicious trading in American Airlines puts was traced back to a U.S.-based options trading newsletter, distributed via fax on Sunday, September 9, recommending the trade. *The 9/11 Commission Report* also noted that the SEC and FBI expended enormous resources in investigating the issue.

BIBLIOGRAPHY

BOOKS:

Bamford, James. *A Pretext to War*. New York: Anchor Books, 2004.

Griffin, David Ray. *The New Pearl Harbor*. Northampton, MA: Olive Branch Press, 2004.

Kaku, Michio. *Parallel Worlds*. New York: Random House Books, 2005.

Morgan, Rowand and Ian Henshall. *9/11 Revealed*. New York: Carroll & Graf Publishers, 2005.

National Commission on Terrorist Attacks. *The 9/11 Commission Report: Final Report of the National Commission on Terrorist Attacks Upon the United States*. New York: W. W. Norton & Company, 2004.

WEBSITES:

9-11 Research.WTC7.Net. "9-11 Research, An attempt to uncover the truth about September 11th, 2001." 9-11 Research website. http://911research.wtc7.net (accessed September 23, 2011).

AirNav.com. "Liberty Municipal Airport." AirNaav.com website. http://www.air nav.com/airport/T78 (accessed June 10, 2011).

BBC News. "President Clinton's best defence." BBC news site. http://news.bbc. co.uk/2/hi/events/clinton_under_fire/profiles/259798.stm (accessed August 10, 2011).

Chicago Times. "Blame Plentiful in Brown Crash." Chicago Times website. http://articles.chicagotribune.com/1996-06-07/news/9606080183_1_brown-crash-air-force-commerce-secretary-ron-brown (accessed October 25, 2011).

Cotsalas, Valerie. "The Unsold Warhol." The New York Times website. http://travel.nytimes.com/2006/09/08/travel/escapes/08warhol.html (accessed September 29, 2011).

Friends of Firefighters website. http://www.friendsoffirefighters.org
(accessed August 10, 2011).

Global Security.org. "Fort Knox Bullion Depository." Global Security.org website.
http://www.globalsecurity.org/military/facility/fort-knox-depository.htm
(accessed June 10, 2011).

Google Maps. Multiple pages. http://maps.google.com (accessed last on
October 24, 2011).

Israel Defense. "A Revolution in Israel's Air Defense." Israel Defense website.
http://www.israeldefense.com/?CategoryID=472&ArticleID=465
(accessed August 28, 2001).

Los Angeles Times. "Bermuda Skirted by Storm." Los Angeles Times website.
http://articles.latimes.com/2001/sep/10/news/mn-44113 (accessed April 23, 2011).
Ministry of Hajj. "The Rituals & Stages of the Hajj." The Ministry of Hajj
Kingdom of Saudi Arabia website (accessed August 2, 2011).

Montauk Life. "Andy Warhol in Montauk." Montauk Life website. http://www.
montauklife.com/history/history_warhol.html (accessed September 29, 2011).

Snopes.com. Multiple pages. http://www.snopes.com (accessed last on
October 24, 2011).

White House Website. "Eisenhower Executive Office Building."
http://www.whitehouse.gov/about/eeob (accessed on September 21, 2011).
Wikipedia. Multiple pages. http://www.wikipedia.com (accessed last on
October 24, 2011).

Williams, Mike. http://911myths.com (accessed September 21, 2011).

The Willard Hotel. "The Willard – America's Hotel." http://washington.inter
continental.com/ (accessed on June 10, 2011).

PLEASE CONSIDER REVIEWING

Thank you for reading this book - I hope you enjoyed it. Now that you've finished my book, won't you please consider **writing a review?** If you could, take a few minutes out to write a review of this book on Amazon, Goodreads, Facebook or any other place you feel like sharing.

Reviews are the best way readers discover new books. And, believe it or not, the sheer number of Amazon reviews affects how Amazon lists book titles. So swing over there and jot down a couple of sentences. Good or bad, every review helps increase the "social buzz" of the book. I would truly appreciate it. And thank you!

— Greg Enslen

About the Author

Author and columnist Greg Enslen lives in Ohio with his wife Samantha and three children. He's enjoying the small-town life after two decades in Washington, D.C., and Los Angeles. All of his books are available on **Amazon.com** and Kindle, and several have been published by Gypsy Publications in Ohio. For reviews, news updates, and more information, please visit his website at **http://www.gregenslen.com**.

Greg Enslen